KARA

Lovers and Liars

The second story of the lives and loves of Kara
Gilbert and Greg Sheppard.

Kathryn Gillings and Gary Baxter

Cover Design: Yazoo Designs
Interior Layout: Cecily Potter

Printed in Australia

First Printing: 2023
Republished July 2023

Paperback ISBN: 978-0-6458751-2-6
E-book ISBN: 978-0-6458751-3-3

Acknowledgements

First and foremost, to you… as a reader, thank you.

Selecting this book from a list or a shelf and being inspired to buy and read it… that is a wish come true.

If you have enjoyed our first book and are returning for more, we cannot thank you enough. As co-authors and friends, we have walked alongside each other in this writing journey, to bring Kara to life…

However, no authors produce books without friends or other skilled professionals and these people deserve our heartfelt thanks:

To Jo, Maggie, Tanya, Kelly, and other dear friends, for your enthusiasm, being champions of the story and your sharp eyes to once again give us raw feedback to correct those never-ending little oversights…

Vanessa from Yazoo Designs, for your creativity and patience, bringing the Kara stories to life, with wonderful covers, to promote and 'expose' them beautifully.

To Cecily for your design and flair for the interior of our books.

To all the brave, sexy individuals and couples who have contributed their stories and engaged with us online and in person in our research and, of course…

To the real-life 'Kara Gilbert' and 'Greg Sheppard' who continue to willingly share the story of your most unique friendship, love and experiences.

Your relationship, connection and sexual adventures will forever be inspirational.

Thank you.

Kathryn and Gary

Chapter 1

*H*er favourite fluffy throw rug had worked its magic. Somewhere, during the first minutes of snuggling onto the couch watching the first scenes of the movie, she'd drifted off. It was close to 9.00 p.m. when she was woken by the ringing of her phone. The adrenalin pulsed through her body from the sudden return to being awake. She grabbed her phone from the coffee table. *Who on earth would be ringing me now?* Through awakening blinks, she saw it was Greg Sheppard.

She sat upright and with a smile said, 'Hello Greg, what a pleasant surprise.'

It was the moments of silence that concerned her first.

'She's gone, Kara… she's dead.'

A cold chill ran through her, His simple statement was horrific. She knew it was him, but the voice was almost unrecognisable. She grabbed her chest, and swallowed hard, holding herself trapped between wanting to hear the next words, but not.

'My God… Greg, what's happened, who's dead?' Panic had risen instantly inside her, her back straightening further. She'd never heard her friend so distressed; he was barely getting the words out. 'Greg! What's happened?'

Between more breaths, she started to hear him let some words escape.

He just repeated, 'She's gone. She's dead, Kara.'

It could only be one of his daughters or Tess, that would render him in such an inconsolable state.

Kara's voice now rose, reaching fear-filled shrill notes. 'Greg, is it one of your girls?'

'Tess was killed in a car accident.'

'Where are you?'

'The Royal Adelaide Hospital.'

Kara immediately felt that swell of the formidable. *If he's at the hospital—Oh God!* She drew in a breath. *I need to stay calm here.*

Her reply was firm and steady 'Greg, I'm coming to get you. Stay there. I'll be there soon.'

Kara ended the call and jumped off the couch. Greg was the only man for whom she would forsake anything to help. He was the one person who searched for her, found her and saved her, and now he needed her, and this was all that mattered.

As she scrambled around her apartment to grab clothes, her phone and keys, she thrashed through other thoughts from the day. She'd heard a news bulletin earlier on the radio as she drove from her hometown of Clare to Adelaide. She hadn't taken a great deal of notice of the terrible news that a forty-four-year-old woman and fifty-nine-year-old taxi driver were the victims of a fatal collision involving a truck on Greenhill Road.

Surely that isn't what has happened to Tess? But he said she was gone. My God, it must be.

That sick, empty feeling started to tremor through her. Kara had never met Tess, but she felt she knew her well. After all, they'd shared the same lover.

I've got to get to him quickly.

It was only a fifteen-minute drive to the hospital, but all the while her mind was burning with thoughts and the concern for what she was about to find.

As she pulled up to the emergency entrance, she could see Greg standing outside the hospital entrance. She barely recognised him. The tie discarded, the crumpled jacket, and a shirt more rummaged into his waistband than tucked, said it all. Kara already knew he was a mess. He was just standing there, nearly motionless, clutching what looked like a plastic shopping bag in one hand, while holding his forehead with the other.

As she approached, her heart lurched at the sight of him. It took only a second to see that her beloved friend was totally wracked in despair. His face, a shocking shade of white, his eyes red mapped and brimming with tears, and hair in disarray. Stooped forward as he leant against the wall, appearing many inches shorter than his six-foot stance. As if his heart had drawn in his stature to shield it from pain. His body simply looked like the spirit that characteristically powered and energised him, had been drained away, leaving a very vulnerable, bare shell, empty of the usually buoyant and enigmatic man she knew.

Kara parked in the 'patients only' pick up zone, next to the emergency entrance, close to where he stood. She jumped out of the car and ran to him. He turned toward her, dropped the bag to the ground and nearly fell into Kara's outstretched arms. She could feel his whole body shake.

Kara just held him, saying little more than 'I'm sorry. I'm so sorry' repeatedly, until his shaking subsided and he could once again breathe slowly.

Once she knew he had settled enough to hear her she said, 'Let's get you home. My car's just here.'

Greg nodded, allowing Kara to lead him by the hand toward her car. She opened the passenger door and Greg moved slowly to sit inside. She shut the door firmly, her action telling him not to dare attempt to get out. Kara ran back to the hospital entrance, grabbed his suitcase, and picked up the shopping bag he'd dropped when she arrived. She glanced inside. It contained Tess's belongings. She tied up the bag and raced back to the car.

Greg sat, staring ahead, not saying much at all, other than the address to his and Tess's apartment. Kara knew he needed sleep, and was in no state to make decisions, or be left alone.

'She picked out her wedding dress today,' he said almost to himself.

Kara tried to drive with her hand resting on his leg. She decided it best to just listen and ask no questions. As she turned into his driveway he said, 'And just like that she is gone.'

Once inside his apartment, she helped him take off his jacket, and said, 'How about you head to the shower, while I sort us some food?'

He offered no protest, responding with little more than a nod or 'Okay' here and there as if on autopilot. He was obviously still in shock, suspended in that awful state of exhausted numbness.

While he showered, Kara ordered some food to be delivered, then found a bottle of wine and a couple of glasses. She poured the wine before finding cutlery and plates. *There is no way I'm leaving him tonight. He needs someone to watch over him.*

Somehow, she needed to make sure he took the sleeping pills given to him by the doctor that he'd tossed onto the table. *I won't let him sleep in his bed tonight. Not their bed.* The bed she suspected he'd woken up in, with Tess beside him, only a few mornings before.

Greg took a long time in the bathroom. Before he undressed, he found himself just standing in front of the vanity, staring without focus into the mirror. He took a crumpled card from his pants pocket and the ring. That ring. *Our ring.*

He just stood there, staring down at the exquisite diamonds that he had slid onto Tess's finger less than a year ago.

How on earth can this have happened? Only what seemed like a few hours earlier, he'd received a text from Tess, obviously excited at having found her wedding dress. She'd also collected the final draft of their wedding invitation from the printers, which he'd found in her bag.

The same thought kept repeating, over and over. *How can the feelings about such special items be changed in an instant?*

Now a ring and this crumpled card served only as bitter reminder of the woman he loved so much and had now lost.

The dream of what was to be their special day in a couple of months' from now, had just been obliterated in seconds.

Today had been Greg's last day working in Sydney, his time consumed by back-to-back meetings with his clients, the production manager and more, preparing the final details for the filming of a promotion ad, and related TV series launch scheduled for next month. He was travelling back to Adelaide with Matt, the film director, which gave them some last precious hours to finalise the shooting schedule, before arriving back in Adelaide around 6.30 p.m. that evening. On route to the airport around two thirty that afternoon, he had seen Tess's text message appear on his phone. He didn't want to call her back with Matt around, but had wanted to send a text in reply. He quickly tapped out his message as they started to take-off.

> That's wonderful. Can't wait to hear about it. I've got things to tell you too. Until tonight babe. Love you x

He was pleased she'd had a good day and that he'd signalled he wanted to speak with her. He had to tell her all about Kara, tonight.

Greg turned the phone to flight mode and dived back into the discussions with Matt. He hadn't realised until tonight at the hospital that his message had not been sent.

His phone had been on silent all day, so he had no knowledge of the barrage of missed calls and messages that flooded in once he landed back in Adelaide. There were about ten calls from Tess. This wasn't normal. A wave of discomfort hit him.

Something must be up.

He quickly grabbed his bags, said a hasty goodbye to Matt and then dialled Tess's number.

Maybe she can't get to pick me up after all? He had not contemplated anything else. It wasn't Tess who answered. It was Monique, Tess's mum.

'Oh Greg, I've tried for hours to reach you...' Then she stopped. The cry she let escape was devastating. Between sobs and deep intakes of breath, she blurted out something about an accident, before more peels of uncontrollable crying rang through the phone.

'Mon, what's going on? Mon? What accident? What's happened? Is Tess, okay?'

'I told them you are... or were, her fiancé... that you'd be devastated... they need to speak to you... Oh, Greg...'

Mon's voice wailed, then faded.

Greg heard the phone rattle and then an unknown voice, deep and somewhat stilted and formal, responded.

'Mr Sheppard, this is Constable Porter from SA Police.

'I'm sorry to report that Ms Merchant has been involved in a vehicle accident and has not survived. Ms Merchant's parents are here at the Royal Adelaide hospital and would appreciate if you could meet them here as soon as you are able. They will provide you more information about the events of the accident in person. I am sorry for your loss.'

Greg barged to the front of the taxi queue, apologising to those he passed. He was already in a vacuum of near panic, with no sound registering, other than the belting of his heart. After uttering 'Emergency, Royal Adelaide Hospital,' with a frantic tone, the attendant immediately put him in the next available cab.

'This passenger has to get to The Royal Adelaide Hospital. It's an emergency. Go!'

Greg arrived at the hospital entrance within twenty minutes. He stepped out of the cab and into his worst nightmare.

Chapter 2

As he stood in the bathroom now, a few hours later, he struggled to recall any real conversation with anyone when he first arrived at the hospital. It was just odd phrases and words that screamed through him. 'Tess was gone', 'I understand you two were engaged', 'A cab, traffic lights, a truck'. These phrases had kept cycling through him.

He couldn't really comprehend in any sequence what they were saying. He kept insisting that he had to see her. It couldn't be true. *How could she be gone?*

This wasn't the first time in his life he had asked this question of himself.

His thoughts transported back to 1976. His first year of school. As a little boy, after the first few months, he'd finally become accustomed to the weekday routine. He'd awoken to the usual sounds in the house: the shrill alarm. His father's footsteps down the hallway to make his morning coffee.

The front door clicked, signalling that his dad had left for work. He was a mechanic at a Service Station, his days always started early.

He once again heard his mother's voice, firmly ringing out. 'It's time to get up, Greg, come on, hurry now and help your sister' flinging open his bedroom door, as she briskly continued her walk toward the kitchen. 'Breakfast time.'

He'd dressed as usual, woke his sister, helped her to dress, then led her by the hand to the kitchen. His mother was busying herself opening and closing cupboards and putting items into boxes strewn across the floor. He now could recall her vividly, dressed in a blue floral print shift dress and a teal blue cardigan. Her dark shoulder length hair pulled back loosely; held clasped by the same tortoiseshell clip she always wore at the nape of her neck. While seated at the kitchen table, eating his cereal, he could still see her pacing around the kitchen. It was in that moment, his whole life, changed.

'Greg, I want you to go to the shop before you go to school this morning. I need you to get some more boxes for me. I have things to sort today. Run along now.'

He'd done as he was bid and had thought nothing more of it.

When he'd arrived home that afternoon—his mother was gone.

No goodbyes. No hugs. No explanation. It was another fifteen years before he saw her again.

Today had belted his heart with the same unexpected jagged pain, as it had back then.

When he'd approached the room where Tess lay, he didn't need the nurse standing with her to lift the sheet which covered her. He could see Tess's hand. It was hanging limp off the side of the barouche and moreover, he could see the ring. The ring he'd had made especially for her, that signalled she was to have been his wife.

The doctor spoke. 'Sir, if you would like to wait in the foyer, we will arrange for Ms Merchant's belongings to be brought to you. With your consent, we will remove her jewellery and give you the items that came in with her. Her mother has told us you are the person who should have them.'

Greg had just stared at him, nodded and uttered a quiet, 'Thank you.'

He didn't need to hear the words. The only other woman he'd truly loved unconditionally had gone.

Again. Without notice.

There was no chance to say goodbye, to look into those sparkling blue eyes, to hold her or to linger in a last kiss.

The doctor nodded to the nurse standing next to Tess. She waited until they had all left the cubicle, before removing the ring and her necklace. The nurse could not help but stop and admire the ring. It was exquisite. A ring such as this, clearly symbolised just how much the man who gave it to her was in love and connected to her. This was always so painful to witness. Rather than put this into the bag with the other belongings, she held it in her hand, as if to keep it alive in the warmth of her palm.

Greg had thankfully stopped himself from wanting to see more of her body at that point. *That is my Tess. That is our ring on her finger. Those beautiful fingers that will never touch me again.* He'd shut his eyes and saw her face on that night on his boat at the Marina, her beautiful eyes glistening with tears of surprise and her smile filled with love when he had proposed to her. How she had held him so tight. He didn't want to see or hold a memory of any other image of her.

The nurse, who had witnessed his shocking realisation that Tess was truly gone, had found him minutes later standing aimlessly in the corridor outside of the cubicle. Taking him by the arm, she escorted him to a private room near the entrance to the hospital.

'The doctor would like to speak with you again, but, just for a couple of minutes. I'll be back soon too, to see how you are going and bring her things.'

She offered a soft affirming look that rendered him to simply sit and wait. Greg responded with thankful eyes, and barely a nod.

His gaze fell to the floor, as he sat, head drooped between his lap, elbows on his knees, hands clasped frozen together. He stayed there motionless, noting only the scuff marks on the linoleum until the doctor returned to stand in front of him, clearing his throat.

As Greg raised his head up to the guttural sound, he barely heard the doctor muttering some obligatory awkward condolences, before quickly handing Greg some sleeping pills and a script for more if he needed them.

The nurse returned and after the doctor left, quietly stepped forward and handed Greg the bag containing Tess's belongings. With a knowing sensitivity, she carefully opened her hand, which held the ring and gently placed it into the palm of his hand. As his grip enfolded around it—she said, 'I am so sorry for your loss.' She felt her own heartstrings yank as he looked at her. Before he could see the tears starting to well in her eyes, she composed herself and briskly handed him papers to sign to confirm his receipt of the items. There was an awkward silence between them as she instructed him where to sign.

After signing the release papers, she asked him gently, 'Do you have someone who might come to get you? It's not a good idea to be on your own.'

He had thought for a split second... 'Err, yes, thank you, I do have someone; I'll call them now.' The nurse smiled at him and as she turned to leave, she stopped to face him.

'Now promise me to take those pills—you won't think you need them, but at least for tonight you will.'

Greg nodded and smiled meekly.

'Yes, Okay. Thank you again for everything.'

Tess's parents appeared from around the corner. He stood and hugged Mon with tears suddenly freely flowing from them both. 'I can't fucking believe this Mon.' He shook hands with her father, then hugged him. The depth of their loss held and shared in a second. No words were needed. Without anything else that could be said, they left to go home.

He then took out his phone and rang Kara's number.

She was the first friend he thought of, and the only person he wanted to call. Immediately she had responded, as he had known she would. The forever dependable and caring Kara. She had known just what to do and had been there in an instant for him.

Thank God she's here now. At least, she hasn't left me... yet.

He undressed and eventually stepped into the shower.

With Greg safely in the bathroom for a time, Kara could actually breathe for a moment. She'd never visited this place where Greg and Tess lived together. Kara moved awkwardly around the apartment for the first time, now truly realising where she was. She'd been so focussed on wanting to comfort Greg in such a time of need, she had not given a thought about entering this part of his life, into a place where she really didn't belong.

This was their place. Tess's domain. The home Tess and Greg had created for themselves. And of which Kara always considered she never should, or dare not, encroach. In that moment, she felt like an intruder. This was the place where the two of them had created their lives as a couple together. She, his ex-lover, was never supposed to have entered. But here she was, in tragic, exceptional circumstances.

She called out and poked her head into the bathroom to see that he was alright. He was standing in the shower, water cascading over his motionless body. She stopped to gaze upon his statuesque form. His response to her eyes on his nakedness would've always inspired some excitement in them both. Tonight, they both only longed for cleansing.

'I'm okay,' he said flatly.

As Kara moved around the kitchen to grab some more items in readiness for the meal that would soon arrive, she couldn't help but notice the many little things that signalled she was in another woman's home. She saw photographs of them together, the reminder notes and invitations to both of them displayed on the fridge. She was handling crockery and utensils purchased by Tess for their future lives together and saw the piles of brochures and papers about their forthcoming wedding plans on the end of the dining table. A jolt of guilt shot through Kara.

Stop it. This is Greg's place. He needs you tonight.

Before anything else could penetrate her thoughts, Greg emerged from the bathroom as the doorbell rang.

Kara answered the door, collecting their food delivery. She knew that eating would be the last thing he felt like, but that he needed to, so she served up a plate of food and placed it in front of him.

She was sensitive to not ask questions directly about the accident or Tess, but chatted lightly. She tried to make it as casual as possible and easy for him to eat, sit and share as little or as much as he wanted. As he poked at his food, he spoke about the work he'd done in Sydney and he listened as Kara told him about what she'd been doing lately. Greg appeared pretty well composed, Kara sensed, while he was verbally responding, yet all the while, his mind was in overdrive in another place. It didn't matter.

The only mention of the hospital was when Kara suggested he followed what the doctor had recommended, to take the sleeping tablets—for tonight at least.

Greg took the tablets and muttered something about 'probably not needing them really, but I promised the nurse I would…' then poured himself another glass of wine. Rather than suggest that wasn't a good idea to drink any more after taking tablets, she decided to wait and remove his wine, as soon as she could.

Kara cleared the plates, along with the wine bottle and was in the kitchen, loading their dishes into the dishwasher, when she heard him come in.

'I've got so much to organise; I'll need to speak with Mon and Trev about the funeral. I hope Mon's going to be okay? I don't

know how she'll cope without Tess; she was her baby girl. Tess…
er… Kara, can you pass me my notepad please, I've got to make a
list…'

Kara sensed Greg was trying desperately to regain some sort of
control of what was happening, and to sort his thoughts, feelings
and actions. She figured he was running on the last few drops of
fuel he had in his tank.

The sleeping pills were taking effect. Kara knew he needed
sleep. Despite his vain attempt to be in control, he was fading fast.
The exhaustion and sleeping pills now close to becoming all-
consuming.

She didn't miss the slip. He'd nearly called her Tess. So
understandable.

She avoided answering him directly, as she emerged from the
kitchen, 'I know you have heaps to sort out, but why don't you
leave the list until tomorrow. It's okay, you won't forget.' She led
him to the couch and made him sit. She placed a cushion at the
end of the couch and guided him to lay back. All the while he held
a deep frown on his forehead, clearly still desperately trying to sort
and process and plan.

Planning. This was what he did best.

Greg Sheppard could read the situation, the needs of the client,
create solutions, anticipate problems, and take charge with
bravado and confidence. He was focussed and the outcome would
be absolute. Perfect beyond expectation. His work was sorted like
compartments—giving each project and client, dedicated focus
and precision in the moment, and he attempted to apply this
approach to all parts of his life. It was what made him so successful
professionally in much of his daily life. It was his instinctive way
to deal with anything, or anyone. You always felt like you were all
that mattered when Greg Sheppard was with you. However, Kara
knew his heart and soul were shattered, and dealing with this
trauma would ultimately test him. This was something he could
not fix, or initiate a plan B.

Kara put a throw rug over him and once she had him covered and made him as comfortable as she could, she perched by his side on the edge of the couch and just sat. She stayed very still, just watching and listening. After a while, she gently removed the wineglass from his hand and placed it on the coffee table next to them.

'It's time to rest now,' she said softly.

He eventually looked at her, with rather glazed eyes saying, 'Yeah,' with a sniff and a nod. Kara took one of his hands in hers and stroked the back of it, softly over and over, hoping that the rhythm of her touch would settle him to sleep.

Greg started to close his eyes and sink back into the lounge, still half talking to himself. Kara just kept stroking his hand. Opening his eyes, his grip tightened on her hand as he turned his head to face her.

He looked straight into her eyes and held his gaze for a moment, before uttering softly and slowly, 'Kara, thank you for being here for me.'

Kara smiled gently, 'I will always be here for you.'

Before she could say another word, he rolled onto his side, slipping into an uneasy sleep. Kara just sat there, staring at him for a long while. She saw his body twitch now and then, but at least he'd crashed for hopefully a few hours. She whispered, 'Sleep my special man, it's been a tough day. And you have a horrendous week ahead.'

She softly walked around, quietly tidying and strategically putting some of Tess's items away out of sight, picking up her shoes by the door, removing the makeup left on the bathroom vanity, her mail on the desk, to soften the sting of those incidental reminders when he woke.

Kara thought about the fact that Greg had called her in his hour of need. She knew he truly thought of her as a special friend, but she also knew he would barely recall anything he said or did tonight. As she thought about what he had said, she felt uneasy.

It was true. She knew if the circumstances were reversed, he would be the first and only person she would want by her side to offer her comfort. She also knew how she'd told him about how connected she was to him and how much she adored him, but never told him how much she still loved him or in what way. He'd shared so much about Tess and his love for her. Despite never having met Tess, Kara had never asked him to leave her or insist that she and Greg spent more time together, although she knew that he loved them both.

In reality, Kara knew exactly why she had never pressured him. There were many times when she wanted more. No more than when they were first reunited, however, she realised she was so raw, hidden, and alone back then. She'd never had any man treat her or make her come alive in the way that Greg did. Since then, they'd come to understand each other in a very different way. After their initial lust-filled connection, there was more beneath the surface than either of them knew. They'd bonded in a unique way, unlike any conventional relationship between a man and a woman. They both shared the same type of fantasies, lust and openness about their intimate desires and needs. They loved each other, but not in any traditional sense. There wasn't a category, type or way to describe it. Perhaps only that they had brushed, caressed and fulfilled each other's secret parts of their hearts and sexual fantasies. They were so easy together, sharing all and the best of each other with a pleasure and trust that let them enjoy and have fun with others, while intensifying their connection as the deepest of friends and lovers.

But all of that was fine until now. He'd always been so open about his love for Tess, and Kara had never wanted to intrude on that. Now, here she was. In Tess's apartment.

Kara resolved in that moment, that she would only ever be here, in this place, as his friend and *never* as his lover.

Kara poured herself a wine, found another blanket and pillow from the guest bedroom, then settled on the two-seater couch opposite where Greg was sleeping.

She sipped her wine slowly, letting her thoughts wander as she watched him. His breathing was slower, finally now in a deep sleep. She placed her glass on the coffee table and curled up. She had better get some rest too. *Tomorrow is going to be another tough day.*

Before reaching for the lamp to switch it off, she turned her head toward him and whispered again, to her sleeping friend...

'Greg, I do love you. I know that I will never be able to describe it in a way that you might fully understand. It's nothing like the love that you and Tess felt. I also know you love me in a unique and special way. You must realise that I can never replace or be a substitute for her, or that kind of love. I'm not Tess and never will be. There are so many things that I'd love to say to you about us, but dare not. Especially not now.

'Looking at you, I am feeling so much of your pain and already I see you trying desperately to project the façade that you can cope when I know you can't, and won't find this easy to deal with. I already dread for you, waking in the morning and those seconds when the pain will flood in with the realisation of what has happened today. It would be so easy to wrap you up in my arms and profess my desire to want to be with you, and protect you always. But that is not for me to do or to even suggest right now.'

Greg Sheppard was her lover, but equally a true friend. As such, she believed as a bonded mate, she would offer love and care unconditionally, without any expectation of reciprocity.

As Kara sat there, staring at her sleeping friend, she just knew he wouldn't really know how to deal with this loss right now. She made a promise to herself.

As much as you love him and will always want him, Kara, you are not her. You must promise to wait until Greg approaches you and you can see yourself reflected in his eyes and not Tess. Yes, you are his friend for life, but cannot be his lover again until he's ready.

She also knew that Greg was not going to sit still. He'd cope best if he was busy and had some sort of routine. But people reacted differently, having experienced trauma, especially so suddenly. There was always the risk he could derail. She would be there whenever he needed her.

Kara drifted in and out of sleep during the first couple of hours, rousing frequently to check on him, but the enormity of the whole shocking event crept up on her, and she eventually succumbed to a deep exhausted sleep.

She awoke the next morning around 8.00 a.m. startled and surprised by Greg's face looking at her as he patted her gently, saying, 'Good Morning Kara, I've made you a coffee.'

'Oh, thank you,' she said, moving to sit up quickly, still adjusting to where she was.

The realisation of the events of the day before came flooding back. 'Greg, I'm sorry, I had planned to get you breakfast this morning. Did you get much sleep?' She accepted the mug of coffee taking a comforting sip.

'Actually, I did sleep. I haven't been up for that long.' The flicker of a smile appeared, punctuated by the escape of a small sigh.

Kara noticed that while he looked pale and drawn, he'd already showered, dressed in what looked like his work clothes, appearing a much more composed person than she'd ever expected to see this morning.

As if he could read her thoughts, he said, 'I thought I would head to the office quickly to clear some appointments. I expect there will be lots to do today.'

'Good idea.' Kara paused. She knew it was important for him to hear her name.

'There will be lots to get through. I'm sure you will want and need to be with Tess's family today too, but please don't overdo it.'

She saw the slight flinch in his eyes at the mention of her name, but she just kept speaking. 'I'll head off now and let you get going.' She had already slipped on her shoes, grabbed her handbag and keys, before rushing up to him, to say goodbye.

Greg took her by the hand, drawing her into a gentle hug. 'Kara, thank you so much. I couldn't have got through last night without you.'

'Greg, I am so truly sorry. I know how much you loved her and how much this hurts. I'm here whenever, or for whatever you need me to do. I'm only a call away, remember? So please call me to check in, just so I know you're okay—for my peace of mind too.'

The words exchanged clung to each of them, cemented by their gentle embrace. She kissed him gently on the cheek and turned toward the door.

As she opened the door she said with the hint of cheek in her voice, 'Besides, Mr Sheppard, you know if you don't contact me, I will hound you relentlessly to check up on you, regardless!

Greg gave her a little smile, standing in the doorway, watching as she left toward the stairs. He blinked hard to hold back a tear. He would not let any grief out of its box to take hold of him today. No one, not even Kara, would see him cry.

Chapter 3

For the next two months after Tess's funeral, Greg buried his head in his work. It's what he needed, a distraction from the traumatic loss and continuous thoughts of what could have been. He loved his fiancée so much; he knew he would never love like that again. Tess was that 'once in a lifetime all-consuming love'.

Just the thought of her would start a beautiful feeling that oozed from his heart. He likened it to heavenly hands clasping his heart and squeezing it till the love burst out to spread through his entire body. It used to take his breath away; his heart would race and he'd grin like a dazed teenager. He would sigh as he imagined those hands, those lips and that body touching him, kissing him and loving him. Nothing else in the world mattered in those few moments.

However, that exquisite elixir that used to flood through him was now gone. Replaced by a strangulating ache that would intensify to near unbearable pain every time he thought of her. It still squeezed his heart, but now only hurt escaped poisoning his entire body. His knees would go weak and he just wanted to curl up and cry.

He could see Tess everywhere. He would find himself staring at blonde, slender women, with soft, long flowing hair as they walked along the street or sat in a café, or glimpses of a woman driving past in a black 3 series BMW. He would hear her gentle laugh or see her name written, and without warning she would come flooding back, along with the pain.

He longed for the day that it became more bearable and he could feel relaxed and at ease and just maybe this pain would subside enough to allow happier and more sensuous feelings to override it.

Greg knew one day he probably would enjoy the pleasure of another woman, of course, but he also knew that his heart died along with Tess. That he knows without a doubt. For now, he just worked and tried to focus on the only part of his life that he could control.

During these months he had kept in regular contact with Kara. She would call, text or email him, every couple of days and at least once a week he would call her, talking for ages about everything and anything. Especially in those first days leading up to Tess's funeral and at those times when he privately felt so sad and alone. Not that he would share that much about his feelings, but she remained the one friend whom he knew somehow understood the intensity of what he was going through. She knew him and also the love and connection he had shared with Tess. They talked a lot when he was away travelling, mostly about things that they both had been doing, seen, listened to, read or had enjoyed. Their communication had remained easy and open and caring. Ironically, given their first connection was at primary school where they had hardly spoken a word, they had now become best friends.

Kara's world had shifted dramatically since that fateful night's call. She had returned to Clare to her work, but somehow her head and heart were now linked to the city and wherever Greg was.

She spent every weekend in Adelaide at her Aunt Sarah's, or the odd occasion crashing in the guest room at Greg's after a late-night dinner. Those nights were the hardest. She was forever conscious that Greg had not initiated anything that suggested he was ready to rekindle the intimate and sexual connection they'd shared prior to Tess's death. She kept reminding herself that these were 'early days' really. She'd promised herself that she would wait for him however long it took despite her growing desire to touch, be touched and feel him inside her once again. Alone, she would indulge herself, her fingers enticing the butterfly touch to arousal and her memory flight back to the times together, when they were excited by the sight, groans and elated sexual encounters with each other, and with others.

Together, they'd tasted the world where sharing and exchanging in sexual encounters with others had stimulated them to feel that genuine bond of compersion. Each deriving excitement from watching the other receiving and giving pleasure to others. Rather than evoke jealously, it had intensified their desires for more open, honest expression with each other; building a confidence, the urgent desire to experiment, and express more about their sexual selves.

So, Kara held back. Waiting. However long it took.

Her home in Clare had always been her sanctuary. She'd created it out of the ashes of her past life, but somehow, these days, the predictable country town culture, offered no real solace. Neither did her work- which had always inspired her driving force. These days, she found herself in a strange state of inertia, moving along only until she returned to the city. Somehow, being closer to Greg and being surrounded by unknown people and opportunities was all she desired, which saw her marking time during the days until she could return to Adelaide.

When he worked away, she found herself wandering through her days, suspended in hope that her friend was going okay. Greg had somehow moved into the first priority in her life, and neither of them knew it.

Greg had landed in yet another city for a job, having maintained a gruelling schedule for himself and his team since his return to work. This time he was in Sydney, preparing for a software launch for an ICT company. Greg was unusually restless. He'd focussed firmly on 'life ahead' during the past month, including moving back to his own apartment in North Adelaide. While Monique, Tess's mum, had told him to stay at Tess's unit for as long as he wanted, he was conscious it belonged to them and in reality, it had just been too hard to remain there with so many reminders of Tess.

Having slowly started to regain the rhythm of his work life, the regular trips away gave him a routine that was somehow comforting despite the frantic pace. Part of that appetite for success was also powered by the flavour and delicacy of sex which had always previously featured in his life.

Those feelings were stirring once more.

Back in his hotel room, after enjoying a couple of beers to unwind from a full-on day at the ICT launch with his team, Greg finally relaxed enough to allow himself to indulge in some sexy thoughts. He wondered what it was about hotel rooms that initiated those feelings. He already knew that most people play with themselves in hotel rooms, male or female it was just something that seemed to happen. Maybe it was the clean, sterile and pristine room? The feeling of a little indulgent luxury, the crisp clean sheets or even perhaps the naughtiness of walking around naked in an anonymous room? Who knows, but… it happens. Greg remembered how Kara had once told him how instantly 'naughty' she always felt when she stayed away in a hotel. He remembered her description of how she touched herself and how it had so stimulated and inspired her to indulge in their first phone sex encounter.

Greg pondered this phenomenon more, as he felt the urge to stroke himself. He hadn't even thought of sex or bothered to wank in these past months. As these feelings stirred, he wondered how many others might be engaging in a little self-indulgent pleasure at that same time in that hotel. He then thought that given that there are as many businesswomen in this hotel as men, they have either already done it or were going to when they return from the bar and or restaurant and hop into bed with a toy or some accommodating fingers. By this calculation, Greg considered that reasonably, there should be some of these horny women in the bar.

Suddenly sparked by these thoughts, he quickly showered and headed down to the restaurant to look for a table and have dinner. He went to the bar, ordered a wine and looked around to find that most tables were taken up with only one person probably overnighting for meetings or work tomorrow.

He noticed a blonde lady, around his age, playing on her phone while she waited for her meal to arrive. Given that there were no free tables, he felt a challenge arise, and with a little extra confidence from the drinks already consumed, he strolled over to her table.

'Excuse me, are you expecting anyone else to join you or are you on your own?' He knew she was by herself, as there was only a setting for one. He kept talking rather quickly, 'But please… before you answer, my name is Greg and I would like to ask if I could join you? There are no free tables and I promise I am a nice person, without an agenda. I'm hoping you might simply enjoy some company—as would I.'

Megan looked up, offering only a hint of a smile. He at least had her attention. He smiled back, continuing, 'How about this? I will be on a five-minute probation and if I haven't impressed you enough in that time I will up and leave you be, and just admire your beauty from a distance… and besides… by that time your meal will be here.'

She smiled at this unusual attempt at a pick-up. 'Five minutes, hey?'

He nodded. 'Yes, just five.' Her smile widened as a faint glow rose in her cheeks.

'Okay, just so long as you don't try to chat me up. I have no intention or desire to run off and jump in the sack with anyone.'

'Sure—deal!'

'Then, please join me, I'm Megan,' as she stretched out her hand.

'Nice to meet you, Megan,' shaking her hand as he took the seat opposite.

Greg's smile always made any woman feel comfortable, and Megan had certainly warmed to it. He knew confident professional woman were so much easier to talk to, as often their jobs required them to be outgoing and able to communicate well. He asked Megan all about her work, what brought her here, and the parts she enjoyed about being in Sydney. She told him about her role as a middle manager for a real estate company, how she mostly handled property management and some of their national conferences, which is why she was there. He briefly told her about his job, careful not to disclose too many connections, and played down his position.

The five minutes had well and truly lapsed, both having slipped into an engrossed conversation. Greg casually asked if he could order and eat with her.

'Please do,' she said, her smile now replaced with a grin, 'Besides, I think you've passed the probation period!'

Their meals arrived, his being served only a short time after hers. He ordered a bottle of Penfolds 389 and in no time, they were talking freely and openly. They started to talk about the other people in the bar, as they'd spotted a couple of rather intoxicated men, making poor attempts to chat up some other single women.

'Hey, would you like to play a game? It's something I do sometimes when I'm away and sitting in a dining room on my own. It's just a bit of speculative fun,' he said.

'Sure, why not?' Megan said, clearly relaxing as she was enjoying her second glass of wine.

'Okay, we each choose someone and then we say what we think might be their 1. Occupation. 2. Marital status and 3. How they satisfy their sexual appetite while they are away from home.'

Megan laughed, 'Sounds like fun. Who first?'

Greg pointed out a gentleman sitting nearby. 'You first.'

Megan glanced at the man sitting at the table adjacent to them. After only minutes she said, 'He's an easy one! He looks like an insurance assessor, works full time and is sick of it. Clearly married. Too boring and programmed to do anything too naughty, but I think he'll be tempted to watch a porn movie, then have sexy dreams before going home to his wife and assuming the missionary position once a month, if he's lucky!'

'Well done, I have to agree!'

'Your turn.' Megan said. She glanced around the room, spotting a lone woman sitting in the corner of the dining room. She was dressed in a suit, her mid-length dark hair was neatly shaped into a tailored bob reading papers as she ate, stopping between mouthfuls to write a few notes. 'Okay, what about that woman?' asked Megan.

Greg smiled. 'She's middle management for sure. Trying hard to make sure she's ahead of the rest. Probably finance or planning, something where she has to compete with mostly men in her job. She's divorced and now career focused. She'll go back to her room, allow herself enough time to use her compact vibrator to escape from her day and to help her sleep.'

Megan laughed out loud. 'You've certainly done this before, haven't you? That's so like how I was thinking! So, who next?'

Greg looked around the dining room very carefully this time. He singled out a lady, he estimated to be in her forties, attractive, with shoulder length mousy blonde hair.

'Let's imagine her life together this time, shall we?'

'Okay,' Megan said, now clearly relaxed and enjoying the game.

'I think she comes from money,' Megan continued. 'Just look at that dress, her hair, her jewellery, clearly no expense spared there. I think she's married by the looks of it. Well-travelled, and away from home a lot.'

'She seems pretty comfortable on her own.' Greg said as he poured Megan another wine. Greg decided to take a risk at this point and boldly asked, 'So do you think male escort, vibrator or self-love for this woman?'

'Vibrator for sure,' she responded without hesitation. There was a moment of silence while Greg took in Megan's answer. She blushed slightly, sensing his reaction to her bold, near self-exposing response.

She hurriedly continued... 'Anyway, what makes you think she will indulge in pleasuring herself while she is here?'

'I think just about everyone touches themselves in hotel rooms when they travel on their own.' Slowly Megan nodded in agreement, as Greg continued; 'I think she is a fingers girl. She's clearly a confident woman and knows exactly what she wants and how to get it.'

'Is that right?'

'Of course!' Greg said with a smile.

'Hey, would you like me to tell you how I think it would go?' he asked. 'I could even describe it for you in detail if you like.'

Megan's eyes widened slightly. 'I'm intrigued.'

'Okay. She'll go back to her room. Everything is exactly where it should be, because she is a perfectionist. As the door closes, she places her glass of wine on the table, still half full, left over from her dinner. She kicks off her shoes, reaching behind to lower the zip of her dress, gliding it down slowly off her body as she watches herself in the mirror. She hangs her dress, and faces the mirror again as she removes her bra, admiring her beautifully shaped breasts. Just this is arousing for her. She runs her hands over them slowly then heads to the bathroom to clean her teeth, enjoying the fact her breasts, while still perky, just sway with the movement of the brushing motion. She quickly removes her make-up, before heading back to the bedroom and slides off her knickers. This time, not placing them in a neat pile, just recklessly kicking them aside. What she has planned won't require underwear.

'She takes a sip of her wine, which is a little tainted by the toothpaste, and stretches out on the bed, laying her head back, and closing her eyes, she thinks of a work colleague she met today. Immediately her hands explore her soft skin. She caresses her breasts, nipples, her tummy, imagining her hands are that of a lover seducing her. While one hand stays clenched to a breast, the other is sliding down her leg toward the creases in her groin. Her legs fall apart slightly, and she brushes her now swelling lips. She is wet and can feel it without touching. She pinches one of her nipples as her other finger caresses her clit for the first time. Sliding it down to her soaked pussy, then gliding up to begin massaging her now firm button. She strokes it like only a woman who knows what and how to turn herself on, can. She rubs it with more pressure and speed until she feels the warmth start to build inside her. As the heat envelops her, she twitches, feeling her ultimate pleasure building inside. Her knees are now bent and wide apart, feeling the ecstasy about ready to leave her soul and exit through her hot vagina. She stops, letting the bubbling orgasm settle, and breathes deeply. She struggles to let her fingers lay to her side and her body calm down, despite wanting more. She waits until her body subsides, until only a hint of arousal remains tingling inside her. Taking herself again, this time aroused to that point, the ultimate place, so much faster than the time before, and so it was only after a short time that she stops her touch again, just poised before her climax. Leaving it a little longer this time, allowing nearly all sensation to subside, knowing the next time she won't be stopping. Her pussy is still twitching slightly, but her legs have stopped quivering and shaking. She starts again tentatively, anticipating that this will be the one. Her clit is hard, her pussy swollen and her groin so wet. Her head falls back as she builds the rhythm, fighting to keep her fingers moving softly and ever so slowly, relishing in the excitement of knowing this time will be it. Despite the urge to rub hard and fast, she deliberately lifts her hand, positioning it to allow only the slightest and most delicate touch. Her index finger rolls over her like a slow, whisper. How she wished someone was there with her. She breathes hard and deep once more. She's now desperately concentrating on other thoughts, anything other than what her fingers are doing, allowing only her body to succumb to the sensation. Once again, the heat rises, the tingles rage through her body, starting at her vagina and radiating to every inch of her. She can feel it building so much bigger than the first two. An explosion is sparking, her entire insides are going to exit through her and out between her legs, and she doesn't care. Her head is fully thrown back, her hips thrusting, as she imagines her colleague filling her. She can almost smell him, taste him, as he pounds deep into her. It started from a place so deep and continues to build till she explodes. She lets out a cry that could have been heard from two rooms away, but she doesn't care. She feels her pleasure gush from between her legs, her juices flowing, squirting from her pussy, to run down to her arse. The orgasm doesn't stop as she convulses with total ecstasy. As she slowly returns to earth, still quivering and shaking, she takes some deep breaths. "My God, that was huge!" she whispers to herself.'

Greg looked at Megan, perched on the edge of her seat, leaning forward to listen. She had barely moved since he first started to recount the story. Her cheeks were now flushed and her mouth agape. Greg just smiled gently.

Megan eventually found her voice, 'I am in room 1226. I'll be ready in about ten minutes, if you'd like to join me.' With that, Megan stood up from the table, grabbed her bag and headed straight toward the lobby lifts.

Greg sipped the last of his wine as he intently watched Megan walk off. For a split second he saw Tess in Megan, a sharp pain stabbing him in the heart. He closed his eyes as the pain pulsed through him. When he opened them, Megan was gone.

He breathed in. 'I can do this,' he replayed to himself, as he finished his glass and grabbed the still half full wine bottle to take to her room. He signalled to the nearest waiter, then confirmed the night's tab for this table to be charged to his room.

The door was slightly ajar in welcome when he arrived, inviting him to enter.

He walked inside, his eyes scanning furiously. *Megan must be in the bathroom.*

He called out a gentle, 'Hello.'

'Just a second.'

Megan appeared from the bathroom wearing a loosely fastened hotel robe, looking very attractive, her hazel eyes held wide, as she smiled at him with a somewhat shy, yet seductive grin.

He stepped up close, placing a hand on either side of her face. He stared into her eyes, moving slowly to caress her lips with his. Soft, but purposeful. He teased her with small kisses and sucked her lips. As the passion built, so did the depth of their kisses, as she removed his shirt, belt and pants. He kicked off his shoes and within a flick, he was naked, all bar his socks. Her robe now fell open revealing her curved slim form with silky alabaster skin, underneath. He slid the robe off her shoulders, allowing it to fall to the floor without resistance. He put his hands on her waist, deftly leading her toward the bed, before laying her back across the sheets. It was only then that he moved decisively, to position himself between her legs. All the while he held himself above her. Greg, now fully aroused, already knew from the gentle rise of her hips that she was ready to receive him. 'Do you want me?'

'Yes,' escaped from her lips, in a barely audible whisper.

He lowered himself on her. Megan instinctively wrapped her legs around his waist as he penetrated her, slowly at first, then building to rhythmic thrusts, deep and hard. Megan arched with every stroke, ensuring she received every millimetre of him. It had been a long time since Greg had a woman. He was instantly transported to that place of lust and passion that too few people truly get to experience. He was lost in the moment, with her soft long blonde hair floating over him. Her delicious womanly scent and taste, a mix of perspiration, perfume and sex, now ultimately blended with the sensation of him deep inside her. He luxuriated in how wet and warm she felt, how she rose to each thrust, moaning each time he filled her. He had been here before.

'I love you, Tess,' he whispered in Megan's ear. She stopped moving immediately. She fell limp as Greg stopped and returned from that place of passion with a thud. Megan gently pushed to roll Greg off her, as she softly asked, 'Greg, who is Tess? Is she your wife?'

'What?' Greg was still hazy. 'How do you know about Tess?'

'You just called me Tess, is she your wife?'

Greg moved to sit upright in a flash. He felt the heat of embarrassment and confusion rush through him. He muttered quickly, 'I'm really sorry Megan, it's a long story. I really can't talk about it now. I am so sorry, I'd better go.'

He turned away, to sit on the edge of the bed with his head in his hands, as she quickly grabbed her robe and sat next to him. She placed her hand in the middle of his back rubbing him softly 'It's okay. It's cool if you're married. I understand, let's keep going.'

Greg didn't say a word. He started gathering his clothes, he wanted to leave as fast as he could. She sensed his discomfort and touched him gently on the arm, saying, 'Greg, you don't have to go or tell me any details. Please stay.' Greg shook his head. 'Well just know that I'd love to see you again, when you're ready.' Greg swallowed hard. He didn't really want to talk about it at all, but knew she deserved some explanation.

'I'm so sorry Megan, Tess was my fiancée, and she was killed in a car accident some months ago.' He continued, 'I thought I was ready, but I'm clearly not. I'm so sorry about tonight, but I would like to see you again, one day.' He stood and moved to grab the rest of his clothes.

The room was silent as he dressed and gathered his phone and keys. In the seconds before he closed the door behind him, he turned, placing one of his business cards in her hand. 'This is me.' He put his hand gently on her cheek. 'I'm really sorry Megan, I hope we can meet again sometime.'

Megan watched him leave. His head and shoulders drooped as the door clicked behind him.

Greg was completely despondent as he left Megan's room and headed to his suite. He didn't know what to feel, just that the whole experience had engulfed him. More than even the embarrassment of this encounter, all he could think about at this moment was his Tess. The pain of her loss was nearly insurmountable.

He'd thought he was dealing with his grief so well, that enough time had passed that he could once again enjoy the touch and feel of another woman. *But maybe not yet. Maybe not ever?*

He missed her, he always would. From the first touch of Megan, he had been consumed by the fragrance of Tess. Megan had become Tess. The sheer essence of her had overtaken his sense of touch, smell and taste and had penetrated his flesh through this other woman.

He slept badly, woken by turbulent memories of beautiful times with Tess throughout the night, tempered by the image of Megan's face staring at him with confusion. Waking well before the alarm, he dragged himself into the shower.

As the water ran over him, he allowed the events of the night to wash away. 'It was just one night. Forget all about it,' he told himself. But despite how much he tried, the thoughts of Tess and the resurgent pain of her loss lingered with him all day.

When he entered his room that evening, he undressed, poured a wine and ordered room service for his evening meal.

No dining room encounters tonight, he thought.

He opened his laptop, ready to check a few emails before his meal arrived. The phone rang. It was Kara. He hesitated, but then answered, 'Hello Kara,' he said in a subdued tone.

Kara sensed he was in a quiet mood, and replied accordingly. 'Hello there to you too. Lots on your plate tonight?'

Greg, wanting to quickly recover his usual casual demeanour, replied 'Nah, I'm good, just tired. I had a tough day.'

Kara recognised that tone. He had Tess on his mind, but she didn't want to press. She knew to just let it go. He would share if and when he was ready. She replied, 'Well, you're not alone there! It's been a crazy day for me too!' Kara told him about her day, noting he was not fully engaged.

Kara stopped talking. Took a breath and said, 'Hey look, you do sound really tired. I'll let you go, I just wanted to know you were alive and…'

'Kara, no, please don't go. I do want to talk to you. Something happened last night.'

'Okay, sure. What happened?'

Greg proceeded to tell her all about how he was still having reminder flashbacks and catching glimpses of Tess everywhere. He told her about meeting Megan, how they shared a meal together and played the 'sexual preference game.' He shared how retelling Kara's account of playing with herself, had resulted in an invitation to Megan's room.

He paused, then continued. 'Kara, I told her I loved her and called her Tess, as I was making love to her. I didn't even realise. Everything just stopped. Right there. For her and for me.

'I didn't really know what to do. I couldn't believe what I'd done. It was all I could think of, to just get out of there. It was embarrassing for both of us.'

Kara listened. She could imagine the scene, and her first thoughts were how bad he must have felt. After a while she said, 'Greg, that must have felt awful! But it's understandable.'

'You think? It can't be!'

'Actually, yes. It's quite natural to have flashbacks and its only early days still. Hey, tell me, did she have long blonde hair?'

'Yes, she did.'

'Well then, that makes even more sense! It was one of the things you so loved about Tess, so it's only natural you associated this Megan lady with her, especially during sex. Did you say anything to her about why?'

'I wanted to disappear through the floor, but yes, I did. I told her that my fiancée died and I apologised.'

'How did she react?'

'She was really calm and very understanding. She just said she was so sorry, it was okay, and she'd like to see me again one day, if ever I wanted.'

'Sounds like you picked a nice woman. It could have been lots worse, you know.'

'You're dead right—it could.'

There was quite a time where both were just thinking over the phone, before Greg asked, 'Kara, do you think I will ever be able to make love to a woman again without Tess being there?'

'Of course, you will! Please don't be too hard on yourself. It will be alright, just give yourself a bit more time.'

Greg let out a sigh. 'I suspect you are right. Thank you, I needed to hear that.'

They continued to chat for a while before ending the call with a promise to catch up for a meal when Greg returned to Adelaide the following week.

After the call ended, Kara's thoughts started churning. She felt for him, knowing how bad he would have felt to have exposed his vulnerability, especially during sex, and how confronting this would have been to happen in the arms of a completely unknown woman.

Kara knew he would've hated not being in control of a situation and that Megan had unknowingly hit that underlying 'Tess' nerve that was omnipresent in him.

However, Kara was confronted with unnatural feelings of her own in that moment. As Greg spoke, she could feel herself becoming agitated, the heat in her cheeks rise, and she kept moving uncomfortably.

It didn't take much to really understand why she felt so rattled. She instinctively knew Tess was clearly in his everyday subconscious thoughts, indicating he was still feeling her loss deeply. Kara also realised that she had felt the pangs of a combination of jealousy and complete inadequacy. A response she hadn't expected. She'd been so prepared to wait and not apply any pressure until Greg was ready for sexual connection with someone again. Now she realised that secretly within herself, she'd expected it would be her he would reach out to; but instead it was another woman. A complete stranger.

Kara scolded herself nearly as quickly as she started to lament the situation. *You know you can't control 'horny,' especially when an opportunity arises. One can really never know when or where or with whom ignites it!*

Nonetheless, Kara was feeling a tiny bit hurt. She didn't begrudge her friend for a second, pleased that he had at least reclaimed the urge for some fun again after all the pain of the past months.

She was shocked by her own reaction. She felt nothing so strongly like this before, not even when she was watching him have sex with another woman right in front of her, or when he had spoken of how beautiful and attractive Tess or another woman was.

'Kara, you are being crazy girl—stop it!' she told herself firmly. 'He's your best friend, and he loves you for that. Listen to your own advice. This has nothing to do with you. Let him heal.'

Chapter 4

As the taxi approached her street, Megan felt the shiver vibrate down her spine. Arriving home didn't feel the same tonight. Much of it was due to the guilt she'd felt for having betrayed him. She had shamed him in one selfish moment by inviting a man to her room.

Throughout the flight home, she kept asking herself how she had so easily forgotten that she was a mother and a wife. How had she succumbed so easily to give herself to a stranger that she had met in a bar. She was shocked that it had been so effortless, easy and exciting. Even worse, she had to face Michael, her husband.

At the time she gave Greg her room number, she knew Michael was home with Matt and Tracey, checking their school and Uni assignments and cleaning up after their dinner. She had never done anything like this before.

She knew her justifications were feeble, but somehow, she kept trying to make them shout out louder to drown out her behaviour two nights ago in Sydney.

It pained her that Michael hasn't really been the same since his job had become redundant, opting to accept a payout and assume home duties. He still works out and looks good. He's as calmly proficient as he'd always been.

She knew his love for her was still buried deep inside him.

At first, it was fun and a welcome change for them both to have reversed roles, but the spark has dimmed. Well, truthfully, it's borderline extinguished.

He had never complained about working part time as a simple technician at the local computer store, slotted in between the demands of their two typical 'live at home', indulged older kids. He'd never made her feel bad about being the bigger income earner now, yet she knew how that quietly ate away at his pride and self-worth, with each dollar more that she made. His life was now predictable, his world had narrowed from that of the innovative corporate leader, to that of the local school council chair. He shops, cooks, cleans and manages each day with precision, organises everything for everyone else and has become exceptional manager of their lives.

It is, however, the same almost every day, week and month. His life is now one big 'to do' list. The household itself had somehow developed needs that have subtly overtaken their individual lives.

She felt that even sex and intimacy was scheduled in on the third Friday of every month, as routine as the trash being taken out. Now she felt like she'd shattered the balance and code of their safe, yet predictable life.

She got out of the taxi and her mind continued to pound the thoughts about her actions and what she should do. Her steps slowed as she walked up the driveway.

Should I confess? Tell him everything that happened? Tell him I'm sorry and that when they had both realised that nothing about this encounter was right, the man had left.

But I can't tell him that, because it's not true. Actually, I revelled in the reawakening of my unadulterated desires, and I truly and desperately wanted more of him, to finish what he started.

Maybe I should ask Michael if he has ever succumbed to desire when he was away on all those executive trips? That if he did, I totally understand. I now know how easily it can happen. It's just sex. It's not love. No! He won't accept any of that! Oh God! Should I just leave?

Stop. Get a grip, woman. It was a completely momentary lapse of judgement and in the end, you found yourself supporting a nice man who was caught in his own grief. That was it. You will never see him again. Find that homecoming smile and let it rest. No good can come from telling him.

She reached the back door and stopped. She drew in a breath, rubbed her hands down her body to smooth her dress, her back straightening just slightly. Megan opened the back door and walked inside. She looked at Michael, standing right where she knew he would be, at the kitchen bench, checking the plans for tomorrow.

'Hi darling, it's so nice to be home.' She found the smile that outwardly looked as warm and bright as the one she gave him when she left a week ago. Deep down, she knew her life would never be the same.

During the next few weeks, Megan was busy, she barely had time to revisit those thoughts of her last trip. But here she was in Melbourne for the third time this month. Michael had not been pleased that she was leaving again, and his parting words had smarted.

'Another work trip—seriously? Just think of me back here at home while you enjoy Melbourne again.' She thankfully had swallowed her first response that was sharper than a slap across his face, after herself having spent years in the shoes he now wore. She had once before spoken similar words too. Megan simply gave him a hug and headed out the door.

After a full day of meetings, she walked the six blocks to the hotel to shed the contractual debates and deadline reminders that were still swimming in her head along with Michael's last words, that were still stinging.

Only one more day, thank goodness.

Strolling along Collins Street, she settled into a casual pace, enjoying how it defied everyone passing her, as they pushed on with sombre end of day faces that were focused on just getting home.

Walking through the elegant entrance to the Treasury, she stopped and looked up as she always did. She loved staying in this hotel. The huge chandeliers suspended from a height two floors above, the marble floor, stone pillars and long proud cedar counters of this historic bank now blended with elegant modern décor, evoking such an eclectic sense of grandeur. Hearing music coming from the bar, in the wide-open area to the left of the entrance, she broke her usual routine of going straight to her room to shower before dinner, deciding to enjoy a quiet drink and listen to a song or two.

Settling on a stool at the end of the bar, she smiled as the bartender approach.

'Good evening, what is your pleasure tonight?'

'Good evening. May I have an Espresso Martini please?'

'Certainly Madam.'

Waiting for her drink to arrive, she looked around the bar, watching all the different people coming and going and taking seats at the tables nearby. A grin emerged. The bartender's innocent question, 'What's your pleasure?' had sparked a restlessness and a tingle inside her. Tonight, she was shedding work, and leaving home behind her, and just going to enjoy being a lone woman in a city and place she loved. Nothing more.

She remembered the game she played with Greg and began looking at individual patrons with secret delight.

I wonder how you will pleasure yourself tonight? she smiled to herself. It wasn't long before she indulged in fantasising about secret sexy self-indulgences.

I wonder which guy might be stroking himself while watching in-house porn movies? Which lone lady might rub herself while luxuriating in the spa bath in her room? I'm thinking that couple might be at the hotel for a naughty secret hook up.

As she sipped her drink, she was lost in her mind game, completely unaware of her body swaying to the music and the innocently devilish smile on her face as she pictured their sexy indulgences in her mind. She glanced at the two guys creating the music, one on a keyboard, and the other singing while playing the guitar. Sounds she had lost herself in. She threw the singer a smile and gave a little clap at the end of the song, in appreciation of the song choices which she had loved: Elton, Bruno, and Robbie had seemed to be just right tonight.

He smiled back and winked.

Was he winking at me? She stole another look. He was staring right at her. *Oh my God, he's so young. He can't be a day over thirty. Surely, he isn't really looking at me? Oh! Yes, he is.*

The blush that flooded her face was a heated cocktail of embarrassment and excitement.

What IS your pleasure tonight, Megan? Is it him? Stop that! She scolded herself. Now you're just being silly and you need to go and order dinner. Flattering? Of course, it is. Silly? Well…?

She stood, ready to walk to the other side of the lobby to the dining room. *You're being ridiculous. Time for a quick meal and up to your room. You've got the final meetings for this audit tomorrow.*

Suspended in her own mind talk, she hadn't noticed the music had stopped and switched over to the pre-recorded soundtrack. The touch of a hand on her shoulder startled her. She turned abruptly to see the singer standing right behind her.

'Excuse me. I just wanted to thank you for listening. I knew at least one person appreciated the music.'

She swallowed the first feeling of embarrassment about her own recent thoughts and quickly found the words. 'Why, hello… err… well, you're welcome. I thoroughly enjoyed your music. You guys are very talented.'

'Thank you, I play here most Thursday nights. I'm Sam, by the way.'

'Hello Sam, I'm Megan.'

'Nice to meet you, Megan.'

There was an awkward silence before Megan asked, 'So are you finished for the evening?'

'No, I'm on a break. We've got one more set to go.'

Something inside her just didn't want the conversation to stop there. 'Sam, let me buy you a drink. Consider it a thank you from a new fan.'

'That would be nice, thank you.'

Their drinks were served. The recorded music was loud from the speakers overhead. Megan winced and pointed toward the Bistro tables away from the bar. As they walked to a table and sat down Sam asked, 'So, Megan, I hope you don't mind me asking, but please tell me what was making you smile tonight? I couldn't help notice you lost in your thoughts.'

'Oh, you *were* watching me? It was nothing, really. I just like people watching and making up stories about them. It helps to stop me feeling awkward, when I'm in a place on my own.'

'That's clever. Not many people stay long in a bar on their own without friends or at least a work mate to keep them company. I'm not a fan of travelling for gigs either or staying away from home on my own.'

Megan laughed. 'Well, sadly, that is mostly the story of my life. I work away a lot. This is my third trip here this month. Thankfully, I head home tomorrow.'

'So where is home?'

'Adelaide.'

'I love Adelaide. The Fringe Festival is incredible. Blake and I actually played there last year.' He had tossed a smile with his reply that made her swallow hard before replying.

'Really? That's brilliant.'

Their exchange ebbed and flowed, and while mostly superficial information about each other, Megan was enraptured. Something about the fact he visited Adelaide added even more attraction to the delicacy of their conversation. The combination of his natural, sultry looks, his voice and the connection to home grabbed her instantly like the first taste of a smooth new flavour. They both lost any sense of time.

Just then Megan could see a hotel staffer walk up behind him. She nodded towards him, signalling Sam to look around. 'Excuse me, Sam, you're on.'

'Yeah, sure. I'm coming.' Turning back to Megan, he grinned. 'I think I'm in trouble! Sorry, Megan. It's only a few more songs— I hope you'll stay.'

'I'd love to, but I'm thinking it's really time I headed to my room, I really should be getting ready for my meetings tomorrow.'

'Oh, come on… you have to eat and why not enjoy a little more music to end your day? Hey… pick a song and I'll play it for you.'

'Really? I can't think of one, I really don't know…'

Sam had picked the suppressed restlessness swirling inside her. It was as if she was bursting to let her inner freedom and feelings escape. He sensed she only needed and wanted someone to open the door. He was a willing doorman.

'It's okay, I think I've got just the song. Please stay. One of the songs in this set will be for you. You can tell me after which one you think it was and tell me if I got it right.' With that, he stood up and headed back to his guitar.

Megan signalled a waiter and then ordered a table and some food. She'd unconsciously pressed herself firmly in the chair. Her body had already made the decision not to leave. She stayed, enjoyed her meal, serenaded by Sam and Blake's music and the indulgence of a night on her own, as simply herself.

It was the second to last song, and she caught it. It was subtle, yet resounding and beautiful. She loved Charlie Puth's songs. That was the first chord that struck. The lyrics did the rest.

Sam had not turned his gaze from her throughout the entire song.

There had been no hesitation or second thoughts as she waited for Sam to load up the sound equipment into Blake's van. Nor when he met her at the night entrance to the hotel and she led him by the hand to her suite. Not a flicker of self-consciousness as she pulled him into a deep embrace within seconds of closing the door.

His lips melted into her neck like the song had graced her soul, so softly, and yet with fierce piercing intensity.

They shed their clothes in seconds, all the time, their hands never seeming to lose connection with each other's flesh. His tongue traced from her neck, across her left shoulder and then down between her breasts. He paused to kiss each of her nipples, suck them and then resume his kisses. 'Just stand still,' he murmured as he moved his body slowly down to his knees, kissing and sucking on her skin inch by inch, until he reached her wetness. Here he stopped.

Kneeling in front of her, his fingers and his tongue found her, already her clit was so firm and her pussy was dripping with anticipation. Megan's whole body was nearly convulsing at his touch. She reached down, gripping his long dark hair in her hands, curling the locks around her fingers to pull him closer. She kept holding him in close between her legs, as she sat on the edge of the bed, laid back and kept drawing his tongue deeper inside her. She had not felt like this for so long. As his tongue and lips savoured her, it took only seconds before she succumbed, coming in his mouth and letting out the first of many moans. Barely waiting for her orgasm to subside, she pulled him up the length of her body, now clamouring to feel all of his pounding muscles on her and inside her. Sam was huge, the biggest man she'd ever had. She could feel his cock so thick and deep inside her, she already knew she would be sore. She didn't care. This was a delicious pain she could take all night.

They made love for what seemed like hours. As if suspended in time, Megan was completely lost in sheer sexual indulgence. She loved the feel of this younger man desiring her, thrusting hard deep inside her, bringing her to climax over and over, with the thrill and excitement that only a stranger can. Her passion just kept rising, wanting more and more each time.

Sam's own arousal and enjoyment of Megan's heightened response to his every touch was escalating too, beyond anything he had ever experienced before. He had not expected such passion or such near insatiable desire for more in any woman. He eventually could resist no longer and whispered, 'Oh God, I'm going to cum... can I fill you?'

'Yes, Oh God. Yes!'

Sam exploded, filling her with his seed with deep, hard pounding. She felt the pulsing of his cock as he kept squirting inside her.

As his breathing slowed, so did his thrusts. He had given her everything, now totally and blissfully spent. Megan was reeling with the feel of the warmth and flood of him that still pulsed deep inside. She felt so satisfied, but despaired at the withdrawal of the warmth as his thick flesh pulled out of her.

They laid back for a short time before he rolled to move closer toward her. As he softly brushed a strand of hair from her face, he leant forward to kiss her gently on the cheek.

'Beautiful, I need to go.'

He quickly dressed, kissed her on the lips once more, thanked her and he was gone. As the door clicked closed, she lay back, both exhausted and exalted on the bed. This had been everything she had secretly yearned for. A buried fantasy that had finally come to life.

She whispered to herself, 'I'm a really bad girl' smiling on the inside.

She immediately knew there was no going back. She'd indulged herself in this drug, and she wanted more. Sleep followed within seconds, while her dreams continued to replay the delight that her body had exhausted.

Chapter 5

This morning, her stirring thoughts were of the night before, and not anything about home or her family. That was the true guilt. Right there. She had enjoyed herself, loved the escape and the fact she had not considered any consequences or anyone's feelings other than her own. She had indulged her own fantasies and secrets, and it had felt wonderful.

As the normality of another workday and travel back to Adelaide enveloped her, only then she felt the pangs. She hadn't yet wanted to admit that her worry and anxiety was more about fear of now needing to suppress her desires and resume her 'normal life' when she got home, rather than the guilt she felt before about having betrayed her husband. Little did Megan realise how much her sexual desires had infected her, or that there was no simple antidote.

She was surprised at how quickly that initial shame had near engulfed her when she had previously returned home after meeting Greg. It had only flickered in her and subsided so swiftly, as she walked into her home once again on the Friday night. In fact, she was feeling quite liberated.

'Hello darling,' she called out as she walked up to Michael, giving him a big hug. 'Oh, you've kept some food for me, you are so sweet, I'm starving.'

'Of course, don't I always?' Michael paused; Megan seemed unusually bubbly after arriving home from her work trip. 'So, it all went well? You seem pretty happy.'

Keep it in check girl, she told herself. 'Oh, no. Well, err… yes. I suppose, this trip ended up with some very unexpected but positive results, I ended up with everything I needed.'

'That's great. Come on, time to eat.' As Megan sat down to eat the meal, she breathed in, her vagina still stinging from the abuse it copped last night while gulping and swallowing in her own justification. *Well, I didn't lie, really. I just didn't say exactly how my needs were satisfied.*

Aware how much her inner glow was pounding against her, Megan had worked hard to regain her normal demeanour and approach to life at home. She tried not to let her thoughts drift back to those memorable Sydney and Melbourne encounters, or indulge her now raging desire for sex and intimacy. Just looking at Michael, she now could see his body before hearing any of his words. She saw, heard, and could nearly taste sex everywhere.

However, she tried to remain outwardly composed and slowly fell back into the routine.

It lasted for just over a week. She and Michael had hosted friends for a BBQ lunch the following Sunday, which typically extended to dinner and quite a few wines into the night. Megan had loved how she and Michael had shared the preparations to host their friends, finally seeing him so relaxed and able to put his 'responsible self' at rest for some hours. She noticed he'd often glanced at her tonight, giving her 'that grin' that reminded her of the times and pleasures they had shared in those years pre-kids before their now advanced professional lives.

Her thoughts kept rolling. *Deep down, he is a lovely man. I just need to help him find who and how he was. We've both got lost in these past years.*

After clearing up the aftermath of lunch, dinner and bottles as much as their tiredness allowed, they headed to bed.

Lying there next to his warm body, breathing rhythmically, she couldn't help her thoughts indulge. She desperately wanted to feel it. The sensation of skin on skin, moisture, fingertips, a tongue, lips, his cock inside her, her body lifted by his chest, heaving from his escalating breaths as he penetrated and enjoyed her.

Michael was asleep. He had rolled from his side to his back, as his usual gentle snoring started to escape. Megan couldn't sleep—she was horny as hell. Should she just touch herself?

But why, when I have a man lying next to me?

Still under the covers, she edged herself down to the end of the bed, wriggling gently to position herself between his legs. She slid her body upwards, allowing her fingers to rub his inner thighs. She felt him stir, but before he could register, she slipped all the softness of his penis in her mouth. She drew him into her, her lips clasped around his base, drawing him into her mouth, all in one delicious taste.

She held him fully in her mouth, suspended until she could feel his shaft fill and thicken. He was hard and erect, starting to a rousing consciousness that alerted him this was beyond a dream. Megan started rolling her tongue around him, circling and flickering across his knob, before sliding her mouth up and down him from base to tip. She didn't stop.

She thought she heard words 'Megan… what the?' that faded to pleasurable groans. Michael's hands reached out, grabbed her hair, and his motion just followed her rhythm. Up and down, faster and faster. Megan did not stop. She worked him, near devouring him, so desperately wanting him to release and lose total control. His breathing raced and, in a minute or two, she could sense he was so close to coming. In a flash she moved to sit astride him, grabbing him and guiding it deftly and swiftly inside her. He reached out now to grip her by both breasts, as his moan and seed both shuddered into her.

She kept riding him, calling out, 'Come baby… God, just let it go!' Her orgasm engulfed him in return.

Both of them rasping for breath, Michael finally opened his eyes wider and wider, just staring at her.

'Megan, wow, I can't believe...' He couldn't find any more words.

Megan smiled and simply said, 'Sshh now, I've wanted to do that to you for ages.'

She climbed off him and moved to her usual position on her side, facing away from him. She could feel herself sink into the cool sheets, feeling blissfully content. Michael rolled to cuddle her, tucking her close in his arms. He too hadn't done that, in what seemed like years.

'Goodnight darling.' he whispered.

Monday morning dawned with everyone awake early—with the usual routine falling all too easily into place. Michael was up first to make breakfast, made sure showers were staggered, that lunches were organised, found car keys, checked who's in or out for dinner, reminded her to grab her laptop and watched Megan head off to work. The little grin and lingering kiss she left on his lips was the only mention of the unexpected passion she had unleashed on him last night.

Michael stared vacantly at the soapsuds as he washed the dishes from breakfast and the remnants of their Sunday night meal with their friends. As he rolled the dishcloth over the plate repeatedly, he was lost in rumination.

Something isn't right. Megan has changed, she is not the same somehow. She's pleasant, happy, maybe too pleasant and too happy? I don't know. It just feels strange, he thinks.

He grabbed the tea towel to dry what he just washed.

And as for last night... where the fuck did that come from? She's not done anything like that in years!

He nearly dropped a dish, realising he was almost shaking. He tossed the tea towel and took a seat. *Could it be anything to do with the business card I found a month or two ago in her work pants after her trip to Sydney?*

He chided himself. *Stop being ridiculous. Every trip since then she's been to Melbourne, you idiot. Sure, she was quiet after Sydney and then excited after the last trip- but that's business. You've been there. Remember those highs and lows of trips and negotiations? How you hated to talk about the details of work deals when you got home. Stop being stupid. Besides, this is Megan. Mrs professionally responsible.*

Okay, you both really haven't made love like that for ages, but you loved it, and she probably has missed it like you have.

Michael allowed a relieved smile to spread across his face. He did enjoy every part of their Sunday. He had no reason to spoil it now.

Megan had driven to work with a sneaky smile of satisfaction on her face. She knew the near effrontery of her sex imposed on Michael might arouse suspicion—but still; it felt so good. Maybe now she could find all the pleasure and adoration she craved at home from now on.

She could only hope.

Let's wait and see, she thought. *I'm in your hands now. It's over to you, Michael.*

Three weeks later, after returning from a colourless trip to Perth, Megan arrived home to nothing more than the life she had experienced before Sydney and Melbourne. Michael had initiated nothing and her body was stirring. The switch that had been flicked on was sending jolts through her again.

She now kept revisiting every minute of her two encounters again. Her thoughts kept drifting back to that first taste of adulterous passion.

I wonder how Greg is? Could he be ready and want more now?

Oh, stop it woman, he was grieving the loss of his fiancée, he wouldn't have given you a thought! But maybe, just maybe, he has?

The lingering fantasy of them enjoying each other's bodies that had halted so abruptly, still held with her so vividly.

Could I be the one to help him? I nearly did before, so maybe I could now?

She was sitting at her desk at home and started looking through her wallet. *Where did I put his card? I'm sure I put it in here?* She was becoming near frantic to find it. She was now overcome with the desire to contact him.

Then she remembered. She'd put his card in her pocket, so as not to let it get mixed with the many cards that had crammed her wallet after so many trips. This one had been special.

Shit, my pants… Michael would have washed them by now!

That evening she asked Michael casually, 'Hey, you didn't happen to find a business card from an event manager in my pants, did you? It was probably a while ago, after Sydney, I think.' She continued to explain, internally straining to keep a 'matter of fact,' tone in her voice. 'The next company event is looming—I might contact him to handle it. This guy handed it to me as I left the conference. I thought it would be a waste of time, but as it turns out, it might be useful. I haven't got time to organise it with all of my other deadlines at the moment.'

Michael looked strangely relieved as he went to the laundry and came back. He handed her the card. 'Is this the one—Greg Sheppard? I found it, it nearly got washed.'

'Oh, yes, thanks, darling.'

He hesitated for a second. 'Do you think this Sheppard guy is any good?'

'I have no idea, really. His company evidently coordinated the majority of the Sydney event, which was extremely well organised. I'm sure my team will let me know. I'm pleased you salvaged this card, though. Saves me one more job to try to find these guys.'

Megan had watched Michael closely as she spoke. She saw his brow soften, and he returned her gaze. She knew she had told him enough.

Chapter 6

$\mathcal{J}$t was Friday and as Kara was driving from Clare to Adelaide, her phone rang. She expected to be her manager, so she answered without a look to identify the caller. 'Kara Gilbert, Regional Development' she responded automatically.

'Why so formal today, Ms Gilbert?' said the voice. She recognised the voice instantly, it was Greg.

'Oh, hello you,' she said with a laugh, 'Sorry, I expected this to be a work call... How are you? *Where* are you?' she replied quickly.

'I've just landed back in Adelaide and on my way home, where are you?'

'I'm on my way to Aunt Sarah's. I've spent weeks in Clare and touring everywhere, so I'm treating myself to a weekend in town!'

'Want to join me for dinner tonight? Something easy, I'd love to see you.'

'Yes, sure, love to. Is 7.30 too late? I'd like to unpack and say hi to Sarah first, if that's okay?'

'Absolutely. no problems. How about we meet at *La Vigne* on Norwood Parade? We can decide where we want to eat from there. You know there are plenty of places on the Parade that are open till late.'

'Okay, sounds good. I've never been there. It's been a long day, so a taste of France is what I need tonight! See you soon.'

Greg was already sitting on a stool at the bar by the time Kara arrived. He greeted her with a big smile and had a glass of Rosé ready and waiting for her. Kara laughed out loud... 'I so love having a friend who knows me so well!' She climbed onto the stool next to him, accepted the glass and took a sip.

'I really needed this!' she said.

So started their night. It took barely minutes before they'd melded into their usual banter and conversations about all sorts of random topics, as easy as they always did, and time slipped away. They wandered along the street and enjoyed a meal at one of the Asian restaurants, barely stopping their conversation while they paused to order their meal and drinks. They both had drunk too much, but were so enjoying such a relaxed and simple time together.

After main course, they still had the remainder of their bottle to finish. 'I'm toying with the idea of having dessert,' Kara said.

'*I* could be your dessert?' a cheeky suggestive smile crept across his face.

Kara halted. She didn't know what to say in reply. She just looked at him.

'Kara, would you like to come home with me? I've been wanting to ask you that question since you arrived.'

'Are you teasing me?'

Greg's voice lowered. 'No, seriously, to be honest, since the accident, I've felt you've been a step away from me and I wondered if you didn't feel attracted to me in the same way anymore? Are you seeing someone?'

Kara was suddenly reeling with his questions and the overindulgence of wine.

'No, I'm not seeing anyone right now. Yes, sure... um, if you think that would be okay?'

Greg just stopped and looked straight into her eyes. She didn't need to say more. He could see, despite her attempt to sound calm, light-hearted and to avert his stare, that her face betrayed her. He knew instantly that she genuinely missed him, still wanted him, that there was much more behind her words. His heart went out to her in that moment.

'Kara,' he said softly, 'Let's go, shall we?'

Kara, feeling the flush rising to her cheeks, just nodded, trying hard not to look at him for too long.

By the time the cab arrived, Kara had fought and found her composure as best she could and tried to chat with Greg naturally, suppressing the heat rising inside her. When they arrived at his unit, Greg escorted her inside carefully, as if on a first date. He gently took her bag from her shoulder and led her into the lounge room, saying, 'I'll fix us a drink' and disappeared into the kitchen.

Sitting side by side easily on the couch it was after the second sip of wine, that Kara suddenly blurted out, 'Greg, I need to tell you something. I wasn't that happy about something you said about me.'

'Really, I'm sorry, what is it?'

'I can't believe you told Megan the story about how I bring myself to orgasm!'

Greg just smiled. 'Really? That? It's just that you described it so well, I'll never get that story out of my mind!' he laughed, still not sure if she was serious or not.

'I know. But it was my story, our story.' Kara said.

Greg was a bit surprised realising, *she is serious*. 'I'm sorry, I didn't say anything about you, she thinks I just made it up.'

'Well,' Kara said, the wine fully helping her to speak freely, 'you know, I was a bit jealous when you told me about her.'

'What?' asked Greg, now a little surprised.

'Yes, I hate to admit it, but when you told me, sure, I was upset for you about what happened, but I also was wishing—actually hoping, it was *me* you were having sex with. I'm so sorry, but it's honestly how I felt. It felt worse, because you used my story to lure another woman to your bed.'

Greg was motionless for a second or two. He stared at her and could see she was feeling embarrassed, and yet, he knew she spoke of genuine hurt and feelings for him.

Without a thought he moved closer to her, raised his hand to stroke her face and drew her face toward him.

He leant forward to kiss her and said, 'Kara, I'm so very sorry. But you need to know, I don't ever want to upset you. I just didn't want you to be the first after Tess. It just needed to be *us* in our own way, when the time was right. Like now.'

That was all that needed to be said.

From the second their lips met; they were immersed once again. Hands roamed everywhere without question, clothes were discarded, and their bodies were entwined in embrace in every way, that tempted arousal. Frenetic, impatient, and hot, they touched and tasted each other, as if with a hunger and thirst, each desperately needing to be satiated.

Both naked, lying on the floor, touching, kissing, and holding each other, Greg paused as he moved to lay on top of her. Kara could feel him so hard, grazing both her thighs as he inched all of his body even closer.

He looked straight into her eyes. 'I have really missed being with you like this, Kara.'

He entered her in that moment. Her body arched as a satisfying groan escaped her, as deep in sound as was his penetration. She came fast and furiously, likened to the first time when their bodies had connected those couple of years ago.

Their lovemaking moved to his bed, the reclaimed heat and sheer enjoyment of sex which had been dormant for so long in both of them, continued to burn feverously until sleep finally found them, snuggled in a gentle embrace.

Greg woke first and immediately felt the warmth of a body next to him. He looked to see Kara cradled under his arm and sighed with a strange sense of relief. For the first time in so long, he awoke to find the same last image of the night before, to be real and alive in his mind and his arms. *Yes. It was Kara who was here last night, and she's here this morning.* He'd slept truly and soundly for the first time in ages. He hadn't awoken to the stark realisation of loss or emptiness, but just that afterglow of having enjoyed a night of passionate lovemaking.

He smiled as he looked at her. She was sleeping soundly, facing away from him, but as much of her body as possible was pressed against him.

As Greg recalled the intimate events of last evening in detail, his smile widened and he reflected, whispering to himself, 'Kara Gilbert—you have often talked about the many 'firsts' we have shared. This one was so important for me. Thank You.' While she didn't hear his words and wouldn't ever fully realise, Kara had given Greg a fresh 'beginning' experience that, as she would soon discover, had sparked the start of more that neither ever dared to imagine.

As even more of his body started to waken, he let his fingers gently trace down her back.

She responded instinctively in the way, only he could inspire…

Chapter 7

They started the next day blissfully enjoying each other's bodies, in the same way the night before had ended. It was late in the morning. They sat up in bed sipping coffee. Kara couldn't help but notice that Greg seemed more like his old self. Not just that they had enjoyed some amazing sex without any apparent flashbacks, but that he was listening attentively, joking and talking openly.

As Greg told her about his next few projects, Kara sat there, wondering if it was too soon to talk about stepping back into the swing scene again. She hadn't been able to stop thinking about the last time they had enjoyed sex together, which was in the company of another couple. It had been such a turn on.

Greg noticed she wasn't fully listening to him and stopped talking.

'Kara, you are not here, are you? It looks like you've got something on your mind.'

Kara smiled, drew in a deep breath.

'Well, okay, I'm just going to say it… it seems like sleeping with me hasn't upset you too much… so I was wondering if you might be keen to add a couple more bodies into the mix again?'

A grin appeared on his face as he replied. 'So, you've been thinking about *that*, too, have you?'

Kara laughed and slapped him gently on the leg. 'It's such a turn on.'

They both laughed. Kara's tone became a little subdued. 'Look, it was just that our last ever time together was with another couple, and I wondered if you would ever really think about trying it again?'

'Yes, definitely.'

'Perhaps we could try a club?' Kara suggested. 'I know we could find one somewhere, and it might be fun to just look and check out who's there, without having to post ads, wait, chat, and all of that. Besides, if we don't feel like playing with anyone—we don't have to.'

Greg's eyes glistened. 'Sounds like a good plan!'

'Okay, great. But I don't think there is much around here, only private parties. Perhaps we should look interstate?'

'Alright, I'll check what's around in New South Wales. That's where my work is taking me most these days and if I find something promising, perhaps you could grab a weekend away and join me to have a look?'

'Great idea.' Kara's smile was so wide with her reply.

Although this had been a little tentative exchange about starting to consider swing again, inwardly, both of them were getting quite aroused and excited by the idea of exploring some kinky fantasies once more.

It didn't take Greg long before he had researched some clubs, sending a message to Kara, only a couple of days later.

> Found a couple of places that sound alright in Sydney and another in Brisbane. Want to come to Brisbane with me next month on the 10th? I have a short trip for 4 days: Thursday to Sunday. Club is only open Friday and Saturday. Want to try?

Kara was surprised at how quickly he had located a club and loved his enthusiasm. She quickly replied.

> Wow! You've been busy! I'd love to join you. I'm excited. Tingling already!

They set about planning their time away, Greg decided to drive to Brisbane as he had some props to return and have a car at their disposal to visit any location they desired. It was all set. They were to leave on the 8th February, giving them time to arrive comfortably in Brisbane for his event and be there for the Friday and Saturday evenings when the clubs were open.

The anticipation and build up toward their trip had stimulated much discussion, sexting, and speculation about what may or may not happen. It had been so arousing that on a few occasions, it had led to some amazing orgasms for both of them, even when apart.

As the plans for their road trip were taking place, Kara suddenly remembered the messages. She told Greg about a very unexpected exchange, which she had all but forgotten.

Kara had nearly forgotten that she'd updated their ads on a couple of swing sites, posting them in different states, in the hope that through some of them, it might score some possibilities one day.

There had been little response, and Kara had stopped checking the site regularly until a notification popped up on Kara's phone.

Sent from a woman, middle-aged, who provided her name from the outset. This in itself was unusual, with many people reluctant to identify themselves, especially in their first message.

This message had sparked Kara's attention immediately.

> Hi there,
> Really like your profile and we have the qualities you are as we are a genuine couple. We are nice, friendly and carefree, and so want to explore our sexuality further and are open to sharing with others. Still rather new to this. We're based in Brisbane, but willing to travel. Please make contact.
> Thanks, Veronica.

Kara replied straight away.

> Hi Veronica,
> Thank you so much for your message. We travel and work all over the country, so I post in a few states in the hope we might find some like-minded people to meet and get to know as we travel. I can't say when we might next be in QLD, but I would be most happy to keep in touch and see if you would like to meet for a coffee, drink or chat sometime when we are nearby.

> Thank you so much for your reply, Kara. Please give me a call or text whenever you are next in Queensland, hopefully on a weekend we are free, and it most certainly would be lovely to meet you. Warm regards, Veronica. 0411222366

Kara responded, sending her own phone number too, and confirmed that she would keep her contact details. She received another final message from Veronica, with a promise to keep Kara's number and to say that she could contact her whenever they next visited, no matter when.

Kara had saved the messages to her photo stream, aware that they would not remain on the site for long and these were people worth a follow up one day. But that had been ages ago.

'So, what do you think? asked Kara.

'Sounds like they're genuine. Especially as she's offered her name and number, up front.'

'Yes, I thought so too. The messages don't read like a guy pretending to be a woman.'

'Why not send her a message and let them know we are heading to Brisbane? Perhaps they might like to meet for a drink?' suggested Greg.

'It was some time ago—but it can't hurt.'

Kara half expected that Veronica wouldn't likely even remember her but sent a text message to her mobile. It was quite a surprise, when she responded within minutes to say that she and her partner, David, were thrilled that Kara had made contact again and they were still very keen to meet her and Greg.

There were numerous messages exchanged between the two women until Kara suggested they create a group to enable the four of them to join in the chat. So, in the days before Greg and Kara left, there had been some fun, open, sexy messages between them all, and definite plans in place to meet on the first night Greg and Kara arrived in Brisbane.

Chapter 8

It had been about three weeks since they had last seen each other in person, despite speaking or messaging every day. Kara had travelled from Clare the night before, staying at her Aunt Sarah's, ready for Greg to collect her in the early hours of the next morning.

Greg met Kara at 5.00 a.m. at her aunt's apartment and they headed north on the highway to Queensland. Loaded with a full tank of fuel in his utility and both with coffees, they were off! It wasn't long into the trip before they were talking about their chats with the couple they had arranged to meet, and their anticipation of what opportunities might present at a swing club. While the words flowed casually, the air in the car became thick and filled with hot anticipation. Sitting side by side, after weeks apart, their lustful chat flicked the switch in them both. The craving to touch was so magnetic, Greg needed to find a roadside parking bay. Neither could travel another kilometre—he simply had to plant himself between Kara's legs.

This was always going to be a challenge in a ute, but necessity and desperation always find a way. With the passenger seat extended back as far as it could, Kara's skirt pulled up, her knickers removed, Greg's pants around his ankles, they managed to have sex right there in the passenger seat. Steamy and near frantic, it was as fast as a pit stop. Each of them came quickly, responding to the simple sheer relief of accelerated sexual tension, and the longing for their bodies to touch once more.

With their heightened lustful desires satisfied back to a gentle purr, they again hit the road. They didn't stop talking about everything, singing loudly to playlists, and reminiscing past encounters, which helped the kilometres and hours to just roll on by. They stopped for fuel, a quick lunch, and worked out where they would stay that night. It was about three hours after lunch, with still a further three hours from the destination, Kara decided to read, allowing Greg to drive in peace for a while. After about twenty minutes, she snapped the book shut and tossed it in her bag at her feet. 'This book is boring.'

She looked out of the window, across the expanse of the countryside. Miles and miles of the same flat, open land. She suddenly blurted out, 'I'm feeling restless. You know, right now, I feel like some dry crackers, not soft, a little crunchie, a smooth cheese, maybe a Brie or a Camembert… and a glass of wine, a soft red but not too soft, a Pino or young Shiraz!!'

'Well, I can do the wine,' Greg said.

'Really?'

'Yes. Just behind the seat there, I brought a couple of bottles for when we meet our new friends, I was planning to sit back with Veronica and a glass while we both watch you undress David.'

'Do you mind if I drink while you drive?' asked Kara.

'No, go right ahead.'

'Have you got a glass somewhere?'

'No. Sorry, but how badly would you like a nice Barossa Shiraz?'

'Real bad now, I can almost taste it,' Kara laughed in reply.

'Well, sip it out of the bottle then. It's quite okay, I don't mind.'

'I can do that!'

He reached behind her seat and passed her a bottle. She removed the top and took a sip.

'Well, not quite the casual intimate picnic scene I had in mind, but I am feeling better already!'

After a couple more minutes, she couldn't help but ask…

'So, you were planning to watch me undress David?'

Greg grinned 'That was just one of the little scenarios I've had go through my head.'

'Tell me all about what you had in mind. I want to hear it—with every detail. I've got heaps of time and a bottle of red,' Kara said as she took another little sip from the bottle.

'Well, I imagined we would all arrive at our room and I would get us all a drink. I kiss Veronica as I hand her a glass and then continue to caress her, allowing my fingers to gently get to know her, while we both turn to watch you and David do much the same. I pictured you starting to undress him as he soaks up the attention. I stand behind Veronica with one hand around her just below her breast, pulling her against me as we watch you. You bend down to remove his pants and jocks and take him firmly in your hand. You stroke him for a little while before putting him in your mouth.'

Greg noticed Kara reposition herself in the seat. *God she is wet already*, he thought to himself. He took his eyes off the road for a second to glance at her. He saw her skirt lifted a little, her legs slightly parted and her hands in her lap, the bottle of Shiraz sitting in the cup holder. Greg was sure she'd started touching herself.

'Tell me more,' she murmured.

Greg just smiled to himself and continued.

'David now stands you up and with no hesitation or finesse removes your clothes. He lays you on the bed, his hand straight between your legs as his lips meet yours. He teases you with a combination of rubbing and penetration, you taking his two large fingers with pleasure, groaning with each thrust. As Veronica and I watch we are getting aroused ourselves, you whisper in David's ear, "Fuck me, David."

'Without hesitation he climbs onto you and enters you fast and hard…'

Greg shot another glance sideways. With her knees now slightly wider apart, her head was pressed back hard against the seat and her eyes closed, her breath escaped in fast gasps. He could tell she was definitely touching herself. He noticed she'd slid her knickers aside and a finger was hovering over her clit. She couldn't smother a moan. 'Fuck, I am so wet, babe.'

'Are you picturing him pounding you while we watch?'

'Oh, yes, I am.'

She didn't try to hide her self-pleasure in any way. The orgasm now erupted, shuddering through her for what seemed like minutes.

Finally. she opened her eyes, turned to look at Greg, 'My God, I'm really enjoying this wine.'

Greg burst out laughing. 'I'm so pleased.'

Inwardly Greg felt a warm glow rise. He was smiling on the inside. It was fun to see that Kara had been so aroused by his story and felt comfortable to masturbate in front of him, but more so, that she had once again relaxed completely in his company.

He thought back to how she was when they first reunited a few years ago, some thirty-five years since their first ever kiss.

The Kara sitting beside me is no longer quiet or reserved. She hasn't changed as such, but the real Kara has emerged and sparked boldly. It's nice to see. She's unique and special. I'm pleased she's here.

Chapter 9

*K*ara and Greg had often spoken about how it was near impossible to pick anyone from a crowd who might be a swinger.

There was none more surprising than Veronica and David.

They'd arranged to meet them at a relatively public seaside Bistro, crowded just enough to make their meeting casual and ordinary, but offered the perfect setting to enable them to chat discreetly about what they might look to enjoy.

Having settled into their room at the hotel, Greg and Kara wandered the beach path and then found their way to the bar at the Bistro. Scanning the crowd, it didn't seem that their 'friends' had arrived yet.

As they enjoyed a beer and the open-air bar, so close to the expanse of sand and Pacific Ocean that stretched out in front of them, they chatted speculatively about whether they might actually play with this couple.

'Veronica mentioned she had been the one who was experienced with couples, but I think that had been with her ex. I wonder if her current man is okay with all this?'

'He must be, if he's agreed to meet us,' Greg said.

'Possibly… but as you know, chatting and meeting is one thing —but it's another big leap actually watching your partner with someone else.'

'Yeah, I suppose—they might not be as liberal as us!'

Kara giggled before asking, 'Have you got an idea about how we might start, if we decide to play with them?'

Greg thought for a moment. 'Well, perhaps like the fantasy I shared with you in the car? She and I could watch you and David undress each other, perhaps? Then you both could watch us. How does that sound?'

'I think that sounds like a nice gentle way to start. You already know how much I enjoyed that in the ute!'

They both started laughing, neither noticing the couple appear at their table.

'You must be Greg and Kara?' said Veronica with a smile, moving to take a stool opposite Kara.

'Hello,' Greg said warmly, as he stood and walked around the table to give her a welcoming peck on the cheek. He and David shook hands firmly as they both nodded.

Kara stood up and walked around the table to give both David and Veronica little hugs, 'Well hi there, thank you for meeting us here. Greg was just reminding me about how I try to overcome boredom when we travel.' Greg and Kara laughed, and the others joined in—without any real idea about Kara's little solo wine tasting pleasure.

Veronica was quick to reply, 'Sorry we are a bit late, we had hoped to be here much earlier, but we got a little lost. Sorry to keep you waiting.'

'It's not a problem,' Greg said. 'What would you like to drink?'

David jumped in. 'I'll get the drinks. What would you both like?'

'Kara's drinking a dry Rosé and just a beer for me, thanks David.'

Veronica just started talking brightly, nonstop.

'I hope you had a smooth trip. You've had such a long way to drive.'

'Yes, it was a long way, but it's all worthwhile,' Kara said with a slight grin. She glanced at Greg. David arrived back at the table with the drinks, and they all took a moment to settle and take a sip.

It was Greg who got the conversation going in earnest.

'So, tell me,' as he looked directly into Veronica's eyes and then David's, 'Have you enjoyed this type of thing before?'

Veronica responded immediately.

'Actually, I'm the one who has had the most experience, from quite some time ago.'

Kara shot Greg a sideways glance, before returning to give Veronica her full attention.

'It was with my ex-husband. We were quite active and had a few regular couples with whom we had quite regular hook-ups. We all enjoyed it, we all got along so comfortably, and it was easy. But after a time, well... it got a bit out of hand.'

'Oh, how was that?' asked Kara, gently.

'Well, some of it, or us—I should say, got carried away. The relationships splintered, not in the way it should have. My husband ended up leaving me for our play friend's wife.'

'That must have been tough,' Greg said.

David suddenly spoke, slowly and carefully. 'It wasn't that long after that, when Veronica and I met. We had a number of years together before she suggested she'd like to introduce me to the pleasurable side of swinging. To be honest, I wasn't that keen at first. She'd talked so much about the negative side. But then she shared some fantasies with me during our lovemaking, which was very hot and stimulating. It ended up with us visiting some clubs, then parties. And I started to actually enjoy the whole scene.'

Veronica chimed in, 'It took some time to convince David that this was just sex and not about falling in love with someone. We are both sexy and horny and have such a full-on sex life, this just takes it to another level.'

Kara couldn't help but grin before saying, 'I know exactly what you mean! I get such a thrill from seeing Greg enjoy someone else, while he's looking at me. I think it brings you closer, if you approach it in the same way. It's about shared pleasure, not an individual thing.'

'Are you sure you two women haven't met and been talking before?' David said and laughed… 'Veronica tells me something similar all the time.' Greg looked at Kara. He winked. She nodded.

'Well,' Greg said, 'would you two care to grab a drink and maybe join us at our hotel? It's only a couple of blocks from here.'

'Sure, we didn't have time to organise some drinks. Is there a bottle shop nearby?' asked David.

'There's one just about a block away,' Greg said as he stood up from the table. 'Well, how about I take you there?' suggested Kara.

Before David could reply, she took him by the hand. 'Come on, it won't take long. Besides, I won't bite!' Kara looked at Greg and smiled. 'Greg, perhaps you and Veronica can head back to our suite and get some wine glasses ready.'

Greg moved to stand next to Veronica, placing his hand on the small of her back as he looked at her and smiled. 'My pleasure, this way Veronica.'

As Kara led David past Greg and Veronica toward the door of the club, she whispered, 'Now promise you two will behave and don't start without us!' and laughed.

Greg smiled. 'Well, don't take too long, you know I never make promises!'

Kara and David chatted as they walked to the bottle shop. Kara felt that his hand had become clammy and sensed he was still rather nervous.

'Are you feeling okay about this?' she asked.

'Yes, I'm fine. I feel better having met you both. I do enjoy this type of fun, but it takes me a little while at first to warm up.'

'I understand. It's why we always like to chat and meet people first. We both will only do what everyone feels comfortable with.'

David selected some beers and a bottle of wine for Veronica, paid for them, and they headed back toward the hotel. It was light chatter as they walked, mostly about Kara and Greg's trip, how long it took and the contrast in weather.

As they approached the elevator, David stopped and turned to Kara. 'Kara, you are a lovely lady, thank you for your kind comments before.'

'My pleasure. I wonder if they have started without us?' she giggled.

On entering the room, they found Greg and Veronica sitting on the edge of the bed, just chatting.

Greg stood up as they entered.

'We got some more glasses from the bar downstairs,' Greg said, as he handed Kara a wine he'd poured for her. David poured Veronica a drink and taking his beer, he sat down beside her on the end of the bed.

'Thank you. So, what have you two been chatting about while you were waiting?' asked Kara.

'Well,' he said slowly, 'Veronica has been telling about how she is quite a prolific squirter!'

'Is that so?'

'She sure is,' David jumped in, 'you will be quite amazed.'

'Really?'

'Oh, sometimes I have completely drenched David and soaked the bed. I hope I don't mess up your bed tonight!' she said with a wide smile.

'Sadly, I've only done that a couple of times and certainly nothing like that,' Kara said.

Greg jumped in and brought the moment back to start some play.

'We spoke more about what we all might enjoy. We both agreed that it would be nice to see you and David undress each other.'

'What a lovely idea.' With that Kara gave Greg a little nod and smile, put her glass down and walked up to David. She took him gently by the hand, guiding him to stand. Veronica stood up too and moved to stand in front of Greg a few paces back from Kara, so they could both see clearly.

Kara took David's beer and set it down next to her glass on the table. She stood facing him, now in the middle of the room, and slowly unbuttoned his shirt. She slipped his shirt back over his shoulders, letting her fingers glide over his skin, down his arms as the shirt slid off onto the floor.

She ran her fingers across his chest as she turned around, her back now toward him. David unzipped her dress and let it fall to her feet. As she stepped out of it, he leant forward, pulled her body back up close, to allow his flesh to press against her. As he kissed her earlobe and nape of her neck, his hands reached around to feel the form and shape of her breasts over her bra. 'There is nothing better than the feel of a soft earlobe between one's lips and the scent of a beautiful perfume,' he murmured.

Kara kept looking at Greg and Veronica the whole time. Greg gave her a little wink. She smiled back, noting that Veronica's hand was obviously feeling and rubbing Greg through his shorts. Both of their pleasure was clearly rising. David unfastened Kara's bra and removed it swiftly. He started kissing Kara's back, moving lower and lower, sliding her knickers down as he dropped to his knees. Kara was completely naked in front of the three of them now. She could tell by the look on Greg's face that he was getting off, as she watched his hands find Veronica's breasts underneath her T-shirt. She could see her nipples hardening through the sheer cotton, just as hers were in response to both men's first touch of each of them.

The feel of a little slap on her left butt cheek suddenly startled Kara.

'Please, can you not do that?' Her request was uttered gently, but adamantly. David wavered. He stood up and looked at her.

'I'm really sorry, it's just that Veronica likes it a little rougher sometimes. I thought you might like it too?'

'It's okay. It's me, not you. Don't worry. Hope you understand.'

'Absolutely.'

Kara nodded and smiled gently. Not wanting to dampen the mood. 'Alright then… I think it's time I took off those shorts of yours!' she said quickly as she grabbed his hand and pulled him to stand closer, up in front of her. She slowly undid the button of David's shorts, sliding them down, along with his jocks at the same time. He was now finally naked as well. And very erect. Kara dropped to her knees, taking his erection in her hand and slipped her lips over the tip of him, circling her tongue around the thickness of his shaft down to the base. She sucked him firmly all the way up again, very slowly. This is what she and Greg had imagined she would do. She felt his knees buckle slightly and heard him exhale. She let her lips glide up and down him at a slow, gentle pace.

When he let little sighs escape involuntarily, she knew he had finally relaxed.

Kara slipped her lips from him and wrapped her palm and fingers around his shaft.

'I think we need to let Greg and Veronica see this too,' she said as she turned around, his cock still resting in her hand. He looked down and then up again into Kara's eyes.

'Of course, my God, that felt so good.'

As they both turned around and focused on where they expected Veronica and Greg to be in front of them, their next vision wasn't what either expected. Greg's now naked body was lying on top of Veronica, also having shed her clothes on the bed. Veronica's hands were firmly gripping his butt cheeks, pulling him into her forcefully.

Without saying a word, Kara kept hold of David's cock and led him to lay next to them.

'I think we need to catch up a bit here!' she said as she released her grip and wriggled closer to them. It took no time for David to move on top of Kara and suck on her nipples and the soft flesh of her breasts.

Kara turned her head to look at Greg and Veronica, now fucking at full pace beside them. Greg's eyes found Kara's. He stretched out his hand, feeling for her breast. Veronica's words cried out more and more, responding to each time Greg pushed into her.

'Oh, God. I'm loving this. David, watch me. I can't hold it...' She was vibrant, loud and lost in the sex itself.

Kara couldn't help but watch her and Greg.

While Kara felt, and delighted, in the wet soft warmth of his lips as they ascended up toward her inner thighs, she was still mesmerised by the sounds and activity of the two bodies beside her. This wasn't what she'd expected to happen so fast.

So much so, she had lost any connection with what David was doing to her. He had moved to taste her, his head now buried between her legs, his hands running up and down over her hips and thighs. She suddenly realised that she had been reeling from not even seeing the two of them undress, and how much Veronica was commanding Greg's body, that she had all but forgotten David was there.

She quickly reached down and ran her fingers over his arms and over her own body. She pulled him to reposition, signalling he could enter her if he wanted. He knelt between her legs and slowly guided himself into her. Kara looked up, only to see his gaze was fixed squarely on Veronica. He had a mix of wanting and hesitance—all in the same moment.

He looked back at Kara, who smiled and pulled him close enough to be able to hear her whisper. 'Only as much or as little as you want, remember?'

David looked at her, smiled meekly and eased inside her. Kara lay still, letting him lead by his own desire. David started thrusting into Kara, groaning with each press.

In that moment, Veronica let out a series of moans and high-pitched gasps. David hesitated at the sound, clearly distracted. He was not relaxing into this at all.

Nearly without a breath of recovery from her orgasm, Veronica could see David wasn't coping too well.

'Kara, it takes him a while to warm up- shall we swap back for a bit? I'll get David going, watch this…'

Veronica, now on top of Greg, rolled off onto her hands and knees and said, 'David, do me from behind.'

Kara wriggled closer to Greg and whispered, 'So much for watching,' with a little giggle.

'Sorry, she was unstoppable. I'll tell you later. Come sit on me.'

By the time Greg and Kara could turn their heads, Veronica had smothered David's cock with lube. 'God, I love anal. Come on Greg, give Kara some of this…' as she handed him the lube.

Greg took it and squeezed some over himself. 'Want to try again?' he whispered to Kara softly. He knew she'd not found it that comfortable in the past.

Kara nodded.

Poised above him, Kara was about to slide onto Greg. She looked over to watch David thrusting into Veronica, her head tilted back and hear her now crying out, 'Feel me squirt! My God, can you see, Kara, God I love to cum.'

Veronica grabbed for Kara's hand and drove her fingers down between her legs to feel the stream of fluid gushing from her while David was continuing to pump her. Kara had never seen or heard a woman whose orgasm was such an effusive outpouring of emotional juices.

'Wow!'

'I don't do this all the time, but like I said, when I'm really turned on, I let go all over the place.'

Veronica sat up and she and David repositioned, so she could stroke him and watch Kara and Greg at the same time. 'Let us watch you ride him, Kara. You'll love anal, I promise.'

With Greg's hands gripping her breasts, Kara started rising and lowering herself over his still rock-hard cock, slowly at first, enjoying him rim her and then just enough to allow his knob inside her. She breathed in and out slowly, relaxing more with each exhale, allowing herself to take him deeper and deeper each time. He pulled her body close to him and started to bite hard on her neck. Kara moaned as he started to thrust fast and deep. Kara was lost in the sensation. She couldn't distinguish which part of her he had penetrated, and she didn't care. The sensation was thick, firm and completely exultant. As he came, her body climaxed in unison, oblivious to everything and anyone else around her. This was another first for her. She couldn't believe how much she had enjoyed it, despite feeling exhausted.

Greg held her close to his chest for what seemed like ages. Kara just melted into him, allowing her body to rise and fall with each of his breaths.

'I knew you'd love it,' Veronica whispered. Kara smiled meekly, before rolling to lie at Greg's side.

'I know she did,' Greg said.

'Drink break?' suggested Kara, changing the subject adeptly.

Greg shot her a look and a knowing grin as he slipped off the bed and headed to the bathroom.

Veronica sat up and David moved to sit by her side. Kara handed them both a drink. He looked at his watch.

'Did you know we've been at this for over two hours? No wonder I'm feeling hungry!' he exclaimed.

Returning from the bathroom, Greg said, 'There's a nice little Asian restaurant downstairs, what say we have some dinner together before you leave?'

'Sounds good,' said David.

Throughout dinner, the four chatted about their work roles and their families. It became clear to Kara and Greg that Veronica and David had assumed they were a second time married couple like themselves, so they just allowed the conversations to follow on. It had been a light-hearted evening and for any other patrons it would have appeared like any other shared catch up between friends.

As Greg signalled the waiter for the bill it was only then that Kara looked around the restaurant, then leant forward slightly so all three could hear her whisper, 'If only they all knew how much dessert we had—even before dinner!'

Laughing as they left the restaurant, they said their goodbyes, with the suggestion that they might enjoy each other's company again someday.

Chapter 10

*R*eturning to their room after dinner, Greg and Kara both stripped off, brushed their teeth and headed to bed, all the while still talking nonstop about the afternoon's experience. They both were so surprised at how well it all went with Veronica and David, which was in contrast to their outwardly sedate and relatively ordinary, understated appearance and demeanour.

'What happened to us watching you and Veronica undress? One minute you were both standing there feeling each other up, and by the time I turned around, you were already going hard at it on the bed!'

'I'm sorry about that. I couldn't believe it myself. As soon as you both were naked and facing each other, she just raced to take off my clothes, stripped off and pulled me onto the bed saying, "Get that cock into me!"'

Kara was astounded. 'Really?! Wow!'

They both kept repeating the statement jokingly for the rest of the weekend. It was such a surprise command from the lips of what seemed to be a most conservative woman! It had rendered them both speechless and yet somehow delighted them too, adding to the sensation of heated and fervent sex they'd enjoyed from that moment.

Greg laid on his back on the bed, his arms tucked above his head, and let out a sigh. 'What a fun evening. I'm buggered. I'll be asleep in minutes. Did you really enjoy yourself today, Kara?'

'Absolutely!' Kara paused for a moment. 'Actually, I couldn't believe how much I enjoyed you taking me anally. I've never really been able to relax enough to do it—let alone enjoy it before. It was amazing.' She paused again.

'I know you like a little anal touching yourself. Have you ever come when someone's played with you in that way?'

'Well, no, not really. It feels great, but I've not had a situation where I could experience much of it,' Greg said.

'You know that guys evidently have a 'P' spot?'

'No, is that something like a G spot?'

'Yes. Evidently the prostate stimulation can give a whole new feel to a guy's orgasm.'

Kara and Greg lay quietly next to each other. Their bodies just touching.

After a couple of minutes Kara turned to Greg and said, 'I want to stroke your body until you fall asleep. Is that okay?'

'Sure, you know I love that.'

Kara moved to kneel between his outspread legs. She let her fingers trace up over the top of his feet, around his ankles, then slowly glide up his inner calves and thighs, then rolled down the outer sides of his legs again to his feet.

'Oh, that feels so good,' he murmured, his eyes now closed as he breathed deeper, his entire body sinking farther into the sheets.

She didn't say a word, just kept her fingers rolling up and down his legs, letting them tease the inner creases of his groin as she relished touching every inch of skin that she could.

This was a most sublime moment for Kara. She loved seeing Greg completely relaxed, dozing and feeling that rare, suspended time of no demands, no expectations, nothing but pleasure having his body caressed into the anticipating arms of sleep.

Her fingers scrolled up the length of his body again, this time venturing farther up over his stomach, out across and around his hips. She circled them up through the middle of his chest, out and around to his sides and down again.

By the third cycle over his body, this time, she let her fingertips wander lower to graze the tip of his penis and then circle down through his pubes. Stroking his balls and taint lightly, she then let her fingers rim his hole.

She didn't rest there, but just included these parts of him, as she ran her fingers all over his body again.

Greg's breaths had become deep and slow, now purring. Kara sensed he was still awake, luxuriating in every part of him being gently stroked.

'Can I grab some lotion?' He nodded.

Kara slipped to the bathroom, getting the lotion, she turned on the hot tap at the basin, and held the bottle under the steaming water.

Returning to her position on the bed between his legs, she poured a generous amount of now warm silky body cream into her hand and allowed some to drizzle over his thighs.

She focussed her massage and stroking on only his lower body now. Her fingers glided across his skin, letting them linger in each of the spots she loved. She felt so aroused herself, just by touching him. The delicate tender skin of his taint—between his arse and base of his cock, the soft line of skin at the top of each leg—the inner fold of his groin was always so soft and warm to touch. She loved watching the ripple of delight that would pulse and respond to her touch. As she cupped his balls gently in the palm of one hand, the fingers from her other hand softly anointed them. She could see the base of his cock thickening.

She couldn't resist any longer. *I need to explore him inside and out.*

While his eyes remained closed, she could hear small sighs escape as he breathed in her touch. He was clearly still awake. Grabbing a couple of pillows from her side of the bed, she tapped his bottom.

'Lift up please.' Greg raised his hips high in response as she slipped the pillows beneath him. She wanted to see and stimulate him in every way.

She coated her fingers with even more lotion and let her fingers start. She whispered, 'It's my turn.'

One finger from her left hand eased inside him. She paused, the tip of it just inside him, to allow that initial discomfort and pulse of resistance to subside. 'Is that okay?'

As he exhaled and nodded, she felt his muscles relax and she was welcomed inside further.

She penetrated a little deeper, feeling for that firm little spot, covered in the delicate smooth flesh that was purely like softened silky butter to touch.

'Am I in the right spot? Tell me if I'm hurting you.'

'Yes, it's on the spot,' he breathed in slowly and then sighed. 'Ahh, that feels so good.'

Having found the rhythm, her finger moving as if beckoning, stroking his prostate inside him, while taking all of his cock in her mouth. She sucked him slowly, from base to tip, matching the sliding movement of her finger inside him. She moved her right hand to hold his shaft, to focus her lips and mouth on her favourite part of him.

Kara loved her tongue to feel the ridge at the bottom of the head and to let the tip of her tongue flick, taste and slide over the most delicate flesh. This was another of his sweet spots.

He was thick, hard and now pulsing. His hips were rising gently up and down, he was lost in the sensation of being finger fucked, sucked, tasted and stroked at the same time. He grabbed for her hair with both hands.

Kara's pussy was pulsing—feeling his orgasm rise and giving him this much pleasure was exhilarating, and her body was hammering inside with her every movement too. She let her finger slide out of him gently.

He erupted. With a loud cry and resounding moan, he squirted warm, sweet cum into her mouth. To Kara, the sound and taste was simply delicious. His body kept twitching for a time.

Kara had now stopped sucking and stroking him, but held it between her lips softly, allowing every drop to pulse into her mouth.

He realised he was still gripping her hair tightly and had to force himself to relax his fingers, locked with handfuls of hair. A huge sigh escaped him. Kara remained kneeling between his legs, her head now rested on his stomach.

'My God, that was so amazing. The best I have ever had. It's never felt like that before.'

Kara eventually moved to lie by Greg on her side, facing away from him, but with her body gently snuggled against him. He wrapped his arm across her body and reached for her hand, curling her fingers between his. He let out a little sigh filled with sleepy content. A satisfied smile held on her face and her body shimmered as she slipped into her dreams. She was delighted with every pleasure she had given and received today.

Chapter 11

The next morning, Greg woke first. He looked across at the sleeping Kara. He smiled. Her shock of dark locks spilling over her face and the pillow cradled between her arms. Her right leg and one cheek predictably thrown out above the sheet, with her lightly tanned skin, a glowing contrast to the crisp white hotel sheets. She even slept as eclectically as her personality. From random tangles to smooth silk. He slipped out of bed, threw on some clothes quietly, not wanting to disturb her.

He crept out of the room and headed downstairs to the restaurant and ordered coffees for them both. While waiting for his order, he thought back to the sensation of her touch the night before. It had been astounding. Here was this woman, who despite still holding and emulating her dignified, somewhat shy, professional self, had boldly catapulted headfirst into sexual fantasies and continued to look for new ways for each of them to experience pleasure together and with others. Notwithstanding, she had stood quietly by, had waited on the sidelines, after Tess, until he was ready. Kara Gilbert had to be his most, unexpectedly, genuine friend.

She was sitting up in bed as he walked back into the bedroom, coffees in hand, a wide grin behind them. 'Good morning sexy, I hope I didn't wake you when I got up.'

'No, I didn't even realise you'd gone until just now.' Her hands rummaged through her hair in an attempt to resurrect herself. 'My goodness, you've got coffee too! Thank you. You're a legend.'

As Greg handed her the coffee, he slipped off his shorts and T-shirt and slipped back under the sheet next to her. Sitting side by side and sipping their coffees, their words were silent, but thoughts were loud and bouncing.

Kara was the first to speak. 'I think we had lots of fun with that couple, but I think I loved what I explored with you afterwards even more.'

'I have to agree. That was amazing.'

'I'm so pleased. I was a little scared, I didn't want to freak you out, but just give you a new experience—like it was for me.'

'You've never done that to anyone before?'

'God, no. I just did a little research!' Kara said without hesitation.

'Well, you did an amazing job.'

'Like you did with me. As you heard!'

'Yes, you actually were the loudest you've ever been.'

'Really?'

'Yes, for sure,' replied Greg, 'I thought we may have had a knock on the door!'

With that, Kara leant over and took Greg's coffee cup from his hand and placed it on the side table.

'I'll try to be quieter next time,' she murmured, as she climbed over his body and slid down beneath the sheet.

Greg sank back into the pillows as he closed his eyes.

Greg had found it hard to muster enthusiasm for work that day, after such a big night (and morning) full of sexy fun with Kara and knowing there was more to come.

We've still got the swing club tonight. What a fun trip. Work first though, he thought to himself as he entered Karstens Conference and Training Centre.

After a series of meetings with the manager, the tech team to confirm the audio-visual equipment and the catering manager, he sorted all the final details for the Trade show, scheduled to be held in a few months' time.

Thankfully, the venue was perfect with more equipment and options included than he'd first expected, so he didn't need to meet with other suppliers. He was able to unload the promotional banners and materials he'd brought there in the ute, saving more time the next day. At 6.00 p.m. he tried calling Kara. He left her a message. 'Hey sexy, I'm all sorted and, on my way, back to the hotel. We have plenty of time to have dinner somewhere, before tonight. See you soon.'

Kara walked out of the little lingerie shop when she heard the ping of a message. She grabbed her phone from her bag and called him back.

'Hey, sorry, I missed you. Are you finished already?'

'Yes, I'm all sorted and I'm nearly back at the hotel. I have a free day tomorrow too. Where are you?'

'I'm only a few blocks from the hotel. Not far. I've just been doing a little shopping. I checked the club website and its BYO drinks, so I've bought some wine to take tonight. It also said dress to impress, so I thought I needed something a bit sexier to wear, it is our first club after all,' she laughed.

'Sounds good, see you soon.'

'Hey, I'm getting quite excited about tonight. I'm feeling rather horny again!'

'How can you be? My God you are insatiable! We have to save our strength for tonight!' He laughed. 'I'll see you soon, you naughty woman.'

The cab dropped them outside the door of what looked the same as any one of the endless line of warehouses in the secluded cul-de-sac. An amber light above the door, signalling the only difference to the rest of the corrugated grey buildings.

Regardless of the research they'd done online, as soon as Greg and Kara walked in the door, they knew this club was different to what they were expecting. It emulated a very casual and unique feel. The two of them outwardly appeared casual. Internally, both caught the strange mix of trepidation and heated anticipation. The combination of not knowing what they might find behind the doors, yet the feeling that whatever happened would be kinky fun.

Kara, dressed in a short body-hugging black velvet dress with long sleeves. It was plain, but with its low scooped back and teamed with her knee-high black suede boots, the effect was simple and elegantly sexy. With Greg escorted inside wearing black jeans and a red and white striped Country Road shirt, the two of them made an attractive, noticeable impression as they entered. Walking straight up to the bar, they handed over their BYO bottle of red wine and paid the cash entry fee.

Mike, the manager of the club, greeted them warmly and as first-time guests, gave them a quick walk through the building, showing them where bathrooms were, where to access towels, lube or condoms and explained the basic rules.

'It's quite simple really. If a bedroom door is closed, it means private fun and no entry. If a door is open, but a chain is across the doorway, it signals those using the room are happy for you to watch but not enter, and if there is no chain, people are happy for you to watch and also join them.'

'Sounds simple enough,' Greg said.

'Oh, feel free to use the massage table too,' he said, pointing to the table in a little recess alcove at the end of the large room, filled with lounges and chairs along each wall.

'We just like you to use the massage oil provided, it's specially blended to not wreck the spa. Apart from that, make yourselves comfortable. I hope you enjoy lots of fun tonight.'

'Thanks so much. I'm sure we will.'

Kara hadn't said a word during the tour, just nodded and smiled, but all the while gripped Greg's hand a little tighter as she walked around, taking in the many rooms and people who were clearly checking them out as she was them.

Greg led her downstairs, which revealed another large lounge area, in front of more bedrooms, a few with doors open and a couple closed. Next to this was a spa with four naked people drinking and chatting happily to each other. A quick look around and Greg spotted a couple chatting to some others on a lounge. They looked much the same age as Kara and him, and probably the best option so far. 'Let's do the spa first,' Greg suggested as he undressed.

They are greeted and watched by the four spa occupants as they remove their clothes. The two men admired Kara's perfect body as she removed her dress, revealing the midnight blue and black lacy bra and knickers. Kara could sense everyone was watching as she slipped these off too. She smiled to herself. *I think these little items I bought have had an effect already.*

A spot was quickly made for them in the spa. Greg and Kara slipped blissfully into the warm bubbling water and found themselves sitting next to an English couple who were in Australia on holiday. It's pretty clear why everyone was there, so their talk quickly and easily shifted into what each couple had done before. As the conversation flowed, Greg felt the English lady's hand run up his leg, taking hold of his already half aroused cock. She stroked him slowly as the chat continued. Greg took Kara's hand, placing it on top of the hand that was already stroking him. Kara followed her touch as they both now continued to stroke him.

The English lady looked at Kara. 'It's you I really want, my husband here is not really into this stuff that much, but I love it.'

She stopped caressing Greg and stood, pulling Kara to her feet. She placed one hand on her cheek, her lips on hers and her other hand between Kara's legs. Greg could feel Kara lift her leg to rest on the seat beneath the water, to welcome her fingers. The spa became completely silent, and the temperature clearly rose through the others as they watched the little display which lasted for nearly a minute. As the lady released Kara from her lips, Kara smiled and then slid back to sit on Greg's lap. With no effort at all she slid over him and just slowly rocked back and forth on his erection, as the English lady started chatting again, telling everyone about more of her and her husband's sexual adventures in countries around the world.

Kara moved to sit next to Greg as the other couple, who had been relatively quiet until now, admitted this was their first time in a club. She appeared to be younger than the rest of the group, and while with a rather large, chubby figure, she had a pretty face with alabaster white cheeks and sparkling eyes. At this point, the English couple went back upstairs to the bar, leaving the four 'clubbing virgins' in the spa.

As the lady stood next to the spa, towelling herself dry, she bent down and whispered into Kara's ear, 'Would you be interested in coming upstairs and just playing with me on your own?'

Kara turned to look at her and smiled gently. 'You are lovely, and I enjoyed our little kiss and touch, but,' she nodded towards Greg, 'we only play as a couple. Sorry.'

'That's quite okay. Well, if you change your mind, let me know.' Kara looked at Greg, who had clearly heard their exchange.

'You did that well,' he said and just smiled. He had enjoyed that whole unexpected little encounter.

Buoyed by Kara's display, he took a risk.

He looked at the younger couple. 'As we are all first timers here, would you like to get a room and just try some same room sex?'

The two looked at each other and the pretty girl replied, 'Sounds like fun. By the way, we are Scott and Belinda.'

With that they all hopped out of the spa, wrapped towels around themselves, and gathered up their clothes. They easily found a room, and all lay down, side by side. Scott dived straight between his young lady's legs, munching her furiously, much like a starving lion with its latest kill. Greg and Kara caressed each other, watching this somewhat aggressive display. Belinda was certainly enjoying it from the expression on her face, and the purring moans which escaped her, but she had not yet ascended to an orgasm yet. After a few more minutes, Scott came up for air, wiping his mouth.

Scott then looked directly at Kara. 'Would you like me to lick you?'

Kara was a little hesitant in reply. 'Okay, that would be nice.'

Greg shot her a look. *Clearly,* he thought, *she hadn't caught quite the same image I had of how Scott looked—like he was in for the kill when he ate out Belinda.*

Kara laid back slowly on the bed, parting her legs, ever so slowly, as Scott positioned himself between them. Greg watched Kara closely in those first moments. He didn't want an onslaught to hurt her. Thankfully, Scott had picked up on Kara's flicker of nervousness and approached her with his tongue and fingers slowly and gently. Greg saw Kara exhale and relax into his touch. Noting Scott had tempered his approach and wasn't dripping ravenous, devouring drool from his mouth, Greg could relax a bit. Now sure she would be handled gently, Greg turned toward Belinda, kissing her softly on the lips as his right hand roamed, starting a fluid caress over her body. He let his finger take a slow wandering path to her clitoris, delighting in its firm and beckoning welcome. Offering only the gentlest, delicate touch, he explored every millimetre. Her bead, now unable to hide under the cover of her fleshy folds, was throbbing at his touch. Belinda was starting to twitch between each deepening breath.

Greg was lying on his left side and Belinda on her back as she reached and took his free left hand with her right, squeezing it as each wave of the sensation of his floating fingers rolled through her body. Greg looked over at Kara. She looked back with a brief smile, between breaths which were now getting heavier. He knew what that meant. Scott was obviously still taking things steady, and she had relaxed into the pleasure of his tongue and touch. Greg felt Belinda's fingers straighten, with their two hands now firmly palm to palm, every one of her fingers bending back into their own erection, matching the uncontrollable arch of her back that was relishing in the talent of his fingers. Her breathing plummeted into deep moans.

Kara heard the change in Belinda's tone and knew that Greg's special touch had penetrated her. She looked towards them. She could see only Greg's back facing toward her as he lay on his side, and Kara realised it was his adept right hand and fingers that were working this magic on her. But it was her next vision that held her spellbound. Delicate and simply beautiful, Kara couldn't move her gaze from Belinda's own fingers, reflecting a uniquely profound expression of pleasure.

As Greg was working her clit, his free hand was suspended just in front of his chest next to her. Her hand had found his. Belinda's fingers, which were outstretched above their joined palms, were quivering and flickering around his fingers. As her gasps rose higher, her fingertips started to roll around and glide up and down between each of his, with a near gossamer touch. Close to a climax, each finger slid down, ever so delicately, until becoming completely entwined and melding with his full open hand, before gripping it firmly. She drew in a huge breath, clearly about to come. Her fingers suddenly straightened, flexed and arched back in sync with her whole body, as she cried out in ecstasy.

Kara caught every sensation from just seeing the response between their hands. Unlike anything she had ever witnessed before, Kara could not help but look away with a pang inside. Checking herself, she realised this wasn't jealousy; it was complete awe. So intense and beautiful, it felt like it was an intrusion to watch. That was one of the most intimate connection of flesh she had ever seen, reflected only through fingertips. It was something she would never forget.

It wasn't long before they were all dressed and left the room. Greg and Kara headed to the bar to compare notes about the night so far.

Chapter 12

*A*fter thirty minutes or so at the bar chatting and watching others wandering around or trying to connect, they decided to wander again, into the den of debauchery. They headed downstairs and noticed a couple seated huddled side by side on a couch. They were silent, just perched on the edge of the seat The woman was frozen, as if she'd been placed there. Her head hung down, her gaze fixed toward her lap, looking more like she was waiting for a bus than sitting in an adult sex club.

She was dressed in a sari and he in shirt and pants. It became instantly clear to Greg and Kara that he was the one enjoying the venue: his eyes were held wide, scanning everyone who entered the room, offering a nod and a small smile. She remained fixed to the spot, with both hands clinging to her man's arm, obviously out of her comfort zone. Greg raised his eyebrows, then turned to Kara and winked.

'Let's chat to them,' suggested Greg pointing to the couple.

'Yes, let's.'

'Hello, I'm Greg and this is Kara. Do you mind if we join you?'

'Certainly. Please sit down. I am Vijay and this is my wife, Rani.'

Kara nestled into the lounge with Greg at her side. Greg turned to Rani, on his left, smiled and asked softly, 'So, what do you enjoy about this place?'

With that, Rani's face blushed, and she wrapped her arm tighter around her husband, and buried her face into his shoulder.

Greg and Kara shot a glance to each other, before Vijay spoke again.

'It's okay. As you can probably tell, this is a fantasy of mine. We've come here as a couple a few times but haven't ever done anything. We, or rather I, just watch. My wife doesn't want to take part but is happy for me to maybe try.'

Greg noticed Rani's fingers grip tighter to Vijay's arm. *She looks like she wished a hole would swallow her up*, he thought.

'Fair enough… You are a very supportive wife,' Greg said softly. Rani turned her head to sneak a look at him and smiled appreciatively in response.

Greg headed to the bar to refill their glasses. Returning, he found the couple he spotted when they first entered the club that evening, now also seated on their couch. Nathan and Sue introduced themselves and soon a conversation flowed between the six of them, mainly focussing on drawing Rani into the chat, but with a little about the swinging experience times they'd all had.

Greg and Kara started flirting with Nathan and Sue, offering smiles and suggestive comments.

A connection was building, especially with Nathan, whose nods and comments signalling his desire to explore things with Greg and Kara. After a few whispered exchanges, he and Sue stood up and excused themselves.

'We'll be back in a moment,' she said. They stepped back into the darkened corner, still in Greg's line of sight.

'I think they're talking about joining us,' whispered Greg.

'I'm not sure she's as keen as he is. Let's wait and see.'

After a couple of minutes, the two returned. They remained standing and Nathan blurted, 'It's been lovely to meet you. We're headed to another club. Have a great night,' and with that, they both turned and left.

The disappointment showed on Greg's face. The words toppled over him like a glass that had been knocked off the table, spilling into his lap.

'It's okay. We'll have a bit more fun tonight, I'm sure.' Kara whispered.

'Yeah, we probably will. Shame we didn't qualify though; I would've loved to have fucked her.'

'It's not that, I'm sure. We actually did qualify—a bit too much for her liking. Remember, she said she liked to play, but he was only supposed to watch?'

'She did mention that. You could be right.'

Vijay and Rani had continued to sit quietly next to them. Vijay turned to look at Greg and Kara.

'She was quite an unusual woman. She was a bit too scary for us, too I think.'

With no more than that, his words confirmed Kara's thoughts and Greg nodded affirmingly.

'We don't do scary, just horny nice people,' Kara said. They all laughed, even Rani. That was all it took.

'Would you guys like to watch us have sex, closed door, just us?' Greg volunteered.

Vijay looked at Rani who shrugged her shoulders, gave a hint of a nod, and blushed again. 'Sure.'

They all stood slowly. Greg took Kara and Rani gently each by the hand, led them to a room farthest away from the lounge area. Greg noticed the room had been vacated and cleaned earlier and was the most private. Once all four were inside, he closed the door. Vijay and Rani sat closely huddled to each other on the side of the king-sized bed, motionless, again perching as if in a waiting room. The air thickened with the humid mix of heated arousal, anticipation and fear of the unknown, emanating from the two of them. Greg and Kara stood directly in front of them, only an arm's length away.

Greg looked closely at Rani. Her eyes were wide open, but she kept her body still pressed firmly against her husband's side. He still couldn't tell if she was terrified, embarrassed, or was just caught by the thrill. He turned to Kara and removed her dress to reveal her perfectly rounded breasts, body, and midnight blue and black lace knickers. Vijay's eyes widened, and they all heard his intake of breath.

Kara removed Greg's shirt as he kicked off his shoes. Next, she undid his pants and slid them down, taking his jocks with them. Greg's turn in this alternate striptease finally removed Kara's undies. Greg and Kara now stood only a foot away from their audience, completely naked. Greg, already aroused by being watched, noticed Rani looking at them both directly and no longer averting her gaze. She had released her grip of Vijay's arm, which she had clutched so tightly since they all first met. She'd finally started to relax.

Vijay's bulge was loudly showing his approval of this private porn show. Kara slowly turned her body full circle, standing in front of Greg, allowing his fingers to roam and dance over her breasts, stomach, back and up her arms, gracing her neck and back again. Positioned close behind her, Greg reached around her body to let the fingers of his right-hand graze down slowly from her navel, over her mound and slip between her pussy lips. He held her close, his other hand firmly cupping her left breast. Rani and Vijay had a full-frontal view of him working her pussy the way he knew she loved, all the while his hard cock pressing against her from behind. Kara had started nervously, concerned by Rani's apparent reluctance, but now the strength of Greg's tenderness, by word and touch, had shifted them all.

Kara glimpsed Vijay rubbing himself through his pants, Rani's eyes were now glistening towards Kara, watching intently as Greg's fingers beckoned rhythmically inside her. Kara now with her head back, eyes closed and moaning with pleasure was such a turn on for them both. Kara let go, completely lost in the voltage that now permeated throughout her body. She was the only person who did not hear the deep guttural moans that escaped her as she came.

With Kara still convulsing from her orgasm, Greg moved to stand in front of her, stroking her body gently to help her settle.

As Kara's eyes opened and her breathing slowed, she hugged Greg and glanced over his shoulder.

'I think our friends need a little extra help to get started,' she whispered.

Greg turned and could see them both still dressed, Vijay's penis bursting to escape his pants.

'Would you like Kara and I to undress you for each other?' he offered.

Vijay shot Rani a glance, and Kara thought she caught a little wink.

They both nodded in reply.

Kara stepped up to Vijay and took both his hands in hers, drawing him up to stand in front of her. Greg did the same to Rani.

Kara reached for the button of Vijay's pants and opened it quickly with her left hand as she unzipped his fly with the other. She dropped to kneel in front of him, easing both his pants and jocks over his profound erection, pulling them down to his ankles. She slipped off his loafers and stood up again. As he clambered to step out of the clothes at his feet, Kara stroked her hands over his chest and shoulders, before unbuttoning and opening his shirt. He was a large man, and now with his body becoming fully revealed, Kara winced slightly at the folds of flesh and his very rounded belly. She swallowed hard, pushing a memory from her past, underground where it belonged.

She walked around behind him, only then easing the shirt from over his shoulders and slowly down his arms, before tossing it on the floor. She had kept an eye on Greg the whole time, watching to ensure they both had co-ordinated the undressing so their 'friends' were ready at the same time.

Greg's hands at first fumbled around Rani's waist through the layers of her sari.

Rani could feel the excitement building inside her own body as her eyes darted back and forth between Kara and Greg.

She surprising took the lead, taking Greg's hand, placing it on the golden clasp at her shoulder. Unfastening it, he watched as she guided the first soft folds of silk to drop away from across her chest. It revealed a midriff blouse, in the same apricot colour as the flowing material of the sari, and the first exposure of her dusky, dark wheaten flesh. She bent down and scooped up the folds, placing the edge of the fabric in Greg's hand and she turned around, untucking the material from the band of her underskirt as she went, slowly unravelling and revealing herself with each turn.

As she turned to face him again, he placed his hand on her shoulder to stop her, kissing her cheek. 'Thank you. I can see now. Let me take it from here.'

She gave him a gentle smile, with her eyes lowered. With that he walked around her, unwrapping the remaining layers from her body and once removed, he stood behind her and unclasped the button of her blouse at the base of her neck. She pulled the little top off over her head and tossed it aside quickly, within seconds wrapping her arms around herself to cover her chest. He glimpsed the honeyed flesh of her small pert breasts and the darkness of her nipples and areola. Greg slipped his fingers inside the elastic waistband of her underskirt and pulled it down toward her knees. Greg had half expected she might be more traditional with knickers under her sari, but this was a mere fleeting thought as what she was offering was so intoxicating. He had unwrapped a gift. While full bodied, this was nonetheless, a special reveal. One of timid trust and wanting.

Carefully, he slowly slid her skirt down further, inch by inch on either side to the ground. She was now completely naked.

Greg took Rani by the hand, guiding it toward her husband's erection. Only a flicker of resistance in its journey, she followed, letting Greg guide her to wrap her fingers around his cock and the rhythm to stroke him.

Greg turned back to Kara and pulled her into an embrace, allowing the couple time to dissolve into each other's touch. As he traced little kisses up Kara's neck, he heard the sound of flesh pounding between heavy breaths behind them. He stopped and whispered in Kara's ear. 'That was a good idea. You okay if we do more? I know he is a large man.'

'You've made me come so hard already. Your touch and them watching us was just so hot. Do you think they will cope with more? I think I can deal with him. He's nowhere near as big as my ex. You'll know if I can't.'

'Okay. Let's take it slow, though. Even if they just enjoy each other, while we watch.'

'Alright. Let's show them more.'

Kara walked up to the bed and lay down right beside them. Greg lay on top of Kara, drawing her arms above her head, then sucked hard on her neck. In the next swift motion, while still gripping her wrists firmly in one hand, he pushed his cock inside her with the other. An escalating moan escaped her, the sound building as he penetrated her deeper with each thrust. The combined feeling of Greg's heat sliding deep inside her and the intensity of again being watched so closely by this first-time couple catapulted her into an orgasm that all but screamed throughout the room.

As the throbbing inside her subsided, Kara could feel her body land back into the gentle fold of Greg's arms. She looked at Greg and then turned her head towards Vijay and Rani, smiling gently. 'I'm sorry if I was loud. He just makes me feel so good.' It was then that Rani spoke directly to Kara for the first time.

'It's good to say what you feel. He made you feel very good, I think.'

With that Rani turned to Vijay, and they whispered together. Vijay looked up at Greg and said, 'I would like to watch you give this same pleasure to my wife too, if you will?' Then turning to Kara, 'Only if you are happy to share him, please?'

Kara and Greg shot each other a glance. They then both realised what the whispers had been about. Kara looked back at Vijay.

'If Rani is happy, then I am,' she said.

'If it is my husband's pleasure, then it is mine also,' Rani said.

Kara and Greg looked at each other again, rather surprised. They were suspended for a second, not sure that her words were truly her own and how to proceed.

Kara leant forward and spoke to Rani. 'It's alright. Greg is gentle and lovely. Enjoy him.'

Greg laid down on the bed as Kara took Rani's hand from around her husband's body and placed it gently on Greg's penis, wrapping her fingers around his shaft and motioning to stroke him. Greg looked up at Kara, his eyes wide, searching to check she felt alright. Kara nodded and smiled, turning back to face Vijay.

She reached for his hand and brought it up to her mouth.

Starting with his little finger, she put each one between her lips, sucking them one by one, slowly from base to tip. By the time she reached his index finger, he reached out with his other hand and started stroking her between her thighs.

Rani's eyes had widened and smiled back at Kara's when she spoke to her about Greg. Rani had stroked Greg's cock tentatively, before moving across the bed to lie up close to him. He rolled onto his side to face her. He kissed her softly on her mouth and ran his hand carefully down her neck and over her breasts. Her kiss was not what he'd expected. She'd returned his gentle pecks so willingly. Soft, warm and gentle, and surprisingly passionate. His hands roamed down her body, sliding between her legs. He found her wet, his fingers instantly sending an invitation to explore her.

Greg glanced over at Kara. He knew she would not want Vijay on top of her. She didn't need any reminders of that obese, oppressive, bearded beast of an ex-husband. He could see Vijay kneeling at the bedside with his face between her legs, her head back and groans of pleasure escaping her.

As Greg fell between Rani's legs, she whispered, 'No real sex.'

'That's okay. I will just touch you. I will stop whenever you want me to.'

Greg lowered himself to hover over her body, his knob lightly caressing her lips and clit, grazing her wetness. He kept gently rubbing her again and again, back and forth. She let herself melt back into the sheets, near falling deeper into another world. He then lowered himself a little farther and pushed gently against her opening, just parting her wet bulging lips. Greg felt the resistance of her tight vagina as he pushed ever so carefully. He pulled back and then pressed against her again. Then once more. Each stroke a millimetre deeper, yet she still didn't resist. Without warning she reached out, grabbed his shoulders in her hands, pulling him closer to edge his knob even deeper inside her. Greg, despite his urge to push harder, and her first physical request for more, he held back. He would not go further without her complete desire and consent.

Rani could feel herself about to explode, having now completely succumbed to the tenderness of his touch, the warmth of having a body fully wrapped in her arms, and the fullness of his cock poised to enter her. She now wanted him so badly. *This wasn't the plan at all. I Can't. But I want this. How can I? It feels so good. Can I?*

With his knob now completely inside her, her brown eyes suddenly fixed deeply into Greg's as she grabbed his butt cheeks, threw her head back, and for the first time, released a moan that she fought to suppress. Within seconds, she again pulled him closer, bringing him inside her even deeper. Greg, knowing she now cannot hold back her orgasm, gave her the remaining 80% of his erupting length. Their groans in unison told their story. Greg came so hard, he expected to taste it in her kiss. Eventually, her body's shuddering subsided, and he kissed her lips, cheeks and neck as she slowly returned to the real world. Rani's eyes spoke to him in that moment. She'd never had sex like that before or ever had a multiple orgasm, but she had now. Her eyes thanked him more than anything she could say.

Vijay had motioned for Kara to suck him, while Greg had started to pleasure Rani. Kara had allowed her lips to glide over him, firmly yet gently, as her fingers slipped over his thighs and balls.

Sensing his mounting orgasm, she slowed and stopped sucking him. She signalled for him to turn to fully watch Greg and Rani. She waited until the moment when Rani could resist no more. As she heard Rani let that cry escape and reach for Greg, she pulled Vijay close and said, 'Watch her while you come on me,' as she knelt below him.

He needed no more encouragement. He gripped himself and within a few seconds blew his load over Kara's breasts.

There were no words spoken as all four slowly recovered their composure.

After a short time, they all stood, dressed and moved to leave the room.

As they left the room, Rani and Vijay each took Greg and Kara's hands in theirs. 'Thank you both. We will never forget you.'

After such an intense experience, Kara just looked at Greg and said, 'Ready for home?'

'Yeah, for sure. It's been a big night.'

Greg and Kara stood quietly waiting for their Uber ride and remained quiet for most of the way back to their hotel. It had been an evening which offered so much more, and yet nothing like they expected.

Back in bed at the hotel, it was the recount of alabaster gossamer fingers arching and deep brown Indian eyes, both glowing in orgasmic energy, that sparked Greg and Kara's bodies again into more highly charged lovemaking, before sleeping blissfully in each other's arms. This night had unfolded more of the gift of compersion than either had expected.

Chapter 13

The phone alarm was unwelcomed in the dark hours of morning, however necessary to get the two of them back on the road to Adelaide in time for Kara to get to work in Clare on Tuesday.

Dressed, packed and in the ute with coffees in hand by 6.00 a.m., they had a good start to make it to West Wyalong before evening.

As the ute reached the highway, Greg glanced across to see Kara with her head back, her eyes closed, her coffee perched in her lap, her mouth upturned at the corners with her lips glistening. 'Are you back at the club there, sexy?' Kara blinked her eyes open and turned to him.

She giggled. 'Yes, I was. How could you tell?'

'That smile said it all. What part of the night are you thinking about?'

'To be honest, I still keep seeing you and Belinda caressing each other's fingers. It was exquisite to witness. So sensual and so romantic. It was nearly too much for me to watch.'

'Funny you say that. It was something that stood out for me too.'

'I was okay with it—not jealous or anything like that, but it was mesmerising.'

'I know. It was intimate and quite intense. Quite amazing.'

'It was such a contrast to having watched her with her husband-he was quite ferocious really.'

'Yeah. I was a bit nervous about what he might do to you.'

Kara smiled. 'Don't worry, I was too!' She laughed, 'but I knew you were watching out for me.'

'I always do. '

'I know. You are a sweetheart. Like knowing I wasn't that keen to have Vijay on top of me.'

'Yes, but I think he was extremely happy with what you did.'

'I think his wife had the most pleasure. She was such a surprise package and quickly got totally lost in you. It's those superpowers at work again, Mr Sheppard!' They both laughed.

The kilometres rolled by with music and chatting about their weekend, the work ahead and different parts of the countryside, which Greg knew so well. Greg travelled this road often, and like a professional tour guide, he seemed to know where to get the best coffee, meals and accommodation.

By about 4.00 p.m. they were on the outskirts of Dubbo, when their phones were once again in signal range.

Kara's phone pinged repeatedly. 'I hope Aunt Sarah is alright, I don't know who else might be ringing me so urgently.'

Her brow furrowed; the number alone had smudged her cheerful spirits. 'You can't be serious? Surely you can survive without me for a couple of days.' But clearly her comment was for the sender. She let a huge sigh escape as she hit the button to return the call.

Greg could hear the voice, speaking fast with a tone of urgency and near panic through the phone.

'Kara? Thank God. Thanks for calling back. I know you're on leave, but we've got a big problem. It's a mess. I'm sorry for all the messages, but I really need your help.'

Kara just listened before finally responding.

'Phil, can you please tell me what is going on exactly?'

'Sorry, Kara. But the briefing and outlines with all my region's funding applications for the Board wasn't submitted in time. Your guys didn't get it in on Friday, and I've been on the phone all morning trying to convince the Board to give us an extension. I really need you to get this sorted and want you there to present our submission in a workshop session with the funding subcommittee in Adelaide on Tuesday.'

'What do you mean it wasn't submitted? Paul and Karen only had to enter in the final figures, do a proofread and email it. It was set to go in on Thursday.'

'Paul called in sick on Thursday and still isn't back. Karen did some work on it that day but had to race off as her son broke his arm at school or something, so she only sent if off this morning.'

'Phil, this is *your* region's application. We were just checking it and adding the final touches for you. Why do you need me?'

'Kara, you are the only one who can sell it to the committee. I've not had to present to them before.'

'Phil, you do realise I am actually away? I'm not even in South Australia right now. I won't be back until Monday night. I can't possibly—'

'Kara, this could mean my job. Please. I need you.'

'Phil, I understand, but I cannot even physically get to Adelaide Monday night, back to Clare to prepare and then back to Adelaide, even if I wanted to.'

'I'll send you whatever you need via email. Perhaps you could stay in Adelaide Monday night and I'll meet you there on Tuesday?'

'Phil, seriously, this is a big stretch, don't you think?'

'Kara, I know. I'm sorry. I just don't know what to do.' She paused, then dropped her shoulders with reluctant acceptance.

'Okay. Send me all the files. I need you to pull together all the images and summary of the major projects and key messages you want to get across into a basic power point. I'll see what I can do.'

'Thanks Kara, you are a gem. I'll send you whatever you need. Call me Monday night. Anytime.'

'Alright. We will get it done Phil. Goodbye.'

Kara ended the call and just sat, phone held in hand, as she just stared out of the window.

It was another couple of kilometres before Greg spoke. Kara had not spoken in extensive detail about her work, but when she did, a clouded grey always shaded her eyes. He already knew before this, that she wasn't happy. He'd worked out that her role had morphed from leading to fixing, from exciting to mundane, a change to that of conformity and accountability rather than creativity and true community development. It was choking her.

She was obviously holding back the tears now.

'Sounds like you're wanted urgently?'

'Yes. Kara to the rescue. Yet again.' She breathed deeply, trying desperately to muffle her crying. 'See. I'm indispensable… for other people's problems, anyway. It's okay. I'll get it sorted.' She avoided Greg's gaze as she spoke.

'I know you will and will no doubt, do it brilliantly. But are you okay about it, really?'

'No. truth be known, I'm not. In fact.' She attempted a laugh. 'Could we turn back? I already know I enjoy Queensland more….'

But she couldn't hold it back. A tear trailed down her cheek. 'I'm sorry. It will be fine. I'm just upset that work interrupted our lovely trip.' She swiped at the tear with her sleeve. 'How far until we reach West Wyalong?'

Greg took his left hand from the steering wheel and reached out for Kara's hand, not taking his eyes off the road. He squeezed it gently and didn't let go. After about two more kilometres, he pulled the ute to the side of the road and turned off the ignition.

He pulled her hand to his lips and kissed her fingers gently.

'Kara, it's probably not my place to say, but I know it's not just this call. Work is clearly making you unhappy.'

Kara couldn't stop the wash of tears now trickling down her cheeks.

'You're right. I need to do something. I'm simply so tired of running back and forth between Clare and Adelaide and as you know, I don't get to create anything anymore. I just seem to be the person who fixes everyone else's fuckups. I shouldn't complain, I suppose, but….'

'But It's not what you want to be doing?'

'No, it's not anymore. Not at all.'

'So, if you could do or be anything you wanted, what would you do? Where would you go?'

Kara heard the question and while asked with the softness of a gentle caress, the realisation it provoked struck her like a blade. She swallowed hard, sniffing back the reality of despair that she had been denying about her job. She lamely attempted to compose herself.

'You mean apart from me being a sex goddess in Queensland?'

Greg just looked at her and smiled at her attempt to lighten the mood. 'Yes. Apart from that, of course.'

Kara just looked at him for a moment or two and turned back to look out of the window. She was contemplating his question honestly and confronting her own needs again. As only a true friend does, he'd given her a renewed perspective.

Softly her reply fell out of her mouth, barely a whisper.

'I want to leave Clare. I want to love my work again, for a start. Whatever it is.'

'Then there are some things you can do already. That's great. You don't have to do more just now. But knowing you have some options and things you want to do, is a good place to start. Don't you think?'

Kara leant across the seat and kissed Greg on the cheek. 'Thank you. You're right. It's time for change. I've got some thinking to do.'

'Well, I'm here to help in any way I can.'

'Thank you so much.' Before uttering another word. Kara stopped. Captured in his simple words, she caught the wave of their special connection, even more than when they had relished in each other's pleasure with others.

True compersion.

Kara swallowed hard. Then spoke.

'Now, you can help by picking a great song. I'm on holidays, remember!' Greg started the car as she turned up the music.

For the next couple of hundred kilometres, the conversation and volume were turned up to bright, and filled with everything other than work or decisions, but both Kara and Greg had ideas and thoughts about Kara's future brewing inside. Unspoken, yet the vibrations were felt like the bumpy, unkempt road beneath them.

The roadside stop, and chat delayed their arrival at West Wyalong, rather later than expected. About 10 kilometres from town Greg suggested Kara search for a particular restaurant he remembered, to order some food.

Kara found the site for the Asian bistro he'd described and called to order a couple of takeaway dishes. Greg drove straight to the restaurant.

'It won't be ready for another fifteen minutes, so I'll head to our hotel, check in, unload our bags and come back to get you. I won't be long.'

'Sure,' replied Kara, loving that Greg always had a plan.

Kara went inside and after chatting for a while she learned there was a nearby bottle shop so she walked to the next block to buy a bottle of wine to accompany their meal. The walk in the evening's glow was a welcome stretch for her body. She had used a few different muscles this weekend. By the time Greg returned she had food, wine and a wide smile to greet him.

'I hope you're hungry! We've got plenty here!'

The 2-star hotel that screamed 'stop, stay and go' through the loud bedspread and unloved prints adorning the walls, became the backdrop for a most intimate and sensitive evening. Greg's speaker crooned out favourite songs and they sang between mouthfuls of delicious Kway Teow chicken, rice and red wine, until the need for rest hit them both.

Kara took to the shower first as Greg cleared up the remnants of their dinner and checked his work messages.

As Kara lay back in bed ruminating over the day while he washed away the hours of driving, she could only replay his words. 'What do you really want?'

She knew he was right, without saying it directly. Her next steps needed to take a different path to keep herself professional and emotional self, intact. During dinner Greg had probed more about what Kara had been dealing with at work and what options she might have.

'So, what's really happening at work Kara? Are there other options,' Greg asked.

'I'm not sure. I still love the work I do. But I'm just getting more and more frustrated. My colleagues and staff seem to lack finesse or experience, so I seem to end up doing their work or fixing things. Oh, don't get me wrong, they all try, and I don't want to sound like I'm blaming them. Perhaps it's really time for me to move on.'

'Sounds like you're ready and in need of a change.'

'I've never been interested in the management positions as they're all based in the city, but you are right. I'll sort something out. Hey, isn't it bedtime?' Kara said, wanting to change the subject away from her world of work as soon as she could.

Tonight, she would think no more about herself.

This was her last night with Greg. All she really wanted to do in this moment was thank him.

Greg slipped between the sheets, kissed her and wrapped his arm around her. Lying on his side, his shape and form was the sight that always sparked her.

With her cheek pressed lightly against his chest, she let her hand whisper all the gratitude she felt for him from the day. Kara just took him in, with her eyes and her touch. Her fingers stroked up and down, across and over, lyrically gliding across his naked flesh. His muscular, shapely, hourglass body was to her like a violin she simply could not resist playing. 'I think you're spoiling me,' he murmured.

'Sshh now. I love doing this. Just sleep.'

Kara kept her fingers floating over him until his breathing lowered to the deepest notes.

Chapter 14

Awoken by the warmth from a body and fingers breathing their way over her skin, Kara's morning started as lyrically as Greg's had ended last night, followed by blissful shudders and sounds, which drowned out Greg's alarm resoundingly.

The last day of travel was full of sunshine and recounts of the weekend's events yet again. Chatting about experiences they had only dared to fantasise about two days before, they now had real, explicit accounts of themselves swinging with others. About an hour into their in-depth conversation Kara put her hand on Greg's arm.

'You know, I thought I might feel a bit jealous but it didn't feel like I expected. I sort of felt pleasure through you. Does that sound silly?'

'No. But yes. I know what you mean. I didn't really like seeing another man touching you at first, but it was such a turn on being able to watch you enjoying yourself, sort of by remote control.'

'Yes, that's kind of it. After a while I could sense that you weren't feeling anything emotionally for the women, so I just relaxed and enjoyed seeing how you aroused them. I could feel you with me all the time, if that makes sense?'

'That's exactly how I felt. It was like you were with me through someone else.' 'I know. You were sort of touching me the whole time, but through your eyes. It was quite exhilarating. But I'm still surprised at what and how much we did. It was a record-breaking weekend, I think!'

'Exactly. Me too! As for records, I think you've created a big one.'

'To what record are you referring, Sir?' Kara said with a devilish grin creeping across her face.

'I'm guessing you had at least twenty orgasms, Ms Gilbert! In less than four days. That is a record. I'm certain of it.'

'Umm, well?' Kara stopped and closed her eyes. Still grinning, she recalled and counted through each part of their trip.

'By my count you had at least seven Mr Sheppard. Is that correct?'

He laughed. 'You think? Now let's see, I think it was eight.'

The next stage of their trip was a 'come by come' account for each of them in the past days, filled with laughs and highlights in between. The kilometres flew by and without realising, it was already lunchtime.

Greg refuelled the ute and Kara grabbed sandwiches and coffees from the service station café. As they turned onto the highway, Kara's phone pinged three times.

'That will be Phil's emails. I'd better take a look and see what I can get done now, if that's alright?'

'Good idea. That way you can have an early night before your meeting tomorrow.'

Kara took out her laptop and created a hotspot to her phone.

They were about four hours from Adelaide, and Kara worked solidly nearly the entire time. Greg would look over now and then, as she read and typed. He smiled whenever she started talking to herself, obviously rehearsing sections she had to present to the board. He had not seen her in work mode before. She was focussed and unwavering.

'Sorted!' she exclaimed as she snapped shut the laptop. 'This is the best I can do. His presentation thankfully was quite good, so that only needed a few slides added.'

'You're quite the machine when you're working, aren't you?' He threw her a grin.

'I'm sorry, I haven't been much company. I just knew I wouldn't feel like starting this tonight. Now I only need to check it over once when we get back.'

'It's absolutely fine, Kara. I was just a bit amazed at how you focussed, especially while travelling.'

'Well, I suppose. It just needed to be done.'

'I'm impressed. I'm sure the board will be too.'

'I hope so... Shit!'

'What's the matter?'

'I just realised that I haven't got any work clothes with me. I can't front up to the board in my sexy little black dress!'

'Nothing at your aunt's place?'

'No. I took everything back to Clare last week.'

She checked the time. They wouldn't get back to the city before the shops closed. She thought hard.

'Maybe I can call the boutique where I got my suit from the other week? No, that won't work, they don't deliver.'

'How about you call and see if they have something, and I'll sort something through my office. Andrew lives not far from me at Burnside and he could pick up your outfit and drop it at my place.'

'You sure? You're a lifesaver!'

'You'd better call the shop right now, though.'

Kara did a quick Google search and found the number for Veronica Maine at Burnside Village. After a few minutes, Kara had purchased pants, jacket and silk top. Fortunately, they had the same outfit she had bought, but in a different colour, that had just arrived.

Hearing Kara had sorted the purchase, Greg called the office.

'All sorted, madam!' he said. 'Andrew will be there in the next twenty minutes. Now you can be dressed to impress too.'

'Thank you so much. I think you are a real machine, Mr Sheppard! I love how you don't see problems, just solutions.'

A couple of minutes later Greg threw out a statement. It sounded more like a thought out loud than anything.

'Why don't you come and stay at my place?'

Kara grinned. 'Sure—I'd love to. Your place is much closer than Sarah's to the city for me to make the meeting in the morning too.'

'Actually, Kara, I was thinking a bit longer term. All this driving back and forth from Clare is wearing you down as well as your work. Why not make the break now?'

'What do you mean?'

'I was thinking you would be wonderful as an event organiser. There are plenty of firms who would employ you here in Adelaide for sure. I've got a three-bedroom apartment, and I'd be happy to share the place with you. You could move straight away and wouldn't have to wait until you sell your home in Clare. It would be rent free, we'd just split the costs. You have your own room so you keep your independence.'

'Greg, are you serious? But... what about...?'

'Hey, you don't need to decide this minute. It's just an idea.'

Kara sat quietly as her mind swirled, contemplating Greg's suggested plan.

As they pulled into his apartment driveway, Greg said, 'Look Kara, you don't need to think more about it now. You have other more important work to do tonight.'

Kara turned to look at him slowly. In a serious tone she said, 'You're right. I have much more important business, with you, tonight.' Then she grinned. 'You did have eight. I need to make sure my record is an even 3:1.'

'You are so naughty, Ms Gilbert,' he laughed as he jumped out of the ute and grabbed their bags.

Kara woke over an hour before the alarm. Greg was sleeping deeply; his near snoring breaths were purring. That sound always comforted her. Despite her temptation to touch him all over, she slipped out of bed and snuck to the guest bathroom. He was such a light sleeper, and this morning she needed work, and not her own pleasure to be in the spotlight.

Maybe for the last time. She thought.

Greg's simple statements and his offer of a place to stay had hit the nerve.

She wasn't happy. He was right.

She was sick of trekking back and forth to the city, at the whim of her employer and squeezing only a slither of her personal life in between. Her clothes were nearly as unsettled as she was—from hanger to bag to car, resting barely for a few days, before being traipsed back again for another round of washing, crumpling, ironing and hanging. They hadn't landed in the same place for more than three nights for years.

She hadn't either.

She pulled the clothes from the bag that had thankfully landed on his doorstep last evening. As she steered the iron over each inch of the fabric, holding it firmly, letting it glide to smooth every crease, her thoughts followed in similar detail.

He was offering her what he'd never given to another in the same way. She felt his protective care and knew that it came from the same cradled place where she held him. They somehow shared a fierce, yet delicate bond of understanding, respect and unconditional friendship, wrapped in the delicate touch of their shared fantasies. Its foundation was now strong, beyond mere sex, and she knew and felt it.

But, despite this being a natural and sensible offer, she also knew that underneath, it might scare him—as much as it did her. Promises and commitment, while enticing in some moments, near repelled them both. The past effects of having given the heart of themselves hadn't ever brought either of them their desired lifetime of happiness, but sadly, only pain. Her ex was simply a bastard wrapped in shiny paper, who shattered her sense of worth and ability to trust. His wife was comfort and stability, but without vibrant colour or intimacy. His beautiful Tess, he lost when she was but a second from the finish line. The winning trophy within arm's reach, her death denying him a life with a loving soul.

Kara knew he didn't extend this to her lightly, and it warmed her heart. He was offering the most his heart could give. It was a statement of their absolute, intimate friendship. She already knew she would accept. However, she had to make sure it gave him and her, the elasticity they both still needed.

It was important to tell him. There was a strange but warm blanket of comfort and a foundation for a fresh start that moving to the city and into his home would bring. He'd offered it so willingly, but she knew they had to talk a little more first. There had to be some terms stated. She caught the sense he had more to consider in the seconds after he offered. So, they needed to make sure all the arrangements of shared living didn't give pause.

They'd share his house every day, but only each other's bed at times needed most. Walk tight together at all times as only best friends do but keep things as separate and usual as they like. Plans together should only be as spontaneous and random as they have always been, and other people or partners should never be questioned or denied.

These had to be terms, as she knew it's what was right and needed to be, for both of them. *But how to tell him?*

Kara crept back into the bedroom and stood next to the bed looking at the sleeping Greg Sheppard.

A shepherd he is, beyond his name for sure. Forever the protector, she thought.

She leant down. She dared not touch him for fear of disturbing. She just took in a deep breath. She wanted to take the scent of him with her today.

As she turned to leave, his hand caught her fingers. Drawing her back, she turned and sat gently bedside. 'Hey, I'm sorry, I didn't want to wake you.'

Greg drew her fingers to his lips, kissed their tips and then folded them into his palm. 'You'll be brilliant. It's a done deal. Dinner here tonight to celebrate.'

'Thank you. For everything. I'll bring the wine. Go back to sleep, you Superman.' She drew his hand to her lips and returned the kisses.

Kara's fingers lingered against his, before she turned and slipped out of the room. Only the graze of her perfume remained.

As the front door clicked shut softly, Greg rolled onto his back, folding his arms behind his head.

He lay there, looking up at the ceiling.

Already she'd, without the exact words, signalled she had accepted his suggestions, was ready to leave her job and move in. He'd felt it through her fingertips. He knew she didn't want to leave.

Should I have asked her to live with me? Where did that come from? He dared not even share the secret with himself, but he didn't merely offer. He truly wanted her to live with him. To be there, physically living alongside him, as she had been emotionally, since they reconnected those few years ago. She'd become a friend like no other. He loved her for being just her unique self, and how much she cared about people and him. She did just lighten up his life.

Seeing her so exhausted by her work, he'd felt overcome with a desire to protect her and give her something back after all the time she had helped him. She had become his kinky lover, and while bold and open, he felt her fierce protection and genuine feelings for him. He felt the same about her.

How do I tell her we both should keep seeing other people too? Will she be alright with this?

Chapter 15

By 3.00 p.m. it was smiles and handshakes as Kara walked out of the offices in Victoria Square. She'd given a presentation like no other with a newfound clarity in her approach, fuelled by the decision she had made.

Kara stepped back from the stress and pressure as if she'd already left the position. The board was impressed and had approved all the funding by the meeting's end. Phil was overjoyed and invited her to join him and their boss, Lainie, for a drink to celebrate.

'Kara, that was incredible. You always do a great job, but today you did an amazing job. Thank you,' Lainie said, raising her glass.

'It's always good to finish up on a high note,' she said quietly.

As Phil and Lainie near choked on her words, she calmly explained her decision to move to the city and gave them a month's notice. After the initial shock settled, and another thirty minutes of discussion while still reeling, they both understood.

Kara thanked them both and left, with the promise to meet and sort details during the next couple of days. She just wanted to get to Greg. There was so much to share.

Greg knew this was a big day for Kara, especially if she had given notice about leaving too, so dinner needed to be special. He was, thankfully a very adept cook. He loved creating his own recipes and everything about preparing and sharing food with others. For Kara tonight he had decided on a trusted favourite with the best of ingredients. A three mushroom sauce to adorn two medium rare Scotch Fillet steaks, a potato bake, honeyed carrots, and broccoli. Everything needed to taste and feel just right for her as he also knew they had a delicate conversation ahead of them.

Kara had walked from the office and headed straight to the taxi rank. She sent a quick message to let him know she was on her way. Enroute, she asked the driver to pull into Vintage Cellars near Greg's place, and wait while she bought a bottle of premium red wine. Tonight deserved a rich, full-bodied red wine to celebrate change.

As the cab meter ticked on, she thought *to hell with the expense* as she considered her selection, eventually choosing a Penny's Hill 'Footprint' Shiraz. She raced back to the taxi. Five minutes later she was walking through Greg's door.

'Welcome, how did it go?' Greg called out from the kitchen.

'I think I nailed it! Everything went perfectly, but I'm so glad it's over,' she said accepting the glass of wine from Greg that he had already poured for her.

'How did they take the news?'

'They were shocked at first but understood my situation.'

Kara's eyes looked over her glass as she took a second sip and watched the chef return to the stove. She smiled to herself, loving the contrasting sight of Greg in the kitchen adorned in his business clothes and butcher blue striped apron, as he flourished his master chef style over the hotplates.

'It's just about ready are you hungry?'

'I sure am. I barely had a couple of bites all day.'

Greg served out two generous servings and topped up their wine glasses.

Having a man cook for Kara was a rarity, and there wasn't truly much that impressed her more. The time, planning and care to prepare a meal for her, so delicious, was such a special gift. Greg had given her the perfect celebration already.

They chatted through the meal, mostly about Kara's day and he could see she was happy. Kara was first to finish and sat watching her personal chef have his last mouthful. She loved watching how he would eat the whole meal, always keeping the absolute best pieces for last. She watched with a grin as the last forkful entered his mouth.

With an even bigger grin she said, 'What if you're too full before you finish the plate?' She almost laughed at his little ritual.

'Easy. I just advance straight to the pieces I've saved and leave the rest,. Why? Are you laughing at me?'

'Never!' she replied, covering her mouth to stifle her chuckle. 'I just love that you are a "save the best till last" type of guy… and you are still wearing an apron!' They both laughed.

Greg took off his apron and enjoyed a big sip of wine, swirling it in his mouth, savouring the mix of flavours and swallowed.

'Ahh, that is a great drop.'

'The wine was just right with those sensational steaks, and the company even better. A perfect way to end a monumental day.' She took another sip.

'Congratulations on a great finish and a new start!' Greg raised his glass and chinked it to hers.

Greg's tone lowered a little. 'Kara, I already knew this morning you'd decided to leave work and accept my offer to live here. So maybe, we should have a chat about how our new living arrangements might work?'

'Great idea, what are you thinking?'

'Well, Kara, we are the closest of friends and I will always be here for you whenever you need me as I know you will for me.'

'Of course. That goes without saying, Greg.'

'So, as we are also friends with benefits—'

'Friends with *lots* of benefits,' Kara interrupts with a grin.

'Yes, sorry, friends with *lots* of benefits for sure, and I want that to remain above all else. Please don't take this the wrong way, but I really want us to keep our individuality and fire too, if that makes sense?'

'I totally understand,' replied Kara not showing much emotion either way.

'Is that totally cool, Kara? Please let me know if it's not.'

'Totally cool.'

Again, she wasn't giving much away. So, he kept trying to explain.

'You may come across someone that you just feel the urge to fuck, and I want you to know that I'm quite okay with that. We both work away and at different times, we may feel the need for someone at the time. I want us both to know and feel that it's quite alright, if we want to explore others. Just like I did with Megan in Sydney.'

Kara looked up from her hands that are in front of her on the table and said, 'Of course, that's alright by me. Hey, but you never know there may be a bit of crossover there as well. How will we deal with that?'

'Well I bloody hope there is!' replied Greg with finally a smile emerging. 'Shall we say, no one fucks someone else in front of the other, unless the other is invited to join in?'

'Yes that's a good idea.'

'What about if you found some guy that you would like to invite here to meet you on your own one day?'

'Well, I'm not quite that easy!' She laughed... then composed herself. 'But I know what you're saying. For me, I think it should be no different to what I'd be happy for you to do. We need to keep enjoying ourselves. We should agree that we know we are both free to find anyone we want on our own. That's a given, however, let's add that we will both let each other know if we are enjoying them here—just to respect each other's privacy, but more to make our dates feel okay about being in our shared place. Does that sound fair?'

'Absolutely. Happy with that. Can you think of anything else, Kara?'

'I don't think so. Well, not right now. This red is quite distracting! But, hey what about you? Can you think of anything we need to consider?'

Greg stopped to think. 'There is one last thing. Perhaps it's the most important for day-to-day arrangements. I was wondering how it might work when we each have our separate rooms, but we would like to fuck each other?'

'Probably no different to how we work that out now, living in separate places. We ask, or just start perhaps as the mood takes us? That part's easy,' Kara said with a grin.

It was Greg's turn to breathe a little easier. 'Yes, of course. That's simple. So, we just agree to always plan to sleep in our own rooms each night unless the other is invited in case we have had a big day and need to just be alone and get some sleep.'

'That's it. Sounds like we have a plan.'

They raised their glasses and smiled. It was an easier agreement to negotiate than either had thought. It just needed someone to start the conversation.

Kara blurted, 'I have thought of one more thing. Maybe we can use a swing club rule for starters? Like, if we arrange to play with anyone or couples together—we don't then splinter to sleeping with one of the playmates on our own in this place. We start as two, we finish as two and don't solo with the players, without talking more about it first.' Before Greg could say a word she also said, 'Most of all, if we feel horny we say so. If we don't, we say it too without taking it as rejection or personally.'

'Okay that's fantastic. I'm happy with all of that. I'm sure we'll fine tune it as we go. Hey thanks. I don't think enough people really talk through what they really want or think sometimes.'

'Greg, thank you. I've thought about all of this lots too. You're right. This stuff is important to work through. I didn't quite know how to talk to you about how we might make this work, but I have wanted to. I am so grateful for the place but I need to lighten your life, not make it more complicated.'

'Kara, I'm sure this will continue to be just as it is between us always—a happy, comfortable, and uniquely sexy arrangement! Now how about dessert? Tonight is a celebration, remember?'

'Sure, what is for dessert?' Kara asks looking toward the kitchen.

'Me,' Greg replied with a cheeky grin.

'Ahh, my favourite flavour!' replied Kara as she stood and walked around the dining table and unbuttoned his shirt. Dessert was undoubtably the most delicious ending to a successful and memorable day.

So it progressed that Kara's next eight weeks had been nearly as happy and transformational as when she first reunited with Greg. While her transition to the city happened smoothly, it was non-stop, nonetheless. With the help of Greg's contacts and great references from her boss and the board, she'd secured a position with an event production agency and was enjoying the flexibility and ability to design and plan again.

She'd put her house in Clare on the market, sorted and put most of her furniture and belongings into storage, taking only the things she loved and needed to Greg's apartment.

What made her the happiest was the peaceful way she and Greg stayed connected and didn't miss a beat or drop a note from the first day she moved in. He'd been such a catalyst for change in her life in so many ways in these few years and yet remained so humble and encouraging about her every step. He'd welcomed her into his home with such generosity and care, Kara couldn't imagine her life without him as her most trusted and beloved friend.

He'd even gone so far as to leave a little surprise gift, which she'd found resting on her pillow on her first night at the apartment. The romantic, gentle sensitivity of this man, often veiled beneath his strong and confident shell, was something she adored. She knew no one so incredibly thoughtful and encouraging. The note that sat beneath the little ribboned box containing a resplendent solitaire pearl on a silver chain, so overwhelmed her, she near drowned him in hugs, happy tears and every pleasure imaginable that night.

It read:

A pearl is said to be symbolic of wisdom learned from experience and can protect and bring luck and prosperity. Most of all, they are symbols of the integrity, generosity and purity of those who wear them. Welcome to your new home, job and life Kara. My first and forever. Much love Greg x

It was like nothing about their connection had really changed, just better. Now it was chatting over the dinner table instead of over the phone, and while they upheld their agreed arrangements, they had shared each other's beds on most nights. The sexual energy, fun and pleasure without obligation, which they'd always enjoyed had stayed the same.

Kara loved the discussions that just rolled. Greg was someone who shared so many things in common with her, who was well read, open, innovative and astute. The nights when they were both home and work permitted, were often spent in deep exchanges about more aspects of their lives and views. They shared much more about their marriages, families and the little details and intricacies of the decades of their lives before they had reconnected. Kara had discovered even deeper dimensions and insights into Greg than he'd ever revealed before. She had uncovered more of the hidden compartments behind the outward confidence and simplicity he portrayed. During this time, Greg revealed even more of his innate sensitivity, kindness, generosity and care, brimming with powerful aspirations. He was a person filled with a strength and near impenetrable force. Yet she had found his vulnerabilities, both of which were equally endearing and attractive.

Reciprocally, he had exposed, understood and accepted her for all her strengths and weaknesses and had sparked parts, never revealed so explicitly to herself or others. So, despite each holding some hesitation at first, their unique bond had only strengthened as housemates. They were each other's confidante and sounding board and relaxed knowing that they could tell each other anything.

It was Friday at about 2.30 p.m. and Kara's ring tone sang out from beneath the papers across his desk. He grabbed the phone. This was rather unusual as she rarely rang during the middle of a workday.

'Hi Kara, everything alright?'

'It's more than alright! It's amazing. Sorry to interrupt you at work... but my house has been sold and at the full price I was asking for. I just had to tell you.'

'That is brilliant. We need to celebrate tonight then.'

'Yes, definitely. But, it's also why I'm ringing. I know it's my turn to prep dinner tonight, but I'm making a quick dash to Clare to sign papers for the agent. So, I'll be back this evening—but likely not until just after 7.00.'

'Hey, that's quite okay. I'll sort the food—no problem. I'm so pleased for you.'

'You are a sweetheart. What's say I grab one of Clare Valley's best wines to bring home, so we can celebrate in style.'

'Deal. See you tonight. Can't wait.'

Greg was delighted with Kara's news and looked forward to hearing all about the sale when she arrived home. Just before 5.00 p.m. he dashed out to grab ingredients for dinner and by 6.00 p.m. he had everything prepped to cook their meal. He returned to his desk, now wanting to get as much finished as he could before she returned. It was in this next hour that Greg would uncover even more unexpected news to share with Kara too.

Chapter 16

*M*egan arrived home to an empty house. It was Friday night basketball for Michael and Matt, and Tracey had messaged to say she was going out with her friends after her Uni lecture tonight. She saw the note from Michael left on the bench.

Pasta in fridge. Matt's staying at Jack's. See you about 8.00 x

Usually she was grateful for his organisation and thoughtfulness, but tonight this grated. *He thinks about my meals and clothes, but not about my body.*

She took a glass and poured herself a wine.

Standing in the kitchen, she removed her clothes and started wandering restlessly around in only her bra and knickers. Between her next couple of sips of wine, she peeled off her underwear and relished in the feel of walking naked throughout the house, the feel of doing something slightly naughty while everyone else was out.

Stop it. Behave yourself.

She gathered up her clothes and headed to the bedroom. As she entered, she looked at herself in the mirrored robe. She ran her hand over her breasts and down her body. The urge was stirring frantically inside her again. *My God, I'm feeling horny. Stop it, woman. You shouldn't think about it.*

The feelings rose, and she kept flicking back to the thought of him. It caught her often, like an itch or an undone shoelace she couldn't reach. She knew what she wanted to do.

But it's not that simple, it's not right, I must be strong. Her thoughts debated as she tried to find a distraction. But then that feeling surged again, a warmth inside her. A memory. A need. A desire. *I have to see Greg again- just one more time.*

So far, she has resisted calling him but the urge was becoming overwhelming. She imagined him caressing her, the tingles that radiated through her, his smile that penetrated her, and of course that feeling of having him inside her. Her legs almost gave away as she imagined herself there, her groin pulsing and moist from the virtual sex in her mind.

She tossed her clothes on the floor and raced back to the kitchen to pick up her phone and her glass. She can't take this anymore. There is no overcoming her new addiction to sex and the lingering memory of the close encounter with him.

Megan sat holding her phone for what seemed like ages. She squirmed as she sat on the edge of her bed. She desperately wanted to make the call. She drew in a breath. *You are just checking in on him, that's all.*

She dialled Greg Sheppard's number.

It was just after 6.30 p.m. Greg was back sitting at his home office desk still working on the project proposal for the Melbourne Film Festival. His phone rang, as it had done all day. When it loomed it was like one non-stop phone call for weeks, or so it seemed. He reached for the phone half expecting it to be Kara calling on her way back from Clare, but it wasn't her ringtone. He looked at the number; it wasn't one he recognised. *Had to be work.*

'Greg Sheppard,' he answered in his usual business voice.

'Hi Greg, I'm not sure you remember me but I'm Megan, err, we met in Sydney at the...'

'Wow, yes. Of course, I remember you. How are you going?'

'I'm going really well, thanks. I'm really sorry to call and can go if it's not convenient or appropriate.'

'Don't be silly, it's great to hear from you. I'd hoped you might call so I could apologise again for leaving you the way I did that night. I thought you might have wanted to forget about me.'

Not bloody likely, she thought.

'Oh, I've been pretty busy with work and stuff, but I have definitely thought about you… quite a bit, actually. I hope things are a little easier for you, after such a tragic loss.'

'You're very thoughtful, Megan. Thank you. I'm doing much better now. I've had some great friends who've helped me.'

Megan stumbled as the words tumble out… 'To be honest, I can't stop thinking about you and what we did.'

'Megan, it's okay. Truth be told I've thought a lot about you as well. I'm so sorry about how it ended.'

Greg heard Megan's breath escape. Clearly she had been apprehensive about calling him and she had more on her mind that she wanted to say. 'Please know I completely understand about that night. Although…' she hesitated.

'Yes, I know. You were very understanding. Well, perhaps we can have lunch or a coffee sometime, to make up for it.'

'I would really like that,' Megan purred down the phone. 'Do you really think of me often, Greg?'

'Of course,' he responded politely.

'Greg,' Megan said not able to control herself any longer. 'I'm sorry, but I really want to finish what we started… to be honest you're all I can think about. Could we meet again soon? I'm sorry for speaking like this, I just can't help the way I feel.'

With a slight gulp, Greg's thoughts went into overdrive.

Wow, that's not what I was expecting. She really hasn't left that room. I can't hurt her. She's so sweet.

'Megan, it makes me feel good to know that such a lovely person feels that way about me, but… I need to tell you about what's happened since we met.'

'I am so sorry Greg, I wasn't even going to contact you, it's just…'

'I understand completely. It feels like we had unfinished business.'

'Yes, that's it. So, what has happened since we met?' Megan asked cautiously.

A part of her didn't really want to know what she expected he would say. She braced and waited for his reply.

'Well, as I said, I had a friend who had really helped me since my fiancée's death. One especially. Kara. She has been a rock and is a special friend. We share this place together.'

'I see. Now I feel so silly. I'm sorry.' Megan's reply was crestfallen. *He has someone.*

'Hold up. Well, it's not exactly how you may think.'

Greg realised he had never described the type of relationship, nor the kinky pleasures that he and Kara enjoyed, to anyone outside of this scene before.

'It's sort of hard to explain, but Kara and I are more of… best friends and soul mates, really. We are lovers but we are open to seeing others, if you know what I mean?'

'So, are you saying that you have an open relationship and are okay if you each feel like sleeping with someone else?'

'A bit like that. Yes, we are free to do that if we choose. But it's a little different. We actually enjoy sleeping with others, when we're both together.'

'Oh.' Megan let his words absorb. Greg could nearly hear her mind racing. He didn't say a word, just let her think about that.

After a moment she whispered, 'So, are you saying you have threesomes or are you both bi?'

'Yes, we've had threesomes, but only with other women. We're both straight really. But Kara is what we call bi-curious. She's very open to exploring women too. It's helped her understand more about her own body, and she loves how it gives me pleasure to watch her with someone too.' He paused. 'Megan, I know this is nothing like you expected, and it's probably hard to understand, but I want to be honest with you.'

A rush of heat waved throughout her body as she imagined herself and Greg being watched by someone.

'I've never really thought about sex like that.' Swallowing hard she then muttered, 'it actually sounds a little exciting.'

'Believe me, it is. It might not be what you expected, but you're most welcome to catch up for coffee or lunch and meet Kara one day, maybe? I'm sure you'll like her. She knows all about you.'

'She does?'

'She knows all about me, as I do about her. We trust each other implicitly. It's sort of how and why we can share each other together.'

'Um, sure. I understand. I think. Lunch would be nice. I don't know when I can though, I never know when I can get away—especially interstate. '

'That's fine, whenever it works. You two are quite similar, you know.'

'How's that?'

'Both thoughtful, pretty and very sexy.'

'Stop it, you naughty man!'

Megan relaxed a little on hearing that Kara wasn't quite the usual type of committed partner. *Maybe I might still have a chance to be with him again?*

She was utterly fascinated about what he said about the two of them and sharing people. She'd not thought about it before, but it had got her tingling. The effects of her thoughts, the wine and the sound of Greg's voice hit her like a drug.

'Greg, can you tell me a story, about us? Like you did that night. What it might be like if all three of us were together, naked and sexy?'

'Sure, are you really okay about including Kara? It will be dynamic and very arousing.'

'Yes, sure. As long as it ends with you making love to me.'

'Megan, I take it you're on your own?'

'Yes, I am.' *Well, I am on my own right now,* she thought.

'Okay, let's start with the two of us, you and me, together, naked and sexy. We lay together on my bed. The ceiling fan slowly turning to the beat of our hearts. The curtains move with the breeze from the open window. The door is open to let the air flow through the room. You are laying on your back, I lay beside you but on my front, just our lips touching. I love the taste, the fullness and softness of your lips. I could just kiss them all day, but we both know it won't be long before we are devouring each other. My hands explore your body from as far as I can reach in each direction, teasing you with each pass. Each time my fingers find the top of the inside of your legs, they open further, welcoming my touch. It's not long before they find and converge on your pussy, feeling the wetness that has been desperate for me to touch. I feel your clit stiffening with each rub. I can hear your breath deepen as the sound of the front door opening and closing alerts us. We can both hear footsteps, although the person is being quiet and treading softly.'

'I whisper, "It's alright. It's Kara." Although a wave of panic runs through you, you don't want me to stop. I say, "She may want to join us. She will certainly enjoy watching us."

'You just nod, knowing that you are close to orgasm. You glance quickly toward the door and can see Kara standing there, a gentle smile on her face. She can see our naked bodies touching. She can tell there's a bursting sensation building inside you, from your gasps and moans. You feel her climbing on the bed to sit up close to you. Her perfume and body warmth envelops you. You feel the soft feminine touch of her fingers on your inner thigh. You wanted to resist it at first, but you now welcome it.'

Greg could hear Megan's breath deepening through the phone as he spoke and the groans as he suspected she was now touching herself.

'You feel her hand up close to mine and two new fingers slide inside you. She hits your G spot, and you explode from the double contact.'

Megan was rubbing herself frantically when the beam of car lights flickered across the window. She stopped and listened.

God, is that Michael?

Greg sensed a sudden quiet. 'Megan, are you still there?'

Don't be silly, Michael won't be home yet.

'Yes,' she whispered, breathlessly. 'That was so hot. I think I'd better go. I'd love to call again sometime if that's alright?'

'Sure. We will have to…' but before he could finish his sentence, Megan had gone.

Greg, now sitting back on the lounge, sat motionless for some time after Megan's rather abrupt end to the call. He smiled. She had been aroused and poised to come. It was a whirlwind of a conversation, catching him both unexpectedly, yet predictably at the same time. He hadn't been that surprised when Megan called, knowing that their first encounter had been so heightened and he had abruptly thwarted her arousal.

He was pleased she had reached out as he still felt awful about having left her, suspended in the passion of that night. He hadn't got her details or even her surname, so he'd felt bad about not being able to contact her. Kara had been right. She said she was sure Megan would be in touch somehow. He hadn't picked that she would be this bold when he met her in Sydney. He definitely hadn't expected the apparent urgency for sex that she conveyed in the call this evening either.

As Kara walked through the door, apologising for being later than expected, he called out. 'Hi there, sexy. How did everything go? Don't worry about the time, I've been held up too. I'll get dinner started soon. But hey, come have a wine and sit with me first. You honestly won't believe the phone call I just had!'

Chapter 17

Michael had swung the car around and pulled up at the front of the house. Realising Matt and Tracey were off with their mates, he thought Megan might like to join him at the pub, rather than being home for another couple of hours on her own.

He walked around to the side door, surprised to find the place in near darkness. Only the hallway light to the bedroom appeared to be on. He slid open the door carefully and stepped inside. Something didn't feel right, a wave of caution stopping him from calling out. He placed his keys down carefully on the table and tiptoed across the living room towards the light.

Megan was still laying there, hot, and still throbbing inside from having listened to Greg's sexy, dulcet tones through the phone. She felt bad for hanging up, but she was sure she'd heard a car arrive outside.

She listened again, but everything was still. It must have been a car doing a U-turn. *Damn it!*

She had been on the brink of coming fiercely from rubbing herself so furiously, she could barely stop herself from exploding.

She wanted more.

Should I call him back? No, I won't risk it. I'm so close, anyway.

She cupped each of her hands under her breasts, squeezing them and rubbing her thumbs over both nipples, still so tight and erect. Two fingers from her right hand soon found her clit and started circling instantly. She was already floating back into the words that had penetrated through the phone, his imagined caress and a woman's gaze and touch across her body. There was no stopping the juices flowing and the moans of pleasure this time. She could nearly feel his body close to her, his finger beckoning inside her. Her index finger from her left hand was now pushed hard inside her vagina. She heard the last words he uttered: *'You feel her hand up close to mine and two new fingers slide inside you, she hits your G spot.'*

Pushing her second finger inside, she catapulted into the ménage imagery that was now fucking her; the stimulation hitting straight from her mind to her body.

Michael's footsteps down the hall towards their bedroom had stopped on hearing the muffled strange sounds emanating from their bedroom. A part of him wanted to turn back, yet he was compelled to keep listening. He took two more steps closer to reach the doorway. in that moment, he was too scared to look, his imagination going wild. *Was this to be every married man's biggest nightmare? To come home and find a man between your wife's legs.*

He heard her moan again, louder this time.

It couldn't be anything else. He could already picture what he was about to see for real. *Who will this man be? is it someone I know? One of my mates? How should I react? Do I stay calm or should I lose it?*

Michael's motion was now suspended, not having floorboards that would creak and give him away, he was able to walk right up to the half-open door. The hall light was directly above him, so he wouldn't throw a shadow as he reached the doorway. He knew the hall light with the door half open would light the centre of the bed perfectly, like a back light for an intimate scene in a film. He took a breath and looked in.

His eyes are now adjusting to the almost dark room.

At first, he saw her clothes carelessly piled on the floor, then her naked form across the bed with her legs spread wide.

His head turned to scan the room. It wasn't where his mind had taken him. He breathed for the first time as his eyes scanned back.

He could see her completely. She was alone. Only her phone lay next to her on the bed.

Her head was pushing hard back into the pillow. Her eyes shut tight. Her pussy lips pink, thick and glistening. Her fingers inside her moving in near desperation. Her toes twitching and her hips rising, as she worked herself adeptly.

Michael was mesmerised. He'd never seen her masturbate before, let alone witness any woman rise to orgasm at the hands of their own skilful touch.

He could feel his own arousal. Now, so intense, it started to near burn through his clothes. He felt like he was there for ages, but really maybe fifteen seconds.

'May I join you?' he said softly.

Megan screamed at the shock of someone appearing, breaking the spell she was in. Her hands are quickly removed, and her legs snapped shut. 'Oh My God,' escaped her as Michael entered the room fully.

'Can I join in or is this a solo event?' he asks again softly.

'You scared me, my heart is racing, but yes please.'

He quickly removed his clothes and stepped up onto the end of the bed, crawling on all fours until he was kneeling between her legs. He let his hands glide up over her calves and thighs softy. Relaxed by his touch, it took only a second to recover herself back into the lustful fantasy.

She pulled him onto her. It was deep, hard and fast. While it was Michael thrusting into her, Greg had been the one who penetrated her completely and she could nearly see him as her story came to the orgasmic climax.

Laying back on the bed side by side, they were silent for some moments, both of their chests heaving to regain their breath.

'Megan, that was such a surprise. Don't get me wrong, it was amazing.'

Her cheeks, still bursting with pleasure, hid the blush of the guilt beneath. Her mind jumped into a fast sprint.

'I feel a bit embarrassed; I didn't think you'd be home for a long while.'

Michael's face flushed a little. He now realised she must do this often. He'd never really thought about her pleasuring herself before. He hadn't expected that this was what she would say. He flashed back to those weeks ago, when she'd surprised him between the sheets. This was a step back to the daring, sexy Megan he knew when they first dated.

'No, it's okay. Don't be embarrassed. I loved it, I also do it when I'm home alone during the day.'

As he turned and cradled her in his arms he whispered, 'I love you, Megan.'

From the moment he started blinking in the morning the recollection of last night rippled warmly through him, like waking to the delightful realisation that it wasn't a workday.

He looked across at Megan, still curled up soundly next to him in their bed. He chided himself for his ignorance and suspicions. *Of course, a sexy woman like Megan masturbates. Why didn't you ever think about it? I'm being ridiculous. There's no way she's having an affair. Last night was amazing, a plus for our marriage.*

He rolled over toward her, sliding his arm beneath her pillow to cradle her gently. Something cold touched his arm. He felt around and pulled it out. Her phone. It had been next to her on the bed, obviously lost in the folds of their fervent lovemaking. He smiled again as he reached over her to place it on her bedside table. *She'd have been in a frenzy if she couldn't find it.* As Megan stirred, she turned and looked up at him perched over her body.

'Good morning.'

'Good morning, my little surprise package.'

Megan's eyes widened as a cheeky little smile spread sheepishly across her face.

'By the way, I found your phone too. It was buried beneath your pillow.'

'Oh, thanks.' *God, I hope he didn't look at it?*

'Megan, tell me, did the phone have anything to do with you pleasuring yourself last night?'

She coughed back the panic rising in her throat. 'No. Why ask that?'

His voice lowered. 'I just wondered if you liked looking at sexy sites or something?' he asked gently before volunteering; 'That would be quite okay too, you know.'

Her relief sparked her to reply. 'Maybe we could watch some together tonight?' She started to run her hand down his body. Only their bodies spoke for the next hour.

Chapter 18

$\mathcal{K}$ara listened intently as Greg told her all about the random call from Megan. 'I had said that she'd try to contact you some day, but, Wow! That was much more than I expected she would do.'

'Yes, she was quite a surprise really. I could sense straight away she'd wanted to reconnect with me, but I didn't think for a minute she would respond the way she did about you, or what we enjoy.'

'Yes, I knew she'd want you, but I'm rather impressed at how she reacted to you telling her about me, and that we play with others, though.'

'I actually think she really got excited about the idea of the three of us.'

'We may have found a new and different friend and future playmate here?' giggled Kara.

'You could be right. I'm sure she hung up so fast because she was about to come from hearing about you and me touching her.'

'That's a good sign,' Kara said with a cheeky grin. 'I bet you'll hear from her again soon, you know! Hey, do you really think she hung up because she was coming?'

'Yes, she did. I think she didn't really want me to know she was touching herself.'

'Or someone interrupted her?'

'You think? Nah, I'm not sure she's had phone sex before. Besides, she said she was on her own when I asked.'

'Maybe. But if it was me, and you'd got me that steamed, I don't think I could stop!' Kara laughed.

'But you need to remember that you are now, these days, an insatiable unique horny cat, Kara!'

'That is so true! I'm so liberated, that I'm now technically horny and homeless, thanks to you.'

'Yes, you are! I'm sorry, tell me how everything went with your house?'

Thoughts about Megan slipped from the room as the two of them discussed Kara's deal with the house, the buyers, settlement and Greg's upcoming Film Festival plans. Greg's delicious pasta eventually hit the plates on the balcony. Accompanied by Kara's bottle of Paulet's Polish Hill River Shiraz, their late dinner serenaded the two of them into a memorable night of celebration, filled with laughter and lovemaking.

Spooned in Greg's bed, just as they each drifted off, with the full contrasting colours of their day still clinging to keep them awake, Kara remembered.

'Greg?'

'Yeah?' He replied dreamily.

'Remind me to tell you about the messages.'

'Okay… what messages?'

'With all of today's news, I forgot to tell you about the couple who replied to our message. It can wait.'

'Sure… sounds good,' he murmured, his words barely audible, as they both slipped into a blissful sleep, one that only sex can provide.

It had been out of the blue that Kara found another couple had messaged her in response to one of their original ads, posted over a year ago.

This was a quite different message. A couple, both married, who were 'Friends with Benefits' who admitted to meeting secretly each week or so, were looking to add further spice and heat to their liaisons.

Kara had replied, and a number of messages were exchanged. They'd checked out as being quite genuine, so Kara said she would arrange a possible time with Greg. There were long breaks between messages, so Kara had all but forgotten about them. While on her way to Clare to sort her house deal, her phone had signalled a message from this couple via the swing site.

At breakfast, Greg reminded Kara.

'Did you say something about a message you wanted to tell me?'

'Ooh, yes. I got a reply from that couple who messaged us ages ago. They now want to meet us for lunch and maybe play next week. They're Friends with Benefits. Both are still married to others, but it seems like they enjoy each other regularly.'

'Do they seem genuine?'

'Yes, seems like the real deal. I've only had contact with him though. I get the impression they haven't played with others much before.'

'We can at least meet for lunch and see how it goes.'

They both smiled. Inside and out. It was always exciting when they had the possibility of a bit of naughty play again.

Kara sent the messages to meet the couple who identified themselves as Rick and Sally. Everyone was all still keen and the catch up was organised for the following Friday at 1.00 pm. They arranged to meet at a restaurant in a hotel with accommodation in North Adelaide.

Greg and Kara had coordinated their plans for work that morning to keep the afternoon free. Wisely, Greg suggested the two of them meet at a café nearby in the hour before, to catch up quickly ahead and make sure they arrived together, to meet their prospective playmates.

Greg was already seated at a window table when Kara arrived. 'I've ordered a cheese platter and a beer for us both, just in case we decide not to stay for lunch.'

'Planning ahead as always, Mr Sheppard?! I love it. Still feeling excited? It feels like ages since we've enjoyed a bit of naughty with others!'

'That's for sure. Lots has happened since Queensland. I can't wait.'

Both enjoying the cold beer, and their constant chat about possible fun to come, filled the hour. She checked her phone for the time. 'Shit, we don't want to be late, we'd better go.'

Slightly nervous as they really didn't know much about this couple, Greg and Kara entered the door of the dimly lit hotel, compared to the blistering sun outside. Greg held Kara's hand to guide her, as they both took a moment for their eyes to adjust and focus and walked toward the lounge bar area, both looking around, checking every patron in the bar and dining area. They kept glancing at each other, their hands now gripped firmly, holding the only sign of tension with the anticipation and some trepidation, while trying to find a couple they don't even know. They had only a somewhat loose description from their messages. The guy was a bit older than Greg and Kara, describing himself as a medium build with greying hair and she with long blonde hair, quite tall, attractive and a Scandinavian look about her.

Greg and Kara couldn't see them immediately, so decided to order a drink, take a seat in a booth and just wait until they were found.

'Well they did see pics of us,' Kara said, 'so surely they will recognise us.'

After only their first sip of wine, they notice a couple, hand in hand, walking directly toward them, clearly fitting the description.

As they approach, the guy inquired softly, 'Kara? Greg?'

Both nodding and with a grin, Greg immediately stood to shake hands with Rick and kissed Sally on the cheek. Kara slid across the seat of the booth and also stood and kissed them both offering a simple, 'Hi.'

'Hello, nice to meet you both,' Greg said as he motioned them towards a different booth table setting along the rear wall of the dining room. 'I reserved us a table. It should be a bit quieter.'

After a few telling shy looks, nods and giggles, they got seated and ordered drinks. Rick was quick to share. 'This is our first time. We haven't been together that long really, but we've advanced so quickly sexually and are keen and excited to look at some same room sex, as I explained in my messages. We both agree it would be a turn on having a couple watching us and us them.'

'We are fairly new to this as well and the same, it's quite a turn on,' offered Greg in reply, throwing Kara a little smile.

Rick leant forward and in a more hushed tone said, 'I have a room upstairs, when, or should I say, *if* we feel ready.'

'Great,' says Greg. He noticed both Sally and Kara were nodding approvingly.

Intimately seated close to each other in the rounded booth, with the two women in the middle. Kara kept one hand resting on Greg's thigh as he did likewise on her, as they all chatted freely. Sharing about what each might enjoy about swinging and same room; all of them were getting aroused. It hit a whole next level, after both women each confessed to having been so excited by the thought of meeting, that they'd decided on their own, to come to lunch without wearing any knickers beneath their dresses. This was the final icebreaker, and everyone laughed.

They all enjoyed a light meal and as Sally drained her second glass of wine, she then dared to admit to them all about what she had fantasied about, ever since Rick had told her about this meeting he'd planned.

'I've actually kept thinking about the idea of, well maybe, having both of you guys watching me and Kara enjoying each other, without either of you guys being able to touch us until we have fully satisfied each other.' She continued, 'I'd imagined we are sitting in the middle of the bed facing each other, our legs wrapped gently around each other. We kiss deeply, our hands moving over every inch of our bodies, caressing each other's breasts, pinching each other's nipples and letting our lips and tongues journey across all of our soft flesh.' Looking at Rick first and then at Greg, she whispered, 'now… I want you to watch us each taking turns to kiss and taste our pussies and see us each with vibrating dildos penetrating each other. You guys are sitting on either side of the bed, hard and stroking yourselves.'

Kara and Greg listened attentively, quite surprised at such a disclosure, but completely enjoying hearing Sally sharing her fantasy so openly. It was refreshingly, enthralling and arousing.

Rick, however, tried to hide his surprise at what Sally revealed in all its explicit detail. Greg could sense instantly that this was not quite what he had planned. Rick finally spoke, 'Let's maybe just try the same room and see how it goes, shall we?' It was clear that he was feeling he'd lost control of where this hook up was heading.

The next moment, Kara felt Sally's hand touch her thigh and slowly work her way to touch her now moist pussy. Greg felt Kara gently inch herself closer toward Sally. He suspected instantly that the two ladies had connected somehow. He threw a little glance Kara's way and smiled.

Kara responded by opening her legs a little wider, inviting Sally's touch. Kara's hand, near instinctively, explored Sally's thighs and worked to allow her fingers to feel her warm and moist vagina. Both women were now well on their way to wanting much more than a 'same room' couple experience. It wasn't long before both the men realised what was going on, and they smiled at each other. Greg noted Rick's grin, but also sensed his growing apprehension.

Greg felt Kara's hand rubbing his thigh, now sliding deeper into his crotch and her grip getting firmer. He knew she was getting really turned on. He felt her hand, now gripping his cock firmly through his shorts.

He assumed Sally was doing the same to Rick.

Kara whispered in Greg's ear, 'Glance down. Feel this.' He reached down under the hidden safety of the tablecloth and felt Sally's finger rubbing Kara's now firm clit.

Kara muttered in his ear again, this time near breathless. 'I just want your fingers to enjoy this too.'

Kara rubbed him harder now. She was gripping him, as much to hold onto a shred of her own composure… *I can't cum here, not at the table,* she thought. Barely able to contain a whispered tone, she near gasped, 'Greg, for God's sake… get us all upstairs to a room now, PLEASE.'

Greg smiled. He too needed to regain some physical composure before leaving the booth. 'Hey Rick, did you want to grab another bottle of wine, and then let's take it to the room—I think we need to let our ladies relax and get more acquainted, don't you?'

Rick nodded, stood and headed to the bar. They waited for him to return. By this time, the women had stopped exploring, knowing it would only be a short wait until more.

Greg signalled for Sally and Kara to slide out of the booth, before standing and leading them to the elevator. It started as a quiet trip to the fifth floor, but breaking the silence Sally again suddenly exclaimed, 'I hope you both like my breasts, I've just had some work done on them.'

'Really? They look great but was it painful?' asked Kara.

'No, not really. I'm loving my new look and Rick does too,' she said with a grin. There were smiles all round.

As they entered the generous suite, complete with two queen-sized beds, Kara and Greg could sense Rick's discomfort rise, and Sally's fever dim a little, now facing the uncertainty of what might happen in this moment. Greg excused himself for a minute to go to the bathroom, so Kara knew she had to take the lead.

Kara quickly dived into her handbag, pulling out her little portable speaker.

'I think we need some music.' She quickly paired it to a playlist from her phone. 'Hey Rick, would you mind pouring us some drinks?'

Before they could speak, she removed all of her clothes. Once completely naked, she moved to stand close up in front of Sally.

'Your turn, I'd love to see your new tits, Sally. I'm sure Rick, you'd like to help her? Besides, Greg and I would love to watch too.'

With that, Sally and Rick looked at each other and smiled. Kara could sense the horny lust re-emerge to fill the room. Rick quickly shed his shirt, pants and jocks moving over to sit behind Sally who was now kneeling in the middle of the bed, having already kicked off her shoes.

By the time Greg emerged from the bathroom, he found Kara naked, kneeling on the bed, with Rick starting to undress Sally. 'Wow!' was all he could say.

'Hurry up, you. You're missing all the fun!' laughed Kara as she beckoned for Greg to join her on the bed.

It took Greg no time to discard his clothes and start kissing and rolling his hands over Kara's body from behind her, watching as a now naked Sally kneeling on all fours, was being entered by Rick from behind and Kara's hands were starting to roam over Sally's shoulders and neck and then down toward her breasts.

'May I touch them?' Kara asked. Sally nodded with a smile.

As Kara's hands started to cup Sally's breasts in each of her hands, Sally edged forward closer toward Kara kneeling up in front of her. With Rick still pounding her from behind, Sally allowed her cheek to graze up and down the side of Kara's face and in seconds the two women were kissing deeply.

Both men stopped, nearly at the same time, held poised to watch as the two women got lost in exploring each other by hand and by mouth.

'I've never done this before, it's so wonderful,' was all Sally could say, in moments caught between rolling her tongue deep inside Kara's mouth.

After some time of enjoying tasting each other, Kara again sensed Rick's restlessness, signalling he wanted Sally again—badly.

Kara murmured, 'You are delicious, but let's let our men have a taste, shall we?' as she turned to face Greg who was now lying on his back on the bed next to them, stroking himself as he watched and enjoyed the women explore each other.

'Having fun?' he whispered with a grin as Kara climbed onto him.

Kara smiled and leant forward and whispered, 'Yes, I am, but I think he's struggling a bit, let's just watch them and let them see what we can do...'

Greg whispered back, 'Yes, I noticed. Come on sexy, let's just enjoy ourselves...'

Kara sat astride Greg, grinding into him, and both relished the sensation of being fucked while watching the other couple enjoy themselves on the bed only a metre away...

Greg whispered to Kara, 'Shall we invite them to join us on our bed?'

'Ooh yes.'

'Would you two like to join us over here?' he called out.

'We'd love to,' responded Sally, who pulled Rick by the hand over to lie close up next to Greg and Kara. Rick climbed on top of Sally and they resumed fucking hard. It didn't take long before Sally's hand reached out to feel Greg.

He responded by reaching out to let his fingers trail down along the side of her body.

Out of nowhere, Sally called out, with Rick still pumping hard inside her... 'Kara, I've always had this fantasy to be taken by two men at once... Would you mind if I could try this now with your man?' Kara shot a look at Greg.

He mouthed: 'Okay, if you're okay?'

Kara replied to Sally, 'Sure, but please be careful with him!'

In a flash, Sally had manoeuvred from Rick and was clambering to get onto Greg's body.

Kara led Rick to stand behind his lady, motioning him to enter her, as Sally mounted Greg who was lying on his back. Kara stroked Rick's back softly as he let his cock rim Sally's hole and motioned to slide gently inside her.

Noticing him withdraw as Sally is riding Greg feverously, Kara sensed Rick was letting jealously creep in.

Standing beside him, she whispered, 'It's okay, this is only sex. Don't overthink this. I know it might feel weird, but this is just fun and Sally is just exploring. Nothing more. Enjoy her fantasy.'

He nodded and turned back to Sally, caressing her body with his hands, and moved to re-enter her from behind.

Kara moved to sit on the bed, just above Greg's head, with Sally on top of him, Rick behind her, and she just watched, enjoying her first sight of a double penetration scene.

However, it wasn't long before Kara could see Sally lose herself in Greg's penetrating force.

Suddenly, Rick exited to the bathroom. He'd obviously caught how she slipped away from him, too. When he returned, he walked with a near defiant stride straight up behind Kara, and started kissing her neck. He signalled her to lie on the bed right next to Greg and Sally, who were still grinding away. Rick lay on top of her and entered her slowly.

Kara accepted him, but with the first touch of her hands around his body, she could feel both his aged flesh and his insecurity. The tone, vibrancy and genuine passion had long left this man and Kara could not only sense, but feel that clearly, he was only here to play at Sally's pleasure. He didn't look or really respond to Kara at all, his eyes all the time fixed on Sally and Greg.

Kara waited until Sally had fully enjoyed Greg and her shuddering climax, before whispering to Rick, 'I think she wants you back…' He quickly pulled away from Kara and moved to lead Sally away to the other bed.

Rick quickly started fucking Sally hard—this time anally, with clearly a desire to pleasure her with all his might, as if competing with Greg. All the while, Sally kept calling out about how much she loved it all.

Greg and Kara knew they had entertained this couple enough, and it was now time to just enjoy each other. Greg held Kara's arms firmly above her head, kneeling close in between her legs which she wrapped around him, high, nearly above his chest. Biting hard on her neck as she loved, he thundered inside her, each thrust more powerful than the last. He had held his raging desire to cum until now. Kara's body quivered and near convulsed, as if every muscle and nerve was being penetrated, the illicit delight of being restrained by his powerful hands, while he thrusted deep inside her.

Their orgasms were resounding. They laid back, watching Rick and Sally, who were still at it.

After laying there for some time, Greg and Kara nodded to each other. They quietly slipped off the bed. It wasn't until they were both fully dressed, and Kara moved to grab her speaker before Rick noticed them. 'Oh, you're not leaving, are you? Have you had enough?'

'Yes, I think we'll leave you to it. Thanks for a great time,' Greg said.

'Yes, thanks so much,' Kara said as she grasped Greg's hand and they walked out the door, leaving the sounds of the others still pounding flesh behind them.

Greg and Kara were both quiet, standing hand in hand in the lift, until it started its descent to the ground floor. As if cued, they both started. The exclamations were nearly in unison.

'That was not what he expected, I'm sure. She was a dynamo!' Greg said as Kara blurted, 'He wasn't ready for any of that at all. She wanted everything and anyone, I think.'

They suspended any further comments as the lift opened and they crossed the reception area out to the carpark.

As they approached his car, Greg turned to Kara. 'Shall we order in some food tonight?'

'Great idea. All the more time to talk about this afternoon! But my shout for dinner, okay?'

'Deal.'

Kara scrolled through her Uber eats app and ordered some salt and pepper squid, Mongolian beef and some fried rice from a little restaurant not far from Greg's. 'It should arrive in about forty minutes.'

'Perfect.'

Just as they arrived at the apartment, Greg's phone pinged with a message.

'Not a number I know. It's work, I bet. It can wait. Our food will be here soon.'

They opted for a lounge room easy meal and chatted throughout with little recounts of their afternoon.

'Did you see how jealous he was getting?'

'I know. For a first timer, she surprised me. You know when she first climbed on top of me, she whispered, "You're so sexy."' Greg tried to copy her sexy Scandinavian accent.

'Really? But that doesn't surprise me actually. You look and feel amazing and such a contrast to him. She was bursting to get hold of you.'

Greg grinned. 'She wasn't afraid to play with you either!'

'I know. Quite amazing—I think she was ready to try it all. I've got a feeling she will have more new friends soon and leave Rick in her wake!'

'I think you're right there. He was clearly punching above his weight.'

Greg's phone pinged again. It was the same number. He looked at the time. It was nearly 9.00 p.m.

'Seriously? Who on earth is calling me now?' he lamented.

Chapter 19

'Someone must want you, Greg. It might be important.' Kara said.

'Fuck! It's Friday night. If they do, it had better be good or really urgent!' he said, swiping the phone firmly.

'Hello, Greg Sheppard,' he said briskly.

'It's Megan here. Sorry, if I've called at an inconvenient time.'

'Megan? Umm, hello. Sorry, I didn't recognise your number.'

Greg looked at Kara, his eyes wide at first, that fell into a frown that was a cocktail of mild exasperation, surprise, and curiosity. Clearly, he hadn't expected this call at all. Kara's look was inquisitive for a second until she heard the name.

Then she just grinned and nodded. She mouthed 'go ahead.' As she stood to clear their plates to the kitchen, she tapped him on the shoulder as she whispered. 'I told you she'd want more!'

Greg gave Kara a wink and focused back on the call.

'Yes, err, I have interrupted you. I should go. Sorry again.'

'It's okay. Kara and I have just finished dinner. Is everything alright?'

'Yes, I'm fine. I really didn't even consider the time. I just thought of you and decided to call, to, well, ask you something.'

'That's nice. You're forgiven.'

'Thank you.'

There was a long pause before Greg asked. 'Megan, what did you want to ask me?'

'Well, you mentioned we could catch up one day and I should meet Kara, and was trying to work how that might happen?'

'Yes, sure. It would be nice for us to meet for a drink, coffee or a meal sometime? Where do you live?'

'I would love to, but I live in Adelaide,' Megan softly replied.

'You have to be kidding… we live in Adelaide as well, North Adelaide. Would you like to meet somewhere for lunch?'

'Here in Adelaide? Really? So, you don't live in Sydney?' Megan sounded puzzled.

'Sydney? Oh, I see. No, when we met, I was in Sydney for a couple of days for business.'

'I hadn't realised that. That makes it a lot easier, but I'm not that familiar with that side of town. Could we maybe just catch up, at your place?'

'Sure,' he replied slightly taken aback by her sudden request to meet at his place over a restaurant or café, after only having really met fleetingly and spoken on the phone once. 'When suits you, Megan?'

'I am free tomorrow, if that works for you?'

'Tomorrow? Saturday. Hold on a minute and I'll see what Kara has on tomorrow.'

Greg put the phone on hold and went into the kitchen. 'Kara, Megan wants to come and have lunch with us. Here, tomorrow! Are you free for lunch?'

Kara pondered for a moment. 'That should be alright. I've got a late hair appointment—but I'd be home around 1.30 p.m. You could invite her over and start without me. Lunch or whatever!' she said cheekily.

'You really are a naughty woman, Kara,' Greg replied as he headed back to pick up his phone.

'You there, Megan?'

'Yes, I'm here.'

'Kara has an appointment, but will be here by early afternoon, around 1.30 p.m. Would that work for you?'

Megan stopped and thought for a moment. *Michael is working around the house in the morning, but will go straight to watch Matt's game at 12.30 p.m. They'll be home by 4.00 p.m. As long as I'm home before them.*

'Is it alright if I come a bit earlier? I have somewhere to be by 3.30 p.m.,' she said.

'Sure, that's fine,' He signalled Kara to come closer, so she could hear his reply. 'Perhaps you could get here about 12.45? We can start with a drink and maybe lunch and Kara can join us as soon as she can?'

He looked up at Kara, mouthing 'Is this okay?'

She nodded and mouthed back, 'Of course.'

It was then that Megan's true admission burst forth. Kara heard it too.

'I don't really need food. I just want to meet you in person again. I want us to do what you told me in that story too, umm… with Kara,' her words cut across his.

'I'm sure Kara and I will really enjoy that too, Megan. So alright, I'll see you around 12.45. tomorrow then. I will organise some lunch and wine. I'll text you my address. Please call me if you can't find the place.'

'Thank you. I really can't wait. Until tomorrow. Goodbye.'

'Look forward to it Megan, bye.'

'*Wow!*' The exclamation burst forth from both of them as Greg ended the call. Neither Greg nor Kara was surprised at her request to meet, however this expression of wanting to explore a threesome was unexpected. Clearly his phone sex story had sparked something inside her.

'I would have thought she'd be a restaurant girl, before she would want to come and meet us at home, let alone ask to play?' Greg said, his tone conveying a mix of disbelief and delight, rather like finding a forgotten fifty dollar note in a coat pocket.

'She certainly is keen. She sounded near desperate to meet tomorrow. I wonder why?'

'Who knows? She sounds pretty eager though.'

Kara paused and pondered for a second or two. 'She's probably excited. I can't judge! Remember, I jumped on a plane and flew across the country to see you the next day, rather than wait?' She laughed, and Greg joined her.

'Yes, you did. This is definitely refreshing! Let's just wait and see what happens!'

Kara had risen early to select clothes ready for her visit to a salon, but mindful of the fun she might encounter on her return. She wanted to make an impression on Megan. She'd set the table for their lunch guest, before readying to set off for her hair appointment. Greg emerged from his room and headed to make coffee.

'Would you like a cup before you go?'

'Sure. That would be great.' They both loved starting their days savouring a quality coffee and Greg was the master barista of the two of them, so she delighted in his offer.

'I'll try to get back as soon as I can. This will be fun. Would you like me to organise the food?' she asked Greg.

'No, it's fine. I thought I'd order a couple of dishes from that little noodle bar in Norwood.'

'That's a great idea. Thanks.'

Checking the time, she jumped up off the kitchen stool.

'I'd better get going...' as she headed for the door, she called out, 'Now Greg, don't go having too much fun or use up all those superpowers of yours without me!' Then she stopped. She turned back and walked up to him.

'Hey, seriously, Greg, if you get the sense that she really only wants to enjoy you, send me a message and I'm happy to give you time alone, and I won't come back until you message me.'

'Kara, I appreciate that. But she's asked to play—so shouldn't our swing rule apply here?'

'Yes, but this is a little different this time. You and her met first, when you were both on your own. Perhaps, let's take this one a little carefully, maybe? There's something that feels unusual.'

'You're very thoughtful, Kara. I'm sure it will be fine. I'll see you for lunch and I'm sure we will all have fun.'

'Yes. you are probably right. But just know it's okay. Whatever pans out.'

'Alright. Thank you. Now go, you don't want to be late home!' As he stood in the shower, he thought about what Kara had said.

Jumping back to that first encounter with Megan, he realised that in a couple of hours, he would be readying himself to invite in the lady he tried to make love to, until she became the face of his beloved Tess. He had never forgotten how he became so overcome with grief and had left her bed so abruptly. He had barely seen her as 'Megan' that night.

A flicker of doubt entered his thoughts. *Kara might be right—but not just about her wanting to join us. I've only spoken to Megan over the phone since then. Will the sight of her bring it all back again? This may be a terrible idea.*

After more minutes of the warm water running over him, he settled and resolved not to think too much more about it. Besides, Kara would be here and so much had changed in recent times. He would let the excitement of Megan's enthusiasm to meet them, take hold of his thoughts.

Greg called his favourite noodle bar and ordered a couple of dishes for delivery. At 12.30 p.m., the doorbell rang, and he braced himself slightly for the first sight of Megan. He opened the door. 'Your noodle delivery, sir.' Greg breathed out a sigh, smiled and tipped the delivery lad.

Megan arrived at the address early and parked down the road. She sat in her car watching the delivery man arrive, drop off food and return to hop in his car and leave.

She dropped her head in her hands and said to herself, 'My God! What am I doing?'

But the adrenalin pumping lust inside her far exceeded the guilt or any consideration of consequence, other than the urge and excitement that was building inside her. She got out of the car, locked it and hurried to his door and knocked, before allowing another thought to halt her approach.

Greg opened the door with a big smile and a kiss on the cheek. 'Hello, Megan. Welcome, come on in. Perfect timing, the food just arrived,' he said as he escorted her into the dining room.

'What would you like to drink, soft or hard?'

'I would love a wine, if that's okay? Thanks, Greg.'

'Certainly, red okay?'

'Thank you, that's perfect.'

Seated at the dining table, they picked at the food and talked casually about work, the weather and a few local political issues, both avoiding the elephant in the room.

Greg's phone signalled a message.

'Is that Kara?' asked Megan.

He picked up the phone and looked. 'Yes, it is.' He read her message aloud.

> Hope you and Megan are enjoying lunch. I'll be there in about 30 min. Can't wait to meet her. K x.

Megan smiled as she rolled a section of her long blonde hair between her fingers and looked across the table, but it was obvious to Greg that she hadn't fully relaxed. 'Kara seems like a lovely lady.'

'She is. She's very kind and bright. I'm sure you'll like her, Megan.'

'So, how long have you two known each other?'

'We first met in primary school. We were each other's first kiss. But we lost track for decades, and only found each other a few years ago, but we've been the best of friends ever since.'

'And lovers too.' Then she flushed a little and sat there quietly. She was fascinated, but also now feeling nervous about meeting Kara and what might happen. She also knew she was becoming desperate to touch Greg, and he was right here in front of her.

Greg cleared the leftover food and dishes to the kitchen, returning to stand beside her, still seated at the table. He reached out, taking her by the hand to stand. 'Let's finish our drinks in the lounge, shall we?' He guided her slowly to the sofa where they both sat side by side. Greg looked at her. 'Tell me, what would you really like, Megan?' Megan looked down at her drink and paused to take a sip. She slowly turned to him.

'As I said when we spoke, I do feel like we have unfinished business. I was actually so turned on by your story—I just had to know what that felt like, for real.'

Inwardly Greg sighed. But he had to know a little more—to be sure.

'We do have unfinished business. But are you really sure about this, experiencing a third, Megan? Kara is happy to sit out.' He said, looking directly into her eyes.

'Yes, I think I really do.' Her eyes widened, and she leant forward slightly, her body and lips poised as if on the doorstep, in the last chance moment at the end of a first date.

He looked down for a second and hesitated. Her desire was filling the room.

He reached out, removing the glass from her hand, and set it down gently on the coffee table. He raised one hand to her right cheek with his left, he steered her face to meet his until their lips touched. The small pecks soon built into outrageous passion. It wasn't long before he stood, took her hand and lead her to his bedroom. Starting with their shoes, they removed one piece of each other's clothing, kisses unleashing, and landing everywhere over each of their bodies. Greg gradually laid her on her back, positioning himself on his side facing her. He caressed her body for as far as his hands could reach, watching her quiver as she tingled and relished his touch. His feather like fingers teased the insides of her legs, her stomach, her breast, her neck, her cheeks, and her lips.

Eventually, she murmured, 'My turn,' boldly pushing him onto his back.

Megan moved to position herself on the end of the bed at his feet. She started by kissing his feet, his toes, calves, and all over his thighs. She ran her tongue up the inside of his groin, brushing his inner leg and balls with her tip at the same time. Her cheek brushed his now hard cock as she headed north with her kisses, sucking in his flesh, until she reached his wanting lips. After holding in a deep passionate kiss for a minute, she made her way down his chest and teased his balls with her tongue again, before running the tip up and down his throbbing shaft. She tantalised him for minutes before taking him in her mouth and began sucking him with no mercy. His moans were proof of his escalating pleasure. Bringing him to a precipice, he responded, before he could take no more, swiftly lifting her to lay her on her back. He had to take her now.

Megan's legs fell apart as he positioned himself between them. Without delay or effort, he put himself inside her, between her soaked lips, signalling his presence with hard, deep thrusts. It only seemed like seconds before she succumbed to the thick strength of him, from her vulva to her cervix, filling her completely, each press seemingly begging her inch by inch to come. Her ecstatic cry near screamed its way to the front door.

Kara heard the sound the instant she unlocked the door and stepped inside. She recognised it instantly. Greg hadn't messaged to signal she wasn't going to be welcomed, but she entered quietly and cautiously, nonetheless.

She rested her keys and bag down gently and slipped off her shoes. Dressing down to only her underwear in the hallway, she tiptoed to Greg's bedroom door. She looked to the bed. Greg and Megan lay naked on the bed. Greg's back was facing her, his hands gently stroking Megan to settle her from her explosive orgasm, the sound of which had greeted her at the door.

Greg caught the scent of Kara's perfume, and turned to look at her, his smile secretly welcoming, as he gave her a beckoning nod. Kara reached to unclip her bra, slipping it over her arms and let it drop to the floor. She slid down her knickers, stepped out of them, leaving them similarly abandoned in the doorway.

Kara moved forward and slid onto the bed, ever so quietly to lie alongside Greg. She let her hands run across his back. She could see the hairs on his back electrify, as he reached behind to touch her. It was the welcome, and the signal, that the time was right. Greg edged over a little closer to Megan, giving Kara a bit more room. He leant over her and kissed her.

Kara rolled to her back to prop on the pillows, with only Greg between her and where Megan's head was resting. Kara kept her left hand rested to keep squeezing gently on his butt cheek. With the fingers of her other hand, she rubbed her own labia, slowly and rhythmically. Round and round, up and down, every circle grazing her clit, the moisture increasing each time her fingers passed across her pussy lips.

Megan was still settling from her heaving breaths after her vibrant orgasm, while her mouth clambered for his lips, and more of his body. Greg kept the flow of his gliding finger strokes over Megan's body, while feeling the warmth of Kara's flesh pressing against the length of his body from behind. After a few minutes, Greg rolled himself on top of Megan's body, and reached out to find Kara's free left hand. His fingers wrapped between hers to squeeze them tight, before sliding himself down Megan's body until his head rested between her legs.

As his mouth found her mound, he resumed his kisses, each edging closer to her swollen pussy that was still humming for more. His tongue flicked as Megan now became fully conscious of the heated presence of Kara's body by her side. While momentarily startled, and a little afraid, as she hadn't heard or sensed Kara's arrival nor ever experienced a woman masturbating next to her, Megan was revelling in suspense. Being licked deliciously by a man, while simultaneously feeling a woman's rising pleasure beside her, was like a forbidden treasure. She exhaled the apprehension before then breathing it in afresh.

Kara was rubbing herself faster and faster, building on the intensity of their awareness of her being right there with them. She could feel their mounting pleasure and her own. Instinctively, she reached out to grip some flesh as she started to climax. She found Megan's hand to grip it tightly as she moaned. She could no longer stay quiet.

Megan was electrified. Caught in the moment and her gasps, she responded to Kara's outstretched grasp. She felt and gripped Kara's breast. The sensation of Kara's soft flesh and the vibrant shudder of her body that filled her hand, while listening to her orgasmic groan caught Megan's body, making her rise harder against Greg as he now pushed two fingers deep inside her. Every part of her was rising. Her hips lifted, she wanted more of Greg's touch as deep as he could; she didn't care if he broke her. She was lost in the feel of the flesh of a woman's breast in her hand, with him working her to a frenzy at the same time. Megan had not felt the overwhelming rush of desire like this before. The cry that she released as she came was loud and long. Megan near collapsed back into the folds of the quilt beneath her.

Both Greg and Kara stopped for a second. They looked at each other, paused and smiled. Both knowing that Megan had felt it. That euphoric moment where the body succumbed to pleasure that had crashed through the stifling taboo. She had allowed herself to feel and completely enjoy two bodies, regardless of their gender—just how they felt. It was just a taste, but it was enough. Megan had enjoyed both of them.

Greg moved up over Megan's body and kissed her on the cheek softly before whispering in her ear. 'Watch us,' as he slid gently off Megan's body, moving slowly toward Kara.

Megan slipped out of the bed and headed as if toward the door. Greg watched, checking to make sure she did not just walk out. He sensed her hesitation, knowing they couldn't let her leave in this moment, especially if he'd made her feel uncomfortable without talking through it.

To Greg's surprise, Megan suddenly turned, walked around to the other side of the bed away from him and crawled across to lay next to Kara. As one hand brushed over Kara's hair and down the side of her cheek, she leant forward, kissing Kara deeply. Kara responded, matching the delicacy and pressure of her tongue and lips exploring her. To Megan, it was like having dared to flavour the petals of a soft pink rose, finding the bouquet through a sensuous touch of lips. It was a more arousing fragrance than the intake of any scent she had ever smelt.

Greg watched, mesmerised by their intense, yet sensitive passion. He was still hard, now barely able to hold back from wanting to explode at the sight of them locked together so intimately. Between kisses, he caught Kara's eye. She smiled and motioned Megan to lie on her back. She trailed her own kisses and hands down Megan's body, over her stomach and breasts. She knew what Greg wanted and needed to do and what Megan had really wanted since Sydney.

She pulled Greg closer and whispered, 'Take her, just give me your hand.' As he moved quickly to mount Megan, he also slipped his fingers between the moist lips of Kara's vagina. He pounded into Megan, near galloping, like a racehorse to the finish line. He could feel her orgasm build, as was Kara's in response to his touch, his fingers pushing inside her at the same time. The sensation and sounds from the two of them was nearly too much. He couldn't hold back any longer, ejaculating at full force into Megan. He slowed his thrusts as he felt the last drop of his cum transfer to Megan's body. His fingers remained deep inside Kara, whose muscles were still pulsing and thumping against them. She too had climaxed at the feel of his touch, and the sight of him and Megan fucking so hard alongside her.

They all lay there spent before Greg realised, he was probably squashing poor Megan, but also being so aware of both women's despair at withdrawal. He waited, poised in them both, waiting to ease out of Megan and fingers gently from Kara, after each of their pulsing bodies subsided.

Greg laid back on the bed between the two of them. No words were spoken. There was no need. The shared caresses across the three of them were soft, but still heated. So, it took no time before all found themselves back into exploring and pleasuring each of their bodies yet again. Greg found himself so aroused for the second time as a result of two women's escalating passion, and response to his, and each other's touch, that he found himself once again, releasing his seed deep, again. This time Kara felt his full power, as he shuddered hot bursts of cum inside her throbbing vagina.

After such heated lovemaking, they all near collapsed, laying still side by side, panting heavily. This lunch was much more than any of them had expected.

Megan just lay there in the middle of the bed on her back, panting. She did not want to move, fearing it might break the euphoric and near magical satisfaction that surrounded her.

Kara leant over and kissed her softly on the cheek. 'Well, that was amazing. Thank you, Megan, I'm so pleased to meet you.' They all laughed. This was the first time the two women had actually spoken.

She smiled. 'Thank you, it has certainly been my pleasure, Kara.'

She leant over and kissed Greg deeply and passionately. 'I am definitely so pleased I let you sit at my table in Sydney!'

'I think we might need a drink,' Greg said as he climbed out of bed and pulled on his jocks.

Megan glanced at the clock on the bedside table... 'God! I'd love to, but I'd better get going,' she said suddenly, and she jumped off the bed and looked for her clothes.

'Work? on a Saturday? That's tough,' asked Greg inquiringly.

'Oh... um... yes. There is always somewhere else I need to be,' she replied, not wanting to reveal that the afternoon had slipped away, and she was close to the time when she would be missed at home.

Five minutes later, after a hurried goodbye, Megan left Greg and Kara's apartment, darting glances up and down the street as she headed to her car. She quickly started the engine and moved off. But once around the corner, she turned into a side street and parked.

She needed to just stop and breathe. Her emotions had been nothing less than turbulent for the whole day. As if she had been skydiving for the first time. She had jolted between initial determination and fear as she prepared herself, swallowing the reticence that rose as she headed to the plane in anticipation, again feeling the excitement and adrenalin building. Finally, she took that one step and just allowed herself to indulge the bold release and discovery of sheer joy as she floated under the canopy of both Kara and Greg's vibrant touch. She had leapt—and loved it.

Now back in her car, she experienced the thud, landing at ground level as she faced the reality of returning home. But it was an overwhelming sadness, more than guilt that really struck her. This didn't feel like home anymore. It was just where she resided.

After about ten minutes, she regained her composure, started the car, accepting that her passion and happiness now lived beyond where she was driving to. She knew her newfound desires could not be satisfied without more of what she had today.

Kara and Greg could not believe it. It had been two hours of quite incredible sex, with someone who had never met Kara and had not ever dared attempt a threesome before. Megan had leapt into their bed and their lives in such contrast to what they'd expected. Kara had privately been convinced that Megan would only really entertain Greg, so also was very surprised at how she has responded so warmly and willingly to her as well.

Yet there was still something unusual and a little perplexing about the afternoon. There was an air of desperate intensity in her that contrasted with the calm professional Megan whom Greg had described when he first met her in Sydney. He'd even commented that he hadn't expected she would so boldly express her desires and so readily explore the two of them physically and as passionately.

Kara had also noticed the subtle change and near panic when she realised the time, before hurriedly exiting.

Stop overthinking everything, like you do, woman. Nonetheless, something about Megan left her wondering.

Chapter 20

Megan had arrived home barely in time. There was no time to shower without it being questioned, so she changed her clothes quickly, and started busying herself around the house, before Michael and Matt walked in the door.

Damn, I must have a shower soon, the smell of sex is all over me. Find your normal. Keep it inside. Pull yourself together, she kept repeating to herself.

'Did you win?' she called out, in her usual mum 'I'm trying to be interested' tone.

'Yeah, we did.' Matt was booming with pride. 'Killed them. 5 to 1—I'm starving mum, what have you got to eat?'

'There's some snacks in the pantry. But take it easy—I'm making pizzas tonight.'

'Great. Alright mum.'

Michael walked into the kitchen and kissed Megan on the cheek. 'Hey there. Have you had a good day?' Before she could answer, he gave Megan a blow-by-blow description of the game as she started preparing dinner. 'He played really well today; you should've seen his goal. Brilliant, right from the corner…'

'Like to pour us a wine?' asked Megan, hoping this would suspend the commentary.

'Sorry, yes, of course.'

'So, what did you get up to today?' Michael's question was innocent, but Megan nearly choked on it.

'Not that much. I did a bit of work and cleaning up and I caught up with some friends for lunch.'

'Did you catch up with Janet and Mel?'

'Amanda and Gail, actually.'

'Amanda? Do I know her? asked Michael.

'No. She's someone new I met through work. I met her and Gail, whose one of her friends.'

'Did you have a nice time?'

'Yes, it was surprisingly most enjoyable.'

'That's great. Do you want a hand with the pizzas?'

'I'd love you to grate the Mozzarella. Then everything will be just about done for later. You could grab the pastry from the fridge. I might go have a shower and get changed, if that's alright?'

'Sure. Great idea. I think both of the kids are heading out tonight after dinner, so we have the place to ourselves,' he said with a little wink.

Megan turned as the flush filled her face. *Oh God! He's thinking a date night. It's alright. Just stay cool, but I've really got to wash the scent of Greg and Kara from me.*

Standing in the shower, she calmed and relaxed, the soothing hot water and her hands washing all over her body, allowed her indulgent reflections of four other hands caressing her, the power of Greg's body taking her, and the sensation of kissing another woman's lips, to also flow.

Everything about the day had been heightened with colours that burst through her every nerve. In contrast, coming home was predictably grey, dull and drab. Now, even Michael's suggestive inference to the opportunity to spend a night alone together, paled like a faint shadow, to that of the excitement and rush of orgasmic pleasure, after having spent the afternoon with Greg and Kara.

Only weeks ago, if Michael had initiated anything, I would have been excited. What on earth are you doing? She thought, as she dried herself and pulled on her jeans and T-shirt. After she carefully anointed her body with perfume, lotion and makeup to add the final touches to her camouflage of her day, she let out a sigh. *Ok, go enjoy pizza night woman.*

Michael had enjoyed the best Saturday in ages. He'd held a light-hearted mood all day. Cooking breakfast with all the family was a favourite, and he'd found that time allowed him to get the lawns mowed before getting to watch Matt's winning game. After a couple of celebratory beers with his mates at the club, he now had a lovely night still to come. Megan wasn't away for work, so prepping dinner together before sharing an intimate night on their own at home was perfect.

Couldn't be better really, he thought as he slid the cheese rhythmically over the grater.

He enjoyed nights like this. Simple food. Uncomplicated and relaxing. Just him and Megan. He loved having the kids still at home, but it seemed like an eternity between the nights when the kids were both away and he could totally unwind to just fully enjoy being alone with her on a day when she wasn't working either. He ruminated on the possible shared pleasures to come. *Maybe she'll masturbate in front of me again before I take her? Or we both could do it in front of each other?* A shiver of lust shook through his body. It could be a fun night indeed.

Noting the time, Michael grabbed the pizza trays, oiled them lightly and took the dough from the fridge. Covering his hands and the rolling pin with flour, he started kneading, rolling and massaging the rounds for the pizza bases. Matt and Tracey both wanted to eat before they left. He'd finished fitting the bases to the pans and had them in the oven to blind bake for a few minutes, then topped up his wine. He took the bases from the oven to let them cool.

It was then that Megan's phone next to him on the bench started vibrating and buzzed once, signalling a text. He glanced and saw the notification 'message' on the home screen. It showed it was from GS.

It pinged again.

No work for her tonight, I hope, he lamented to himself, as he picked up the phone. The message had appeared as a banner on her home screen.

It was then everything went cold. The chill spread right through every one of his bones in a shudder, rendering him unable to breathe or move. He stared at the screen for what seemed like minutes, but was only a second or two before his heart shattered and his mind hit overdrive, frantically muttering to himself like a mathematician deciphering a code.

She said she had lunch with… Amanda. Yes, Amanda. And a Gail. Gail Who? Is that GS? But why a kiss? Fulfil what? What had she started with this GS? A special lunch? What is she playing at?

He read the message again.

> Dear Megan, just to say it was certainly a special and most enjoyable lunch today. Thank you. So lovely to finally fulfil what we started. Until soon. G x

Strange there was no name—just GS as the sender? GS? Then he remembered. They were the initials of the guy with the business card that she was so keen to find. Michael resisted the near overwhelming urge to hurl the phone straight into the wall. Placing it down carefully, he just glared at it, as if the phone itself was to blame. He stood there with one hand, steadying himself on the bench as he tipped and drained his glass with the other.

The message didn't say it outright, but this was the clincher. Everything else added up.

Her moods—swinging from flirtatious to dim between trips away. Her increased sexual appetite. *God, the phone on the bed when she masturbated that night! The bitch. It was him, I bet.*

He had to get out. He couldn't look at her until he sorted his head. Grabbing his wallet and keys, he paced down to Tracey's door.

He knocked and called out, 'Hey darling, can you please tell mum I've left my wallet at the club. I'm walking back as I've had a couple of wines. Tell her to go ahead with the pizzas without me.'

She called out, 'Okay, fine, Dad.' By the time she appeared at the door, he was heading out the back door.

He had to walk.

Fast and hard.

His stomach, thoughts and emotions, all churning.

She has to be lying to me. How could she do this to me? To us? After everything we've created together. God, what will the kids think? What did I do? What didn't I do? What has he got that I don't? I will kill the bastard! His feelings somersaulted with each street he passed, from competitive anger, to jealously, to self-recrimination and then simply numbness.

Eventually his pace slowed, as did his breathing. Eventually arriving at the club, he simply asked the barman about his wallet that was knowingly already safely tucked in his pocket. He slipped out before anyone he knew stopped him, being in no mood for anyone tonight. He walked to the next hotel and stayed there quietly, seated at a table in the corner of the lounge. After sipping his way through four single malts, he finally decided exactly on what he had to do. *If you don't know what to do, do nothing until you know exactly what to do—then do it right, I will lose any advantage by giving away what I know right now.* He stood and steadied himself for the long walk home.

It wasn't until after 8.30 p.m. that Megan got a bit worried. Michael still wasn't home. She knew it was quite a hike to the club on foot and had scoffed and giggled a little when Tracey told her that he had elected to walk. 'He'd only had one glass of wine, I'm sure. But you know Dad, he wouldn't dream of doing anything improper.'

She consoled any sense of alarm by telling herself he'd probably got caught up with Bill or another of his mates, and he would've called if something was really wrong. Besides, she secretly hoped that date night would somehow be averted. She wanted to savour the feeling of her special afternoon. So, after clearing up the dinner dishes, she headed to bed and was sound asleep by the time he returned home.

Unbeknown to Megan, Michael was similarly relieved that she was not awake.

Michael awoke from a restless sleep with the reality of the whiskey and that message of the night before thumping into his head. He looked over at Megan sleeping next to him.

I have to find out.

He climbed out of bed, pulled on his track gear and headed out for a run. He needed to clear his head. Today he had to stay calm.

Megan rolled over and stretched. Realising Michael was already up, she just lay there and let her thoughts fill with the warm delicious tingle that lingered from her lunch date with Greg and Kara. She still couldn't believe the overwhelming heat and passion that they had sparked in her.

She grabbed her phone. I must send Greg a quick message to thank him. She saw she had a message from him already. She opened it excitedly. *How sweet and even better that it sounds like he wants to see me again too.* She smiled. She tapped out a reply.

Dear Greg,
Thank you. I can't stop thinking about you and our special lunch.
Sorry I had to race off. I'd love to share more delicious times with
you soon too. xx

She didn't even bother to look to see when his message had been sent.

She rose, showered, and had started to cook breakfast by the time Michael returned.

'Enjoy your run?' She walked up to him and gave him a big kiss on the cheek. 'I missed you this morning,' she said with a little grin.

Michael swallowed hard. 'Did you now?' he replied, trying to sound normal. He felt anything but normal. Sort of numb and still very confused. She was flirty and light-hearted again. 'Sorry about our date night. Tracey told you about my wallet?'

'Yes, she did. Did you catch up with the guys again? You were gone for ages.'

'Yeah, for a bit.'

'That's nice. You don't spend time with your mates enough, you know. Would you like a shower first before breakfast—or eat first?'

'I might grab a quick shower. I won't be long.'

Michael let the shower drown out his turmoil a little. This was going to be a long day.

Monday morning had not come fast enough for Michael, his whole body now aching from suppressing his rumbling volcanic emotions, now overwhelmed by his urgent need to find this 'GS'. The wait for Megan and the kids to leave was agonising, nearly in slow motion, until he could hear the house sounds dull to confirm he was alone. He stood in the kitchen, staring down at his phone on the table.

It's now or never.

'Damn it. Just do it.' Michael picked up the phone and stopped. He remained poised, holding his phone in one hand, with the paper on which he'd written the 'GS' number from Megan's phone in the other. His own thoughts still in shock and debate with themselves. *It must be this Greg Sheppard guy. You already know what's been happening. Well, it has to be? There was no Gail to be found in her contacts or any other GS.*

This is the only way to fix this. Make the call.

He carefully punched in the numbers on his keypad. Every peel of the ring tone was shouting in his ear, with a part of him hoping it wouldn't be answered. Not only fearful of the confirmation about his wife, confrontations had never been his specialty.

'Greg Sheppard.'

Michael hesitated for a split second then said, 'Greg, my name is Michael Munday, I would like to catch up with you for a chat. Today, as soon as you're available.'

'Sure,' Greg said, hopeful it was a new client but suspicious by the lack of enthusiasm in his voice. 'Can I ask what you would like to talk about?'

'I would like to talk to you about my wife, Megan Munday.'

'Megan Munday? I don't think I know a Megan Munday. How would I know her?'

'I found your card in her pocket.'

Greg wracked his brains. 'Munday.' The name wasn't at all familiar, and he was usually great at remembering contacts. 'Is she in film, TV, who does she work for? What does she look like?'

Michael was getting more and more agitated. *My goodness, he doesn't even remember her! Or, even maybe, I have got this all wrong.* 'Megan is a very beautiful woman with long blonde straight hair. I think you met her in Sydney. She works in property management.'

Greg heard Sydney and the alarm bells started sounding. *Megan. Oh, hell. Surely not?* He paused and then replied calmly, 'Okay, where would you like to meet? I'm at Burnside at the moment.'

'How about the Red Café at Norwood at 2.00 p.m.?' said Michael sharply.

'Fine, see you there.'

As Greg hung up, his heart was racing. This had never happened before. Greg dialled Megan's number with no answer. He left a message 'Please call me ASAP.' He called a few more times, still with no answer.

Greg arrived at the café, taking no time to identify Michael. He could see a man, tall, well-built, perched at a table on his own. His head was down, staring at his finger circling the lip of a cup of an almost finished short black. He finally looked up as Greg approached.

'Michael?' asked Greg.

'Yes,' was the short greeting as they curtly shook hands. Michael gestured for Greg to sit opposite him at the table. The instant Greg sat down, Michael focused, his eyes fixed directly on Greg.

'I will get straight down to it,' said Michael. 'I suspect my wife is having an affair and want to know if it's you?'

'I know a Megan Proudman that fits the description you gave, I have tried calling her this morning, but she hasn't answered.'

'She is in meetings all day,' Michael said, as he pulled out a photo of their happy family, snapped on a beach somewhere with two children beside their parents.

'This is my wife, Megan.' Michael slowly slid the picture across the table for Greg to see with his fingers still holding onto it tightly at its corner. Greg looked at the photo in front of him—everything fell into place. It was the same Megan. The one he and Kara had just slept with this past Saturday.

'Oh, I see,' Greg said as he slowly lifted his head to look at Michael.

Michael could tell by Greg's look that they are talking about the same person.

'Okay, clearly, there has been quite a bit of deception here on a few levels.'

'What do you mean? You've either been with her, or you haven't.'

'I mean, she didn't tell me her real name, or that she was married.'

Michael looked at him and said, 'But you are the one she has been with?'

Greg knew it is best to say as little as possible in this type of situation, where a person's voice is simmering between words. Greg simply nodded to confirm.

It was then his phone rang. It was Megan. Greg cancelled the call quickly. 'Is that her?' Michael asked, his voice rising.

'Yes.'

'I don't want you to tell her we've met. Just tell her that it's over between the two of you.'

'How can I possibly do that?' Greg asked.

Greg's phone rang out again. This time he recognised the ringtone.

'Is that her again?'

'No. It's actually my friend Kara.'

'I don't believe you. Enough of the bullshit. I just want my old fucking life back, and that's not going to happen with you between her fucking legs. You end this. Now!' says Michael, his demeanour having heated from simmer to boiling agitation.

'I truly hope you and Megan can sort it all out for the best,' Greg said, trying to calm the situation. Michael got up sharply to leave. He stood and turned back to Greg, his whole body shaking from adrenalin and pointed a shaky finger at him.

'Stop fucking my wife!' he shouted, loud enough to turn every head in the café.

Greg stood quickly and left five dollars on the table for the coffee that still hadn't arrived and quickly exited as well. Every eye in the place turned to watch him leave.

Back in his car, his head was spinning. *Why on earth didn't she tell me or Kara? Well, at least he didn't try and stab me,* he thought to himself, as he dialled Megan's number.

'Hello gorgeous, what's up?' she answered excitedly.

'I just had coffee with your husband.'

There was a long pause while his statement sank in, while Greg waited.

'Oh, my God! Shit!' blurted into his ear.

'Would have been nice to know who you were, honestly, Megan,' Greg said as calmly as he could.

'My God! What did he say?'

'Well, basically, he asked me to stop seeing you. He also asked me not to tell you he contacted me.'

Greg could hear Megan starting to cry on the other end.

'I'm so sorry. I'm so sorry. What the fuck have I done?' she cried out between sobs.

'Megan,' Greg said in a softened voice, 'you need to have this out with him. Use this as a chance to work out what you both are going to do. You must have known this couldn't go on forever without something like this happening, so now is the time to make some big decisions. Kara and I will always be here to support you, but you need to sort this out.'

'I'm so sorry Greg. I should have told you. It was just meant to be some innocent fun. Now look what I have done, I've fucked up everything.'

'Just sort it out Megan, let me know how things go,'

'Alright. I'm very sorry.'

'Goodbye Megan.' Greg hung up.

Megan was now walking laps around and around her own speedway thought track on the footpath outside her office building. She didn't see any of the many people moving past, trying to avoid colliding with the woman pacing and muttering. Everything was crashing inside.

Michael must have sensed something. *How long has he known? I can't believe he phoned and met Greg. What did he say? Greg wants me to work it out. I don't know what I want. I can't lose my kids. Or my home. I want Greg too. Sex with him and Kara was so exciting. God. Oh God!* She couldn't decide what to do next. She couldn't go home. *Not yet.* She had to work out how to fix this.

She paced more with despair for her own salvation than guilt. She was desperately thinking of excuses rather than how Michael or Greg might feel after such a shocking revelation for both of them. Megan had become her own nightmare without realising.

Then it came to her. Megan remembered what Greg had said about Michael not wanting her to know about the meeting. Greg just told her to work it out and decide. In that moment she had, but not in the way he had intended.

She decided to not say anything to Michael, unless he brought it up. She would let things settle down at home. Then she would be right in telling Greg that things were working out and that she would just like to be friends with him and Kara. As for any future meetings with them, she would just need to be extra careful. Especially if she needed benefits.

Chapter 21

Greg phoned Kara the second he stepped away from the café.
'Hi Greg, thanks for ringing back. I was just wondering…'

Before she could finish, Greg just let a massive, 'You won't believe what just happened!' He hadn't heard a word Kara had said.

'What on earth is going on?' she asked.

'Sorry, Kara, but I've just had a meeting, and a dressing down by Megan's husband.'

'Megan's husband, as in yesterday's Megan? You aren't serious?'

'Yes. *That* Megan.'

'She never said she was married! My God, are you okay? He didn't punch you or anything, did he?'

'No, he was relatively cool under the circumstances. He just told me to stop screwing his wife, in no uncertain terms! He did it rather loudly, standing in the Red Café. That was very embarrassing to say the least, I didn't look to see if there was anyone I knew.'

'I bet it was. That's terrible. She's been silly not to say anything. Especially when you told her about me, *before* she came for lunch.'

'I know. Oh well. I've spoken to her since and told her she needed to sort it out.'

'Hey, I'm on my way home—are you home now?'

'Yes, I am. That's good. I'll see you soon.'

'You can tell me all about it. We might need a drink!'

As Kara drove to the apartment, she thought hard about Megan and her situation. She couldn't blame her; despite the mess she'd created. As they knew so little about her, there were many reasons that could cause her to need more than what her married life may offer. Her husband might suffer a health condition. Sex is tired, stale, and routine. They have mismatched libidos but are great friends and parents. So many reasons why so many seek sex with others. Kara thought back to her own torrid years with her ex. There was no doubt she escaped to others, while only imaginary, she would have given anything for sex or even a connection with someone else. She had sometimes wondered if she and Greg had reunited earlier, if she would have had the courage to fulfil her fantasies with him. But in those days, she was just surviving a fearful life, and lived on eggshells most of the time, daring not to do a single little thing wrong. She doubted, no matter how much she might have wanted Greg, or discovered how lovely he was, she always knew the price she would have paid would have been her life or even his. *There are so many reasons why couples should have more people in their lives, especially when it comes to intimacy,* thought Kara. *Monogamy shouldn't be the only marriage.*

The hug she gave him as soon as she got home was huge and comforting.

'Greg, I know you would've handled it well, but it's not a nice thing to happen.'

'Thanks, sexy. I needed that. I really didn't expect to have a day like this one.'

'I know. So, tell me, what did he say? Tell me everything.'

The two of them sat on the lounge and talked for hours. They shared and dissected much about Megan's situation and Greg's meeting with Michael for a start, both realising her abrupt end to the phone sex, wanting to have lunch at Greg's place, and her time-conscious fast exit, were all little signs that she had another life she hadn't been open about.

The conversation got deeper and strayed into the musings about relationships and marriage that Kara had reflected upon on her way home. 'It's a pity that couples can't negotiate and work out what they need and really communicate about what works for each of them. Like we did, before I moved in. Couples just seem to get together and think everything will just work itself out. But what people need and desire and how they connect alters and needs to be talked about, especially intimacy,' she lamented.

'I agree. Relationships are complex and tenuous; they can be challenging. It would've been nicer if Megan had discussed her needs with Michael, and if she'd wanted to play with someone else as well, then they could've set terms. It can, and has been done between couples, amicably, ethically, and reasonably. It just needs communication.'

'You have thought about this before, haven't you?' Kara said, with a hint of surprise.

'Yes, I have. For a long time. I've never told you. As you know, I'd told Tess about you and I meeting, long before we got engaged, and while I didn't explicitly tell her, she knew underneath and accepted that we'd hooked up. When I lost you for that time after I proposed to her—it made me think about what could be different, especially as I felt different types of love for you both. It felt like I was being forced to make a choice that shouldn't have to be made. After each time you and I met, I knew I had to talk to Tess about you. I'd struggled to find the right time and a way to start the conversation.'

'I hadn't realised. That's very brave and impressive, Greg,' Kara said softly.

'I realised eventually there is never a "right time" so I sent her a message, but...' He stopped. Kara caught the lump of remorse sitting in his throat.

'But what happened?' she near whispered.

'I'd finally decided that I had to speak up, so I replied to a text from her to say I had things to talk to her about when I got home that night. I was on my way back to Adelaide. She'd sent me her message, from the cab.'

'The day she died?' Kara asked softly.

'Yes. But I never got the chance.'

Kara blinked hard. She didn't want anything to make this day harder. She swallowed the rising lump of anguish that had risen in her throat. He was such an honest man. His sensitive disclosure made Kara fully realise the depth of the pain he harboured at Tess's death.

'Greg. It is actually the best thing now, given what happened, that you hadn't said anything. She left her life filled with love, and just for you.' Greg looked at Kara earnestly, then smiled and nodded.

'Thank you. I needed to hear that.'

They sat for a while, sipping their wine, without saying a word.

'As for Megan,' Greg spoke, the words tumbling out of his mouth, 'I think she's been silly, but I do hope she's okay. She's a nice woman and there's something I really like about her,' Greg said.

'Yes, I feel that too and she's quite sexy,'

'Like someone else I know,' grinned Greg.

'Is that so?' Kara was already placing her wine onto the coffee table and moving to kneel up in front of him. 'I think you've had way too much to handle today, Mr Sheppard. It's time I help you relax.'

Kara leant forward, motioned Greg to take another sip from his glass, her hand poised waiting to take it from him. He drew in a mouthful, gave up his glass to her and smiled, before resting his head back sinking into the lounge. She had instantly dialled down his day, from pressure to pleasure in seconds.

Kara leant forward, her fingers unbuttoning his shirt. As she pulled it back to reveal his chest, both her hands circled across his torso, each finger touching lightly and delicately. She could see his body respond. It was like every strand of his body hair was rising to be felt, his flesh tone colouring and shading, as the anticipation of her lips and pleasure ran beneath his skin. As she leant over his body, her nipples grazing his, she pressed light kisses up toward his neck, resting on his left ear. She bit his earlobe gently, and whispered, 'We've done enough talking tonight. Let me drain away the pressure of today.'

He turned his head to kiss her on the cheek, before she started her descent back to kneel between his legs. She stopped only to undo his pants, take hold of them, and in one move, slide them and herself to the floor. She discarded his shoes and socks and slipped his pants over his feet, tossing all aside. Her lips started sucking and kissing the soft skin inside his knees, while her hands ran up and down both of his inner calves and thighs.

He was warm and pink under her touch, and she let her touch roll slowly toward the destination she knew he was waiting for. Kiss by kiss, she crept closer. Her tongue finally wedging in the soft creases and fold of his groin. One side, then the other. From near his arse—up over and around his pubes, across to his hips and back. Each pass of her tongue licked closer to his cock, now firm, and near twitching in anticipation.

This time, she let her tongue find the soft tiny spot at the base of his erection, where it touched and connected with his balls. She loved the contrast, that ridged fold of his sack where it seamlessly glided into firm, hard flesh at the base of him.

Her tongue traced ahead. Every part of her was warm, radiating a need to taste all of him desperately.

She let her tongue anoint him all over. Up and down his shaft and over his knob. She resisted drawing him completely into her mouth until she knew he was ready. No lube or lotion tonight.

She needed every slide to be soft, wet and flowing. She wanted to taste only him. He was rock hard, throbbing against her tongue. Kara lifted herself a little higher, poised over his splendour, and let her lips take the lead. Slipping her moistened shining smile over him, her mouth was open and eager.

She glanced up at him. His head back, eyes closed, with his whole body pressed back into the leather. Her mouth sucked. Rising her lips up and down, slowly at first, drawing in his heat and the sweet taste of him, the pulsation of his every nerve and muscle against the inside of her mouth, sparked the sensations inside her at the same time. Her pussy was pulsing nearly in sync, with each time she rode her mouth over the length of him from tip to base. As her right hand kept stroking the bottom inches of him, her left-hand index finger, slid up and down between his cheeks, grazing his hole, her mouth keeping pace.

Greg started to moan. This sound was all Kara wanted to hear. She knew he needed to release this day, to let go all the woes from his mind, and his body too. He reached out and placed his hands on each side of her face, stroking her gently from chin to cheek. As she maintained the rhythm on his cock, his hands suspended all motion, then without warning, he gripped a handful of her hair on each side of her head. As he clenched tighter, she knew exactly what was about to happen. His body arched and tensed, before he let everything go into her. It took all her concentration to maintain the rhythm of her lips and fingers working him, her own body responding, and shuddering beneath her, until the sweet liquid burst down her throat. She drank him in, swallowing every drop. It was sublime. Everything about this man to her was sweet and giving. His thoughts, ideas, care, body and his cum. Simply divine.

Greg didn't move for what seemed like an eternity. As he lay back, resting in the afterglow, Kara just quietly started to lick and roll her tongue over his knob with a featherlight touch. 'Let me clean away everything from today, all of it,' she said.

Chapter 22

When Megan finally arrived home Monday after her day of meetings, Michael made sure he greeted her warmly, had a meal ready, and then just watched. While he wanted to genuinely try to make up for any of his own shortcomings, he also wanted to look for any sign that Greg Sheppard had alerted her to his meeting with him.

However, Megan was unexpectedly bright and cheerful and chatted throughout dinner about her latest job and there was nothing Michael could sense, nothing that indicated Greg had spoken with her. *He hasn't told her it's over yet, though. She doesn't seem to know about me contacting him. That's something,* he thought.

He started to breathe a little. *Hopefully, by the week's end he will finish this with her, and it will all be behind us. It's just a blip. I need to take some responsibility. I've probably focused more on the kids and mastering jobs around the house than her in recent years.* But he was still watching her every move.

Megan knew she had to keep things very cool and try to restore Michael's confidence and trust in her, especially in the next few weeks. Remembering Greg had said she wasn't supposed to have any idea about his meeting, was the easy solution. She deliberately waited for a couple of days, then just before she left the office, she sent Greg a quick text message.

Need to talk. Could you please give me a quick call? I'm free about 5.30. Megan x

Just after 5.30 her phone rang. *Perfect timing,* she thought. *I'm nearly home.*

'Hello Greg. Thanks for calling.'

'That's fine, Megan. Is everything alright?'

'Yes. It's okay, I just wanted to say how sorry I am about all this mess. I know I should have told you I was married. I know that I've put you in a very awkward position.'

'It wasn't good, that's for sure, but I sort of understand. It wouldn't have mattered to me or Kara if you'd told us. I hope you realise that.'

'I understand that now.'

'So how are things going between you and Michael?'

'We've sorted everything out. I told him what I needed, and he's calmed right down. He's agreed for me to see other people, but he doesn't want to know about it.'

'Megan, that's nice and great news you've arrived at an understanding with Michael. You must've had it out completely, if he's able to accept that sort of arrangement already. That's quite amazing!'

'I know. But it can work, I just need to keep him happy too,' she said, lying through her teeth. 'But...' she hesitated. She had to tell him what she really wanted.

'But what Megan?' Greg asked gently. He knew what she was going to say, just by the lowering of her voice.

'I want more of you, and Kara, and for us all to be close friends. I really need to see you both again, soon. You are both so lovely... and sexy,' she added with a lilt of hope and lust in her voice.

'We feel the same. Perhaps we can catch up soon. Let's wait a bit, shall we? Give you some time to let the dust settle.'

'Okay, thank you. You're right.' She drew in a breath, then near purred down the phone, 'but Greg, please remember, I'll be thinking of you every day. A girl can only touch herself for so long.'

'You are a sweetheart. We'll be in touch soon.'

'That would be nice. Is it alright if you email me? That might be best, under the circumstances.'

'Sure, text me your email address. It's fine, Megan. Take care. Until soon.'

'I'll send it now. Thanks for calling Greg, again, I'm truly sorry. Bye.'

Megan had arrived home and kept talking just until she walked inside. As she entered the kitchen, she gave Michael a look, before ending the call quickly. She didn't look at him but walked past and headed straight for their bedroom. As she sat down on the edge of the bed, her bags tossed next to her, she knew Michael would walk in soon. Predictable as ever. He entered, 'Hi honey. Everything alright?'

'Yes, sure. Long day, that's all. I'll be out in a minute,' she said, her head lowered to her lap, finding the hint of tension, hurt and melancholy she needed in her tone and demeanour.

'Okay, I'll have a wine ready. No rush.' As Michael turned and headed for the kitchen, he let out a sigh. *She's trying not to show she's upset. He's called her. He must have. It's done. I hope she'll be alright.*

'I will make you happy Megan, I promise,' he whispered to himself.

Megan undressed. It was only small, but her smile said it all. Everything was working to plan. Michael could rest, thinking his approach had stopped Greg Sheppard. She just needed to remain calm.

During the next three weeks, Megan executed the best of her resolve for her home life to recover, to restore the feel of work, routine, dependency and sanctuary for everyone. She had not dared contact Greg again, having regained some small sense of balance. *Maybe my 'fling and exploration' phase has passed?* She wondered. Michael had showered her with attention, especially at night, to satisfy her desires.

However, it was short-lived. The entrenched routine was creeping back into Michael and their life. It was, thereafter, only a while before her thoughts drifted back to 'that' feeling. The adrenalin rush of heat and delicious sensation that filled her, often when least expected, found her touching herself at every opportunity. Daily, she imagined, and indulged the fantastic, erotic desire to be bold. Desperate to again be daring and naughty, she imagined fantasy scenarios once more, where she was absorbed in exploratory kinky sex with anyone other than Michael. She didn't care if it was with another man, another woman, being watched by others or watching them having sex—anything that aroused and excited her that was directly opposed to what she experienced in her everyday life. She loved how it seemed to satisfy her inner cravings.

The flirtatious temptation, being adored and wanted by someone else was intoxicating. Greg Sheppard had wanted her. So had Kara. Now all Megan wanted was them again.

After Megan's message and subsequent phone call, Greg arrived home. The recount of the latest contact was the first thing he shared with Kara.

'She's still clearly keen to meet both of us again. She said that it's all sorted, and she has an agreement with her husband, but she just needs to keep it private. She was brave enough to say she should have told him from the beginning about her need for more sex and tell us that she was married. She also said she wanted to see me, and you again. I told her that was nice we'd like to see her too.'

Kara's smile was loaded with apprehension, querying both Megan's spoken and underlying meaning to what she'd told Greg.

'I think that was very nice, but do you think she has it all sorted, really? I'd like to catch up with her again for sure, but I'd like to know that it's definitely all okay. It might sound crazy, but something feels a bit off. I'd love to enjoy her more with you, but we don't need to end up in the middle of a couple's disaster! At least it sounds like it's not been too hard for her to return home.'

'I think you might be right. He was desperate to keep her, that's for sure,' Greg said.

'I'm pleased things aren't angry and she's safe. He must be a nice guy, really.'

'He was actually pretty good, considering. Not sure how he'd cope if he knew she'd been with you as well though!'

Kara smiled. 'Well, sadly, that's not easy for many people to deal with! We are unique!'

Greg laughed. 'So true! Let's see what happens. Maybe she could just catch up when we're away for work?'

'The film festival is three weeks away. She might like an escape by then?'

'That could work, but we'll see. In the meantime, we can always have some of our own naughty fun,' Greg gestured, turning slowly and unbuttoning his shirt, exaggerating like he was starting a striptease. 'Let's watch porn and fuck the night away, Ms Gilbert!'

Kara giggled. 'How about you find the video and leave all the stripping to me!' as she walked up to him and unzipped his pants.

Any thoughts of Megan were instantly suspended. The near thunderous penetration and sounds they created drowned out everything other than each other.

Chapter 23

*F*riday afternoon. What bliss. The end to a week that seemed like an eternity had finally arrived. Megan was only hours away from when she could escape to Queensland. After all those tough weeks, she would soon get to touch, taste and feel him and Kara once more. The two of them held such a fascination and elixir of pleasure, Megan could hardly wait to be close to both of them again.

Megan had been instantly wet with excitement when the email from Greg had arrived a week ago. It read:

From: Greg Sheppard <Greg@PrecisionEvents.com.au>
To: Megan Munday <mmunday@hotmail.com>

Good morning Megan,
I hope things have been good for you since we last spoke.
Again, I can't tell you how much I enjoyed being able to finish what we started in Sydney, at my place. To let me be back inside you and fill you with my cum, was just amazing. I'm so pleased that you also enjoyed meeting Kara so intimately as well. I know you said you would like to catch up again. If this is the case, please accept this invitation to you to attend the Brisbane Film Festival as my VIP guest starting on the evening of Friday 27th of this month. You will be wined and dined, and of course, my body will be yours afterwards for anything you may desire. Let me know if you're free and would like to attend. I'll send details and help with arrangements
Regards Greg.

She replied immediately.

From: Megan Munday <mmunday@hotmail.com>
To: Greg Sheppard <Greg@PrecisionEvents.com.au>

Dear Greg

Thank you so much for the kind and generous invitation to join you in Brisbane. I accept with pleasure, and will delightfully welcome your invasion of my body once again. I will arrive on the 27th. Hopefully, I will be able to stay for the weekend and until the 31st. Appreciate if you can send me details of where to meet etc. I'm so thrilled—I've never been treated like a VIP before. Can't wait!
Please say Hi to Kara. Megan xx

Barely able to contain her excitement, she'd struggled to keep her elated and horny feelings in check all week. She'd nearly pounced on Michael that night, so filled with thoughts of sex and Greg's body again.

The pillow-talk which followed was when she chose to tell him she had another work trip ahead. Her near sultry whisper, 'But I don't leave until next Saturday morning and I'm back by Tuesday, so it's only really three nights before I'm back here with you like this.' As she ran her fingers over him, it was received as she had hoped, Michael still groggy in the afterglow of his orgasm, accepted her every word.

'Oh, okay, that's fine.' On hearing his reply, Megan rolled over. The smile said it all. Now she was really satisfied.

She'd spent each night packing and re-packing her bag. She wanted to take the right clothes to look sexy by day and night. Besides, packing for this trip just reminded her of what she was going to enjoy once she landed in Brisbane.

However, Wednesday night, she'd nearly lost it.

She'd snapped at Michael for the simplest of questions about her forthcoming trip, but it caught her unprepared. The week was laboriously long, and she was impatiently awaiting Greg's reply to her message with the details of where to go when she landed.

Michael's probing had jangled even more. 'So, you're leaving to go on Saturday? Is there something special on? You usually leave mid-week before a conference.'

She'd stumbled at his words, thought with haste and tersely replied, 'For goodness' sake! It's just the welcome dinner for delegates. I don't usually go, but they asked me to be there this time. Alright?!'

'Of course, it's alright. I was just asking,' he replied, a bit taken aback.

'Sorry, but I've done lots for this event and I suppose they appreciated it. I hadn't expected they'd even send me an invitation,' she replied. Again, checking herself. She was lamely tying to sound truthful. After all, she hadn't expected an invitation from Greg so soon. That was the truth. And she was delighted.

Michael had caught the brief tremor of panic in her voice and the see-saw of her mood again this week. It hadn't been there for a few weeks now. He felt a wave of suspicion wash over him again. He watched each day. The little signs were appearing again. So here she was on the day before departure, and the spring in her step was even evident to her kids.

'What's got you so happy today, Mum?' asked Matt as he plonked himself down on the stool at the bench.

'Nothing in particular. It's just the last day for work and it's a lovely day,' she said hurriedly.

'Yeah. Okay,' was the reply as he started diving into his breakfast.

Michael had looked at Megan and winked. 'Your mother is simply happy because I'm making her coffee, Matt!'

'Alright you two, I get it. Enough.' He walked into the dining room, breakfast bowl in hand.

They both laughed.

Megan arrived home from work that night, brimming with electricity. She greeted Michael heartily as she poured them both a wine, asking him about his day.

'Darling, I've just got to check some details for tomorrow, I'll grab a shower and then I'll give you a hand with dinner if you like.' She headed to the study.

Michael picked it—*right there. She was leaving tomorrow, and she was excited.* Work had never inspired her this much. He had to work out what was really going on. If she did have a work trip, the details would be on her computer. He waited for her to leave the study,

KATHRYN GILLINGS & GARY BAXTER

thinking he could try to catch the computer before the screen timed out in 30 seconds. He had a rough idea of what her password was, but now suspected she'd probably changed it.

As soon as he heard her footsteps, he dashed to the study, grabbed the wireless mouse and slipped it into his pocket. He could continue to keep the screen active by remote control. Every ten seconds he would turn the mouse wheel, keeping the screen alive.

The click of the bathroom door and sound of the shower signalled his opportunity.

Michael quickly returned to the study, sat himself down, gripping and scrolling the mouse now firmly on her desk to find her email. It took only seconds to find Greg's messages and her reply. She hadn't been smart enough to empty her deleted folder. As he read, the stark confirmation of his suspicion changed his glare from frozen to boiling point in a split-second.

Megan strolled back down the hallway and was about to head into the kitchen when she realised Michael was standing in the middle of the lounge room.

She had no opportunity to speak from the second after she said, 'Oh there you are darling…'

His feet were planted, arms folded across his chest, glaring upright in his stance. His voice was frightening in its depth and delivery. She stole a glance beyond him toward the study. The computer screen was glowing from the desk. She tried to swallow the rancid taste caught in her throat.

'Megan, stop it! Please don't call me that. Don't say another fucking word. I found the email from Greg Sheppard. You lying bitch. There is no work trip. You're going away to fuck him again. After I'd spoken with him and told him not to contact you again. But I expect you already knew that.'

Megan's already flushed cheeks reddened further. She just stood there, motionless. That was enough.

'I thought so.' He started a slow, loud clap with his hands, each slap jeering as they hit together. 'I really must applaud you for being such a brilliant actress. To think you truly convinced me that all of this was over.' His tone was acid, dripping with sarcasm. Anger seeping through his every word. He didn't allow her a second to find one word, regardless of the fact she couldn't find her voice anyway.

'I don't really know what to say to you, Megan. You've just proven that I can't trust you or him. To be honest, I can't even bear to look at you right now. All I can see is a woman who was once my beautiful wife that I loved, was proud of, who's now just behaving like a lying slut who's happy to throw it all away by screwing around. Fuck knows who else you've been fucking on all those nights away? My God! You need to take your bags and get the fuck out of my sight. Now! You need to work out what the fuck you want because I can't—no—I won't live like this. It's 8.00 p.m. I'm going out until 10.00 p.m. You'd better be gone by the time I return.'

'But what do I tell the kids?' were her first and only words she offered in a limp, pathetic reply.

'I don't give a fuck right now. Hang on, how about you tell them the fucking truth for once? That you're leaving for your fucking sex romp in Queensland.'

With that, he turned and left, not waiting for a reply, avoiding the sobs he knew would fill the house behind him.

And they did. It took all the next twenty minutes to curb the tears enough to even see her way to the bedroom. She'd walked in circles, the reality of what was happening still sinking in. He'd never spoken to her like that. Not ever. He was kicking her out of their home. She was just reeling, not able to consider anything, other than to grab what she could think of, and go. She had just over an hour. She couldn't be here when he returned. His tone alone had sent her that message loud and clear. For the first time in all her years with Michael, she was frightened of him.

Her bag for Brisbane was already packed. That, at least, had most of her favourite outfits and jewellery inside. She raced to her robe and grabbed out another suitcase, pulling items randomly from the shelves, hangers, and drawers. Shoes, jackets, pants, undies, jewellery and dresses, whatever she could focus on or glimpsed—she took. She ran to the kitchen and found a roll of garbage bags. Peeling them off, she ran from room to room, the ensuite, office, lounge and kitchen, frantically grabbing any items that she recognised as her own and shoved them inside. She filled over eight bags and dragged them out to her car.

It was only after putting them into the back of her CRV that she realised she had no idea where to go. Until now, it had just been about getting out. She checked the time. It was 9.43 p.m. She had to be gone within the next 15 minutes.

There was only one person she thought to call. She rang Greg's number.

Chapter 24

*K*ara and Greg had not long been in bed when his phone rang.

This can't be good at this hour, she thought as Greg answered immediately, the worst of thoughts already in his mind. Kara could hear only his broken replies to a jumbled voice on the other end.

'Oh, hell... Tell me—are you hurt? That's good. Okay. Of course, you can for now. No problem at all. Sure, we'll both be waiting. Don't rush. Just take it slow. See you soon.'

Greg ended the call and turned to Kara, explaining. 'That was Megan. Michael found out about the invite to join us at the Film Festival—so he's turfed her out of the house. He gave her two hours to pack and go, and she's on her way here.'

Greg and Kara looked at each other, with the knowing sigh in both their eyes. Kara said what they were both thinking, *the arrangement she had with Michael about seeing other people was too good to be true.* They both climbed heavily out of bed, pulled on some clothes, and headed to the living room, readying for the onslaught. Megan would bring a mess of anguish and words that would need a lot of listening, sorting and comfort.

'Oh My God! That's so not good. Poor woman, she'll be a complete mess. I'll put the kettle on,' Kara said.

'Let's see how she is when she arrives. She sounds like she's in a real state.' Greg paused. 'Kara, look, I'll take care of this. It's my fault she's landing here. I was the one who started this with her. I'm sorry. You wondered about her.'

'Greg, it's alright. For a start, she lied to us, she made the choices, not you. We both entertained her. It doesn't really matter how any of this happened, she's been turfed out of her home. She'll be scared, upset, and needs our help as friends tonight. Besides, you've got to leave early for Brisbane tomorrow, and… I've been where she is and understand what she's going through right now.'

'Kara, you're really such a kind person, there aren't many people who would ever be this understanding, you know.'

'Yeah, I'm a true saint… who swings,' she smiled.

Greg grinned in return.

It was then that the doorbell rang once. Then three more times, hurriedly.

'Megan. Hello, dear one. Come on inside. Don't worry, we'll help with your gear.' Their greetings were as metered and light as they could muster, tainted with the hesitant heartbeats about what her unexpected arrival on their doorstep might unfold. Far be it for them to get closely embroiled in a separation or heated argument between a couple. This was nothing they wanted or had ever encountered, but it was someone in need.

Megan entered their apartment similar to the hesitation and anticipation of walking through an airport security scanner. Despite her most recent intimate encounter, these circumstances evoked even more unknown feelings. None of them were familiar enough for this situation. She was a veritable stranger arriving at their door.

Kara gave Megan a big welcoming hug, as Greg's kiss grazed her cheek at the same time. 'Give me your keys, I'll fetch your gear from the car… I expect you have more than this?' Megan let the keys drop into his hand, with the heavy confirming nod that there was much more to unload than just the story of her night.

As Kara led her into the lounge room, she kept the flow and invitation alive, her voice like warm cocoa. 'Megan, it's alright— you're safe here tonight. Think of nothing else. Now, have you eaten? Prefer a drink? Or both, perhaps? Just come in and sit down.'

With her cases, garbage bags and recount of their journey from the email to their door all received, it was three hours later that Greg and Kara lay side by side in bed, whispering their exclamations of their crazy night, and satisfied that they had sufficiently listened, consoled, fed, and medicated Megan, to have her now sleeping soundly in the guest room.

'I'm fine for her to stay for a few days. Until things settle down. Are you okay with that though, Kara? This is your place too, and I'm the one leaving in a few hours, with all this mess I've brought in. I'm so sorry!'

'You get some sleep, and just wait until I wake you. I'll get you to the airport in the morning. As for everything else,' Kara threw her head toward the general direction of the guest room, 'it's baby steps. I've been there, so it might be better if I'm the one to deal with this right now, anyway.'

Kara made an exhausted attempt to end their day with a smile. 'Besides, Mr Superman Sheppard, I may only be Wonder Woman, but I can manage for a couple of days—even without you and your superpowers, so please don't stress and just sleep now.' She rolled over to her side.

'Come here, Wonder Woman,' he murmured, snuggling his body close behind her, drawing her back into his chest and wrapping his arms around her. 'You're the one with amazing superpowers, Kara. Thank you.'

With her body melded into his cradling warmth and his butterfly kisses across her shoulder, sleep found her swiftly.

As he held her body, all the reflections of her warmth and care this past year breezed across him vividly. This rediscovered, original 'first kiss' sweetheart had become so alive and had given him so much more than he'd ever imagined possible. He'd not encountered a more eclectic, unusual or genuine woman. What had started as basically a fanciful attempt to find her, he'd relished in the suspended fantasy sexual encounters that finally realised when they reunited.

Somehow, she'd not only ignited, but had since managed to change and spark him too. In this year alone, she had become his constant. She'd consoled and been his mainstay after Tess's death, then listened, unbelievably accepted, and was now dealing with his first 'post-Tess encounter' woman, who was sleeping in his guest room. She'd willingly held his hand, boldly shared in sexy swinging encounters, watching and enjoying his pleasure with others. Notwithstanding she'd changed jobs, moved house and just remained forever at the end of the phone, whenever he needed. She was unselfishly kind, nice, bold and sexy. Those were real superpowers.

'Kara, you will always be a wonder woman to me,' he whispered as he finally let his eyes blink to close off this day.

Chapter 25

Megan had awoken with a jolt; her dreams of Friday night having become the morning's nightmare reality. She looked around the room, startled at first, with no recognition of where she was. The stack of garbage bags to the side of the bed brought comforting realisation and relief. Greg and Kara had taken her in. Busting for the bathroom and something to silence the thumping 'pub beat' killing her temples, she climbed out of bed, creeping to the door.

She looked in every direction, desperate to remember where to find the bathroom without disturbing anyone. As she stepped out of her room to venture down the hallway, a note crinkled under her toes. She looked down. The note was for her.

Good morning, Megan. Hope you slept okay. I'm taking Greg to the airport—then grocery shopping and back to get you a late breakfast. See you about 10 am. Kara x

PS. fresh towels in the main bathroom for you. Help yourself to toiletries, makeup, coffee or just the couch or whatever you need this morning!

K x.

Megan's body instantly calmed and clung to the note's sentiment, like it was a mother's morning hug. By the time she'd showered, dressed and sorted through the rumble of packing she'd brought with her, Kara arrived back, filling the kitchen with grocery bags, and even more warmth in her welcome cheer. Kara was speaking to her from the moment she'd entered, before Megan had emerged from the bedroom.

'Hey Megan, I'm home. Sorry I took a bit longer than I thought. I'll fix us something to eat as soon as I can. Perhaps we can make it brunch? Maybe a Chicken Caesar salad? Oh, you must let us know if there's anything you don't like to eat, by the way.'

Megan's height and spirit already rose by inches at the sound of her voice. By the time she reached the kitchen, her own words started to reflect the hint of carefree that comes with a clear blue-sky Saturday.

'Hi Kara. Good morning. A Caesar salad sounds wonderful. Can I give you a hand?'

There were moments when Megan slipped back into pensive and blue, but for the most part, she had smiled through her day, eased by Kara's bright and natural attention. The two women each talked and listened. They sat quietly busying themselves and grazing through the Saturday with usual chores mixed with only a couple of delicate discussions about what had happened between Megan and her husband. In fact, Kara reflected, there was a lot of time spent responding to Megan's questions about Greg and Tess and how he and Kara had met.

As Kara took Megan for the fifty-cent tour through the apartment to show where to find things, Megan checked out every photograph and item carefully. 'Kara, tell me more about Greg. What's he really like?'

'What do you mean? You've met him and know all about the sexy romantic charisma he exudes so naturally!' Kara replied with a devilish grin.

Megan smiled. 'Yes, of course, but I suppose I'd like to know more about what he thinks and how he gets on with other people at work and stuff?'

'Okay, well, this is from how I see him. Greg's what I call a true man. He's a social animal but likes his own space too. He mixes with anyone quite effortlessly—anyone, really. Greg is what you see and feel. Always the consummate professional. He never sits still and puts his full attention and detail into whatever he turns his hand to.'

'He lives well. This apartment is divine. So, has he always been a classy guy?'

'I don't really know what you mean by that. Greg does love the finer things in life but doesn't judge or ignore those without. He's highly intelligent, worked hard for everything, and respects others who have done the same. He's a bit of an adrenalin junkie, loves to be bold, daring and kinky too.'

'He seems perfect,' Megan said, quite near drooling at Kara's description.

'No one is perfect, Megan, but he is a very genuine, rare and special man.'

'How did you two first meet? The way Greg told me, from what I remember, it sounded like you were sweethearts as kids.'

'Sort of. We were each other's first kiss, at our end-of-year social, back when we were 12 years old. We were in the same Grade 7 class at school, and I had a major crush on him from a distance for the whole year.'

'After he kissed you, you were his first girlfriend then?' Megan asked with the escalated interest of a gossip columnist.

'Completely the opposite, Megan!' Kara laughed. 'I was actually the one who kissed him, in the flickering last moments before our parents collected us. We'd never spoken and didn't ever say a word after that kiss for years after that. I later discovered he'd looked for me for years, however we only truly spoke and connected a few years ago.'

'My God, Kara, that's given me goose bumps! It's so romantic. So, what about his fiancée? Can you tell me more about her? The Tess lady who was killed. Did you know her?'

'No. I didn't ever meet her. If I may say, Megan, it's probably best if I leave questions about Tess for Greg to answer.'

'Oh, I understand. Yes, of course, you're probably right.'

'Alright now, it's your turn, Megan. Time to tell me all there is to know about how you and Michael first met? I bet that's a lovely story?'

For the next couple of hours Kara listened to the story of Megan's courtship that was near lifted from a sweet 'pretty in pink' high school textbook, flirting through university bars and work until she and Michael eventually arrived years later at the little Uniting Church in Stirling.

The combination of bourbon, bath, wine, along with her long recount of her love story, and the tears of regret after these turbulent days, was enough for Megan to need the extra comfort of bed, soon after she and Kara finished dinner.

By the time Greg's ring tone sounded just before 9.30 p.m., Megan was asleep. The day had tucked her in safely away from her hassles at home.

Kara answered and heaved a sigh. 'Hi, Superman. How did it go? You must be exhausted after such a long day.'

'I think you are the one who must be bombed. What happened today? Is Megan still there?' He asked, clearly still worried about the whole situation.

'Yes, she's actually in bed already. In the guest room. I just kept her busy for most of the day, so everything's fine. Tell me about the Festival. How did the opening go?'

'It was brilliant. The media guys did an amazing job with the film segments and the red-carpet idea I had for the producers, worked like a charm. We've exceeded our expected attendance numbers already, so all of it, is going perfectly so far. Actually, already one film distribution company director has approached me about possibly managing a film debut event in Sydney next year. I've left the dinner early though, you're right—it's been a long day.'

'Greg, that is so wonderful to hear. Well done you! I'm so pleased. You've put in so many months of work for this, I was just a bit worried about you needing to respond to any glitches on the back of last night's little drama and no sleep!'

'Kara, you know me. I'll push through anything.'

'I do. I knew you'd leave the home box behind and jump into the work mode the second you arrived at the airport. Once in that zone, there is no stopping you, Mr Sheppard!'

'You know me nearly too well, Ms Gilbert!' he laughed. 'But hey, what do we do about our guest?'

'As you said, let's let her have a few days here and wait and see. I will suggest she reaches out with at least a simple message to her husband to start them talking, and perhaps we wait until you're home, before suggesting much more. You know, quite a few times today were spent discussing you. Megan asked me lots of questions.'

'I bet she did! Our story is unique, as you know!'

Kara chuckled. 'Yes Of course! It's very kinky cosmopolitan, especially recently!'

'Did she ask more about us swinging?'

'No, not really. She wanted to know lots more about you, Tess, and how I came to be here, more than anything.'

'What did you tell her?'

'Not much. Just the basics. I didn't want to say too much. I don't really know her enough to trust her with all of our stories.'

'Good thinking. Kara, you've done a great job today—I hope you're enjoying a well-deserved wine.'

'I am, I'm heading to bed. Have you got one in hand?'

'Yes, I have. I'm actually in my favourite position as a matter of fact,' Greg replied, a little smugly.

'Naked on your bed with a full-bodied red close at hand and searching for a nice little bedtime video?'

'You really do know me too well,' he laughed.

'Perhaps I could tell you a bedtime story instead?'

'I'd love that Kara. What do you have in mind?'

'I don't think I've ever told you about my other ménage à trois fantasy? '

'No, you haven't. Hang on, let me get comfortable.'

Kara waited for a moment and then said, 'Are you all comfy there? This might take a little while.'

'All good. Let me have it.'

Kara started picturing the delicious scene that was already making her naked pussy glisten as she found the words to share.

'I have been fantasising about experiencing an 'Eiffel Tower' with you and another man. It starts with me undressing you both.'

'An Eiffel Tower?' Greg had not heard the expression.

'Yes. It's where I'm on all fours and sucking a guy's cock, while you are fucking me from behind at the same time. When you both high five above me between you—that's supposed to look like the Eiffel Tower!'

'Really. Wow. Two guys? Sounds interesting.'

'This is how it might go… A guy we've casually invited to join us, let's call him Andrew, arrives and as we all enjoy a beer and chat, I move to sit between you both on the lounge. I casually unbutton his shirt and pull it wide open, then I sit back, with one hand scrolling gently from his neck down over his chest and stomach down to the button of his shorts, and up again. I do this, while we finish our drinks. I turn and kiss you, run my hand up over your flesh beneath your shirt and whisper, "Watch it all. Don't take your eyes off me." I lean forward, put down my beer on the coffee table, I remove my dress, swiftly moving to kneel up snug between his legs. As my hands circle across his chest, they slide down to unzip his shorts to reveal the thickening of his cock against his boxers. As his head tips back into the lounge, you come behind me and adeptly unclip and remove my bra, letting my awoken nipples join my hands in caressing up and over his chest. Your fingers are running up and down my back. I can feel you getting harder and harder as you press closer in behind me. You watch as my hand rubs him over his jocks, you can see his knob now protruding and searching hard for more.

'You just got harder Greg, didn't you?'

Greg, now forsaking his wine, held his phone close, listening intently, his fingers of his right hand now gripped firmly at the base and starting to slide.

'Yes. I'm stroking already. Don't stop.'

'You shed your shorts and jocks in a blink, as I remove his, and you move to again press firmly into my back, allowing me to feel you, warm and hard against my body, sandwiching me between the two of you, both wanting more. I reach my hand behind me to take one of yours. I guide your arm around me, leading the tip of your finger to follow mine, to trace softly over the eye of his knob. You can feel the silky first drop of his urgent wanting. I can feel you trembling now. Andrew leans forward and kisses me, and near swallows me. You are both ready.

'We are all in the bedroom now. He's standing in front of me, sucking on each of my breasts with desperate thirst. He moves to slide his tongue down my throat, but I push him backwards down onto the bed firmly with my right hand, reaching for yours and pulling you close behind me with the other. I clamber onto the bed fast, to kneel between his knees, still leading you with me.

'"Stay close," I say, "I need you right here. I want you to see every mouthful. Fill me as you watch me suck him, Mr Sheppard."

'I take him between my lips and wait until I feel the first press of your knob enter me, from behind, poised to just an inch inside me. As you grip my hips, I can nearly feel your cheeks clenching, suspending yourself, waiting until I suck. His groan triggered you to thrust, deep to your hilt inside me, my mouth swallowing him to his base, together all in one motion.

'Hold on, watch as I suck him, you will hear him. Can you see me Greg? Watch me. I can feel his cum rising… you will know when you need to fill me.

'We are both coming *now*, Greg…' Kara called out into the phone.

Greg had exploded violently at the other end of the phone. His moan was near deafening, mirrored only by Kara's cry as her story was overtaken by the orgasmic pulsing, she'd finally allowed her fingers to bring.

It was quite some minutes before Greg eventually breathed out, 'Kara, you were right. This has been a big day. Monumental, in fact. I've near blown all over the bed.'

'I hope we didn't wake Megan. Or everyone at your hotel, but I hope you liked the little tour to my Eiffel Tower!' giggled Kara.

Their little laughs at each end of the phone said it all.

'That was amazing, Kara. Thank you so much. I think it's time for sleep, we both have another big day tomorrow.'

'Yes, you certainly have a big day Greg, I'm hoping for a quiet day with our guest here!' she yawned.

'Goodnight, sexy.'

'Goodnight, Greg. Sweet dreams.'

Chapter 26

The blur of her waking vision disappeared as soon as she saw the time on her bedside clock. It was after 10.00 a.m. The smile crept over her face, enjoying a rare Sunday morning sleep-in. Kara uncurled herself, rolled over and lay there outstretched, delighting in the memory of her bedtime story for Greg. She wriggled as the horny little shivers awoke too.

Her fingers twitched. *Maybe I can start the day with a little rub and glow!* As she roamed her hands over her body, she heard the footsteps down the hallway. *Megan! Hell, how could you forget? You must have slept well. You'd better get up, woman.*

In the absence of PJ's, forsaken years ago, Kara scrambled through the drawers to find her trackpants and a T-shirt, giggling at her thoughts. *Perhaps I should have one nightshirt? Usually if Greg and I have had guests here, they're already naked and often in bed with us too!*

She headed out to greet Megan, who was circling the kitchen, clearly doing the cupboard shuffle in search of gear for breakfast.

'Good morning, Megan, the mugs are in the top left,' she said warmly. 'What can I get you for breakfast?'

'Hi Kara, sorry. Thanks. I forgot where they were, but I can handle the coffee machine. Shall I make us pancakes?' she offered.

'That sounds great, let's make breakfast together.' Kara synced a playlist to the speaker to have some lazy weekend tunes to cook by.

It was the best beginning for two women thrown together. A recipe of daggy clothes, flipping batter, hot coffee, and gentle banter that made the day easy for them.

By early afternoon, they had each learned so much more about their lives as kids, professions, girlfriends and milestones, peppered between jokes and observations.

'Come on, Megan, let's get moving. Feel like coming for a walk?' Kara said. 'We shouldn't just talk and eat all day, no matter how tempting!'

'Yes. You're right. I would've been to the gym three times by now. I'll just go find my shoes,' Megan said, enthusiastically.

After about a kilometre of striding along, Megan asked more about Greg and her.

'How long have you been living with Greg?'

'Not long at all. Only since I moved to the city. I used to live in the Clare Valley.'

'Oh, okay. What did you do in Clare?' Kara could tell Megan was aching to ask more about her and Greg's relationship, but thankfully had stopped short of probing. For now.

The next conversation focussed on Kara's hometown of Clare and her family, when after a time Megan asked, 'Kara, if you don't mind, telling me, but what sort of people does Greg like most?'

As they paced along, Kara thought hard before answering. Something about Megan's many questions about Greg, more than her current estrangement from Michael and home, made Kara a little uneasy. She cautioned herself, and moulded her replied as openly as she could, formed by a hint of alarm bells buzzing beneath the surface.

'When it comes to people, he gets along with anyone, from kids to older people. It's fair to say he can stand in other's shoes, consider their perspective, and always looks for the best in them.'

'Does he ever get angry?' asked Megan.

Kara thought this was rather strange, but replied, 'No, not angry. Sure, he gets frustrated and pissed off like we all do;

however, I haven't heard him lose his cool with anyone. Not ever. He's a bit self-sacrificing, in that he will rarely say "no" to anyone or anything, even when he doesn't want to do something, but that's his unselfish nature. I can say that he has little time for lazy or self-absorbed people, that's for sure.'

'I see.' Megan thought a little more before asking, 'so do you think you and Greg will get married one day?'

Kara stopped and looked at Megan, trying to hide the first words that rushed with aghast into her mouth.

She drew in a breath. 'Actually, Megan if you think about it, as lovers who like to explore our fantasies, we already have a very different kind of relationship. I don't expect you to fully understand. The best thing I can say is that both Greg and I have arrived at a place where marriage is not really something either of us consider or are likely to ever contemplate again. The only thing I can say is that I think everyone has a forever friend born for their time, for whom you each catch and hold an innate vibrating connection. Someone who fits and protects you and your happiness like a glove. Greg and I are more like that. We want and are committed to what's best for each other—whether we're together or apart.'

Megan just listened and looked at her. Kara could see that this wasn't what was expected or understood. It was time to change direction for home, and the conversation.

'Megan, I'd love to know more too. Tell me what Michael is really like?'

Megan halted for a split second before answering. 'Hmm, Michael is steady as a rock, and perhaps more the Tortoise than Hare. He's always been a bit shy but appears very confident at the same time. He's one of those sensible, smart hardworking men really, who's a high achiever, but doesn't put himself out there, if that makes sense? Michael is always trying to do the right thing and is a bit of a worrier.'

'It sounds like he's quite a good man, Megan. I just wonder, if you say he gets worried, do you think it might be a good idea to contact him, just to touch base? He hasn't heard from you since you left.'

'You're probably right. But I just don't want to speak with him right now.'

'I get that completely. To keep my ex at a distance to stop his imagination and anger getting out of control, when I couldn't dare speak or face him, I sent him very simple text messages.'

'What would you send?' asked Megan.

'Just something very short and simple like "I know you're upset. I'm not ready to talk right now. Will be in touch."'

'That's a good idea. I might send one tomorrow. Then he's had the weekend to calm down.'

Kara just nodded and smiled in reply, but inside, something jangled.

By their return to the unit Kara had steered the chat to them, opting for the best afternoon and evening plans, and so movie titles led them home. For the most part, both women had a much needed, relaxing day.

The first three quick knocks at the door were deliberate, firm and businesslike. The next were hard, faster and sharply commanding.

Kara jumped, so startled by the sudden intrusion into her finally quiet end to this weekend, that her wine spilt on the magazine in front of her.

'Damn it!' she said out loud as she jumped off the kitchen stool and grabbed for a cloth to mop up the mess.

Who on earth is this impatient on a Sunday evening? I was so ready for a peaceful night in after all the events of last two days.

As Kara approached the front door, the third round of door banging hit. This was sheer impatience, now forceful and nearly frightening. Accompanied by a voice, 'I want to see my wife!' It was demanding and angry.

Megan had jolted upright from the lounge to the sound of the thumping and stood, suspended in her tracks and trembling in the middle of the living room.

Instantly petrified, she was mouthing, 'No! No!' her head shaking side to side, before looking around, clearly as if desperate to find a place to hide.

Kara called out loudly toward the front door, 'Hold on, I'll be there in a minute.' The knocking stopped, but she could hear the loud fall of footsteps pacing the tiles of the entrance porch. Kara didn't need to look through the peephole. She knew it was Michael.

Kara moved quickly to Megan. She whispered, 'Quickly, get into Greg's bedroom. His ensuite. Lock the door. Stay there and be very quiet. Let me handle this.'

Kara waited to hear the sound of the bathroom door locking. She walked and shut Greg's bedroom door firmly and turning; she wrapped her robe around her body and pulled its cord tightly around her waist before marching to the door. She drew in a breath and opened it briskly, braced and steadied for the imminent battle and the gale force greeting that followed.

'Sheppard, I know she's here and I want to see her now!' The blustering raging red of Michael's face, shaded to crimson, startled at the sight of Kara. 'Oh, I'm looking for a Mr Greg Sheppard.'

'I'm Kara Gilbert. You must be Michael,' she said, extending her hand. 'Yes, this is Greg's and my residence, but Greg is not here right now. I take it you are looking for Megan?'

Michael's thoughts were instantly scrambling. *Kara. She is a real person. What should I say? Did he say he was married? No, friends, wasn't it? Regardless, he has his own woman—If he's not here, where is Megan? I bet she's with him.*

He ignored her outstretched hand and stepped closer toward the door, urgently looking past Kara to see if anyone else was inside. 'Yes, I am, and I want to talk to Greg Sheppard now. I'm not leaving until I speak to him.'

Kara stepped across to shield his view, standing firmly in the doorway. She spoke slowly and gently, using her best calm, considerate—but underlying 'don't dare mess with me' tone.

'Michael, as I said, this is Greg's and my place. Greg's not here, he's away on business this week.'

'You know that he's having an affair with my wife and has invited her away with him. He's probably fucking her right now behind both our backs!' The words spat out at her like vinegar.

Kara braced and replied, 'Actually, Michael, Greg has told me all about how he and Megan met and connected. Greg and I have an open relationship. Megan reached out to him. And as he has already told you, he had no idea that she was married. Neither of us did. Please understand that we have both become just friends of Megan's. She did come here last night, quite distraught—as I can see you are now too.'

Michael just stared at her and took a step back. *What?*

Kara could see she'd quelled the raging storm of anger and hurt at her doorstep. Now that he was more startled by confusion, she was confident he wouldn't lash out at her or burst in; she softened her tone.

'I understand what you are feeling. I really do. It is not my or Greg's place to interfere between you and your wife, but I know Megan is not ready or able to talk now. The two of you do have things to work through, and both Greg and I are encouraging her to do that. She'll definitely see you, when she's ready. But now is not the time. Especially not for either of you, when I can see you're both in such a heated and emotional state. Please give yourselves some time and a little space for now. She is safe here.'

Michael looked at Kara, now with focus for the first time. 'I'm so sorry, Ms Gilbert.'

'Call me Kara, please.'

'Of, course, Kara. Thanks. I must apologise for landing here like this. It's just…'

'I understand. No apologies. Relationships are tough. But I really must ask you to leave now and please not to come back, unless Megan invites you. I hope you understand.'

'Yes, okay.' Michael turned to leave. He stopped and turned back with a parting comment, 'Kara, please… Um, tell her that her children and I miss her, and I'm sorry.'

'I will. Goodbye Michael.' With that, Kara shut the door firmly and flicked the lock.

Kara kept hold of the front door handle, leant back against the door, her chest heaving in and out, trying to dispel the aftermath of the potential attack that somehow, she'd just shielded Megan and herself from.

Megan on hearing Michael's voice, so angry in the first moments after Kara opened the door, she had collapsed into a huddled ball on the floor, cramming herself between the shower screen and the wall in Greg's bathroom. Her hands were still folded over her head as Kara walked in.

'Megan, Megan… it's alright. He's gone now.' It was all Kara could say at the sight of her. She'd been reduced to a shivering, cowering, tear-stained mess.

Kara reached out her hand. Megan took it and slowly rose to her feet. 'He was so angry. What have I done? What if he comes back? I don't know what to do?'

'You don't need to do or think anything right now. He won't be back without contacting you first, I'm sure. He's just as upset and confused as you are now. Guys just show it differently. He's sorry and misses you. He asked me to tell you that.'

'Really?'

'Yes, really.'

Megan's eyes turned to hers. 'Kara, thank you so much. I'm so sorry. You shouldn't have had to deal with all of this. I've created such a mess for you and Greg.' It was followed by a shuddering wave of tremors that Kara saw rise from her feet, through her whole body.

'Come on, we need to get you warm and stop that shaking,' Kara said with a gentle smile which hid the adrenaline still running through her veins.

Kara took her by the hand and led her to the main bathroom.

'Hot bath first with wine and music, I think. It was always a comfort for me.'

Megan didn't say a word, simply grateful for the comfort of being taken under a wing and not needing to think in that moment.

As Kara ran the bath, Megan undressed slowly.

'You just get in when it's full and try to relax. I'll go grab the speaker and get you a drink. I think we both need something! I'll be back in a moment.'

Megan nodded and let her fingers scroll through the mix of water and bubbles that Kara had running. She climbed in tentatively, her arms guiding her slowly to sit, inch by inch, eventually allowing her body to be engulfed in the comfort the warmth of the water offered.

'I've selected my favourite songs for strong women,' joked Kara as she re-entered the bathroom, with a glass of bourbon and speaker in hand. 'Here you go. Now just listen, sip very slowly and soak.' Kara turned to leave.

'Hey Kara,' Megan called out quietly. Kara turned to see Megan looking up at her, her eyes welling with tears. 'Thank you so much.'

Kara smiled back. 'You just sit back and relax. It will be alright.'

Kara headed back to the kitchen and poured herself a neat bourbon too. That was not the weekend she had anticipated. Friday night had been enough. She just had to ring Greg.

He needed to know.

Moreover, she needed to just hear his voice. She opened her recent call list and just hit his name. He answered straight away.

'Hi gorgeous, tell me, how's it going with our escapee?' he asked lightly, expecting Kara's usual giggles.

'I've just met Michael. A very angry Michael who arrived here thumping on our door.'

'Oh Shit. Kara, are you alright? How did he get the address?' His tone had plummeted to serious in a split second.

'Yes, it's okay, I'm fine. So is Megan. Well, she's pretty shaken up, so I've put her in the bath with bourbon and some tunes and I'll get her sorted. We'll be alright.'

'My God. What did he do? Did he try to hurt either of you?'

'No, thankfully. He was really angry, demanding to see you, and that he "wanted his wife back" right away! I knew instantly it was him, before I opened the door. I made Megan lock herself away in the ensuite. So, I think I shocked him, because he didn't expect me to be the one to open the door, or the fact that I could say I knew about you having met Megan in Sydney.'

'Kara, are you sure you're okay?'

'Greg, I'm fine, but I am sipping a neat bourbon. No! It's alright, really. He was a bit fired up when he landed here. I somehow talked him down. He was much calmer when he left and seemed to accept that he couldn't come back unless Megan invited him. She was a total mess from the second she heard his voice. So, she didn't see him at all. I'll ring work and maybe spend the day with her tomorrow to keep an eye on her.'

'Kara—sounds like you handled it all perfectly. But this so wasn't easy for you. Just hang in there. I'll be back Thursday night. Call me, I want an update every day and call anytime—whenever you need to. For whatever reason. Promise?'

'Yes. I promise. But I'm sure we'll be fine until you get back.' She paused for a moment, then said, 'but I can say I might need a bit of TLC when you get home.'

'You definitely deserve lots of TLC! and more for sure! Kara, as you know, it'll be my pleasure as much as yours,' he added, hoping to end the call on a lighter note.

Kara actually found her laugh. 'You know just how to make me feel better, Mr Sheppard. Go on now! Get to bed and I'll speak to you tomorrow. I'll want to know all about how day two goes. I'd better go and check on her.'

'Okay, off you go. Goodnight beautiful. I'll call you tomorrow. Stay safe. I'm here, remember?'

'Yes, I know you are. You are a sweetheart. We'll be alright. Goodnight Greg.'

Kara took another sip of her drink, before heading back to the bathroom. She knocked gently. 'Everything okay Megan? Can I get you anything?'

'Do you mind if I have another drink please, Kara? I don't usually drink bourbon—but it's actually going down nicely.'

'Sure.' Kara walked in and took the glass from the edge of the bath. Megan was lying back, neck deep in the water, blanketed by the puffed mounds of bubbles floating over her. 'I'll make it a small one, I don't want you falling asleep in there!' Megan offered up a meek smile.

'Actually, Kara, don't worry about the drink. Do you mind keeping me company for a while?'

'No problem. I only stopped trembling when my Aunt came and stayed with me in those first few days.' Kara sighed as she perched herself on the wide marble tiled edge of the bath.

'Was that when you left your husband?'

'Yes. I remember the panic coming in waves. My body would just shake uncontrollably, even if I saw his name on an email or message. It sounds crazy now, but it was very real and scary at the time.'

'Did it take long to stop, before you could see him and speak with him without being so frightened?'

'No. But Megan, Michael is very different to my ex, I think. '

'What do you mean? Will I ever be able to see Michael without feeling like this?'

'Oh Megan, my ex is a long story. He was a narcissist, a bully, a thug, and an abuser who had to have his own way. He wouldn't have knocked on the door, he'd have knocked it off its hinges. You've already told me you've never seen Michael angry like this before, so it'll be alright. Right now, I think he's just as scared as you are.'

'You think? He was so angry, I don't know how you dealt with him so calmly, weren't you afraid?'

'No one enjoys being deceived. They deal better, even with the painful stuff, when they hear it straight. So, getting upset and angry is normal. But today was more about his fear, not mine. He's just scared of losing you. His pride is hurt, and he's even probably angry with himself too for thinking he didn't satisfy your needs enough to prevent you needing to be with someone else.'

'Kara, I'm sorry. I didn't handle this very well.'

'Megan, I can't really comment too much as I don't know Michael or you really at all, but I look at things a bit differently. I think it's neither of your faults, really. We all have different needs as we get older, so I think it's hard for just one person to fill all our needs in life. But you were both wrong, by not talking about the important things. From what you were telling me yesterday, I think perhaps you both should have spoken out. Sex, romance, intimacy and caring for each other are the core of any relationship, yet often couples rarely talk about it. I bet you spoke more about what to eat for dinner!'

'Kara, that's true. We stopped talking years ago. We just talk at and around each other about really mundane things. But I don't know if I ever could have told him I wanted another guy or about my fantasies. He would've been horrified.'

'Maybe. He might have been shocked at first, or he could have been excited by it, and shared what he wanted too. It may have turned out badly, but regardless, I'm sure you both would still be talking though. Lots more, I'd say. It has to be better than not speaking at all. But I've now said too much!'

'No, you haven't, Kara. We've both been making mistakes, all through our marriage, not just these past few years. Thank you. I've got lots to think about.'

'Enough serious stuff, for now Megan. Hey, you must be getting cold in there!'

Megan smiled as she leant forward and turned on the hot tap. 'It's still quite warm. I'll just top it up a little. I need to wash my hair and then I'll get out.'

'Would you like me to wash your hair?' Kara asked.

'I'd love that. You don't mind? My mum used to wash my hair in the bath and would massage my scalp. It was the best feeling.'

'Okay, hold on, I'll be back in a sec.'

As Kara turned and walked out to fetch a jug from the kitchen, Megan watched her leave, with an admiring smile now emerging. *Greg was right. Kara is a lovely person. I can't help but like her.*

Returning, Kara knelt up close next to the bath. With Megan's head tipped back, her neck cradled in one arm, Kara scooped and poured water carefully over her hair with the other, stopping to smooth the water away from her eyes and down back over her head. Her fingers washed over her forehead, gently stroking and wiping, as if soothing a baby's tears.

'Time to sit up a little for shampoo and conditioning.' Kara said.

Megan moved a little further upright as Kara re-positioned herself to sit on the bath's edge. Kara's touch was delicate and rhythmic, rolling her hands and fingers around and down through the strands. Sedated by the caressing lullaby of water, lather, sweet scents and fingers, Megan let out a sigh as her mind calmed and drifted. She was nine again, happy, safe with the sound of her mother, and '*What the world needs now... is love*' humming around her.

'There we go, all finished,' Kara said as she gently gathered up Megan's blonde hair from her back and shoulders into a long swatch between her hands squeezing the last of the water down its length. Kara stood, reaching for the one of the big soft grey bath towels, ready for when she got out.

Megan blinked back into this Sunday night, before slowly easing herself up, reaching for Kara's hand to steady her as she climbed from the tub. As she guided Megan to stand, Kara couldn't help but notice the slim grace and form of her body, firm and toned, yet with gentle Barbie doll-like curves, which exuded softness. Kara smiled to herself. *No wonder Greg wanted her.*

Kara stepped up to face Megan, holding the towel wide in each hand before wrapping it tight around her in one big hug like motion. Kara tucked in the folds over Megan's back, between her shoulder blades, and gave her a little comforting hug. As Kara stepped back, Megan whispered. 'Thank you.'

Kara just looked at her and smiled. 'My pleasure. It's been a couple of rough days. It'll get better. Now you go get into something warm and I think it's a cup of tea before bedtime.'

'Now you really are starting to sound more like my grandma!' teased Megan.

They both laughed, each grateful that this day was ending, rekindled to the lightness of its morning. They had survived the storm.

Chapter 27

Monday came with Kara rising first, having arranged to take two days off work to be with Megan. The two of them then spent breakfast time working out a plan for each day: a mix of the tough stuff and treats to help Megan feel more settled and together, before diving into any other major decisions.

'As Greg said before he left, you're welcome to stay this week to get yourself, and things at home, calm and sorted. My Aunt used to encourage me to organise every day to do the tough essential stuff or something I didn't want to do, and then make sure I had something I enjoyed or nice afterwards,' Kara said.

'The worst first?' asked Megan.

'Yes. But I like to flip it around to think of it as *saving the best until last*,' she giggled. 'It's like how Greg always eats his meal.'

'Does he really?' asked Megan.

'Yes, he believes I think it's silly because I tease him, but don't tell him, it's actually how I eat too. So, let's get started in Greg style shall we?'

Over the next two days Kara stayed close by, to be the listening ear and shoulder, a few moments of tears while Megan tackled the harder emotional stuff first each day. She'd messaged Michael, spoken with each of her children and to her own mum too. That call was nearly the toughest. She rose early Tuesday morning to head to meet with her boss before her colleagues arrived. She'd been very understanding, giving Megan a few days off and the ability to recommence work remotely, without the need to venture into the office. When Megan returned, Kara could finally see some of the more relaxed, confident woman whom Greg first described having met in Sydney.

By Tuesday afternoon, seated side by side in the rumbling massage chairs choosing shellac colours for their toes in the nail salon, the two of them chatted constantly. They'd found real company and a warm, genuine rhythm in each other. By the time Wednesday morning arrived they'd become real friends.

Kara welcomed the return to work, and some sense of 'normal', having felt like a being on a roller coaster since last Friday night.

'Megan, I'll probably be back here around 6.00 p.m.; I'll grab some groceries on my way home. Are you going to be right here on your own today?' asked Kara as she scrambled together her briefcase, phone and keys.

'Absolutely, I'll be fine. I think I'll actually do some work too. Is it alright if I set up my laptop on the dining table?'

'Of course. I'll see you tonight. Don't work too hard. Maybe you can find us a good movie to watch this evening, we still need something nice to "eat last" remember! Bye.' Kara's voiced trailed out of the door.

It was well after 6.00 p.m. when Kara landed back, lumbering through the door laden with bags. Megan was laying on the couch, feet up, going through her social media on her phone.

'Hi there, roomie!' Kara said, trying to sound bright, after what turned out to be an exhausting day. Megan jumped up to help her with the groceries, taking half the shopping bags, and carried them to the kitchen bench.

'How was your day?' Megan asked.

'It wasn't too bad, just exhausting. Things were a bit more demanding than I expected,' Kara replied, still not able to find her smile.

'Well, let's get this stuff put away, and you can put your feet up for a bit,' Megan said with upbeat confidence in her voice.

The two girls put the groceries away in no time, Megan loading the fridge and Kara filling the pantry. 'Phew! I'm going to get changed,' Kara said as she headed for her room.

'Can I get you a drink?' called out Megan from the kitchen.

'Yes please, a wine of any kind would be great,' Kara replied sliding out of her black pencil skirt. She unbuttoned her sheer blouse and bandeau top. As she was about to put on her bra, she stopped.

A bra really? Why on earth! It's just us girls.

Tossing the bra on the bed, she popped on her tracksuit pants and her old sloppy high school windcheater. It was thin, faded and barely holding together, but a soft comfy favourite, nonetheless.

Kara made a beeline straight for the couch and was greeted in perfect timing by Megan with a glass of red wine.

'Cheers,' Kara said as they chinked their glasses and Megan plonked down on the couch next to her.

After a quiet minute, both enjoying their first sips, Megan asked, 'Was Greg coming home tonight or tomorrow? Sorry I've forgotten.'

'No, not tonight. The festival finishes after the gala dinner. He'll manage the wind up of the venue in the morning and be home tomorrow night,' Kara replied.

They both sipped on their wine and chatted more about their respective days. 'I surprised myself and actually worked most of the day,' Megan said. 'Once I started reading emails and started checking the property sale reports, I just kept going. Sorry Kara, you look exhausted, what shall we do for dinner? Maybe takeaway? Something easy.'

Kara thought for a moment. 'How about we make a huge lasagne, and then we can freeze most of it for any other time that we don't feel like cooking?'

'That might be every night for the rest of the week!' Megan said with a grin.

The wine blended with each other's company, instantly helped them find relaxed and light moods once more.

Kara stood and reached out a hand to Megan, helping her to her feet and said, 'If you're happy to chop, I'll cook the mince and throw it all together.'

'Let's do it!' Megan replied.

Megan watched as Kara assembled the ingredients, it was such a mixed array.

'It's not your normal lasagne,' laughed Kara on seeing the little perplexed frown. 'I just make it as it goes depending on what's in the fridge.'

Kara handed Megan two onions, a carrot, capsicum and a handful of mushrooms for her to chop. Kara manned the hotplates, heating the frying pan with oil ready for the mince. Megan had been quiet as if deep in thought while she peeled, chopped and diced the vegetables standing at the island bench on the other side of the kitchen. They were working without words for a long time, before Megan's reflections were revealed.

'What we did the other night with Greg, was quite a turn on for me, you know,' she said with a slight quiver of embarrassment.

'It sure was,' Kara replied, a gentle smile appearing on her face as she remembered Megan responding to her touch. 'Hopefully we can do it again,' she added, still watching the pan with her back to Megan.

'Can I be honest, Kara?'

'Of course,' Kara said, now looking at Megan over her shoulder.

'I can't believe how much I enjoyed kissing you, no whiskers, and beautiful soft lips,' Megan said, starting to feel a long way out of her comfort zone. But she had to know.

'But Kara...' She now gulped, 'Does that make me a lesbian deep down, you think?'

Kara let out a small chuckle. 'Of course not. As much as I love kissing Greg, there is nothing as soft and sensual as kissing another woman. And he loves it too. He gets so aroused and lots of pleasure from watching. Most men do, let's be honest. Both of us love seeing each other give and receive. It makes us both happy. But it's more than that, as I've said before. There is a term for it. It's something called "compersion" where you get as much thrill and even stronger connection from sharing in sex with others. For me, it's nearly like having sex "through" him and "with him" all at the same time,' Kara said.

'I'm beginning to understand,' Megan said. 'As you say, it is a very different way of thinking.' Megan paused before continuing, 'You and Greg really have it all sorted, don't you.' It was more of a statement than a question, as she turned back to finish chopping the last of the veggies.

'That we do! It is just perfect. No jealousy, no demands, we're just great friends and love sharing unencumbered, unlimited and adventurous sex. You know, even if we have sex with others on our own, we now share every detail.'

It fell quiet again in the kitchen. *Kara, you've overstepped and said too much again, I think.*

She jumped, startled by a touch. Kara hadn't seen or sensed Megan standing there, until she felt her arms wrap tightly around her.

Megan hugged her from behind, her chin resting on her shoulder. 'Thank you so much for letting me stay here and see a little part of your amazing lives,' she murmured into Kara's ear.

Kara put down the wooden spoon, motioning her body around. Megan released her grip, allowing Kara to turn to face her.

'You are a darling. It's been our pleasure to have you here,' Kara said softly, raising her hands to her shoulders. She leaned forward to give Megan a light kiss on the lips. Megan's hands moved from Kara's waist, gliding up over her shoulders, reaching forward and around to cradle her neck, drawing her body closer. Megan's mouth and lips pressing even deeper into her.

Kara had only intended it to be a tender, small peck of a kiss, more a 'thank you' than desire. Megan clearly had other thoughts and feelings swelling. Kara responded accordingly with each sharing their tongues and bodies, all rolling and rubbing around, against each other.

Kara pulled back and away a little. She had to take a breath, not from the passion or kiss, but more the surprise caught in her throat.

Eventually she spoke. 'Megan, let's maybe take this up later, shall we? Or our dinner will burn.' Kara kissed her again, with a feather touch of her lips before turning her attention back to the sizzling pan on the stovetop.

'I'm sorry Kara, I didn't mean for that to happen,' Megan said, making her way back to the other side of the bench.

'Well, I'm glad it did. You made my nipples hard and my pussy wet. Look at this!' replied Kara as she pushed the material of her windcheater tight against her to show her nipples poking firmly erect against the fabric.

Megan just laughed, still with a slight blush in her cheeks. She pushed the sliced vegetables across the bench for her. 'We need to get this finished or we'll be eating at midnight!'

'You are so right!' Kara said, quickly busying herself to assemble the lasagne. Kara pushed the bechamel sauce ingredients over to Megan with a small frying pan, asking if she could melt the butter and mix the rest in, 'I'll talk you through it,' she said.

The two girls stood side by side at the stove top as each did their part of the process. More and more thoughts were sifting and brewing inside them both. Each wondering what the other was thinking, all the while as their hips continued to bump, graze and rub as they cooked.

Kara grabbed a little spoon and took a sample of Megan's sauce. 'It's delicious Megan. Here, taste,' as she took another spoon tip of the silky white sauce and raised it to Megan's lips.

'That is yum, even if I say so myself!' Megan said.

Kara kissed her cheek. 'It's perfect.'

As Kara returned to her pan Megan looked up and around, scanning the kitchen, Kara and her surroundings, as if for the first time. *My God, how my life has changed in just the last few months, most dramatically in these couple of days. I've gone from being a faithful wife and mother to fucking other men and now women for a start!*

Megan also knew she missed her kids a lot, and Michael too. She knew this was only temporary until she could clearly decide and sort through what she needed, and wanted to do. *But I'm not jumping anywhere, 'till I'm really sure. I'm going to make sure I enjoy every minute, while I can too.*

It wasn't long before Kara slid the large dish full of their efforts into the oven. She washed her hands as she turned to Megan, 'We have an hour, what shall we do?' Kara stepped a little closer, and said, 'Would you like to pick up from where we were?'

'Yes, I would like that... but...' She stopped, dropping her chin as her cheeks flushed crimson. 'God, I'm all shy now? It was easy when it was spontaneous.'

'If it makes you feel any better, you need to know I've never been with a woman on her own before either.'

'Really?' replied Megan, looking up sharply, completely surprised. 'I just assumed...'

'Nope. Never on my own. So, I'm a novice in this space as well.'

'I'm not really sure what to do,' Megan whispered, her eyes now wide as she stepped closer, looking directly into Kara's eyes.

'Well, how hard can it be?' Kara said as she mirrored Megan's steps forward. She reached out, gripping the base of Megan's top, and looked at her. She would not make another move without permission.

There was no hesitation.

Megan's smile and consenting nod gave the answer in full. Kara carefully lifted Megan's top over her head, letting it drop silently to the floor. Megan's nipples were already erect as Kara leant forward to take one in her mouth and taste. Kara had moved to hold her in a half embrace, with one hand behind her back feeling Megan melt back to luxuriate against it.

Kara rose her head to Megan's ear. 'Come to my room.'

With a nod, they each grabbed their wine and were in Kara's room within a few seconds.

They placed the glasses on the dressing table without a second thought. Their desire to sip was now heightened only to each other in that moment. It was near involuntary and yet understood as they undressed each other at a suspended, seductive pace. Not until they were both fully naked, standing in front of each other, having the pause of scanning and absorbing the full appreciation of each other's bodies, did Kara pull Megan onto the bed. Their embrace and kisses were tentatively passionate. All four hands caressed, every fingertip touch savouring the softness and feeling of each other's delicate feminine bodies. Kara was the first to let her fingers find Megan's pussy, the tip of her index circling and sliding over and around her clitoris as she felt Megan sliding and disappear into the next realm.

She was sucking on Megan's earlobe at the same time. 'Let me taste more of you.'

Kara barely waited for the breathlessly moaned consent before she slid off the bed, standing at its foot, and took both of Megan's legs in her hands by the ankles, pulling her to the bed's end in near one motion. Megan lay there, her legs spread, twitching in anticipation, with Kara kneeling between them.

Kara could see how wet Megan was, and could feel her desire, like electric static cling drawing her own skin and touch to every part of her body. Kara kissed her inner thigh, glancing only for a split second at the clock at their bedside. *Damn! Only thirty minutes before the oven calls. Time flies when you're having sex,* she thought to herself.

She gently placed her tongue on Megan's protruding clit, now begging and searching for touch. Kara licked her wanting clit with her tongue, tracing a path from top to bottom, then side to side. She could feel the suspense between her lips and on her fingertips, now pressed inside her. Kara pushed her tongue deep into her vagina, as far as she could, knowing it would be now that Megan would be desperate for a hard cock to fill her. Megan started to arch her hips as Kara heard the moaning start. It got louder as the arching of her back became more pronounced. Megan almost screamed as her orgasm hit. Kara sucked firmer, drawing her clit into her mouth as Megan's body shuddered and shook below her. With precision timing Kara slowly released the suction from her mouth trying to match Megan's return from her elevated climax.

It wasn't long before Megan sat up and said, 'Wow, that was amazing. You are so good at that. Okay, it's your turn, babe,' Megan said, her hand beckoning Kara to lay next to her.

Megan kissed Kara again on the mouth, still as soft and tentative as before, but this time it tasted different. Flavoured not only with her own juices, but confidence and wanting. All applied with the fervent pressure of her lips and tongue. With a hint of apprehensive 'now or never', Megan's fingers suddenly moved quickly well inside Kara's pussy, finding her G spot effortlessly. Megan's mouth had moved to take a mouthful of Kara's right breast. She started to suck hard and bite on her nipple, the tender pain radiated and lubricating straight between Kara's legs. Kara was there. Her orgasm arriving, nearly unheralded in seconds, as she too yelled out in a cry of pure ecstasy. Megan held her fingers in place as she too rode the wave with Kara. She felt, for the first time, the involuntary 'after clenching' pulse of Kara's pussy twitching against them.

As Kara's breathing subsided Megan asked, 'Will you let my fingers play with you a little more during dinner?'

'Yes, sure,' was all she could muster in reply, slowly recoiling as Megan's soaked fingers slid from inside her. Kara looked at the clock and decided to lay there a couple of minutes more. Megan cuddled up to Kara with her arm across her breast. 'Wait till Greg hears about this!' Kara said.

'Will you tell him?'

'Of course, he will love it!' Kara said now looking at the woman she had just made love to.

'Come on, you gorgeous thing, let's have dinner,' Kara said sitting up.

They each reached for their clothes. Megan picked up Kara's windcheater and said, 'Can I wear this so I can continue to smell you?'

'Of course,' Kara said, leaning over to kiss her softly on her lips. Their eyes were locked as they moved apart, enough was said in that moment. Kara broke the stare and headed for the kitchen.

Dinner was easy, shared in the lounge in front of television, with them chatting as if the past hour had been uneventful, but inside each of them, the lingering recollection of those sixty minutes and the feelings rumbled. Despite the superficial external veneer of the casual words, even the fact they were cuddled and wrapped around each other on the couch, spoke volumes. By 10.00 p.m. Kara had yawned for the third time, dragging herself from the couch.

'Megan, I've got to get to bed, dear one. Tomorrow is still a workday for me, and Greg will be home tomorrow night too. So, it's going to be a marathon for sure from start to finish! You need rest too.'

'I've got a pretty easy day though, so I should be fine,' Megan said.

'Megan—I can only warn you once. Greg has been away since Saturday. He's been away from us for the better part of six days,' Kara said with a naughty grin sneaking across her face.

'Hmm, I'm beginning to understand what you mean. It must be past our bedtime then,' she laughed as she leant over Kara to a give her a deep, lingering kiss. 'Goodnight, Kara. I can't thank you enough for these past few days. Tonight especially.' She turned and headed to her bedroom.

Kara and Greg only exchanged a couple of brief text messages that night, given Greg had the Gala Dinner and an early start tomorrow morning.

Hi sexy, how's it going? Hope you and Megan had a good day. All's well. Dinner tonight and still on track for home tomorrow on time. G x

Hi G. All fine here thankfully.
Actually, quite nice evening here. Megan has turned out to be most surprising. Sleep well. We have lots to share with you when you get home. I mean lots! Sleep on the plane if you can—preserve those powers! Miss you.
Until tomorrow, Kara x

Chapter 28

The festival was officially over and the 'roadies', for want of a better word, were flat out pulling the place apart. As the venue for the event was only across the road from his hotel, Greg had dashed back for a shower and a change of clothes. Amid the mayhem that usually came with the last night of any event and its pending strike, he'd somehow managed to find a minute to send Kara a quick message to let her know everything had gone well and was on track to be home tomorrow evening in time for dinner. Greg was pleased Kara had messaged back to say things were now fine after the turbulent few days she'd had to cope with, and that Megan was turning out to be quite a surprise package.

He couldn't wait to hear about *that* story.

Greg found his table for the gala dinner, which was about to get under way.

Accepting a beer from the waiter and taking a moment to take in all that had just happened, he reflected on how particularly good his life really was at the moment, knowing full well, how disaster can strike at any time, as it had done before. He thought of Tess and what could have been.

He closed his eyes and again allowed himself a second to picture that beautiful face. A small pain touched his heart, feeling the moisture forming in the corner of his eyes.

Thankfully, Steve, his second-in-command arrived, pulled out the seat next to him and planted himself down firmly at Greg's side.

Steve was an extravert: a bold, loud, boisterous personality who didn't muck around with his words, totally oblivious, caring not a scrap about how much noise he made. He was nowhere as fit as Greg, despite being younger by a few years, but was strong, and handy to have around. He wore his developing beer gut with a swaggering pride and presence. He signalled to the waiter to bring him the same as what Greg was drinking.

'You looked like you were in another place there, mate,' Steve said as a cold Belgium beer arrived in front of him.

'Yeah, I'm just really happy with how it all went here this week, and the great job you and the team did, Steve.'

'Thanks Greg, a great job by yourself as well,' Steve said, drinking almost half of the bottle in one mouthful.

'Cheers,' Greg said as he held up his beer before taking another swig.

'God, you are one lucky son of a bitch you know,' Steve said after a moment of reflection.

'Why is that?'

'Well, you have a successful business, which I guess can be a little stressful, but it sure is a lot of fun and I'm sure you make a few bucks as well.'

'You know what, Steve? The harder I work, the luckier I get, but don't be fooled, it always looks rosy from the other side of the fence.'

'Never a truer statement said,' cheered Steve as he took another mouthful, which finished the bottle.

'And then, there is that amazing relationship you have with Kara. God, that is a one in a million. How on earth do you find a woman who is happy for you to see other women?' said Steve, fighting back a burp.

Greg turned towards him, 'She is special. I'll grant you that. But you know, she is not only okay with it, she encourages it.'

'You are fucking kidding me?' Steve said, placing his head in his hands. 'How is that fucking possible?'

'It's called compersion, it's about her feeling good that I am doing what I enjoy.'

'Fuck, if my wife found me doing what I enjoy, I'd be out on the street!' Steve said loud enough for other people to hear.

'Doesn't she get jealous? What about if *she* sleeps with someone?' Steve said, really trying to take it all in.

'Let me tell you something, Steve. Take this away and have a think about it. If I got jealous, it would mean I didn't love her enough. If I truly loved her, why wouldn't I want her to have everything she wants? If she meets someone, and has an urge to fuck him, I want her to. She would come home and tell me all about it, anyway.'

'I see what ya mean. Fuck me! That's just unbelievable man.' Steve shook his head. 'Why is it, the only woman I'm allowed to fuck, is the only woman who doesn't want to? Can you please talk to my wife?... On second thought, you stay away,' Steve said holding his empty bottle up to the waiter, signalling he wanted a fresh one. Greg smiled back at him and picked up his phone to read a new message.

Chapter 29

The second he walked through the door, both girls' eyes, smiles and hugs effervesced all over him. Their voices nearly overlapping the greetings, which burst to welcome him home. Greg dropped his bags instantly, extended his arms to both of them, kissing each on the lips and cheeks, beaming widely.

'So, I take it you didn't miss me at all?' he asked teasingly.

It elicited the desired response of fake aghast and scolding.

'No, not one bit! We had plenty of fun while you were away,' Kara said, followed by more laughter and warm hugs everywhere.

Kara tossed Megan a loaded wink.

She responded beautifully, 'We're cooking your favourite dinner, Greg. But we have a new dessert we're sure you will love. Kara and I have so enjoyed preparing it together.'

Megan's statement was delivered so seriously that Kara nearly burst inside. Knowing what was on that plate, her words were loaded with so much more than Greg could imagine. Kara raced to the kitchen to smother her aroused laughter. She loved Megan's boldness, and that he hadn't yet caught the innuendo, despite the text she'd sent him last night.

'Megan, how about you pour us all a wine?' Kara was desperately trying to restore an inner cool for both of them, so they could actually reach the dining table and eat.

Plates, glasses and mouthfuls were all brimming with delicious flavours of roasted scotch fillet, duck fat roasted potatoes, broccoli, carrots and creamy peppered sauce. Greg told them all about the festival as they recounted their days, carefully omitting the Michael storm episode. Unspoken, but each of them knew that while it needed more discussion, debrief was not palatable tonight. A big celebratory welcome home, filled with laughter, and delicious, rich full-bodied flavours were the only things on the menu tonight. Girl's orders.

'That was the most incredible meal, ladies,' Greg said, raising his glass high to theirs.

'I have to be the most blessed and envied man on earth! Thank you both so much for spoiling me with an amazing welcome.'

'Thank you, we are so pleased you've enjoyed it so far. Greg, your efforts this past week deserve acknowledgement and celebration,' Kara said with the tone of uniformed heraldry. Then a little softer, 'Just sit there and enjoy your red. Megan and I will clear up a bit and then we'll bring you dessert.'

'Sorry, Kara but shouldn't house rules apply? You both cooked. I should be on clean-up, while you get first "on couch" privileges?' Greg said.

'Doesn't that rule have a caveat? Surely an exemption applies, when we've both been on leave, and you've worked away?'

'Trust you Kara to find the perfect argument. Okay. Here's the negotiated deal. Let me help you clear the table.'

After the scraping, clunking and clicks of plates, cutlery and bowls, condiments and table bling were quieted away into the dishwasher, cupboards and drawers. Greg was the first to land back on the couch.

Greg looked across at Kara and Megan, both still buzzing around in the kitchen. There was a dance in their steps around each other as they worked together, then a shielded shared smile. It was minute, but poignant. They really had connected. His thoughts flashed to Kara's message about Megan being surprising. *Perhaps she was in fact a delicious surprise?* he thought.

A tiny charge flicked on the switch between his legs. Now wondering if dessert could really be a full on, rich delicacy? He realised in that second, that while the main meal was 'Michelin Star' worthy, the dessert might be X-rated and even more of a delicacy! He worked on his best casual, nonchalant appearance outwardly, all the while struggling to contain the excitement filling his imagination and groin as he sat waiting for what they might serve up for the last sweet course tonight.

Kara and Megan knew he'd caught the scent. As they swirled around each other, with a body brush and touch here and there, while putting fruit, whipped cream and chocolate on the serving platter, they were garnishing it for him with their own arousal. It took only one look, and they both winked, their smiles lust-loaded. Holding each end of the plate in their hands, they escorted the dish to the coffee table, resting it down in front of Greg who looked up with a heated grin.

Megan leant down and kissed him. There was anything but glossy veneer in that kiss and the subtle press of her body against him. Full, thickly volumed lips had tasted his and then she pulled back before his lips could respond. He then saw that Kara had watched, without a flicker and with the hint of a smile. *This is different*, he thought as he just stared, following their every move.

Before he could say a word, Kara tapped Megan's arm gently and motioned for her to follow. Megan instantly turned away, following Kara's lead back toward the kitchen.

'Oh Greg, there's one more thing to go with that,' Kara said, again drawing his gaze to them both as they walked away.

Stopping opposite him, only paces away, the two women turned to face each other and let their arms and lips entwine. Fingers touched cheeks, ran through hair and held each other as their lips and tongues pressed harder, passionate and deep. Greg saw them become lost and absorbed as if huddled and invisible beneath a magical cloak, before they eventually released their kiss, and turned to look at him. His eyes were now wide, his lips moist over his grin, as he rose from the couch to stand.

'Stay there. We will bring the rest of dessert to you,' Megan said.

He slipped the button to his jeans open and eased down the fly a little, before sitting back down. He needed more room for his emerging hard on. 'I've already decided this is going to be my favourite dessert,' he said with a smirk as Megan walked over to lay on the lounge on her back, outstretched next to him, positioning her head in his lap.

She gazed up at him, 'No tasting yet. It's not quite ready for you,' she murmured.

Kara had stripped off down to bra and knickers and joined them on the couch, kneeling to face Megan between her legs. She looked directly at Greg.

'I did mention that there *is* lots to tell you. We thought it might be easier to show you,' she giggled.

With that, Kara leant forward and pressed her face gently into Megan's groin, using the tip, blade and underside of her tongue to slide and scroll between, in and over Megan's flesh, vulva and clit, awakening every nerve. Megan's eyes closed as her head pressed back into Greg's lap. He couldn't hold his restraint for a second longer. He near tore open Megan's top to reveal her breasts, his hands reaching for the nipples that were begging for his attention in front of him. He ran his hands up and over her body. Megan's writhing body and startling cries signalled how much she was relishing this dual ended stimulation.

'God. Oh God, I'm loving this,' she panted. 'Oh, don't stop.'

Greg had scooped her up from beneath her shoulders and brought his lips to meet hers. He near swallowed the outcry of 'Fuck' that escaped her, as Kara's tongue and now fingers brought her to a convulsant orgasm.

As Megan lay panting across him, he looked straight at Kara. 'I think maybe it's time for bed,' he said with an exultant grin.

Kara nodded as she and Greg helped Megan rise and move to the other room. None of them gave the platter a second glance.

It took mere seconds for all clothes to hit the floor. Megan lay back against a headboard of pillows with Kara resting on her back between Megan's outstretched legs, her hair spilling over her thighs. Greg was already mountain climbing at pace, ascending kisses, bites and his warmth up over Kara's body from her ankles to her neck, not losing hold of the arousal that had followed from the lounge room. As his body smothered over Kara, he glanced up to see Megan watching intently. She smiled and nodded, clearly engrossed and loving the vision and feel of them both against her.

Greg whispered in Kara's ear, 'She's right with us. You are simply amazing.' He sank his lips into her neck and sucked hard. He waited for the moan he knew would follow before pushing himself hard inside her, her wet ridges of flesh enveloping him with the warmest welcome.

Kara gripped Megan's legs, flanking her as her body thundered against her. The week's pressure gushed from her in uncontrollable squirts. The second her juices flowed, Greg let go, with every groan that escaped him growing louder, with each spasming rush of cum he released deep inside her. His orgasm was so powerful it near penetrated both women.

As they all lay cuddled and stroking, entwined without a care, they spoke, sang to tunes, and melded into an easy three. They didn't finish the final course until all were totally spent hours later.

Unspoken, but it was somewhere during the night, Megan decided she would not be returning home in a hurry.

Chapter 30

It all became clear to Kara and Greg some days later. Kara answered the door to the sight of a young man hidden behind a magnificent arrangement of ruby red roses.

'Delivery for Mrs. Munday.'

'She's not here at the moment, but I can take them. Thank you.'

Obviously, these were from Michael. Apart from the deliberate delivery announced for *'Mrs. Munday'*, Kara recognised in a second purely from the abundance and colour of the striking blooms alone. They were from him, sending a clear message of regret and love for Megan.

It wasn't long before Megan arrived home, instantly exclaiming at the display of flowers. 'My God, what beautiful flowers! Kara, where did these come from?'

'They're for you.'

As Megan read the note, a small smile glimmered briefly, before it was replaced by a bitten lip and creased brow.

'Everything alright?' Kara questioned softly, without any desire to pry.

'He wants me to come home.' Her voice was flat as she slumped into the nearby chair.

'You aren't surprised? What's the matter?' Kara asked.

'It's just that… well… No, I'm not surprised, really. But I'm not sure where I want to be. I've been so happy here with you and Greg, and yet, Michael is a nice man and it's home, but I don't know what to do yet.' While she was rambling in her reply, Kara understood instantly.

'Megan, I can only say it's probably time to meet with him. When you're face to face and start talking, I mean *really* talking, you're likely to have a better idea about what you want and need right now. You don't have to know or make any decisions just yet.'

Megan nodded and found her phone. It was time to go home. At least to *speak* with Michael. Little did Kara or Greg realise; Megan had already decided. She had no intention of returning home. The switch had been flicked.

It had been another turbulent week, as Megan brought home her tumultuous exchanges with Michael, ending with tears and her begging to stay at Greg's for a bit longer. She had explained to Michael that she needed more time, which was understandable. She had not dared tell him the real reason. That life as a wife and mother was boring and predictable. She found him to be unattractive in so many ways. As for the kids—they barely engaged with her since she became the travelling bread-winner, now more connected to Michael and involved with their own friends. Being at Greg's place was fun, sex filled and easy. She felt happy here with him and Kara.

Neither Greg nor Kara could find a reason to refuse, having enjoyed how easily she had connected and slipped into their lives.

Within a week after bringing more of her personal things to Greg's, she really settled in.

By the time three more weeks passed, Megan had moved in completely.

The three felt a connection, simply satisfying like a secluded beach walk and a haystack romp melded into one. They fell into a routine of life that was happy, secure and incredibly sexy. They innately understood each other, and shared pleasuring, beds, fantasies and climaxes equally, in body and in spirit.

For Kara, having now two special friends whom she was bonded with so intimately, that enjoy her and each other, with such trust and sensitivity, was the ultimate. Each knew how to give and receive in order to pleasure each other, in every way and in any combination, apparently without games, fear or jealously. They were different, but equal. Greg and Kara both had taken time to explain more about their connection and unique relationship, and Megan had seemed to completely understand and embrace their lifestyle. In no time, the three had found a rhythm and balance with support, care, and sexual pleasures, sharing every part of their lives together. They harnessed each of their strengths and complimented their contrasts. It had seemed like, in the same way that Kara and Greg had found their tune, Megan had added another dimension and harmony to them.

For Greg, he'd found both women were smart, adventurous, sensitive, giving and sexy in their own unique way. While he'd been the catalyst for both of them, what they each offered and what he was driven to provide for them, was different and special. All three of them had become each other's favourite song, for every different mood or time of day.

Kara, most especially, had relished in the shared arrangements, which for the first time, truly felt like a family. She wanted Greg and Megan to both become the best versions of themselves and felt blessed in how much each of them had given her, since they all first met.

It wasn't until about three months after Megan first arrived, that Kara had noticed it. Ever so gently captured in the way Megan had responded to Greg's touch in recent weeks. There was an increasingly intense, electric surge of power. Kara had always felt a sensuous energy between her and Megan during their lovemaking, and it was something that Greg had often commented on during their first weeks together, about how much he loved the radiant connection between them. They both knew how much pleasure it gave him to see them completely absorbed in the sheer indulgence of each other and sharing their aura with him.

In the beginning they were all so happy and natural together, forever respectful and aware of each other's sensitivities and vulnerabilities. Everything was talked about and nothing was withheld. They held no secrets that compromised or isolated them. They'd been open about any hint of jealously, fear, likes and dislikes, from the start. Unlike a traditional marriage of two, this connection was richer, as if there was always a third person standing by to watch over each of them, to protect and prevent any risk of breaking their collective bond.

When Kara first felt the change, she was in denial. She couldn't believe it was deliberate. Yet, something was wrong. Very wrong.

Kara could feel the subconscious strengthening of Megan's feelings toward Greg and a subtle withdrawal from touch and sharing anything with her at the same time. Like the first touch of salt water over a graze, it stung a little at first, but then was forgotten. That's what Kara felt when she caught Megan creeping out of Greg's room on the first night after all agreeing they all should either sleep together or be alone. It stung sharper when Greg explained she had just appeared next to him between the sheets. She had inwardly tried to justify Megan's actions within herself, struggling desperately to understand how and why this had evolved.

The second time, Kara's gut feelings hit the silent alarm.

While Kara knew intimately about Greg's heightened sexual appetite and fantasies, she also knew his desire for true love, and how much of his heart he had lost to Tess, coming so close to married with family again. Kara was forever in awe of the adrenal drive and thrill he gave and experienced when he encountered any challenge in his life. Everything personally and professionally that was new and exciting grabbed his attention and energy. This was largely how the shared relationship as a 'man, wife and sister wife' with Megan had developed.

Kara tried desperately to find reasons and justification to why Megan and Greg might bond more closely than with her. She considered perhaps Megan was the one who could offer Greg what he craved and needed most. That of a foundation. A solid platform for his life to vault from with the same energy and colour, but something ever reliable to return to, with a soft landing. Similarly, Megan had previously lost some foundation of her former life. While predictable, stable and boring, she still had children who were around. Megan had made some attempts to reconnect with them, and it was through Greg's children how they'd finally come to meet and enjoy in shared times together.

Kara had always been embraced in the warmth, comfort and fabric of their shared family times together, however, she did, at times, still regret that her own daughter and even her Aunt Sarah— her only family, rarely were a part of this. Throughout her daughter's formative years, Kara had encouraged her to focus on being independent, capable and successful. She had camouflaged everything about the emotionally destructive relationship between her and her father, never discrediting him, but promoting respect for his role as her dad and that both of them loved her in their own way. Kara's husband's true personality or the pain he inflicted had never been truly revealed to their daughter. Since their divorce, while she knew her daughter still loved her, she had all but reverted to the safety of her own separate life, which now was increasingly disconnected from Kara.

Kara also reflected on the similarities and differences between herself and Megan and how she and Megan connected with Greg.

She was the long-lost romance of a childhood kiss, and first love who Greg rediscovered. She was an intelligent, brave and insightful, yet sensitive woman, whom he had liberated, ignited sexually, and emotionally. She too had dared him to explore. They'd become the best of friends—connected by so many first-time experiences and memories.

Megan possessed the same combination of intelligence, success, and confidence as Kara, but she also emulated the essence of something unpredictable, like a delightful secret uncovering her sexual appetite and desires. There was an aura of undiscovered and powerful desire surrounding her. Kara had, as had Greg, found this incredibly attractive and refreshing at the start.

But now Kara couldn't help but feel some fear and kept a watchful eye over the next few months.

Kara had cause for alarm.

Chapter 31

Megan was not stupid. She'd sensed the discomfort, having not kept her rampant desire for sex with Greg in check during the past few weeks. Yet she also knew she could not afford for Kara to be unhappy.

'Good morning, Kara, would you like some coffee. I've just made some?' Megan said.

'That would be nice. Thanks,' Kara said. It had been the first morning in ages, when Megan wasn't either creeping back to her room or be the last to emerge from Greg's bedroom. The fact she had spent so many nights sneaking into his room, after each had supposedly retired, had upset Kara the most. The deception, more than the sex itself was the heartbreak.

'Have you got an early start today, Megan?' Kara asked, trying desperately to keep things light through the mud thick air that had filled between them these past weeks.

'No, I've actually got the day off. But I'm really up early so I could chat with you before you left today. I need to apologise.'

'Apologise? For what?' Kara's response was both cautious and curious.

'I'm sorry I've been rather selfish lately. Kara, you and I haven't had much time together. Greg's away tonight, so perhaps we can spend the evening together?' Megan's head had dropped as her words spilled and her eyes dropped, not daring to look at Kara.

Megan had hit the right notes. 'It's alright, Megan. A night together might be nice, but I'm sorry I have a work dinner tonight.'

'I see.'

Megan walked up to stand breast to breast in front of Kara. Megan's hand raised to Kara's hair, let her fingers scroll down a strand, then brush her cheek, trailing just a tip of a final finger to her chin. 'I really am sorry, Kara.' Her words grazed in the softest tone.

Kara couldn't see it in her eyes, but she'd felt some pinch of insincerity in her voice. She paused before uttering a reply.

'It's okay, your forgiven, but please don't keep things quiet from me or Greg again. We're here to help Megan, so it's important to be really open, and talk about those hard moments. Especially as we are a united three, otherwise it doesn't work. It's why we have the agreement we all have. My dinner tonight is for my team and the company's celebration for the few recently completed contracts.'

'I'd forgotten all about that. It's fine. We can have a special night another time. I'm sure there'll be something on Netflix I can watch tonight.' Megan's voice had trailed away.

'Megan, I'm the one who organised tonight, so if you'd like, I can swing you a seat to join us? It might be a bit boring as it's all work, but you're welcome to come if you don't want to stay home on your own. It's at least a free dinner and drinks!'

'Kara, thank you, I'd love that. It gives me a chance to meet some of your work mates too! I can be your date and we might even have a bit of fun when we get home, hey? Is it formal or casual?'

The two women made a striking impression that night. Kara in emerald-green with her dark curls caught casually up styled, and Megan in shimmering turquoise with her blonde locks free and flowing, arriving at the restaurant without fanfare, but nonetheless, turning every head with red carpet attention.

Kara introduced Megan as her flatmate to a few of her colleagues, before leaving to check the handful of formalities for the night. Megan quickly relaxed into the occasion and the champagne.

At first, Kara noticed Megan at the bar, constantly glancing around the room, checking out and making fluttering eye contact with a few of the younger fellas in her team. Kara didn't really care too much. After all, Megan was quite a stunning woman, with her neatly curved figure, pretty face and that intoxicating long blonde hair. Just before the formalities began, Kara quietly escorted Megan to introduce her to Daniel, whom she had placed to sit next to at dinner. He was her ambitious lead-designer, slightly younger but could hold his own with any client, so Kara knew he would make her feel welcome.

Once the formal dinner was over, most people stood around the bar area and chatted. One young man that Megan had been smiling at all night had come over and introduced himself. There were a few flirting and drunken giggles and a bit of unnecessary touching before Kara noticed Daniel slip Megan his card and whisper something in her ear. When Daniel left her to get another two drinks, another young man approached Megan. She didn't miss a beat, filling the air with exaggerated laughs and strategic flicks of her hair and blatantly flirting until Daniel appeared back with their drinks.

Daniel gave the new suitor a look of *move on* which happened immediately. Megan had smothered Daniel and nearly every man at her table with attention that had moved from *I'm politely interested*, to a brazen, *fuck me now attitude*, with every champagne.

By 10.30 p.m. Kara had had enough of the party, and even more of Megan's performance, so ordered a cab, then signalled to Megan that they would be leaving soon. Megan excused herself from Daniel, and stepped over to Kara, swaying with boozy confidence.

'Kara, you are an amazing boss they all rave about you, and it's been a wonderful night. I'll stay for a bit, if that's okay? Don't be worried, I can find my own way home.'

Kara looked at Megan with a look of *you must be kidding* but said; 'I really think you should come home now, but it's your choice, and I can't force you, but please be careful.'

Before walking to the door, Kara turned back. 'Megan, please remember, I work with these people, and they don't need, and shouldn't hear anything about me personally or our home life. You understand? Okay?'

Megan nodded, gave Kara a quick hug and said, 'I promise. Mum's the word. It's all good, Kara. Go home.'

Megan returned to Daniel, giving him her full attention. After sharing another drink together, he offered to flag a cab to take her home. There were two taxis parked out the front of the restaurant, and they both hopped into the back seat of the first one. Megan told the driver her address, Daniel noting it was only a 10-minute trip from the city to Greg's apartment.

As the vehicle pulled away from the kerb, Megan turned to Daniel, immediately planting a pash on him. It was a drunken kiss, yet passionate all the same. Daniel put his hand up underneath her top to fondle her breast through her bra as her tongue explored his feverishly. They had only got started when the cab pulled up at the North Adelaide address.

'May I come in?' Daniel asked breathlessly.

'No, you'd better not, sorry.' Megan straightened her top and climbed out of the cab.

It was all Daniel could think to do, but to call out, 'Look me up on Facebook,' as she walked towards the front gate.

She turned and said, 'I will.'

Chapter 32

The next couple of weeks were a little icy between the two girls, as Kara was finding it difficult to forgive Megan for her behaviour at the party. Her conduct was quite embarrassing, clear from the hushed speculations about 'the blonde,' which Kara caught from the following days and the whispered chats at the copier and in the lunchroom.

Kara was now worried that Megan, in her drunken state, had told her work mates about their unique shared home life and more.

By the next week, Kara realised it was only one night, that Megan and everyone else had settled down and now she was looking forward to her trip away. Kara hoped that on her return she would most likely have forgotten about that night too. It was probably good that Megan would have some days on her own this next week. With Greg away too, each of them had a little space and time, which Kara knew always sparked homecoming desire.

Megan arrived home to Greg's apartment from her work knowing she had the place to herself, Greg was in Brisbane again, and Kara was Melbourne bound. She was restless and bored within the first ten minutes. Megan hated being alone, and even worse that Greg was away at the same time as Kara.

She loved having him all to herself.

Throwing her bag and coat on the couch, Megan headed for the wine cupboard. After sorting through a few bottles, she picked a red, a nice McLaren Vale Shiraz. She reached for a glass and poured herself a healthy serving. She fell back next to her bag on the couch, careful not to spill a drop of the divine red. Her mood was restless already. She didn't do being on her own well at all. Reaching for her phone with one hand, she cleared the security to tap the email app. Nothing new since she left work, so she checked Facebook, flicking through until she came across Daniel. That was him. The guy from Kara's work who'd brought her home after the dinner. She tapped on his name, and flicked through his profile, thinking to herself, *He really is pretty cute.* Without even a thought, she sent a message.

> Hi Daniel, I'm not sure if you remember me, but I'm Kara's friend. I just wanted to say Hi and thank you again for dropping me home

Immediately Megan could feel the pangs of naughtiness. He was quite a bit younger, and she really should be leaving this alone. *But he did flirt and kiss me that night,* she thought. She exited his profile and scrolled down further to see what her other friends were doing.

Within a minute, a reply from Daniel appeared, she tapped on it straight away.

> Are you kidding?
> Of course, I remember you! How are you?

Megan replied immediately.

> You are funny. I'm at home. Both my house mates are away for work.

> I'm still at work in the city, but would you like to catch up for a drink or dinner?

> That's the best offer I've had all day, but maybe not a good idea? Kara might be pissed if she finds out, she's been a bit off since that party.

> Well let's make sure she doesn't then. Would you like to meet me in town, say Gouger Street for dinner? Is forty-five minutes enough time?

> Easy, send the address. I'll see you there soon.
> Megan x

Megan's heart was racing.

That all happened pretty quickly, she thought.

She grabbed her glass and headed for the shower.

In forty-five mins on the dot, Megan walked through the door of the Hung Wing Restaurant, each stride in that red dress making a statement. From a table toward the back of the dining area, Megan saw Daniel stand and wave.

He went to kiss her on the cheek, but Megan went for the lips.

Okay, going from where we left off, hey. Daniel thought as he pulled the seat out for her.

'This was a bit of surprise, Megan; I mean to say a happy one. I'm pleased you could join me.'

'It's my pleasure. As I said, my roomies are away, and I was playing on my phone when your name came up.'

'Roomies being Kara and...?'

'Greg Sheppard, it's actually his place,' Megan replied, now looking at the menu.

'May I take your order?' asked the waiter.

They both ordered food and wine, and unexpectedly, the food beat the wine to the table. They shared the dishes in the end, with the wine going down quick and smooth once it had finally arrived.

'May I ask, which one of you is sleeping with Greg?' Daniel asked, really not sure if he should.

'We both do,' replied Megan in a rather matter-of-fact tone, as she took another mouthful of the lemon chicken.

Daniel nearly sprayed red wine all over the table as he desperately reached for his napkin.

'Really?' he managed to get out, still dabbing his mouth.

'Yeah, sometimes it's all three of us, but mostly Kara and I take it in turns these days,' Megan replied, looking at him for the first time since he asked the question.

Daniel stared at her, his napkin hanging from his hand like a fallen curtain.

Daniel swallowed, took a breath and started to form a smile, 'You're just kidding, right?'

'Nope,' Megan replied, 'It works really well.' Megan looked at him again and said, 'Sometimes it's just Kara and I, but mostly we both enjoy it with Greg.'

'Really, Kara is bi?' Daniel was now completely shocked.

Megan quickly turned to him, 'Yes, I guess we both are. Well, actually, they call it bi-curious apparently. She likes guys but is pretty good at girls too. She and Greg have been into this type of thing for a long time. They've done couples and all sorts, even swingers' clubs. But you'd better not tell anyone that. She will kill me.'

'I won't, but I'm completely blown away. Wow, how good does that Greg have it? You two hot women on tap, and at the same time. My God, is he Superman or something?'

'Yeah, pretty well,' she smiled. 'Actually, that's what Kara calls him,' Megan said, returning with enthusiasm to her meal.

They finished their food and tipped down the last of their wine.

'Shall we go somewhere?' Megan suggested.

'Would you like to grab a drink at a bar?' Daniel asked, as he waved to the waiter for the bill. He was still digesting all this information. Kara, his manager, was into kinky sex. She'd seemed so straight and normal. This was unbelievable.

He sorted the account, and they strolled towards the centre of town. They decided on a bar situated in a major hotel, lots of noise and people, most of them still on their way home from work.

They drank, laughed, and danced for the next two hours. They were getting touchy, and each dance got their bodies closer and more suggestive. Megan was tempted to play the game that Greg had played with her the first time they met, but then decided against it.

They staggered back from the dance floor and landed at their table. Daniel lent over to Megan and whispered in her ear, 'Hey, you're a lot of fun, and very beautiful.'

She now felt the hot breath on her neck that she craved.

'You too, Daniel.' She leant over almost stumbling to kiss him firmly on the lips.

Megan was now quite intoxicated from both the wine and the allure of sex. She put her mouth right up close to his ear and whispered. 'Do you want to take me home and have your way with me?'

'I'll order an Uber. Your place?' Daniel replied with excitement and enthusiasm.

He took the last mouthful of his drink, trying to be cool, but also anxious to get moving. This woman had been a surprise from the outset, and he couldn't wait to discover what she offered up next.

He escorted Megan outside, thankfully it took no time before being greeted by their driver. 'Can we stop at a petrol station on the way please, driver?' asked Daniel. 'I just want to grab something,' he said turning to Megan and kissed her.

The Uber driver pulled into a large fuel station, Daniel jumped out, ran inside and made a quick purchase.

When he hopped back in the car, he kissed her again and said, 'It's just something for us both.'

The car pulled up out the front of the apartment.

Megan, now teetering on her heels from all the wine, fumbled for the door key. She found it and handed it to Daniel to open the door. The door opened and the pair almost fell inside, the fast drinking at the bar now taking effect on them both. The instant the door closed; Megan pushed Daniel back against it without any resistance from him. She planted her mouth firmly on his, which he accepted willingly. Her tongue was reaching deep for the sex within him that she now needed. Megan had untucked his shirt and was frantically looking for the buttons. She pulled the shirt over his shoulders, then laughed as he was now tied up with his cuffs still done up.

They both laughed, which broke the rush of passion.

'Let me get us a drink, what do you feel like?' Megan said, rather dishevelled with her blouse now spilling out of her skirt, her shoes removed and her hair tousled.

'A beer would be great, thanks,' Daniel replied, pulling his shirt back onto his shoulders, enabling him to undo the restraints of his cuffs.

Megan returned from the kitchen with two beers, saying little except… 'Follow me,' with a sultry smile, trailing his beer in temptation behind her.

Once inside her room, beer in hand, he asked, 'Shall I close the door?'

'No. Would you really care if someone watched us?'

'I would, if Kara was watching us. I have to work with her.'

'No one will come home, they're both away, it's just you and me, Daniel.'

Megan took Daniel's beer from his hand, placing it deftly on the bedside table. She was now in charge. She removed his shirt with ease this time. Daniel reached into his pocket and placed the petrol station purchase, on the bedside table.

'How bad do you want to fuck me?' Megan asked as she started sucking his earlobe.

'Really bad,' he replied frantically, undoing enough of her buttons to shed her shirt. Daniel loved the sight of her beautiful blonde hair falling out of her shirt as he lifted it over her head. Her white lacy bra which she filled perfectly, was now presented to him, and only after a few moments of admiring it, he wanted that gone as well. Leaning forward to kiss her, he reached behind to unclip her bra strap. He removed that with ease, as if opening a present you have waited a long time to receive. The bra slipped away and fell between their bodies. Within a second, he tossed it to the floor.

Megan could now feel her breasts skin to skin on his chest. She could feel her nipples harden with each touch and rub across his skin. She wanted to stay in his embrace and savour the kisses of raw passion she was receiving. They both enjoyed the touch of their semi-nakedness with their hands exploring every piece of exposed flesh. Megan now eager to move on, reached for his belt and fly, undoing both with a sense of urgency. It was time to reach what she really wanted. She removed his pants and jocks both at the same time, carefully trying to accommodate his profound erection. She slid them down to his ankles, her face now in his crotch.

There it was.

Before Daniel had barely stepped out of his pants, her tongue slid along the full length of him from bottom to top. Taking him in her mouth, she sucked only just enough to ensure his arousal was ripe and ready to fill her. She wanted him thick inside her as soon as she could.

She stood quickly, helping him unzip her skirt, letting it fall to the floor and he swiftly removed her knickers. Megan turned and climbed onto the bed as Daniel reached for the condoms he placed on the bedside table. With frantic urgency, he tore open the packet, fitting the film of latex over himself with the precision of a card dealer at a casino. He fell in beside her, his hand moving over her breasts then straight between her legs, as his lips found hers.

Megan was in heaven, devouring his tongue as he ignited the fire that was building inside her with his fingers.

Megan pulled her lips away enough to say, 'Fuck me... please fuck me,' her voice sounding as if from another person.

She spread her legs wider as he moved between them, his knob found her effortlessly. He fucked her hard from the start. No warmup required. Her legs wrapped around him, wanting all of him inside her to ravage her, as if to punish her for her naughty behaviour. Her fire built from deep in her soul, slowly converting to a physical burn.

Daniel now had his face above her, watching as she transformed from the enjoyment to a pleasurable pain which was engulfing her. He watched her head tilt back, her mouth open, and with enthusiasm he pounded her harder.

Megan was now in another world. Every nerve ending seemed to be directly connected to that position inside her that Daniel filled. She was almost there, every muscle tightening. The warmth, the heat now completely shrouded her, and then that drain of pleasure that was released like a fireball.

Daniel knew the second, even before the scream, she was there, and so was he. His thrusts were deep and hard as he also exploded into her. He felt as if he had been shot into the sky by a cannon and was cresting the peak. As the final squirt of come left him, he began his gentle free fall back to earth.

They both lay there while the heat and panting subsided. Sooner for him than her, but he stayed in position as to ease her descent back. He saw the smile on her face appear as she re-entered her body; he removed himself and lay back next to her.

'My God, Daniel, we will have to do that again.'

'Yes, that was amazing, I felt I was with you the whole way.'

Daniel removed the condom, placed it on the edge of the bedside table, before turning back to cuddle up to her. *I must remember to take that with me*, he thought to himself.

For a long time they snuggled in a satisfied silence, till he said, 'I'd better get going, I have a big day tomorrow.'

'Of course. I've had an amazing night,' Megan said.

'I'm so glad you messaged me, and yes, so did I,' Daniel said as he started the climb from the sheets and search for his clothes.

It wasn't long before Megan heard the front door click. She stretched out across the bed, let out a big sigh. Her body still hummed from the vigorous love making as she said to herself, 'I hope Kara doesn't find out.' She rolled over, soon falling into a deep sleep.

Next morning Megan awoke with a complete feeling of satisfaction and a bit of a headache. *I think I drank too much, but my god that was fun last night.* She sat up and looked around. Noticing the open pack of condoms, she smiled as she flicked them into her top draw and headed for the shower.

Daniel was still catching himself in his recollections of the whirlwind night with Megan as he arrived at work. As he walked past Kara's office it awakened the revelations about her, that Megan had shared. It took him a while to focus, and he kept checking himself to park those thoughts and stay on task, especially before Kara got back from interstate. She needed the work to be finished, and besides, he couldn't be thinking about her like that.

Thankfully, during the next two weeks Daniel hadn't really seen a lot of Kara since his surprise night with Megan, but he certainly looked at her differently now.

'Beer after work mate?' Tom called out to Daniel as he walked past his office.

'You bet! 5.30?'

'See ya then,' Tom called back as he faded out of view.

The afternoon slipped by and before long Tom was at his office door tapping his watch.

'Just a sec,' Daniel said as he tidied up the last few papers on his desk.

The two men headed down the passageway towards the elevator just as Kara Gilbert came from her office.

'Hi guys. Calling it a night?' She smiled at them as she went past, not really stopping for their reply.

Once out of earshot, Tom bumped Daniel and said, 'I reckon she's fucking hot. I'd do that.'

Daniel nudged him back. 'That she is, more than you think. I could tell you some things about her, but I'd have to kill you,' he said with a wink.

Tom stopped and looked back towards Kara and then turned back to Daniel. 'What? Have you done her?'

'No,' Daniel replied. 'Forget it. I've been sworn to secrecy.' He pushed the down button on the elevator, now regretting that he'd said anything.

'Two Crown Lagers thanks mate,' Daniel said to the barman, as the pair reached the bar at the ground floor of their office building. The bar was still quiet as the crowd normally arrived around 6.30 p.m. They chinked their beers, and each took a swig.

'Come on, tell me about Kara Gilbert,' Tom asked again.

'Mate, I can't, it's pretty personal stuff, and I promised someone I wouldn't say anything. I shouldn't have mentioned it.'

'So, you *have* fucked her then?'

'No.'

'Someone at work has?' Tom's curiosity was on full alert.

'Not that I know of.'

'She can't be a lesbian, she too sexy.'

'Well, not really a lesbian.'

'Not really? Are you telling me she's bi?'

'Yeah, sort of, but for fuck sake, don't say anything.'

'Fuck me! She likes it both ways.' Tom exclaimed, ordering two more drinks. He was really thirsty now, not only for beer, but for more of the mind-blowing stuff from Daniel about their boss.

'At the same time,' Daniel said, swallowing the last mouthful to catch up with Tom, who was now watching him intently.

'Threesomes! Wow! How do you know that shit?'

'I fucked the chick she lives with a couple of weeks ago.'

'Jesus Christ, how did that happen?'

'Kara introduced us at our office party we had. Remember the older blonde who sat next to me at dinner? I drove her home, and we pashed and exchanged details. She sent a message to me on Facebook, one night, so we had dinner, then I took her home and fucked her brains out.'

'Fuck, why doesn't that ever happen to me?'

'She told me her and Kara take it in turns to fuck this bloke they live with, and sometimes it's all three of them at the same time. Kara and this guy do other kinky shit too.'

'You're fucking bullshitting me now, aren't you?'

'True story mate, but don't fucking tell anyone, for God's sake.'

'Do you think that blonde chick would fuck me?'

'Who knows?' Daniel said, now first to finish his beer, signalling the waiter for two more.

'Her name is Megan Munday, look her up on Facebook, but I didn't tell you, alright? Make out you saw her at the dinner and asked what her name was or something. Be cool, she loves the dick, but she's no fool.'

'Fuck yeah, I'll be cool. Do you think Kara would put out? I'd love to do that too,' Tom said now keen to get home and start sending messages.

'Tom, I'd keep away from Kara. She's your boss. Look, I'll need to hit the road after this one mate.'

'Yeah, alright. All sweet. I'm off too.'

They both finished their beers and stepped away from the bar.

'Mum's the word, right?' he reminded Tom as they left the bar. Daniel headed left up the street. Tom followed him out, turning the other way, now hastily pacing down the street.

Daniel knew the instant after he'd gone, that he had made a big mistake in telling Tom anything.

Chapter 33

After leaving the bar, Tom near sprinted to the nearest taxi stand. He couldn't wait to get home to draft out a message for Megan Munday. All the way home, he barely spoke to the driver, as he composed the all-important first message. He considered the approach. Should he be straight to it? Tell the truth, lie a little, or totally fabricate the whole thing?

Landing at home, he fumbled with the keys for his front door lock, swearing as he dropped them. After eventually getting the door open, he grabbed a beer from the fridge, promptly dropping himself onto the couch with his phone at the ready. After a mouthful of beer, he was ready. He placed the bottle on the side table, opened Facebook, quickly typing Megan's name in the search bar. Her profile picture appeared on his screen, and he was instantly excited.

'Oh yeah, I could do that!' he exclaimed out loud. Daniel's words resonated in his head, *'She likes the dick but she's no fool'*. He had to be cool and careful not to drop Daniel in it. Tom pushed the message icon and started typing,

> Hi Megan, I saw you at our work party and haven't been able to stop thinking about you...

He stopped. *Nah that's too corny!*

> Megan, my name is Tom, I work with Kara Gilbert...

No, I better leave Kara out of it. He deleted this message too.

> Hi Megan, not sure if you remember me, I saw you at my work dinner the other night. How are you going? Tom

He thought about that for a while. His finger hovered over the send button. *Here goes!* As he pushed Send. He checked his phone every minute for the next hour, however Megan had not replied.

'Oh well, it was worth a crack,' he said as he took some leftovers from two nights ago from the fridge and tossed them in the microwave. Tom put himself to bed, a little deflated from the lack of response. He'd been so excited about the thought of a hook-up with a sexy older woman.

It was becoming more unusual that both Greg and Kara were home, they had both been busy with work lately. Megan had gone to her room straight after dinner, knowing that Greg had indicated he wanted to enjoy Kara on his own tonight. She hated it when this happened. The threesome sex was thankfully now less frequent too, especially since Kara had sensed that Megan avoided offering anything more than kissing or undressing her. She and Greg would still have great sex, but Megan didn't find it as thrilling during the times she had to share him with Kara.

Since Kara had seen her leaving Greg's room a couple of times, things had stepped back, much to Megan's relief. While she still enjoyed the sensation of having two sets of hands and lips spoiling her, it was only Greg that she adored to taste. Megan simply loved being adored and pampered. She now longed for the nights and days when Kara worked away. She relished in the fact that she had all of Greg to herself, also revelling in her own selfish delight as if she was fucking him behind Kara's back.

She lay back on her bed, flicking through her phone, when she noticed a message from a Tom and read it through.

I wonder who that is? She checked his profile and was still unsure. *I'll worry about him tomorrow,* she thought, settling herself for sleep.

Part way through the night, Megan woke from a dream about the mystery man that had sent her a message. She reached for her phone and sent him a reply.

As soon as Tom's eyes opened, he grabbed for his phone to check for a reply. 'Yes!' he called out, spying a message from Megan was there.

> Hi Tom, sorry I don't really remember you. Do we have a mutual friend?

Megan woke and stretched out trying to get her engine started for the day. She reached for her phone to see if Tom had replied. He had.

> Yes. Kara Gilbert and Daniel Brown.

> Oh, that dinner. How are you Ben? I am sorry I didn't remember you.

> That's ok, would you like to get a coffee or a drink sometime? I thought you were an interesting person.

> Thank you. Sure, a drink after work one day. Maybe this Friday?

That's great, how about North Adelaide somewhere?

Prefer not North Adelaide.

That's way too close to home. That's Michael territory, she thought. Megan replied.

How about Norwood? I live out there and know a few great spots.

Perfect, send me a time and place.

Replied Megan again, feeling strange. *This also is a bit close to home. To this place. But I can do that.*

How about 7 p.m. at the Norwood Hotel this Friday?

Great! See you then.

Replied Megan as she swung her legs out of bed to start the day.

Megan arrived at the Norwood hotel at 7.10 p.m. she knew roughly what he looked like and he her, but to be safe each had messaged to describe to the other what they would be wearing. Tom saw the very alluring Megan, with her long blonde hair arrive. She was at least ten years older or more than him, but nonetheless was a very attractive woman, who caught the stare of everyone she passed as she strolled through the bar.

He immediately jumped up and went to meet her. He kissed her on the cheek, and with his hand gently in the small of her back, guided her to his reserved table in the most secluded corner of the bar.

'What would you like to drink, Megan?' He asked a little tentatively. He had suddenly felt a touch nervous. She had a powerful sexual presence that had nearly rendered him speechless.

'Gin and Tonic please, Tom.'

Megan eyed Tom from head to toe as he stood waiting to be served at the bar.

Yeah, he's not too bad. He's young, but that itself could be a bit of fun.

Tom returned with her drink and another for himself.

They made small talk for a while, loaded with Megan's flirting eyes and innuendo in nearly every comment. Tom figured that he was 'in.' Megan had not had sex for a week now, and only having touched herself once since then.

The more she drank, the sooner she wanted it to happen.

'Did you say that you live around here?'

'Yes, next street, would you like to come back and see my place?'

'Yeah, let's go, I'm ready for a change of scenery.'

They both finished their drinks, then headed for the door.

Tom's flat was only a five-minute walk. He again fumbled with the lock, this night for different reasons than the night he messaged her. Tom was very nervous. This all sounded great in theory, but in fact he hadn't invited many women to his apartment before, or had sex with many at all, really. Megan was quite a stunner, and now that the moment of truth was here, it was a little overwhelming.

'What would you like to do?' he asked innocently.

'Why don't we see what pops up?' she said as she rubbed the front of his pants.

'Sure' he replied, his mouth now so dry, he could hardly speak.

Megan kissed him, not a peck but a full on pash, no warmup. *This is a woman who knows what she wants and how to get it*, is all his mind could say.

Megan had already undone his pants, his fly, and had him firmly in her hand. He yielded to her hold instantly, responding with the speed likened to a clown blowing up a trick balloon. She slid his pants and jocks to his feet, covering his new shiny work shoes. Megan dropped to her knees, taking him expertly into her mouth. 'Oh my God!' Tom said as he looked up to the ceiling, then closed his eyes and felt his knees buckle. Megan stroked and sucked for only about thirty seconds, before she realised, he was about to come.

She stopped immediately. 'Get your gear off, buddy.'

Tom kicked off his shoes, pants, and shirt in seconds, as he watched her remove her skirt and top. She slid her knickers down revealing that she was shaved, another first for him. She then took off her bra and the sight of her firm breasts alone, nearly made him blow. She took his hand, telling him to lie back on the bed. Obligingly he lay there, still and completely fixated. She knelt over him, guiding his erection into her with one swift manoeuvre.

As she sank down onto his shaft, he arched his back, calling out vibrantly, 'Oh fuck, I'm coming!'

Megan rode him hard, trying desperately to get her own tingling pleasure to rise as fast as she could but Tom had blown and faded before she could benefit by even a twitch. She slowed and barely wriggled an inch before he slipped limply out of her.

'I'm really sorry,' said Tom, in hushed embarrassment.

'So, are you a double barrel?' Megan asked bluntly.

'A what?' he asked, innocently having no idea what she meant.

'I guess not then,' replied Megan as she lifted herself from him. She quietly started dressing. Tom just laid there, naked, doing nothing more than filling the silence with despair about his lack of performance.

'That's never happened before,' he offered lamely.

His lie, a pathetic attempt to resurrect his ego and his smile, barely caught Megan's attention.

'No harm done; I better go,' Megan said as she placed her undies in her bag. Once dressed, she gave him a quick kiss, grabbed her bag and left.

As she reached the footpath, she exclaimed to herself, 'Well, that was fucked.'

She walked back towards the pub with her frustration stomping out through each step. However, a new appetite had become exposed. Despite the less than satisfying sex, she'd now tasted and pleasured a much younger man. It was a first blood blonde Cougar who walked back into the bar, 'I want to find someone who can satisfy me,' Megan nearly shouted inside. Such was the rampant desire that she couldn't hold back. It was after midnight when she stepped out of the back seat of the tradies twin cab ute that was parked in the back corner of the hotel carpark. She pulled her skirt down to cover bare arse and adjusted her bra. She didn't look back as she ran her fingers through her messed hair and headed for the taxi stand.

Chapter 34

*K*ara's heart was labouring: both at work and at home. There was something that was *off* everywhere around her. She'd thought she was the only one responsible—she had taken on lots of contracts, was burning the candle and not taking as much care of herself, but somehow this time, it felt like it was beyond her own control. Most of all, home and Megan plagued her thoughts. Not just as a result of the subtle manipulation that Megan seemed to be escalating, but her own rising feelings of mistrust and fear. This was even more disconcerting for her. She resolved to park it for now. She loved Greg too much to indulge her own insecurities. They were all still together, and if Megan was who he needed, she would never stand in the way of that. But something niggled in her.

Just watch and tread carefully, she told herself each morning.

However, today, she could not sit back.

The staff meeting was arranged for 8.30 a.m. and Kara needed to ensure sign off of the stage and showcase displays, budget and tech plans for the Convention Centre. She'd seen all the preliminary designs and reports, and she was expecting her division heads could confirm preferences and it would be green lit by the day's end. She'd been asked to do a flying trip to Melbourne tomorrow to meet the client execs for their final approval of the layouts and program. She especially needed everything to be sharp and ready, without any hiccups. It was Greg's birthday tomorrow night; she wanted a straight fly in, fly out for this deal as there was no way she was missing the special night she had planned with Megan for him, and their friends.

Kara had the agenda ticking, and it was down to the minor choice of the entrance layout and positioning of the delegate reception area. She had no idea how this item would become a lifetime poignant moment and the trigger for some other major changes.

'Thank you, Daniel and Sharon for the layout plans for the entrance. We are down to the last two options, so I'd like to know what everyone's preference is?' Kara heard only one uncomfortable giggle smothered by a cough but noted the wave of little grins across the room.

No one said a word.

'Come on, you guys! I know we've got through a heap this morning. Last decision. I'm not sure, as I actually like it both ways.'

Daniel's cough was loudest, as Kara glimpsed the exclamatory look that he tossed at Tom across the conference table. Tom's eyes flashed, and he couldn't muffle the sniggering laugh that followed. In turn, the reaction of the whole room changed. Heads lowered or looked away, backs straightened, and smothered smiles turned in every direction except towards Kara.

She just stood there. Silent. Staring and suspended by the complete flip and tone of mirthful awkwardness in the room.

Something wasn't right.

Finally, Daniel spoke, mustering every effort to lower his voice a few octaves and sound professional. 'Err, Kara, the design on the left allows less space for general entrance, but it allows for a larger reception desk to process registrations.'

'Thanks, Daniel. Is everyone okay if we go with this?' There were nods all round, and Kara quickly closed the meeting.

As most all stood, near racing for the exit, Kara could not let this go.

'Daniel. Tom. Could you two stay back for a moment, please?'

Daniel knew instantly that Kara's polite, yet firm, request with that commanding look, signalled that leaving was not an option.

They both turned back, returning to stand behind their seats at either side of the conference table. Neither dared make eye contact with Kara, each catching her 'don't dare fuck with me' undertone. Kara, unwaveringly focussed, stood at the head of the table, continuing to sharply tidy papers, without saying another word. She wanted them to sweat for just a moment. She was also strategically waiting to be sure everyone else lingering outside the room, in their childishly desperate attempts to catch an earshot of the discussions, had gone. Daniel shuffled under Kara's deafening silence. He hadn't felt this nervous since he was sent to the school principal's office for letting someone's bike tyre down.

Kara's voice started steady. 'Daniel, thank you for the work on this and your support for Sharon's final design, and… Tom,' as she spoke his name, he snapped his gaze toward her, now also drawn to attention. 'Thank you also, for the extra time you've spent on the tech plans. But I would actually like to know,' as her rise in octave and volume resounded in their ears, 'What the hell just happened then? What's the joke? Clearly there's something I know nothing about.'

Kara just stood there. Staring at them, her arms outstretched as she leant hard on the table, her look shifting side to side from one to the other, waiting for one of them to respond. Tom and Daniel's hooded looks in each other's direction signalled hesitation and trouble.

Kara waited. Daniel was the first to break. 'Kara, well, it was just a private joke. It was nothing, really. Nothing to worry about.'

'A private joke? About what? The whole team seems to know, so why not share? Is it something about me?'

'Kara,' Daniel muttered awkwardly, 'I've made a huge mistake. You haven't done anything.'

Daniel took a deep breath, slipping a desperate glance toward Tom. He drew in a breath before he let the next sentence escape.

His tone dropped to a shame filled *do or die* tone. 'I had a night with your friend Megan, and she told me about your relationships at home.'

'I see. So, what did Megan tell you exactly?' Kara flinched slightly, feeling the impact of his words *at home*, that cut the first blow. She inwardly braced for the next.

'Megan told me you're bi and a swinger.'

Before the reality of the implication of his words slapped her, harder than any hand, she asked, 'Does everyone in this office know about what she told you?'

Daniel looked down, only offering a nod in response to her last question. Kara froze. Stunned, as the horror and impact of what she'd heard, as Megan's poison tremored through her body.

She turned to Tom and asked ever so quietly, 'Tom, so tell me, what is your involvement with this?'

'I've slept with her as well,' his feeble, fading reply.

'Both of you at the same time?' asked Kara, eyeballing them both.

'No, no!' they both fired back in unison. 'I was after Dan,' said Tom, feeling slightly more hopeful he might still have a job after this meeting.

Kara drew in a deep breath before she spoke. 'My God. You two sleeping with Megan is one thing. That's disappointing, but that's your own choices. To be honest, I'm most concerned about what sort of information has been shared with you about me, which now puts me in a shockingly difficult position—not only personally, but professionally.'

She stopped at that moment, drawing in another breath, and looked up to the ceiling, needing the pause to calm the eruption that was building inside her.

'I'm even more worried about my friends. You both do realise that Greg Sheppard is also a colleague, a leading company director in our industry? I cannot have his, or any other client's or colleague's privacy, or their reputations, compromised by any staff of this firm. I hired and trusted you for your talent above your pants.'

Tom and Daniel's faces were ashen, finally comprehending the extent of damage they'd caused.

Kara finally broke the ugly silence that filled the room. 'I need you to tell me the facts in detail. Now, please. I think I deserve that at least!'

They spent the next minutes mumbling and stammering in response to Kara's probing questions, eventually filling in more of the picture of how and when they met with Megan, and the nature of the intimate details she had told Daniel about her and Greg. As they stood to leave, Daniel turned and walked back to stand up close in front of Kara. He extended his hand.

'Kara, for what it's worth, I am truly sorry. I can't speak for Megan, but I am solely responsible for sharing what she told me about your private life to Tom, and in turn, to others here at work. You've never been anything other than professional, and a great manager to work for. Please just tell me if there is anything, I can do to fix this…?'

Kara just nodded, waving them both out. She'd heard more than enough. Her shoulders and head drooped, collapsing beneath her as if every drop of blood was draining from her, oozing to spill uncontrollably out onto the floor, exposing her utter despair. Her palms and fingers, already white and pressed hard into the tabletop, were the only things holding her upright. She held there; completely motionless with her eyes locked on the scratch on the conference room table glaring back in front of her. This little scratch, a blemish on the smooth wooded veneer, somehow epitomising the mark to remind her of this day.

There were no words she could utter right now, despite already screaming on the inside. She had been dropped into a waking nightmare. Her thoughts were raging everywhere, flipping between a desire to commit murder, and wanting to be buried in a grave of death by humiliation and shattered reputation.

As the two men slunk out of the room, each vainly attempting to swallow their guilt and panic about their futures, neither said a word. After closing the door so carefully, not wanting even the click of the latch to disturb.

Daniel stopped.

He stood upright, still, before turning back to glimpse at Kara through the glass. The first manager he'd ever really come to admire, was visibly shattered. Worse still, he knew he was to blame.

As he stepped back to his office, he resisted the impulse to turn back. Such was his sudden desire to apologise and comfort her. Being his first female boss, he had, with his usual bravado, tried so hard to resist liking her. He'd lamented, disregarding, and discounting her abilities at first, then to everyone else in the team. Besides, this Kara bird had just landed there, from the outside of the company, no less in what everyone knew, should've been *his* job. But he'd soon found that Kara was an irresistible force, which had captured him, and he'd found intoxicating, drawn under her spell despite himself. 'I'm so sorry, I'll make it up to you, somehow, Kara,' became the only words he repeated over and over.

It took ages before Kara could stand, even then, needing to steady herself against the violent waves of anger and hurt still beating through her. Eventually she found her feet and determination to walk back to her office. She sucked and gasped life clinging breaths for ages, before finally being able to calm herself and find the salvation of numb autopilot. She had to hold it together for now. She gathered up the reports for the presentation, drove home, focussing only upon the mantra *one thing at a time.*

Kara busied herself in the kitchen, prepping the last of the food for Greg's birthday tomorrow night. Somehow finding a cool, detached place, even mustering the ability to sort the last plans with Megan about the surprise dinner, she kept steady, until falling into bed. She held herself coolly intact until 6.00 a.m. the next morning, when she finally was buckled into her seat on the 'red eye' flight to Melbourne. Only then, she let the tears go, her eyes matching the colour and lonely nature of the flight.

Chapter 35

*K*ara walked out of Greg's apartment and headed to the car.
She hated Monday mornings, but today's dread wasn't the
usual Monday melancholy drag that would fade when she arrived
at work. Leaving the two of them behind as they slept so
peacefully, while she crept out into the 5.30 a.m. darkness to the
office was often tough. But work would offer no solace either now.
Since her horror discovery after the meeting last Thursday, the
office was now a toxic place too.

She had to get through this day. She followed her usual routine
of wiping the dew from the windows of the car, checked her work
bag again, started the car with heaters on to warm the day, sipped
her coffee from her travel mug, and swiped to her driving playlist
to select her first song.

It was at song three when Paloma Faith's '*Only love can hurt like
this*' started, that her tears spilled everywhere. They had just started
to pour out again. She'd barely been able to hold herself together
over the weekend, fighting to quell the urge to spit, scream, and
unleash her despair all over the blonde parasite sleeping in the next
room. Thankfully Megan had spent most of Sunday with her kids,
so Kara could take some breaths to survive until today.

Overwhelmed, she pulled over to the side of the road, turned
off the engine and sobbed. It was like every tense moment she had
held inside during the past few months had just burst out of her
heart, in a river of tears, filled with fear, sadness, anger and regret.

There was only one decision to make, but she had been avoiding and resisting and trying to ignore it for months now. But the events of last week had put the final nail in the coffin. It was time to leave. To leave Greg, Megan, her job, and this life behind. Let the two of them be a couple. This is what Megan wanted. She'd made that abundantly clear to Kara, at least.

She'd tried so hard not to entertain thoughts that Megan had been deliberately manoeuvring for her to leave. She had overlooked the increasing number of times when Megan had created opportunities to have time alone to be with Greg. Kara had arrived at Greg's finding the two of them already having finished dinner and screwing on a number of occasions. Kara had dismissed this at first, but it became obvious when Kara started texting her when she would be arriving home and looking forward to enjoying them both. She'd tried to accept and forgive Megan, understanding her connection to Greg was natural, having lost the grounding of her husband and family so suddenly.

But everything had crashed in, and Kara couldn't deny it anymore. Since her horror work meeting, her mind was now flooded with the many times when Megan had created waves. What started with little things, kept building, and Kara despaired at how to respond. The twisted stories, outright lies, and conniving ways where Megan had gaslighted, inflamed doubt and belittled. The fact Megan's tentacles had infiltrated Kara's credibility at work now crushed her too. The things Kara had dismissed before now came vividly back into view through a much clearer lens. She made herself reflect over all the moments and events. She could now hear Megan, after the night she'd invited her to join her at that work dinner.

It had been the next evening at dinner with Greg, when Megan had looked at her and asked, 'Now Kara, who was that sultry guy that you had your hands all over at the work show last night? What was his name… I remember, Daniel, wasn't it? I think our Kara might be getting bored with us, Greg?'

Kara was rendered speechless, staring at her in disbelief. Greg had thrown Kara a look and a frown which showed it had struck a nerve. Megan's turn away smile should have been a giveaway.

But you were so stupid and forgiving. The ever reliable and gullible Kara! I should have told him then and there, about how it had, in fact, been Megan who'd carried on. She'd been quite embarrassing. She was blatantly flirting with all the guys who were there, especially Daniel. And now it's even worse knowing the little bitch then went on to sleep with him—at our place!

Why didn't I make sure she left with me? Even though she insisted I go. I can't believe she told Greg it was me.

What hurt Kara most was how Greg now looked at her. She sensed from the look in his eyes that he held increasing doubts toward her, and she could feel the connection with her as his closest friend and as a trusted lover, slipping away. Since that night, he'd started to gently question her about the way she'd been responding lately, even suggesting that she seemed to be acting jealously and unfairly distant from Megan.

Kara couldn't believe the extent of Megan's actions that had resulted in the very strained atmosphere between them all. The deceitful way in which Megan had behaved on Friday night at Greg's birthday celebrations and the outright lies she told. It was a deliberate and affronting attempt to repel Kara away. Nearly worse than the humiliation at work; that had been the last straw.

Greg's birthday was always such a special time, when Kara loved to find ways to spoil him every year since they'd reconnected. Kara also thought it would be nice if both she and Megan planned something together, not only to delight Greg but also to help to restore the rhythm between them all. A special celebration, to make sure they both would give him a memorable night. It wasn't only memorable. It was monumental.

Greg had been away for the week, so Kara was thrilled she and Megan could share in the organisation so that it would be a genuine surprise for him. The last-minute work trip to Melbourne and back on the day of his birthday had been a blow for Kara, but when she told Megan about it, she was both relieved and thrilled that she'd suddenly become enthusiastic and jumped into action. She told Kara she would contact their friends to ask them to arrive for drinks and dinner later and even offered to be at the airport to collect Kara.

'Then we both can be home to surprise him. He'd love that,' she'd said.

Kara was alarmed when her messages to Megan from the airport went unanswered. Hopefully everything was alright, and their plans hadn't gone awry. After nearly forty-five minutes without a reply and no sign of Megan, Kara grabbed a cab and headed to the apartment.

Maybe Greg or the guests had arrived early? She hoped everything was alright.

It wasn't! Kara hadn't expected that even more nasty surprises would actually be dumped on her that night. Everything she had feared, and tried to dismiss became a painful truth.

It cut her deeply when she arrived to find that all of her work and preparation had been effectively hoodwinked. Kara had finally realised the extent to which Megan would go to discredit or undermine her in Greg's eyes, the instant she'd walked into the apartment.

As she'd no sooner turned the key in the door, Megan was there to greet her. 'Wonderful, Kara's here!' she'd called out shrilly, as if announcing her arrival to the world. Kara knew instantly that the party was well underway. As Kara walked into the entrance hall, Megan raced up to her, gripped Kara's hand and whispered, 'I'm so sorry. Kara. While I finished the prep, so work wouldn't bother me, I'd put my phone on silent and forgot to turn it off. Then everyone arrived early. They obviously couldn't have seen my message, so I just got carried away and started dinner. Come on, you're still in time for dessert and the best part we haven't given Greg his presents yet. We were waiting for you.' She gave Kara a hug and then whispered, 'I'll make it up to you later… I promise.'

Kara's internal boil calmed a little, subsiding to an underlying simmer.

As she entered the living area, Greg rose from the dinner table and greeted Kara with a big hug. 'Happy birthday, my best sexy friend,' she whispered in his ear. 'Sorry I'm late. There were some unexpected changes.'

'Thank you gorgeous, I'm just pleased you made it after such a day.'

Their friends all greeted Kara warmly and Megan rushed to get her a wine, thus Kara had settled and been able to park her distress. That lasted only for about the next thirty minutes.

Then it happened. The double-blind came into play.

Megan tapped her glass and announced loudly. 'Raise your glasses, everyone. It's time to wish our beloved Mr Greg Sheppard a very happy birthday!' After the final chorus and the last 'Hip Hooray' sang out loudly, Kara stood with the others as they all laughed and shared cheers.

'No speeches, before presents,' jumped in Megan, as she raced behind the lounge, obviously to grab her gift for him.

'Hang on, hang on, Megan, I need to grab mine from my room. I'll be back in a sec!'

Kara had raced to the bedroom. For the first time, after her shocking days, she was now able to feel a little excitement rise inside. As she did each year, she always burst to give him his special presents. It was a time to say, *thank you*' and just made her happy.

She slid open the door to the sliding robe and reached up to the top shelf. She grabbed the bag with the boxed bottle of wine, Tom Ford sunglasses and the portable speaker. They were the *extras* she got at the last minute. This was the time of year, even more than Christmas, when she loved the chance to spoil him. She stretched up to find the box. It wasn't there.

'Come on, Kara.'

'Hurry up!'

'We're all waiting!'

Were the cries coming from the other room, only adding to her now frenzied panic as her hands rummaged across the shelf. She hurriedly grabbed the chair from her bedside, trailing it in front of the robe, and climbed up. Everything from the shelf hit the floor as she scanned frantically, her eyes near begging his special gift to appear. It was to no avail. *Where is it? It was here last week when I showed Megan.*

She stepped down off the chair. *Surely not? She couldn't have? She wouldn't dare. Or would she?*

Kara picked up the wine box and little gift bag and walked back to the living room, where everyone was now seated on the lounges. Kara moved to stand behind the couch where Greg was sitting and put her gifts on the floor.

'Thank God you're back. My present first,' Megan nearly squealed, quickly placing the large rectangular box across Greg's lap. 'Open it, open it!'

As she sat down next to Greg on the couch. Kara took one look at the box and stepped back. Her heart had turned to black in a split second.

She edged farther away toward the kitchen, her hand near leading her from behind, feeling for the stability of the cold marble bench top to grip and steady herself. The sound of each tear of the wrapping paper she had so carefully selected and taped, she felt rip right through her. She'd never felt such pain. Shock, hurt, and rage had combined and rolled into a tight ball in her stomach, and there was nowhere for it to escape.

Her thoughts were screaming. *There it is. You've been played yet again. I can't believe it! Yes, you can. You were right. How dare she? How can she be such a conniving selfish bitch! Stop it, Kara. Get a grip. Not here.*

Not now in front of our friends. Don't spoil his night. Fuck! You are such a fool!

As Greg exclaimed, 'Megan! My God, this is simply amazing. How did you know? It's perfect.'

Kara turned and walked to the kitchen sink. She couldn't watch. Her insides were volcanic. Greg was putting on the leather jacket she had, over four months ago, designed and had custom made for him. Kara's mind was scrambling back to when she'd first thought of buying it for him, and her conversation with Megan at the time.

'Megan, I've finally thought of what to get Greg. His leather jacket is now so worn and brittle, I thought a new one would be a great present. Have a look at some of these designs. I was thinking this one… in tan or maybe even this in black? What do you think?' Megan had looked at the images and had got quite excited.

'That one in black, definitely. Such a great idea, Kara. I've been working on a present for him too. But hey, I'd be happy to go halves with you, if I can't get what I want.'

She hadn't ever said another word to Kara.

Her hand trembled as she grabbed a glass and turned on the tap. She needed water to drown out the sound of his gratitude and excitement and quell her molten emotions. After he'd modelled, praised and let everyone feel and admire the baby soft leather, the others started handing over their gifts to him. It had given Kara the space to control the burning pain and find some composure. As the rousing cheers and thanks subsided a little, Kara walked slowly back to join them.

She stepped up to the end of the lounge next to Greg and bent down and kissed him softly. 'Happy birthday gorgeous,' she whispered in his ear. 'I had something else too, but these are it, for now.'

'Thank you, babe,' as he opened her gifts. 'Kara, wow, these glasses are fantastic. Thank you so much. Hey, did you see what Megan got for me? It's all been such a surprise.'

Kara shot a glance at Megan. 'Yes. It was definitely a surprise, alright. Umm, come on, cake time I think!' Kara said, now finding her hostess spirit.

With the candles blown and glasses refilled for last drinks, Greg raised his glass. 'I have been so spoilt. Thank you so much, Megan, Kara and everyone.'

Surprisingly, it was Greg's little toast, with Megan named first, that helped Kara decide what she now needed to do. It was simple. No confrontation. No drama.

It was then that she knew with a heavy heart that it was time for Megan to be his one and only.

Restoring her thoughts back to this day, she started the car and recommenced the drive to the office. There was so much to do. But again, the thoughts and self-talk kept cycling uncontrollably. Every intersection brought a new route for her mind to turn.

She knew it was Megan's behaviour not his, at fault, but right now, she couldn't muster her usual strength to forgive Greg yet either. She knew Greg had no idea of the extent of Megan's devious ways she'd undermined her or the many lies she'd been telling him, but Kara was still upset with him. He'd obviously noticed the change between Kara and Megan, no matter how slight, yet he hadn't really talked to them about it.

The fact he had seemingly not stopped to think or consider things from her perspective or ask them openly about what was going on, had hurt. He'd always been able to read her so well. Then, how he'd questioned her in a way that suggested he thought she was jealous and behaving unfairly, had burned into her deeply.

On the now rare times they'd all shared Greg's bed, it was Megan who somehow managed always to be the one to receive the most attention and ultimate pleasure from Greg. Kara accepted that in those moments, no man would take note of the choreography going on. It was all sexual pleasure; however, he'd indulged Megan's frequent *sneak ins* so many times, without any attempt to include her.

As she rounded the next corner, Kara scolded herself. *Stop it woman, that's not his fault. You know you are cross with yourself for defaulting to weakness and let it all happen. He's your best friend and a man who'd never hurt anyone deliberately. Sure, he hates to challenge or upset anyone, but he would always stand up to right a wrong or solve a problem. What on earth has she been telling him?*

Kara held the most despair in the full realisation that Megan was taking advantage of him too. Megan was now using his home, his generosity, his body and his trusting nature for herself.

Most of all, she regretted that both she and Greg didn't need to feel like this, or be put in this position. They had both welcomed, embraced and helped Megan so much, unconditionally.

Kara knew it was hopeless, knowing Megan was fabricating, twisting and manoeuvring to benefit herself alone, and also knew that any attempt to expose or challenge her risked even more destruction.

Kara didn't want to create scenes or more hurt for herself, Greg or anyone else, either. She had spent years during her former marriage with an abusive, emotional bully and she couldn't deal with anything as insidious or hurtful like it again. She didn't want to bring any more suffering into Greg's life, he's suffered enough grief already.

The pain of it all was excruciating. Kara had shared, cared and comforted Megan, having openly accepted her as an equal in their shared relationship as a loving three. However, as much as she had tried not to believe it, she had to face the fact that Megan had really only ever wanted to have Greg all to herself. And now even he wasn't enough for her. Kara blamed herself first, and foremost, for not having seen the signs from the outset and stupidly discounting

Megan's actions, like she had done with her ex. Now here she was again, being so unfairly betrayed.

God, you're such a fool. You should've seen it coming. You could see that Megan was desperate, unhappy, and needed to be adored from the beginning. She confused lust and sex with love, and has walked away from her family, especially her kids, looking for someone else to fulfil her needs. She still doesn't know herself or what or whom she wants. She's selfishly clinging to others in a vain attempt to solve her inner self, without a scrap of consideration for anyone. For God's sake, she's still saying she misses Michael, and wants to see him again too. I bet she still hasn't spoken to Greg about that either, even though you asked her to do so.

Kara knew, if you didn't like and love yourself, you would never find real happiness. Megan still needed to learn how to love herself and put the needs of others, first and foremost.

Kara wiped her eyes and pulled down the visor in the car. She opened the mirror, speaking to the reflection. *Time to let it be. One day the truth will hopefully come out. You are now dumped in a* no-win *situation. If you try to speak with Greg or Megan about any of this now, it will only make it worse. You can't control anyone else's behaviour—other than your own. She needs and wants him now, and besides, neither of them actually belongs to you, Kara.*

I hate to see him being deceived. He's my best friend, and he's dealt with enough. I just hope she really does love him and won't hurt him. I will miss him so much.

Kara walked into her office, sat at her desk, and with a strange calm resolve, got to work. She completed her detailed program for the next event, finalised the budget papers, and made numerous calls. The toughest was to her Aunt Sarah. She tidied every loose end she could think of. She had resolved that by tomorrow, she would begin yet another fresh start.

At 7.00 p.m., long after all others had gone, she filled out the form and the note to her boss that explained a little more about her sudden decision well, at least offering only the reasons that made sense. She didn't bother to mention Daniel or Tom, knowing her departure itself would be a lasting reminder of the damage they caused. She'd desperately wanted to complete these alone at the start of the day and then just walk. It was even hard to breathe in this place, let alone see the faces of anyone who now she was sure were undressing and judging her with every uncomfortable look.

However, she didn't want any of her work left unfinished, or cause problems for the company as a result of her sudden departure and personal matters. So, this task had to be one of the last things. She eventually shut down the computer, packed up her desk and collected two last documents from the printer.

She walked into her manager's office and left her resignation and the note in a sealed envelope on her desk. The last two items she grabbed from the printer were letters. These were to inform two people about a departure of a very different kind.

Chapter 36

$\mathcal{K}$ara had one more stop to make before heading back to the apartment. She messaged both Greg and Megan to say she needed to work back late and to proceed with dinner without her.

Her Aunt Sarah greeted her with a huge, warm hug. Kara couldn't hold it back any longer, with the trembling and sobbing starting from the moment she stepped into her arms.

'Oh, Kara, sweetheart, I know darling, I know. It hurts. Let it out,' she said, keeping hold of her crumbling niece, until she had calmed a little.

'Sarah, I'm so sorry. I'm such a mess, but I haven't been able to say a word. God, I've been such a fool yet again.' She tried desperately to pull herself together.

Kara told Sarah enough of what had been happening during the past months to understand why she was leaving and would not be contactable for a while, even to her. However, she had never revealed the extent of the intimacy they all had shared. That was too much.

She explained how Megan had left her husband and sought refuge at their place. Her grateful and loving connection with both of them at first, but how time revealed her intense desire for Greg and she described some of the ways she had more recently attempted to alienate, compromise her role at work, and make it impossible for her to stay.

'Kara, darling, you don't need to apologise, never to me. You're not a fool; you just have such a loving heart and see the best in others. That is a special quality. Especially after everything you've already survived. I'm proud of you.'

'God, I love you. I needed to hear that. But it's...' her eyes filled, and tears spilled in streams down her cheeks again, 'Greg... I don't want to hurt him or leave him, yet I'm running away from him again.'

'Kara, I know, I know. But this time, he needs to find out, all by himself. This is something that you can't fix by being there. You've made the right decision. You're not running away; you're creating space for them. Let her fill it and see what happens. If she becomes what he's wanted, then you have the right to get upset, but only about the wasted emotions you're feeling right now. But please never forget what you've shared with him. He's been one of the best people and friend you've ever had. He changed your life. You've changed his too. Never forget that. I'm sure he won't either.' Kara listened as Sarah spoke at length to remind her of the many changes she'd witnessed in her since that first night three years ago, when Kara landed at her house in the small hours of the morning. Sarah recounted the events and how happy she'd felt when Kara had tried so hard to suppress the excitement at the prospect of flying off to meet a man who'd searched for her for years. The first time after spending years of being on her own.

Her first kiss schoolboy crush, who'd searched for her.

'Kara, he's been a gentleman, honest as the day is new, and has loved you in a very unique way since that time. It became more than just sex, ages ago. My goodness! Even I could see that!

'He's never stopped contacting you, even when he was with Tess. As you said, you were the first person he contacted when she died. Don't ever doubt his commitment to your friendship or his respect for you. Ever. You've stepped back into the shadows when needed and stepped up to help him every time. He won't forget that easily. You've done enough. Now it's his turn, for you. This is the test. If you never hear from him again—which, sadly, could happen, please be prepared for that—it will be his loss. You will remain one of the kindest and truly loving women he's ever encountered. Regardless, just be happy for the times you shared with him, and who you've become as a result.'

Sarah stroked her hair and the small touch of comfort filtered through Kara's pain.

'As for Megan… you can't help her either. She doesn't really know what she wants. Just give her the rope. She will hang herself eventually. I'm sure of that.'

Kara soaked in all of Sarah's words. The first that had given her any real reassurance in weeks. She breathed in and the sigh which followed, let out enough of the hurt and doubt that had been close to crippling her.

'Sarah, I love you so much. I should've come to talk to you, ages before this. Are you sure I'm not being a coward by leaving, really?'

'Kara, you already know the answer to that. You've been braver than many other people I know all of your life. I'm just pleased you're going now. It's only you who'll suffer most by staying at this point.'

'Thank you so much.'

Kara pulled out an envelope from her bag. It contained keys, a business card with details of a paging service and a receipt.

'I'm driving to Melbourne but taking my time. I'm now officially unemployed for the next month at least! I still need to get a new phone, so in the meantime, the card has a number you can call if you need me urgently. They'll contact me wherever I'm staying, in the next few days. I promise I'll call you back as soon I can. I'll let you know my new number once I have one. Please don't share it with anyone. The other things are for you to give to Greg, in the event he contacts you. The keys are for his apartment. The receipt is just for something I bought for him, that he should have. That's about it, really. Oh, if he wants to get rid of any of the things I left behind, you are welcome to them, or please just tell him he can dump them.'

'I'm happy to do all of that, darling. Except, please don't take too long to send me your new phone number. I won't be able to stop worrying until I speak to you.'

'For sure, Sarah. You'll be the first and probably the only! Again, please don't share it. I'm not ready for calls from any other friends just now.'

'Of course. Right now, that's probably the best. You are doing the right thing, darling.'

'I need to get going. I love you Sarah, so much. Thank you for everything.'

'Kara, I love you too. He does too, I'm sure of it.' They shared a long tight hug before Kara turned and dashed to her car. She sniffed back the tears, holding tight to Sarah's comforting words. She had to steel herself a bit longer. There was still the rest of the night to get through. Kara started the car and headed to the apartment.

It was well after 9.00 p.m. by the time she entered the door. Greg and Megan were sitting cuddled together on the lounge. Greg stood up, grabbing the bottle of wine from the table and went over to her.

He kissed her, saying, 'You've had a long day. Everything okay? I bet you need one of these.'

Kara smiled and nodded. 'That would be very nice. I'm going to head straight in for a shower, if that's alright?'

'Sure, I'll bring you in a glass.'

As Kara walked past the back of the lounge to head toward the bathroom, she stopped, turned back and bent down. She gave Megan a slight kiss on the cheek without a word.

'Hi.' Megan replied as she stood up abruptly and turned to Greg, saying, 'I think I might head to bed, sexy. Coming?'

Greg had seen it again. The ever so slight flinch in Megan's face and her quick move to stand, as if to avoid Kara kissing her. Greg saw the wave of melancholy across Kara's face as she stepped back, turned and headed towards the bathroom. He realised it was now time to sort this out somehow. Tomorrow, first up, he would think through a plan and his approach.

'I'll just stay up for a bit and make sure Kara's alright. She looks like she needs a little cheering up. I think I'll wait for her and hopefully she'll join us.' He kissed Megan on the cheek.

'Don't leave me waiting too long, I want you badly tonight!' She said with a seductive smile.

'I'm sure she won't be too long.'

Greg didn't see the *Fuck Kara* scowl that followed when Megan turned and faced away, heading for his bedroom.

As Greg entered the bathroom, with wine glass in hand, Kara was already undressed and about to step into the shower.

'Here you go sexy. You look exhausted.'

The smile was meek as she nodded. 'I am a bit. Today has been one like no other.'

Greg stepped forward, drew her into his arms and hugged her. He stepped back and looked deep into her eyes.

'Come to bed soon, in my room, you definitely need some pampering tonight.'

'I'm probably only cuddling material tonight. I'm really not in any shape for play. I'll only disappoint.'

'Kara, you never disappoint me. But I have been worried about you. Is everything alright, really? Are you and Megan okay? I know something's been a bit off lately?'

'Greg, yes. Err, it has. I'm not up to talking about it all right now. We will talk about it. One day, I'm sure.'

'Yes. Of course, this isn't the right time. But for now… come here.'

With that, Greg stepped up close to her again and kissed her. Slow, deep and tender, unlike any other kiss they had shared for so long. It was beautiful.

She held him, pressed to her body so tight and then stepped back. 'Go on now, Megan's waiting for you.'

'I know. But Kara, I…'

'I know, it's okay, just go.' She stopped him from saying another word.

She held onto the look of his gentle smile as he turned and walked out of the bathroom.

That kiss. His smile and knowing it could be their last. Her heart finally broke right in that moment. She stepped into the shower, her tears flowing nearly faster than the water.

She spent ages in the bathroom, with her music on. Not only until the tears of despair and utter grief suspended, but also to drown out any sound of Greg and Megan's pleasure. She didn't want that lingering memory to be the last she held about this night.

After carefully applying her makeup and fixing her hair, she pulled on her jeans and T-shirt and then packed her makeup and toiletries into a bag. She kept telling herself that she was doing the right thing, and this break will start another new life adventure.

As she tiptoed down the hallway to her room, she could thankfully only hear Greg's purring snores from his room. It took her the next couple of hours to pack slowly and quietly. Most of her clothes and jewellery, her laptop, some books and her quilt and pillow. She took only a few of her ornaments and of course, the pictures of her Aunt, daughter and Greg that she had in frames. The rest didn't matter, this was to be a real fresh start.

The last place she crept into was Megan's room. She already knew she wouldn't be sleeping in there. Kara wasn't worried about the clothes she'd lent her. She could keep them. There was only one thing she really wanted to find and take back. After looking around, she finally found it in a little box in the drawer in her bedside table. She carefully took out her pearl necklace Greg had given her, and Megan had *borrowed*.

As Kara put it on, she muttered, 'It's mine. This was another *first* that Greg gave me. You don't deserve to wear this.'

Kara had parked her car in the street, knowing she would leave during the night. She used the door that led from the laundry to slip out, walk down the driveway and load her gear. It took a few slow trips, taking care not to disturb the sleeping Greg and Megan. Once the car was packed, she quietly walked back into the apartment, stopped, and looked around. One last look. *Do not start crying again!*

She placed the two letters carefully on the kitchen bench.

It was about 1.30 a.m. when Kara clicked the door shut and left for the last time.

Chapter 37

$\mathcal{G}$reg had woken ages before his alarm. Megan was still sound asleep next to him. He lay there for a while, thinking back to how miserable Kara had looked last night. *She's been overdoing it lots lately. I hope she's slept alright. I'll get some coffee started for her.* He climbed out of bed and walked out to the kitchen. It was quiet. He sensed it instantly. Something didn't feel right.

Then he saw the envelopes. There were two of them, propped on the bench, each simply addressed by only their names. He dashed to the other bedroom where Kara kept her clothes and work gear.

All of her things were gone.

'Megan, you'd better come out here.'

Megan wandered out from the bedroom, naked, still half asleep. 'What's going on?'

'Kara's gone. She's taken all of her stuff and she's left. Did you know anything about this?'

Megan's eyes widened. She shook her head. 'No! Not a clue.'

'She's left letters for each of us. Here's yours.'

He handed Megan the envelope.

She took it from his hand carefully. 'I'll just get some clothes on,' as she turned and headed back to the bedroom.

Greg hadn't heard her; he'd dropped down into the lounge and was already reading the note addressed to him.

Dear Greg

This is hopefully a pause and not a full stop. I will carry such special thoughts of you with me, so you will only be but a breath away, always.

As has been the pattern of our friendship, since we reunited, we need to fill some moments between us with new experiences, people, lovers and time apart.

I want you to have only the best of me and never the mundane which sadly, in recent months, is what I've become. Our shared living has become difficult for me, for lots of reasons. Too much to fully explain, but please trust that you haven't done anything wrong. But others have. Not only personally, but it's affected my work too. But most of all, it's just time. Time for me to leave.

It is my hope for you and Megan to see if you can have what I think you really need and desire, but something you have never had. A complete life with one woman who hopefully fills your every day with passion, fun, intimacy and years of love.

It has become clear that this is what Megan really wants too. If she doesn't prove to be right, don't ever regret your time together. I will always be here, somewhere.

Please don't try to contact me right now. I need time to stand alone again. This time, it will be tough.

You remain my closest and most cherished friend, always. You alone understand me completely and hold all my secrets and treasured memories of our times together. You were my first kiss, and I forever hold on to the belief, and hope that you will be my last.

I will miss you so very much.

Just be happy.

All my love, Kara x

Greg just sat there. He re-read the letter over again slowly. He thought back to last night, now realising why she had looked so sad. She'd held him so tight. That was really her goodbye hug. *Why didn't she talk to me? She's always told me everything and never held back before. I know things have been strained between her and Megan, but not enough for this? Surely not? She can't be gone.*

He checked the time and called her number. The phone was off. It was just after 7.30 a.m.. *I'll call her at work around 8.00 a.m.*

Megan had no sooner raced into her room when she ripped open the envelope. She was both desperate yet scared to read its contents. She'd not thought Kara would actually pack up and leave so suddenly. As she read the words, she felt only fleeting guilt. Then came anger. *The bitch. I wasn't that bad. So, I didn't pick you up from the airport big deal! Anyway, I was going to pay half for the jacket. I haven't really told lies. I can sleep with anyone I want too.* Then panic struck. *Shit! Greg shouldn't ever read this. God, what did she write to him?*

Megan emerged wearing a robe, the letter screwed and buried in the pocket of her robe. She asked cautiously, 'Hey, would you like a coffee?'

Greg finally looked up. 'Megan… yeah, sure. Thanks. Hey, Megan, what did she say in your letter? It's your business, but was there anything about why she's gone exactly? I can't believe she's gone without any explanation. It's just so unlike her.' Greg's words started directly speaking to her, but drifted more as if to no one, in sheer bewilderment.

Megan felt relief wave through her. Clearly Kara had written something completely different to him.

'Greg, it's okay,' Megan said. 'My letter said very little, just like yours by the sound of it. Just that she thought a lot about me and you and that we should be together. She felt it was time to leave and made me promise to take care of you. That was it, really. Not much more.'

Megan turned back toward the bedroom to get dressed for work. She was shaking.

Thank God, he didn't ask me to show him my letter. He can never see it. But even if he did, I can explain it away. That Kara was jealous and making things up about me. Besides, I wasn't really that bad.

Her self-talk was lamely caught between the pleasure and pain of the morning. She hated to see Greg so upset, but more than that, she could barely suppress the delight in learning Kara had gone. *He's all mine at last.*

Megan had just finished dressing when Greg walked into her room. She quickly shoved Kara's note into the washing piled in the bottom of her robe. He couldn't see this. Not now or ever. She straightened and turned toward him as she slid the robe door closed behind her.

He seemed nearly dazed and simply lost. 'Megan,' he asked quietly, 'I've seen a bit of separation between the two of you lately. Are you sure she didn't say anything that might tell us why or where she's gone, really? Did you two have an argument, or something I don't know about?'

Megan drew in a breath before she looked him straight in the eye. Stepping up to him and hugging him close, she said softly, 'Greg, I can't honestly say what she was thinking. I felt she was getting a little jealous of me, but I didn't think anything would see her wanting to leave us, ever. She's probably doing what's right for her. I have no idea where she's gone, but maybe let her go for now.'

'Perhaps you're right,' he said pensively. He glanced over at the clock on her side table. 'Hey, haven't you got an inspection today? You need to get to going. I'll try to call her at work. I don't want her leaving like this.'

'Good idea. Let me know if you get hold of her. I'll try calling her later.' Megan motioned towards the door; Greg started to leave, but then turned and walked up to her, giving her a hug.

'That would be nice. I'll let you know for sure.' He took her by the hand leading her to the living room.

Megan grabbed her keys and handbag and headed out the front door. Once in the car, she sighed with relief. Then she panicked a little. She wasn't able to grab that damn letter. *I hope he doesn't go looking for it? No, he wouldn't do that. I'll get rid of it tomorrow. I won't ask to read his. If he asks anything again about it—I can tell him I was upset and tore it up. It will be fine. This will all settle soon. Just stay cool.*

But it didn't stop there.

Megan had left for work and Greg had tried to take in what she'd said to 'Just let Kara go.'

But something just kept biting.

He was frustrated and confused about Kara's departure, especially her slipping away without a word. So much of this didn't make sense. Sure, he'd felt there had been a gap growing between them all, but he really felt the relationship between himself and Kara hadn't changed. He at times could see a sadness in Kara's eyes and kicked himself that he didn't stop and take more time to ask her what was wrong. Megan said she thought Kara was jealous. He thought back. *Kara said that about Megan when I first told her about my encounter gone wrong in Sydney, but that was more about me having attempted to sleep with someone before her, after Tess died. She's been so accepting and welcomed Megan when she landed here. It just doesn't make sense.*

He resolved to call her at work and take her out to brunch and just let her talk.

He could fix this, he was sure. He dialled her number.

'The phone you have called is either switched off or incorrect,' an automated voice informed him.

He tried three more times. He waited until nearly 9.30 a.m., then he dialled her office number.

'All Event Solutions, Maria speaking.'

'Hi, Maria,' he said, 'It's Greg here, could you please put me through to Kara?' he said, trying desperately to sound casual.

'Hello, Greg, Kara is not in today, but please hold, I'll just put you through to her manager,' she said formally, with *on hold* music sounding in his ear before he could say another word.

The phone clicked a few times and then a tailored voice spoke his name. 'Mr. Sheppard. Um, Greg. I am Laura Morris. I understand you are looking for Kara Gilbert?'

'Yes, I am. If she's busy, I can call back, but I would like to speak with her if I may. It's rather urgent. '

'Greg, I'm sorry, but Kara no longer works here. She left us yesterday.'

Her words just wouldn't sink in. 'Are you saying she quit her job or was she fired?'

'She definitely wasn't fired! We would have loved her to stay, she was invaluable. Sadly, she tendered her resignation due to personal reasons. I'm not at liberty to explain, I'm sorry.'

'Yes, of course. I understand. She didn't happen to leave a forwarding address or contact details, did she?'

'Sadly, no. Regardless, I would not be able to share any of that information with you, as you can appreciate.'

'No, of course. Thank you. Thanks anyway.' Greg was stunned.

He felt a wave of panic rise. 'God, this is nothing like she's done before. Where the hell has she gone?'

He kept trying to think. *Where? Back to Clare? No, she sold her house and everything before coming to live with me. Who would she go to? Her daughter? No. They haven't had much contact in recent years.*

Of course! Sarah! Her aunt. She would know. You idiot! She will definitely be the one. Kara's probably there.

Greg raced out of the apartment to his car and headed for Kara's aunt's place. He'd collected Kara from Sarah's before, when they had their fun escape to Queensland. So, he had no trouble remembering the address and getting there, nearly faster than his hopes could take him.

Greg knocked at the door. It took no time for Sarah to answer. Greg was somewhat surprised. He'd somehow imagined Kara's aunt to be old in appearance, grey and more solid in frame and worn for her near sixty or so plus years. She was however, spritely, agile and while her dark blonde hair bore tiny streaks of white and grey, she was nonetheless a lady with an astute spark and surprising youthfulness that he hadn't expected. Her looks emulated the outgoing personality exactly as Kara had described to him.

Sarah greeted him with a gentle hug, blended with a sorrowful, understanding smile.

'Greg, it's so nice to meet you finally, face to face. Kara has spoken of you so fondly. Please come in. I've actually been expecting you.'

Greg stepped inside, having uttered no more than an introduction, and hello.

'Would you like a cup of coffee or tea… or perhaps something stronger?' she asked.

'If you don't mind, I think I need more than tea or coffee.'

'Good choice!' said Sarah as she took out two wine glasses and poured a glass of Riesling for each of them.

'Please sit,' she said, motioning to the lounge. Seated next to each other on the lounge, Sarah turned and asked, 'So, Greg, I obviously know it's Kara's departure that has brought you here. I'm not sure there is much I can say, but I'll answer what I can.'

'Thanks Sarah, sorry, may I call you Sarah?'

'Yes, of course.'

'Sarah, I can't believe she's gone, really gone. I've just called her office, and they told me she's left her job too. Is there anything you can tell me? Like where she is for a start? I really need to speak with her. I need to know that she's alright.'

Sarah could hear the slight quiver in his voice. She could tell he was genuinely worried and was quite desperate to find her. This was going to be a harder conversation than she thought.

'Honestly, Greg, I'm actually not sure where she is right now. She told me she'll let me know where she is once she's settled. She came and saw me last night on her way back to your place. She was quite upset but told me only a little. I understand it's something to do with things changing since Megan came to live at your place. But knowing Kara as I do, I don't think her decision to leave, especially you, is something that she's taken lightly.'

'I agree. I just can't believe she didn't talk to me first. That's so unlike her. She's always been willing to tell me anything. I could see she was rather stressed lately, and I did ask her about it, even last night. But she didn't want to talk. I should've tried harder and asked her much sooner.'

'Greg, this was clearly something she thought was the best way for you and her.'

He picked up his glass, took a sip and just looked down, staring pensively into his lap for a moment. Sarah's heart lurched. She wanted to tell him so much more. But she'd promised Kara.

'Greg, she left me a couple of things, that she asked me to give to you.'

'Really?' His tone uplifted slightly, anticipating, hesitant, and hopeful in just one word.

Sarah stood up and walked to her desk in the other room, took the envelope Kara had given her and returned. She stood in front of him as she handed it over.

'Greg, it's likely the contents won't give you any more information. I'm so sorry. Kara also asked me to tell you that you can bring anything she's left at your apartment to me, or you are free to dispose of it, as you would like.'

Greg just nodded, more focussed on opening the envelope. He had so hoped there would be another note. He felt the keys and his fingers clambered for more. There was paper inside. He pulled out the piece of paper. Not a note, but merely a receipt.

He looked at it carefully. It took only a minute, but the reality of what this transaction was for spoke volumes. 'Kara paid for this. Oh my God!'

He looked at Sarah, now his eyes fired with clarity and resolve.

'Sarah, thank you so much. You've told me so much more than you know. I will find her. I have no idea how, but when I do, I will bring her home.'

'Greg…' she then hesitated. But she knew in that moment that she could not let either him or Kara suffer. He was truly her most genuine and loving friend.

'Look, I will not break my promise to Kara, however, I would encourage you to head east in your search. It could be a grey destination, but there could be some promising work connections. She has turned off her phone and intends to get a new one. So, how about we keep in contact? I'll give you my number too.'

'Sarah, you're as lovely and true as Kara always said. I can't thank you enough. I will keep in touch, for sure.' After exchanging phone numbers, Greg gave her a huge parting hug and left.

The minute he got behind the wheel of his car and backed out for home; his eyes turned to steel. He had not wanted to think about it, but the doubt had been there. His thoughts were reeling. He had pieces, but it wasn't quite fitting together yet. When he arrived home, he couldn't think about work. All he could do was try to figure out what had hurt Kara enough to leave and moreover, not be able to tell him.

He sat down, falling blindly into his favourite lounge chair again, and took out Kara's letter and the receipt, placing both on the coffee table in front of him, and just stared at them for a long time. Thinking hard. He picked up the letter and read it again. The clues were coming together. There was still something not gelling. The receipt, that Kara had left for him with her aunt, had her name and card details and detailed it was for the purchase of a leather jacket. *This had to be the one that Megan gave me?*

He thought back to the surprise birthday night. *Kara had said something about having had another gift for me?*

More questions followed. *Can Megan's letter really be the same as mine? That makes even less sense, if Megan has upset Kara this badly. Have I trusted her too much?*

He had to do it. Greg stood up and went to Megan's room that she hadn't slept in much for over two weeks now and started looking through her bed-side table. He began to think this through in more detail. He traced back through everything.

She went in here this morning after I gave her the letter to dress for work. I walked out of here with her, and she didn't have it in her hand, or even a handbag, so it has to still be in here somewhere. Besides, if she had nothing to hide, and it is the same as mine, it should be easy to find.

He stopped as he saw there was an opened pack of condoms in her drawer. That in itself was strange, as she'd never asked or insisted on using them with Greg. *Who has she used these with? Has she brought people here to fuck at my place?* There was no letter. He kept searching. He looked under her bed, only to find a used condom still containing the dried-up remnants of its user. *That fucking slut!*

He eventually found the letter under a pile of clothes in her wardrobe. He opened it slowly, first looking up to see he was still alone. He knew no one else was there, but he hated not trusting Megan or rifling through her things. But he simply had to find the truth. He read.

Dear Megan

You are an unbelievable woman. You entered my life as a casual friend who first flickered across Greg's life as an unknown encounter, and courageously became part of our rare and unconventional life. You became a friend, a lover, and a major part of us. But it has become very clear in these past months that you had your own agenda. So, I am out.

Only you know what you have done. Sadly, I just wish you had been open and honest about your deepened feelings for Greg and your desire to be with him, without me in his life. My love for you both was unconditional, and as such, I would willingly have stepped back if that is what you both wanted and talked to me about. Your selfish, silly games were not only unnecessary, but hurtful.

Years ago, I vowed I would never let anyone take advantage of me or abuse my trust again. And yet, here I am, having become a victim of selfish manipulation and deception. I can only control my own behaviour, not yours.

This is why I have left, not for you, but to give Greg the chance to share time with you on his own. Let him see for himself and maybe, your apparent need to lie and deceive, will stop now. I hope my departure now gives you the space, confidence and strength to wake up, be honest and make the choices that are right for, not only yourself, but for Greg, Michael and your family. How that evolves is up to you. If you truly love Greg, only you can tell him about the other hook-ups you've had, the stealthy ways you manoeuvred to distance me from Greg, how you've disclosed private information about the three of us, and more, to my colleagues at work, making it impossible for me to continue there. More than anything, I hope you 'come clean,' and tell him the truth about his birthday. That whole night from the airport to the dinner and gift, honestly, was the last straw and you know exactly why.

I understand to some extent why you have acted this way, but I will never forget how you did this or how you have made me feel. All I can say is that any warmth or affection I held for you, sadly, has gone. I'm not angry. I will not seek revenge, despite the fact that you also spread your ruinous tentacles into my workplace, destroying my professional credibility.

Don't panic, I will never attempt to contact you, nor will I ever see you again. I simply feel nothing for you. That also makes me sad.

My last word: More than a lover, Greg has, and will always be my most beloved and treasured friend. So please, don't you dare hurt him or abuse his trust and generosity.

Love him, care for him, and let him be himself. Or leave him be. I will be watching, even from afar.

Kara

Greg's blood began boiling hotter and hotter with each line he read. He reached the end and read it again, this time detailing the critical points. Birthday party, leather jacket. Other hook-ups. Kara's work. There it was. All the evidence he needed.

'Well, she has some explaining to do alright,' Greg said aloud. His mind raced as he formulated a plan, not to entrap her, quite the opposite, to give her time to prepare her defence. Although this was no laughing matter, it was no different to how he would solve arguments between his two girls when they were young. One actually turned out to be a lawyer. He took out his phone.

Megan looked up from her computer as her phone beeped a message. She knew it was from Greg. As she reached to check it, she smiled gleefully to herself. She would have him all to herself tonight. Her smile disappeared the instant she read it.

> Megan, I have found the note from Kara to you, and I would like to discuss that tonight. G.

'Oh Fuck!' Megan said to herself. Her heart raced as she frantically tried to think of exactly what the message said and more importantly how the hell, she was going to defend herself.

Fuck, Fuck, Fuck, why did I not destroy that fucking note. Bloody Kara is still spoiling everything.

As she put her head in her hands. She felt faint, her heart pounding. She thought about her fight with Michael, and somehow this seemed worse, *My God, what have I done?*

Greg strode to the fridge and grabbed a beer. This was going to be a big discussion. In his head he prepared like any prosecuting lawyer would. He took out the letter, making mental notes of each point, imagined what her excuse might be, then thought through how he would counter-question any possible reply. He knew he only had about an hour, if she came straight home from work.

At 6.00 p.m. Megan gripped the doorknob, the cold chrome in her palm, mirroring the reception she was dreading inside. Shivering again, she held there for a moment before entering. *Could this be the last time I walk through this door?*

She could feel his intense stare follow her as she cautiously stepped inside, put her keys on the hall table before slowly walking toward Greg seated at the dining table.

'Hi, take a seat.' He had mustered his sense of calm and control in preparation during this past hour. Perching on the edge of the chair, she held poised there, like the shamed student asked by a teacher to stay back after class. Megan dared not utter a sound.

'May I get you a drink?' Greg asked.

'Yes, anything,' Megan replied, not looking up from her hands in her lap. Greg stood, walked to the kitchen and took his time to fill a glass. He returned, pausing next to her for only time enough to place a glass of Chardonnay in front of her. He moved around to sit directly opposite, waiting until she had taken a sip.

'Is there anything you want to say?' Greg asked. The tone was cool, now internally steeled to remain completely calm. Megan finally looked him in the eyes.

By now, her tears welled and began running down her cheeks.

'I am so sorry. I didn't mean for this to happen.'

'But it did Megan, and now Kara, my best friend, has been hurt, and has gone. Is all of what she said in that letter true?' Greg said, only just able to keep his voice low.

'Yes, sort of,' Megan said meekly, barely loud enough for him to hear. She could see Greg's back stiffen slightly and a deep furrow appear on his brow.

'But, Greg, please let me explain…'

'What is there to explain?'

She scrambled for words, and tumbled her high-pitched reply, racing at escalating pace, 'I just had sex once, not *lots* of hook ups, it was only when you and Kara were away, it didn't mean anything, and I didn't intend to forget her on the night of your birthday. Honestly, it's more Kara. She seems quite jealous; she's taken this all the wrong way. It's not as bad as you might think and—'

Greg could feel himself getting angry. She was not explaining, just making lame excuses. He had to stop her now.

'Megan, we explained when you first arrived here, that we are open. It means we talk and tell each other about everything. That especially includes each other's partners. So, you are saying that you brought some guy here to this place and didn't tell us?'

Megan simply nodded in response.

He pulled the receipt and placed it squarely on the table in front of her.

'Megan. Please tell me about this?'

Megan stretched her hand slowly across the table and picked up the receipt. As she realised what it was, her head dropped, and she muttered a pathetic, 'I said I would go halves with her for it.'

'Halves? You *offered*? Obviously, you didn't pay Kara anything, and even if you did, you still led me to me believe you'd bought me that jacket on your own. It was Kara's idea and gift for me in the first place—wasn't it?' He kept talking. He didn't want to hear a response. 'Megan, that's quite enough now. Don't say another word.' He'd heard enough.

'Megan, we brought you into our home as a friend and lover, we shared everything with you, and yet you took advantage of Kara's kind personality… No! You abused her kind personality, until she couldn't take any more, and now I have lost my best friend, AGAIN… FUCKING AGAIN!' Greg stopped to let the heat inside subside that was building toward boiling point. Eventually he said, 'Is there anything more you want to say?'

'Just that I am so sorry,' replied Megan, now crying uncontrollably, knowing there was nothing else to say.

'So am I,' Greg said calmly. 'I want you gone tonight.'

Megan was now sobbing, her chest heaving, as Greg grabbed his keys and walked out the door.

As she walked to her room to pack her things, she stopped and took out her phone and rapidly sent a text.

Michael can I please come home? I miss you all so much. I know now that you are my soulmate and that with you is where I belong. I'm so truly sorry. Forgive me. Please.

Greg's feelings of anger and utter distaste for Megan paced with him as he took off down the street. As he turned the corner, his feelings had switched to an accelerated desperation to find Kara, and the urgent desire to comfort her. He gulped hard with each step, trying to swallow the guilt for his own blind ignorance. *The signs were there. You knew Megan was trying to manoeuvre herself into prime position.* He'd not had a clue about the extent to which she would go and want to so shamelessly hurt Kara. There was no denying that now, and Greg realised that there was probably much more that went on, that he'd been oblivious to.

While he knew it was pointless, as Kara's aunt had indicated she was likely to have left the state already, he spent the night driving to most of their favourite restaurants, bars and locations that they'd enjoyed together, in the thin hope she'd appear. More than anything, he was overcome with guilt for not having seen this happen. Lamenting the loss of his treasured friend, his heart vainly clinging to the fun, special moments they'd shared. He didn't find even a hint of her anywhere.

He walked into the apartment at 10.30 p.m., marched straight to Megan's room, and then his own. He checked every part of the place to be sure she was gone.

Only then, he opened a bottle of red wine and poured a large glass. After taking one or two sips, he opened his phone and sat staring at the last couple of pictures he had taken of Kara. It was the first day she'd moved into his place, grinning and scolding him for taking photos as she peeked out from behind a packing box.

Then the one sitting with her wearing nothing but the pearl necklace he had given her to celebrate her new job and life in the city. She looked so happy. He stopped and thought back over so many times they'd shared. She had only ever brought happiness into his life. Unconditionally. She really was his *first and forever* girl and his most trusted friend. Now she was gone.

Then he did something that Greg Sheppard rarely ever did. He lifted his glass, raised it as if proposing a toast. He made a promise. Out loud.

'I found you once, Kara Gilbert. I will find you again. I promise.'

A Message from the Authors

The challenges of love, life and relationships are not exclusive to the young, by any means. The dilemma and intensity of relationships as we mature are rarely discussed, but exist, with much more complexity and bravery than we ever dare to share.

If you would like to find out what it is like to give pure ultimate pleasure to someone you love at any age, then you have opened the right story. Kara Gilbert and Greg Sheppard are bonded friends. From a poignant memory of a childhood kiss, the two intimately reconnected, after more than thirty-five years. As first described in *Kara: My First Kiss*, their reunion sparked the start of a rare, unexpected and yet special bond between them that enabled their desires, sexual fantasies and a deeper understanding of relationships to be realised. Open, honest, raw, and uninhibited, this story hopefully will continue to arouse, excite and provoke you to explore and challenge the stereotype of 'one partner for life', and enlighten your understanding of how relationships can continue to evolve and grow sexually. Discovering that sex shared in the company and exploration of others can be a genuine expression of unconditional connection with another and ultimate pleasures that can be realised… at any stage of your life.

Compersion, as opposed to monogamy with jealousy, the paradigm expression of a most unconditional love, is real, and truly exists. Our research was empowering, exciting and a revelation about couples, and the challenges of polyamory. Relationships, love, sex and friendship with multiple people can, and is, an enlightening experience.

We hope you too, like Kara and Greg, will be sparked.

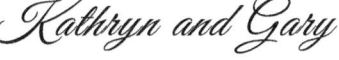
Kathryn and Gary

About the Authors

Despite their contrasting lifestyles and professional careers, Kathryn and Gary's mutual desire to write, has resulted in a unique collaboration between these two South Australian authors. This unique combination has created a bold new genre of sophisticated erotic literature, which dares to explore the complexity of current day physical attraction, desire, sexual pleasure, and how modern-day relationships should be considered and fulfilled.

The male and female influence of their writing brings realistic insight into adult romance and encounters, through Kara and Greg's perspectives and emotions.

Writing and engagement with people has been central to Kathryn's life for decades, with a highly successful and recognised career in education, research and the arts, which continues today. It wasn't until Kathryn's reconnection with the boy she first fell in love with as an innocent 12-year-old, that she found her true passion and talent as an author of adult romance. The real-life encounter with her first true love, became the catalyst into a wonderful renewal of self-acceptance and joy in writing, for pleasure alone—sparking the beginning of the Kara story.

Kathryn is the founding member of a small group of authors known as the Midnight Authors, who enjoy shaping their books for others, often in the midnight hours between their other careers. They support and encourage each other as they create their stories and navigate the challenges of self-publishing!

Gary Baxter's journey as a wordsmith began in his youth, where his natural gift for articulation and entertaining storytelling captured the attention of those around him. With an unwavering love for action novels and a burning desire to create stories that would enthral readers, he embarked on a mission that had been simmering within him for years.

As an accomplished car and motorcycle racer, instructor, entertainer and an esteemed figure in movie action vehicle coordination and stunt driving, Gary's thrilling life has fuelled his imagination and inspired his writing. From the roaring engines on the racetrack to the heart-pounding stunts on the film set, he channels his experiences into words that leap off the page.

Gary's writing has extended into short stories, action and crime novels that will also captivate.

Kathryn and Gary are mature, new-age authors, who bring a refreshing style to romance that is riveting, arousing, and provocative.